SEEDS ON THE WIND

SEEDS
ON THE
WIND

ROGER JONES

MICHAEL JOSEPH

LONDON

MICHAEL JOSEPH LTD
Published by the Penguin Group
27 Wrights Lane, London W8 5TZ, England
Viking Penguin Inc. 40 West 23rd Street, New York, New York 10010, USA
Penguin Books Australia Ltd, Ringwood, Victoria, Australia
Penguin Books Canada Ltd, 2801 John Street, Markham, Ontario, Canada L3R 1B4
Penguin Books (NZ) Ltd, 182–190 Wairau Road, Auckland 10, New Zealand

Penguin Books Ltd, Registered Offices: Harmondsworth, Middlesex, England

First published in Great Britain 1990

Typeset in $11\frac{1}{2}/13\frac{1}{2}$ pt Baskerville and printed in Great Britain by
Richard Clay (The Chaucer Press) Ltd, Bungay, Suffolk

A CIP catalogue record for this book is available
from the British Library

ISBN 0 7181 3255 6

A handful of historical figures make brief appearances in this
novel. It would have been difficult to convey the spirit of
the period without mention of them. Apart from these, all
characters are fictitious, owing no known likeness to any
real person, dead or living.

FOR JILL, WHO SHARES THE JOURNEYS;
AND INSPIRES THE MEMORIES.

BOOK I

LAURA
1893–96

I

—————————

THIS IS DUMA'S COUNTRY, thought Morgan. He alone can chart the way. Lean and dark-skinned, half Kikuyu, half Masai, Duma was a tracker without peer.

It was brazen, blazing country: metallic scrub criss-crossed by long-dry luggas, glittering soil that crumbled underfoot. Blue hills shimmered in the haze, retreating before them no matter how hard they marched. There had been gametracks but they were old and cold, obscured by ochre dust. The herds had vanished: one of those sudden, mysterious migrations many spoke of but none could explain.

That morning, Duma had sighted fresh elephant spoor. It disappeared at midday, lost on a blinding swathe of scree. Duma's gaunt, disgusted glance proclaimed their utter failure. Turning as one, they set course for Mount Kerinyagga's distant, snow-capped peak and the long trek home. They were two weeks older, not one whit richer or wiser.

Evening. A welcome breeze rattled the thorns, a rainbird's call came fluting down the scale. Witless creature, thought Morgan. It will never rain again. The notes seemed to echo, shifting tone, weaving a familiar melody. Duma paused, his brown face taut and suspicious; Morgan shook his head in disbelief. Somewhere near by, a Viennese waltz was playing.

Presently, from beneath a broad-browed acacia, they beheld a truly astonishing scene.

The phonograph stood in the open, its curved black horn aquiver. On the table beside it, amber liquid glowed through crystal glass. Blue smoke billowed behind the tents, bearing a whiff of broiled game-fowl. It was like no camp Morgan had ever seen, like a minor township risen from the wilderness. His mouth agape, he studied the three inhabitants.

Their khaki hunting suits looked new and expensively tailored; their calf-length riding boots oozed luxury. Beyond them, where a trickle of water gleamed, a fourth betrousered figure knelt and scrubbed.

The music faded, and one of the loungers rose to his feet: a fleshy, flaxen pup. As he yawned and stretched, sunlight slid below his solar topee, touching his yellow sideburns and glazed blue eyes. In the same instant, an errant wind struck the acacia, lifting Morgan's thin-leaved cover aside.

''Pon my soul – a bushman!'

Suddenly the glade came to life, with languid gestures and drawling, well-bred voices.

'Robinson Crusoe, I presume?'

'Looks like a beastly Boer to me.'

'There, you see? His very own Man Friday!'

Morgan came forward, doffing his slouch-hat and grinning: conscious, for the first time in weeks, of his own appearance. To these greenhorns, he must present a daunting sight – tall and broad and bearded, clad in hard-used buckskin and down-at-heel boots, plastered from knee to nape in fine red dust.

But the banter continued, undiminished.

'D'ye think it talks, Chas?'

'Doubt it, old boy. I'll wager it *drinks*, though.'

'Done. Have a grog, Robboe, and one for your tame blackamoor.'

Morgan gave his name, ignoring the insult, extending patience and a large, grimy paw. The blond boy touched it fastidiously, bowing low and parodying formal introductions.

'Charles Hardy at your service. Hal, my bro; James Seton, a chum.'

The brother was younger, acned and mousey, cast from the same chubby mould. Seton had full lips, curly black locks and the louche air of a ladies' man.

'A muzzle-loader,' he breathed, eyeing Morgan's rifle, 'a genuine antique. Don't tell me you actually kill things with that?'

'Not recently,' Morgan admitted; then, allowing the first, faint edge to his voice, 'It is a lethal weapon, though.'

In the sullen charged silence, Morgan registered Duma's disdain for their hosts; and that the shorter, younger men had closed ranks between himself and the figure at the stream. They were watching him hungrily, swaying slightly, smelling of hard spirits and French talc. There were echoes of the naval wardroom here, the officer class baiting other ranks. Three years ago in Mombasa, Morgan had jumped ship to escape just such abuse.

'I'm unaccustomed to spirits,' he murmured. 'Make mine a long one, if you please. And Duma takes his water neat.'

'The pitcher's empty, Morgan,' objected Hal, 'and the stream's a long way off.'

'Manners, Hal,' said Charles, 'these fellows are guests. I'll go.'

'No!' Seton spoke sharply, but his dark eyes gleamed with mischief. 'Proceed, Morgan. Make yourself known to the fourth musketeer.' And for some reason, this sally provoked them all to gloating sniggers . . .

Morgan approached the stream with ingrained caution. He intended neither surprise nor concealment, yet made no sound. He had simply forgotten how to move noisily.

This was the youngest Hardy brother, he guessed, noting the slender, blue-shirted back and the tell-tale swell of hips. He had Charles's blondness, too; sunlight played on a mop of golden hair. This observation brought Morgan up short. He must be very drunk; no sane and sober white man went hatless before dusk.

Morgan edged forward, letting his shadow announce his presence. The splashes continued unabated, together with low snarls of effort. Hopelessly unaware, poor child.

'Evening, son,' said Morgan. 'Your turn for the laundry?'

'It's *always* my bloody turn!' The fourth musketeer stiffened, whirled towards him – and promptly changed gender.

'*Son*, indeed,' she snorted. 'Who the hell are you?' Utterly non-plussed, he gawped down into bitter brown eyes and a thrust of rounded bosom against damp fabric. Once again, he doffed his hat, this time in confusion and an automatic gesture of respect.

'Morgan's the name, ma'am. Please excuse the error.'

'A gentleman, are you? You don't look it: didn't think they bred 'em any more.' Her voice was low-pitched, oddly musical despite the scathing tone. 'Morgan, eh. And you think *you* erred?' She bent to the water, smashing sodden khaki breeches against a rounded stone. Spray settled like dew on her long black lashes and mingled with the perspiration on her upper lip.

5

'Let me help,' he mumbled impulsively, surprising even himself.

She paused, tilting her face up in wonder. A rather pretty face, he realised: unusual colouring, even features and fine bones.

'I must be dreaming. He wants to help, he says. Oh *Christ!*' Her eyes widened in real alarm as Duma's slim reflection appeared in the becalmed water.

'My tracker, ma'am. He won't hurt you.'

'But my God, look at his *teeth!*'

'He files them, in the fashion of his tribe. All the better to eat you with, my dear.'

She laughed, with a rich and beguiling chuckle that stirred something deep inside him.

'I asked for that, no doubt. A tracker, you say; so you hunt.'

'I do.'

'Why?'

The question stunned him. No one had ever asked him that before. He squatted beside her, stroking his beard, reading part of an answer from the sweep of green-gold plain and the deepening blue above. 'For freedom, perhaps, and a challenge. To roam as I please and sleep where I fall, beholden to no one but myself.'

'Hm. That's what *he* said.'

'He?'

'James Seton. He lied, as you see.' She was rinsing the breeches, her movements more controlled now. The setting sun lit the line of her forearm, glinting on fine yellow down.

'Then why do you stay, Miss . . .?'

'Howard, Laura Howard. I have my reasons.' She sat on her haunches, her gaze direct but troubled. 'Unlike you, I *am* beholden. To James.'

'I see. So it's always your turn.'

'Very perceptive. And James is very – possessive. Don't provoke him, Morgan. Leave me, now.'

'He's little more than a boy, Miss Howard.'

'Laura. And they are three.'

'Even so.'

She stood, lifting and wringing the trousers. The roundness under her shirt swelled softly, stirring him once more.

'Morgan,' she murmured, 'a knight in battered buckskin, fearless, bold and gallant.' She tossed the dripping material aside and levelled a small pistol at him. 'Take me with you, Morgan!'

A derringer, he thought, the last resort of gamblers and whores. 'What good will it do you, Miss Howard, if you shoot me?' *Is* she a whore? he wondered. It would explain a lot. Her chuckle rang harsher than before, tinged with tension and acknowledgement. 'You can't take me, of course, but I thought the gun might – persuade you – to take notice.'

'Quite. You have my undivided attention.'

'Something happened in England,' she murmured, 'an event which left me infirm and – *bereft*. James proposed this safari, as a healing dose of sport and amusement.' Bitterness overcame her again, putting an edge to every word. 'He forgot to mention that *I* would provide much of the sport. I lost my temper and he lost this.' The derringer flickered, blue and deadly. '*Look* at me, damn you!'

Her free hand flashed upward, tearing at the buttons on her shirt. The material rustled open and down, revealing her shoulder and the upper slopes of her bosom. Bruises stood out starkly, where splayed and brutal fingers had raked the creamy flesh. 'Their hunger is growing, Morgan; I want to sleep without fear!'

Her breathing slowed and deepened, her posture shifted subtly. He was suddenly and acutely aware of her semi-nakedness, and the rise and fall of her breasts.

'Are you never lonely, Morgan? Do you sometimes yearn for solace, out in this fierce land? Or does Duma provide that, too?' The taunt stung, the blatant sensuality rekindled his doubts about her chastity.

'My appetites are normal,' he growled. 'They do not run to ladies who wield a pistol.'

'Then shoot me, for I'd rather die than stay here!' She thrust out her hand, offering the pistol butt-forward. Despair hollowed her features, making dark, clouded pools of her eyes.

'I will escort you to the trading post beyond Kerinyagga. From there, the southward route is easy and well used. You will doubtless find some coastbound traveller who will welcome you.'

She stiffened, drawing herself up, pulling the shirt tight about her throat. Her glance was at once wounded and haughty.

'You are quick to condemn and slow to understand. Some day, you may regret your judgement; you will never regret the decision. I shall be ready at sun-up.'

She returned like a wraith through rising mist and the first pink

7

blush of dawn. Still hatless, she wore the same trousers and a shirt of muted green. She strode freely: slim and eager and erect as a boy soldier.

'What's that?' he demanded, eyeing her bulky brown valise.

'My worldly goods, such as they are.'

'Leave them. We can't afford any extra burdens.'

'I'll carry it myself.'

'God's blood, must I explain everything? Don't you realise that very soon your playmates will miss you, and come thundering down on their white steeds. How shall I elude them, encumbered by this – wardrobe?'

'Don't fuss, man! They will rise mid-morning, bleary and addle-pated – and they won't gallop anywhere today.' She grinned impishly, inviting his applause. 'You see – I freed the horses.'

'That was clever, coming from someone whose brains will fry for the want of a hat!'

'More cleverness than you displayed, even though you wear one night and day. Lead on, and never mind the sun.'

She had dogged him ever since, over ridge and plain, through the slight, slow shift of African seasons. The gods had smiled, and Morgan had prospered. First, he had bought the donkey, to carry the equipment out and bear the ever-growing haul of hides back. Next he'd bought a modern hunting rifle, with a choke barrel and ready-made bullets. The muzzle-loader became Laura's companion, providing pot meat and fowl. Finally, his ambition blooming, Morgan built the cart and took it with them in search of elephant. The cache of ivory mounted; Duma's local status soared.

And Laura became Morgan's lover.

But although he possessed her body, he could not embrace her spirit. She forbade any talk of the past, and would not countenance the sound of Seton's name. Sometimes at night he wondered, as her thighs locked around him and urged him on. It was as though she needed his hardness there, to fill a void within, to cleanse some deep and lingering wound. He said as much, once, and felt the rigour take her. Her breath was warm with loving, but her words as cold as stone.

'Spare me no sentiment, Morgan. Take comfort where you may find it – who knows what the dawn may bring.'

It had troubled him then; it troubled him still.

8

She told him in the full blaze of day. They stood together on hot grey rock, overlooking a plateau where the wind made slow gold ripples in standing grass. 'A week ago, I galloped the donkey until he baulked in soapy lather. The night before last, while you snored, I emptied that bottle of gin. I was sick as a pig at first light, but still burdened.'

He misread the signs, taking it for more of her teasing. 'The sun has unhinged you at last. Tomorrow, I'll make you a hat.'

She turned on him fiercely, with the bitter, brown-eyed glare he thought she had buried at James Seton's camp in Samburu.

'You took the pleasure; I cannot be rid of the price. I am with your child!' Then he knew a moment of total awareness: the wind in his face, the solid earth at his feet; the liquid cry of a coucal, the free, fresh scent of the bush; sunlight glinting on the upward sweep of her eyelashes; and a truth, sprung from somewhere inside him. *This is the way it must be.* I have known it, since that very first meeting in the lowlands.

'I'm waiting, Morgan. What do you want me to do?' Her face was gaunt with a tension he couldn't begin to understand, as if she expected nothing but pain and rejection.

'We will go back, and find a mission and a midwife.'

'You'll stand by me, and give the child a name? Do you swear?'

'Sweet Christ, woman, it's *my* child!'

She turned away from him, and he thought he heard a sob.

'Don't be afraid, Laura. We'll travel slowly and carefully.'

'Afraid,' she whispered, '*afraid?*' As she swung to face him again, he glimpsed a moistness of eye, a softness of expression he knew she owned and might one day explain. Then she laughed, with great mocking peals that challenged the breeze. 'You witless oaf, my time is months ahead! We'll hunt together, you and I, and enjoy the nights as never before.' He studied her gravely.

'Are you sure? Would it not cause – harm?'

And now, at last, she matched his mood, her features clear and sober. 'We will talk no more of this. Some day, you shall know – everything.'

This vow, so solemnly spoken, she had yet to honour. They had indeed enjoyed the nights, until very recently: she was both supple and inventive, despite the bulge. But that brief, bright tenderness had never been repeated.

9

2

THE FOREST HAD ENTOMBED them, smelling of leaf mould and risen dust. Overhead, great boughs wove through shrouds of hanging Spanish moss. It was twilight all day, in the forest; still and cool and dim. Following Duma down twisted green tunnels, Morgan had forgotten the colour of the sky.

Behind him, hooves clip-clopped on packed brown earth. The cart creaked in protest at every turn, laden with hunters' bounty: buckskins and zebra hides, salted meat, curved and weighty tusks. A modest fortune in ivory, he reckoned, and enough victuals to see us through the short rains. All of us.

The pathway opened abruptly, threading a glade beneath an ancient fig tree. Late sunrays pierced the high green leaves and burnished the grass to gold. There was a hint of woodsmoke and a gleam of blackened stumps. Mansign, the first they'd seen for days.

Duma accelerated the pace, conscious, no doubt, of the journey's end; and of the softer sounds Morgan preferred to ignore. They came more frequently now, reluctant, hard-fought whimpers of distress. Morgan frowned and lengthened his own stride.

'Whoa—hold, you men. This is far enough!' Her voice was thick with pain and fatigue. The hoof-sound stuttered, the creaking died away. 'Move on,' he urged Duma softly, 'move on, and she must follow.'

'Damn you, Jed Morgan!' she cried, 'Are you going to desert us?'

Us, again. It checked him, and brought him round to face her and the waning brightness.

She perched, side-saddle, on the donkey's silvered rump. Her belly jutted roundly beneath the long black skirt. She was hatless as always, erect but ghostly pale. Briefly, she sat in radiance. Sunlight made a halo of her tangled, wheaten hair.

'Courage, woman,' he growled, 'the Mission isn't far away. There'll be a bed for your confinement, and white nuns to soothe your pain.'

'I couldn't care less for pious hags and starchy linen! Your son was spawned beneath the stars; I'll bear him the same way!'

'Indeed? On the cold damp earth, like some gypsy's bastard whelp?'

'You said it, Morgan, not I.' He saw the pangs take her. 'Besides,' she gasped, 'we have neither the time nor the choice.' Then, in flawed Swahili, 'Duma, fetch some long straight logs. Split them into two, set them there, in the lowest fork, where those three branches join. Make me a bed, Duma, away from the cold, damp sod!' Her laughter rose, joyous and full-throated. 'He shall be born in the trees, Morgan, as befits the son of a bearded ape!'

'Fitting, to be sure, since he has a cuckoo for a mother. And why *he*? How can you possibly know?'

Colour returned to her cheeks, and with it, the haughty passion he so admired. 'Haven't I always given you what you want?'

'It's madness, Laura, with help so near. I won't be responsible.'

'You will be, before this night is over.' Her tone had mellowed. She said it like a solemn vow.

He paused, undecided, aware of Duma's tension. He was a half-breed, and disowned by both his tribes; but nobody's slave. In Duma's world, women hewed wood and drew water. He was waiting in mobile shadow, the sunlight dappling his rich brown skin.

Laura spoke quietly, sensing the issue, cleaving straight to its root. 'When all is prepared, send him on to the Mission with your precious tusks. He can carry a note, too. It will show our trust and make him feel important.'

'Clever,' he grunted, 'but it won't achieve anything. They won't come into the forest at night.'

'Of course not. We'll invite them to breakfast, chez Morgan-under-the-fig.'

'The joke is over, Laura. No spasms now, I see. Let's go.'

'You moron, you blind, insensitive male! Because I don't cry, you think the pain is gone? Will your son crawl back in and await our convenience? If you're not damned careful, he'll arrive on a donkey's backside.'

He bore her fury calmly, put her to the final test.

'There's a word you've never used, not once since we've been together. If I'm to believe you, you'll have to say it now.'

It stilled her anger, banishing the livid flush. There might have been a flicker of remorse in her eyes, beneath the pain and defiance. Then, to his astonishment, she did say it.

'*Please*, Jed. Do this for me.'

A roosting dove mourned, far above. The donkey snorted, shifting uneasily under Laura's weight. Looking up into her strained, handsome face, Morgan saw how much it meant to her, how little he had to concede. 'Come here, Duma,' he said, 'we have work to do.' And gently helped her to dismount.

Light from high, narrow windows flickered across the valley. The Mission is a hawk, thought Duma, a white-winged hawk with yellow eyes, stooping over the village.

He stood at the edge of the forest, where greenness dwindled into the fall of night. Below him, the huts lay shadowed. Smoke-saplings grew from every roof, thin and tall and grey. There was dust in the air, and fireflies, and a whiff of roasting meat. Here is warmth and plenty, he thought, within easy reach of the lone and sacred fig. He could have told them this: but they hadn't asked.

Instead, he'd swallowed his pride and done as they asked. He had wedged the split logs flat and tight, covering them with fresh-plucked scented ferns. Then he placed a supple zebra hide, and two of the thickest blankets. He'd trimmed the wick and primed the lamp, hanging it from a higher branch. The memsahib had her nest; he, Duma, had built it safe and snug.

Beneath it, he had set a good fire and a tub of water from the stream. He couldn't imagine why she needed such things. It was, after all, a simple birthing. Surely not even white infants ate cooked food and drank cold water?

What strange, pale people they were! The memsahib, though quite mad, had quickly hardened the Bearded One's manhood and softened his brain. How could she give him pleasure, having high sharp breasts and the haunches of a stripling boy? A real woman should be soft and fat like a hippo, so a man could further his line in comfort. He, Duma, had such a one, here in the valley. She would be in bed by now, drowsy and willing. This knowledge, and the thickening scent of meat, tempted him sorely.

He would greet his wife Wanjui before seeking help from the Mission.

*

'I have borne your child,' Wanjui said, from the dim and smoky doorway of the hut.

'Show me,' Duma whispered eagerly; but saw at once that she was sick in spirit. Though fireglow played on her full brown breasts, there was slackness in her body and mourning in her eyes.

'The Healer took him from me. He came feet first.'

Such a birthing was tabu. Its offspring must be carried to the forest and left to the hyenas, lest evil should befall the whole clan. Duma shuddered, picturing carrion beasts growing fat on the first fruit of his loins. He stepped forward, to give and take comfort in embrace. Wanjui's plump pink palms rose against him. 'My teats still ache. Blood still flows from me. You must sleep alone till I am cleansed.'

She turned away from him into the lonely hut-darkness. Presently, he heard her weeping.

Beside him the ass grazed patiently, its teeth rasping on tussock grass. At every moment, the cart groaned like a man in pain. What use are riches, Duma wondered, to us who are so cruelly bereaved?

He gazed up at Kerinyagga's starlit, silvered peak where the great God Ngai dwelt. Cleanse her soon, he pleaded, that we may once more lie together. Get her with a son to heal her hurt and prove my manhood. Do this, and I shall love him all my life, and raise him to bring honour on thy name.

An owl hooted. The evening star gleamed above the dark, still forest. Duma tethered the ass, too grief-stricken to approach the Mission. Farewell, Bearded One, he thought, with your scrawny woman. May she be favoured with a swift and normal birthing. May forest gods smile on fools and little children.

Morgan stepped back, watching firelight glisten on his handiwork.

He'd cut the notches broad and deep, roughly a foot apart. They arced palely up to the platform and smelled of clean, tart sap. The rope dangled alongside, forming a makeshift banister. Not the most noble of stairways, perhaps, but the best he could provide.

Laura huddled near the flames. Her chin and cheekbones jutted in the upward bluish glow, giving her face a peevish cast.

'By God, you took your time,' she snapped. 'I hope it was worth it. What were you making, apart from an infernal din?'

'Laura's ladder.'

'You killed all the snakes, I trust. Here' – she gave him a chipped enamel mug. Tea, tepid and far too sweet; he couldn't disguise his distaste – 'if you don't like it, brew it yourself!'

'Having second thoughts, Laura? Getting cold feet?'

'Don't be absurd! Watch.'

She rose clumsily, steadied herself, pulling tucks in her skirt until she held the hem under her chin. Her voice was harsh but muffled. 'Take them off. My drawers, you fool! Do you think I'd ask if I could do it myself?' Bending, feeling awkward and thumb-fingered, he rolled the white silk downwards until it pooled over dusty bare toes. She lifted one foot, then the other.

He gazed up the slim line of her legs to the shadowed golden gleam between, and the alarming thrust of her pallid belly.

'God's blood, you're a brazen hussy!'

'Blushing, Morgan? No need. The waters are near to breaking. Why soil my best pair of bloomers?' Her voice cracked on the last word, the smile thinned and set in a rictus of pain. 'Brace my back, damn you! Not there, higher!'

Her rigid body awed him and he could feel the writhe of wiry muscle. And somewhere beneath, he actually sensed new life straining to be free.

'Lord save us,' he muttered, 'I never knew!'

'Hah! There'd be precious few babies if men had to bear them.'

The spasm left her. He breathed her earthy odour, and carbolic so strong it made him squeeze.

'Faugh, woman, you stink like a hospital ship!'

'Of course I do, I'm *clean*! Would you have him arrive to squalor?'

She sagged against him, panting. 'He's a Morgan, all right, he fights me harder than you. What shall we call him?'

'Him, *him*, you never stop. Suppose it's *her*!'

'You see? More conflict. Oh *Christ!*' This time, the spasm struck deeper and held longer, hardening her belly, bowing her back. Then there was a squelch, a salty sharp whiff, a cry of relief and triumph. 'There! Now he's truly on his way!'

And so, amazingly, was Laura; a broad dark shadow waddling to the tree, barking out orders.

'Fetch my bag. Come here and help me climb.'

He obeyed, fearful for her. But she managed the crude steps well enough and vanished into the dimness above. He heard the rasp of flint and winced at the reek of paraffin. A yellow gleam filtered down.

'Hmph. One man, at least, has been useful. A cosy lair indeed. The bag, if you please!' He hoisted it, shoved it over the edge. 'Good. Go back to the fire, you'll get in my way up here.'

'Are you sure?'

'Stop dithering, man! Get some rest – you'll need it.'

Alone and uneasy he set fresh twigs among the embers. The platform creaked softly to her movements, her enlarged shadow wavering to and fro. Presently, he heard a sharp rend of some material.

'Laura? What was that?'

'My finest blouse. He'll be wrapped in silk. Now wait till I call.'

Presently, she seemed to settle. The noises ceased, the lamp shone out unshaded. Huddled beneath a blanket, toasting his hands, he shut the forest fears away; thinking only of Laura, in labour.

An ember popped sharply, startling Morgan awake. It was past midnight – he knew by the cold and the wheel of stars through a patchwork of black, jagged foliage. 'Laura?' he called, 'what's happening?'

'Pain, you fool, what else? Tend the fire, and set that water to boil!'

Obsessed with hygiene, heedless of the kettle, he fumbled with the soap and froze his fingers at the tub. Exuding concern and carbolic, he climbed the makeshift steps. How does she know, he wondered, how can she be so calm and certain?

No time to ask, for faint, fresh life was stirring: a mewling cry, an upward crimson scowl, a flutter of tiny fists.

'Support the head,' she warned. 'Hold your child.'

Somehow, she had raised herself. Her serenity stunned him; she wore a pure pale smile of innocence and triumph. 'How do you feel, Father?'

Overwhelmed. Awed by this feeble thing, this living, breathing portion of himself. The lamp flickered, drawing his gaze to her nakedness. Engorged breasts, slackened thighs, the reddened, sodden core of her. 'I'll survive,' he muttered. 'Will you?'

'Of course I will.' The urgency took her again. 'What about his fingers and toes? Quickly, is he whole?'

Morgan counted aloud, teasing her gently. '. . . eight, nine, ten. Fingers too.' Without surprise, his eye rested briefly on the tasselled pink sex, then travelled upwards. 'He has no teeth,' he said, 'and I think his eyes are navy blue.' The child squawled more lustily. And Morgan heard his own voice, choked with pride. 'He's beautiful.'

'And hungry. Give him to me.'

He hesitated, already feeling a powerful sense of possession.

'Please, Jed,' she said, for the second time that night. 'You've no idea how I need him.' He could see, though. She reclined against the trunk, her arms outstretched in supplication; as if, at any moment, the child might be stolen away.

Morgan relinquished his son. She took him gently, crooning, and put him to her breast. He sucked and slurped blindly. Smiling, she cupped a nipple and eased it into his mouth. 'My love,' she murmured, 'my darling.'

Morgan looked away, suppressing a pang of jealousy, sensing a profound unity. Thus it began, he thought, with full-grown maleness at her breast and on her belly. Now we must share her, he and I; and she must share us. 'I'll get a blanket,' he said.

'Not yet.' She was leaning back, her eyes closed, her expression rapt. As he watched, her lips thinned, another ripple shook her frame. 'Twins,' he growled, in alarm, 'God's blood!'

'No, mine.'

A shapeless purple mass soiled the junction of her thighs. 'Afterbirth,' she explained dreamily, 'and no further use. Don't frown, man, everything is prepared. You will find a pair of bloomers there. Wrap it up; bury it later.'

The ugly glisten disturbed him. 'I'll do it now.'

He stooped, wrinkling his nose; shifted her limbs gently, cleaned her as best he could. He stood for a moment, feeling the squishiness inside the material, and tossed it into the night.

'Squeamish?' she murmured, and chuckled richly.

He hovered over her, lowering the wick, reducing the glow, laying blankets across her. She sighed and shifted the baby, giving the other breast.

'Morgan? Remember this evening, something you made me say?'

'A lifetime ago. *His* lifetime.'

'Don't wriggle. I was thinking – isn't it your turn, now?'

He knew what she meant. Knew, as sure as sunrise, that the words would soon be spoken, yet couldn't quite bring himself to speak them.

'I was thinking, too. About tomorrow. A double ceremony, at the Mission. Baptism, and – giving him a surname?' In the dimness, he sensed rather than saw her smile.

16

'Is this a proposal of marriage?'

'He hasn't left us much choice.'

'My, such overbearing passion, such honeyed words. Still, as you say, Hobson's choice.' Her laugh surprised him with its strength and mischief. 'As a matter of fact, I suggested as much, in the note.'

'You are a conniving hussy!'

'Perhaps. It takes two to – connive.'

She sounded drowsy and content; she had ample right to be both. The suckling noises faded, the leaves rustled overhead. Nothing sinister now; just the forest, paying tribute. Morgan lingered, held by her aura. Their aura.

She was sleeping; he could tell by the even breathing. The babe was quiet too. Concerned, he squatted beside her and reached out a questioning hand.

She stirred. Yellow lamplight blazed from her opened eyes: eyes wide and wild, blind with fright and horror that rocked him to his heels.

'Steady, woman. It's me, standing guard.' The wildness faded, softened. 'Will he be all right, Laura? Shouldn't he be swaddled, given a cradle?'

'All in good time.' Her voice steadied. 'Tonight, he has his mother's warmth. I will cherish him, Morgan, now and always.'

He straightened, satisfied. 'I'll tend the fire. Rest as long as you can. At dawn I'll hunt, and give you a tasty breakfast.' He stepped across her and turned to descend the steps.

'Morgan? Promise me one thing?'

'What?'

The tension came back, putting steel in her voice. 'Never, ever, let anyone take him from me.'

Shades of the past, he knew, ghosts he must help her to banish. One day, surely, she would show him how.

He chose his answer precisely, speaking it like a prayer. 'I will die first. Sleep in peace Laura.' And goodnight, my son, he added inwardly, climbing down through the scent of drying sap.

My son, he mused, overseeing the fire once more. My firstborn son; what will he be like? With luck, he will have my stature and her litheness, my strength and her beauty. Not for him the shackles of class and convention, the narrow horizons and dismal towns, the mindless military discipline. Like Duma, he belongs here, by blood and birth and being.

Morgan leaned back, savouring the idea, gazing once more at cold bright stars through darkly shifting leaves. I will buy land, he thought, find a place to set down roots, to raise good crops and livestock; and children. And he shall inherit.

It is good, he thought, as warmth and weariness ambushed him, for a man to have a purpose: dreams to pursue, ambitions to fulfil, people to love and protect.

Nodding, seconds from sleep, he glimpsed the low, dim platform which harboured all these hopes. I will protect you, Laura, he vowed, as long as we both are spared.

For giving me my son.

3

THE FROGS AT THE stream fell silent, sensing a predatory approach. Presently, noiselessly, the rushes parted. A gaunt, bent shadow darkened the starlit water.

The lion was old and crippled. Three months ago, at mating time, a younger male had challenged: bold and blond and massive, under a blood-red dawn. Defeated, his haunches gored to tatters, this once-proud creature limped away. Denied the sunlit killing grounds, shorn of pace and power, he skulked the forest fringes in search of easy prey.

He found it quite soon: a pale blob gleaming under a patch of nettle. He checked, his hackles risen. Manscent, manblood, the musk of ancestral enmity.

Hunger prevailed. Ducking, he snatched the bundle, bit deep and swallowed. Its juices flooded his maw, warmed his gut, surged like sunshine in his veins. Too slim the morsel, too short the relief. He craved more.

Ears pricked, belly brushing damp undergrowth, he prowled the deep shadow along the edge of the glade. He snarled soundlessly at the embers, an enemy older than man. Fear of them cowed him briefly; but, beneath the smoke, he smelled prey.

A smell which rose, inviting, from a huddle near the flames. The lion advanced, feline and flattened, drawn by need no mere fire could deflect. This time, he gauged distance and moment precisely. This time, he lunged – and struck.

Morgan knew a few brief, brutal final moments, with talons raking at him, a great weight on his chest, a feline reek and his own blood coppery in his throat. Every instinct urged him to cry out. A last lost shred of courage held him dumb. If he screamed, Laura would be drawn to mortal danger and the lion would take her too.

So Morgan clamped his jaw, and died in silent agony and darkness, so that his kin might live to see the dawn.

The lion lay in bliss, savouring new richness and yielding flesh. The embers crackled. The animal dragged remains into deeper shadow, slurping at soft intestines, crushing flaccid limbs. Soon, only the hands were left. They smelled of soap, prickling his eyes and muzzle. The lion sneezed and left them, pale beneath the stars.

He settled, by no means sated, bloodied chin on bloodied paws. His cold gold glare slid upwards over the sheltering bush – up to the glow in the tree, from whence came a warmer, sweeter scent.

The scent of meat.

She woke to wind-tossed brightness and a piercing sense of loss: something awful has happened! I am hollow again – barren, alone, bereft. Oh Christ, spare me this pain!

She sensed movement near by, scarcely daring to believe. Remembering how, in darkness, she had swathed the sleeping child, curled herself around him to keep him safe. Oh my love, she breathed, into dark blue eyes and matted hair. She swept him up and kissed him, and let her glad tears fall.

His forceful suckle thrilled her, making her sigh with pleasure. Full, he burped lustily, smelling of warm milk and new birth. 'Morgan?' she called. 'Where's that tasty breakfast?'

No answer, save the soughing breeze. I'll meet him, she decided, surprise him with tea at the fireside and his brand-new, well-groomed son.

She bore him carefully down Laura's ladder, and walked over the dappled grass, dew scattering like diamonds underfoot. The kettle simmered on the dull red embers. The soap lay at the bottom of the clouded tub. The signs betray you, Morgan, she thought, they show your haste and concern. Her heart rose, singing.

Shrugging off her blouse, she laid the child upon it and unbound him. He frowned, grumbling against the indignity; as well he might – was there ever a boy to relish soapy water?

She shredded the blouse and swaddled him again. She was grinning now, conscious of cool bright air on her skin and the way she would look, to Morgan. A blushful bride-to-be, bare-breasted in the woods. Soaping herself blithely, she gasped as the cold rinse tautened her nipples.

The shock brought sudden uneasy awareness. The rustle of leaves was dying and no bird sang. Beware a silent forest, Duma had warned: it signifies death on the prowl.

She turned slowly. Her gaze quartered the sunlit glade, following the flattened swathe that snaked into shaded undergrowth, flinching from dull brown smears, resting in wide-eyed horror on the remnant of Morgan's hat. He went nowhere without it: *I will die first*, he had vowed.

The baby whimpered, sensing the icy clench within her. Not yet, she pleaded, not before his boy is weaned, before we have spoken tender thoughts too long left unsaid. Let this be some clumsy jest, let him spring from these silent bushes, bearded and beaming with pride. She stumbled forward, reaching for the crumpled fabric.

And froze, as a tawny shadow rose across her path, growing shining fangs and sulphurous eyes.

She fought the panic, the urge to hopeless flight. *You have killed my man; you shall not take my child!* In that fierce fearful instant, she heard the kettle hiss, and conceived a fleeting hope.

She inched backwards, rigid and erect. The lion crouched, its twisted haunch aquiver. She laid the swaddled child down gently, touched his unwrinkled forehead once, placed the slippery soap beside him. Her eyes narrow and unyielding, she groped among the ashes. Her scorched fingers closed around a stout ember. Straightening, she stood between her baby and those terrible, hanging jaws.

And went towards them.

She took one pace, then a second, lifting the brand, seeing the sudden flame spill out against the cloudless blue. She could feel the beast's discomfort, and saw, in her mind's eye, the exact shape of its slinking retreat. She lunged forward, snarling in fury and triumph.

Some half-healed birthwound tore inside her. She felt the weakness, the warm wet gout of blood on her thighs. The brand was all at once heavy and it slithered from her grasp.

The lion's head lifted. She saw the flare of bloodlust and knew that she was lost.

The first swipe disembowelled her, flinging her face-down in the grass. Though physical pain seemed distant, her mind cried out in agony and grief. You are thrice cursed, Laura Howard: to lose any man who might love you; to surrender life in the instant it blooms; never to raise a child you have borne!

There was a hideous crunching sound, an ominous numbness below her waist. She was dragged backwards, her swollen breasts jolting, her fingers vainly clawing at soft earth. In a last, tear-blurred vision, she saw the child lying peacefully in the morning brightness, and the sharply smelling soap foaming yellow in the dew beside him.

Desperately, she twisted upwards, driving weak fists into gory whiskers. Bare fangs loomed above her. She fought them bitterly. I will die hard, she vowed, to buy a few more precious moments.

And pray that somehow, *someone* may yet protect our son.

Father Andrew was cross. Veins bulged at his temples and his eyes burned smoky grey.

Joyous braying had ruptured his dawn devotions. Rising from his knees, skidding on red stone, he'd raced to the Mission window and found a scene of sunlit devastation: a donkey had laid waste his lovingly nurtured delphiniums.

It was enough to try the patience of a saint – a status Father Andrew could not yet claim. In this his thirtieth year, he still suffered certain mortal frailties. Denying them and himself, he found solace in drab green cassocks, daily cold baths, gardening and muscular High Church orthodoxy.

This morning, restraint had failed him. Running one hand through his jet-black hair, he let out a most unsaintly bellow. 'Be off, you greedy vandal, you evil spawn of Satan!' The donkey browsed serenely, towing a creaky cargo of slaughter: striped hides and long cream tusks. Pausing, it actually *grinned* at him. Shattered blue petals winked between yellow teeth. 'Damn you!' hissed Father Andrew.

At which point, Duma had invaded his inner sanctum. He stood there semi-naked, smelling of woodsmoke and rancid goat fat. His flesh glowed rudely, matching and mocking the polished wood of the crucifix which hung on the whitewashed wall behind. With his own blasphemy and the sound of butchered flowers in his ears, Father Andrew had been obliged to grant audience.

He did so, mentally counting Duma's vices. A half-breed who neglects wife and hearth to plunder God's creation; who files his teeth and swears foul oaths and scorns the living Word. How *dare* he invoke Christian charity?

Duma made it sound matter-of-fact, this saga of greed and lust and stupidity. A pregnant slut, a bearded wastrel, a babe conceived out of wedlock and born in the trees.

Father Andrew's anger finally erupted. 'The *proof*, man, show me the proof!'

22

The tracker produced a folded scrap of paper from his kirtle, which he tendered reluctantly.

Unknown Father, [he read]
We have dwelt as man and wife for many months, beyond the reach of any church. God has seen fit to grant us a child – and earlier than expected! We invite you to share our joy, to receive our true repentance, to bless our union and cleanse our child of guilt.
Your prodigal daughter in spirit,
Laura Howard-Morgan.

Perhaps I was hasty, he thought. An unlikely slut, who uses smooth vellum and a cultured hand, and displays a subtle wit. An interesting name, too. It carries the ring of wealth.

His eye wandered beyond the window, where the donkey ambled and munched. Reparations might be claimed, new delphiniums sown, the Mission coffers replenished. Even in England, one must pay to enter holy matrimony. And there *was* a lot of ivory.

'You should have shown me this before,' Father Andrew said. 'God's house is ever open. We must make haste.'

At first the forest awed him, with its musty dimness and a thousand stealthy rustles. So vast, so vibrant, so – African. But the path was broad, the going easy. The tracker moved with comforting assurance, a sleek brown shadow utterly at home. Relaxing, Father Andrew followed, letting his hopes take wing.

Stumbling footfalls beside him brought him to guilty awareness. He had neglected Kibe.

Kibe was his one true disciple, the apple of his eye: a chubby, almond-skinned lad whose soft physique belied his moral fibre. Alone among the age-group, alone among the clan, Kibe had renounced all superstition. No sabbath Christian he, pious on Sunday, pagan through the week, but a questing soul who hungered for the Word. In six months, he had devoured the Kikuyu Bible. 'I want to be a priest,' he insisted, 'I want to save my people.'

Ever since, Kibe had served with dog-like devotion, scrubbing floors, reciting scripture, struggling to master English. This morning, wringing his hands over strewn blue petals, he'd whispered, 'You may need help. Where you go, I go.' And met Duma's withering gaze boldly.

23

The path widened. Beyond Kibe's bobbing, white-robed shoulder, between barbed leaves, Father Andrew glimpsed a spread of paler green. Thin smoke curled above grey ash, water glinted in a pail near by.

Then Duma halted.

He lifted his head, with his nostrils flared, his muscles twitching like oiled brown snakes across his shoulder span.

The air was totally still, touched with an ominous sweetness. From the corner of his eye, Father Andrew detected a living presence. His gaze passed uncomprehendingly over the small silken bundle, leaped to the low bush beyond it, and flinched from the fury crouching there. He actually saw the lion's bloodstained lips curl back, and read his own death in its fevered feline eyes.

The snarl froze his blood. Kibe gibbered beside him and turned to flee.

'Stand!' Duma ordered. 'If you move he will kill us all!' He bent his bow; the wood creaked quietly, the string tautened. The arrow glistened, black and deadly, waiting.

And the lion came on, contemptuous.

'Shoot, man!' breathed Father Andrew. 'He's almost upon us!'

'Would you have me wound the child?'

Child? Dear God, thought the priest, it is a child lying there, wrapped in beige silk, beneath those savage jaws! Prayer welled from the depths of his being, burst unbidden from his ashen lips. 'Heavenly Father, protector of the meek, deliver this innocent soul from evil!'

In that same instant, the baby stirred. A tiny pink fist struck upwards, seeming to brush the broad blunt muzzle. The cry startled them all. High-pitched yet lusty, it was a cry of hungry outrage, unyielding, unafraid.

The beast drew back, its bearing visibly altered. Father Andrew saw its bloodied mask twist in distaste, then heard a rumbling sneeze. The child squawled again. The lion snuffled, pawing soap-slimed grass in frustration; then it recoiled, wheeled, and vanished crookedly into the bush.

Kibe sank to his knees, his sallow upturned face washed with tears and holy radiance. 'A miracle,' he whispered, in English, 'oh Father, I have seen a miracle!' then, to Duma, in Kikuyu and joyous scorn, 'Kneel with me, heathen! Kneel before the one true God who answers every prayer!'

It was not to be. Duma started, shook himself like a dog coming out of water. '*Some* god favours this child,' he grunted. 'Let us now see if the begetters were as fortunate.'

'Take care,' the priest advised, 'the beast may return.'

Duma tested the risen breeze briefly, once. 'He is defeated: I *know*.' He moved off, his eyes fixed on a jagged trail of flattened grass.

Kibe was comforting the child, loosening the silk bands with his gentle brown hands. 'A boy,' he murmured, 'strong and well formed. He shall be the first son of the Mission.'

Gazing down on wondrous, living pinkness, Father Andrew's insight woke once more. His parents are dead, he thought, killed in his defence. I know this, as Duma knows.

A son of the Mission. The worldliness stirred within him and would not be denied. I should mourn the dead, he thought. Instead, my heart rejoices at a boy to shape in the service of the Lord, to follow my footsteps and extend my ministry.

He knelt in reverence, touched the warm flesh and replaced the silk clumsily. His glance fell on the clawed yellow soap. Its sharp freshness stung his eyes. She cared for you, he thought, kept you clean, bought your life with her devotion. Rest in peace, Miss Howard–Morgan. Know that your child shall grow in love. For I shall raise him, son of man – and God.

A slim shadow fell across them. Father Andrew looked into Duma's sombre eyes.

'My partner sired him, his mother was my friend. I have a claim on him!'

He's serious, Father Andrew realised grimly. Already, the struggle begins. Aloud, he said, 'The huts cannot hold him, Duma. He is a white boy.'

'A *hunter's* boy, bred to space and freedom!'

'You heard my prayer, saw the lion cower. This is a holy child. He belongs with me.'

The child stirred, sensing the clash of wills. The small face contorted, the hunger-cry sounded anew. 'Look at him!' crowed Duma. 'Hear his need for mother milk!' He thrust his lean brown arm skywards, glowing in the sun. 'Will your God, who dwells so far above, reach down and give him suckle? Yet I, Duma, can show him teats which ache to fill his mouth. *Give him to me!*'

Father Andrew retreated, clutching the silky, fretful bundle tightly: a child reprieved, whose fate now hung between two snarling men.

Until Kibe stepped in.

He walked like a beast of burden, bowed under blankets and hides. A small brown suitcase dangled from his left hand. Sweat glistened like honey on his forehead, dark damp patches soiled the dusty cassock. 'Shame on you,' he panted, 'for blighting his first fair morning with anger!' He straightened, releasing the load, and waved a plump hand through the sparkling dust. And scolded Father Andrew.

'Duma's wife has lost a child, we have found another. Isn't it a sign? Let her feed him, and take him to her hearth and breast. Surely she will love him as her own. For who else is there to wean him?' Kibe smiled, soft as the eddying breeze. 'Trust in the Lord, you said; and I reply – go thou and do likewise.' Father Andrew nodded, struck dumb; and Kibe rounded on the tracker.

'Curb your laughter, heathen, and listen to the bargain we'll strike. You will bring him each day to the Mission, to breathe its holy air. Once weaned, you will renounce him to the Father, from whom he will learn the white man's ways, and reading and writing. Later, perhaps, you may show him beasts and flowers as his parents might have wished.'

Kibe is come of age, mused Father Andrew, marching, and into the Lord's good grace. From now on, no one will dare to mock him. Duma will see to that.

The child squirmed and whimpered in his arms. He glanced down on his unfocused eyes and unformed features, marvelling. What kind of child is this, who in one fierce hour of life has made a lion into a lamb, and made Kibe the lamb into a godly lion? Yet what a testing lies ahead! To live in two worlds, to master conflicting beliefs, to choose the best of both and grow to worthy manhood. Forgive me, son. It is the will of God.

As they returned through vaulted forest greenness, Father Andrew couldn't suppress a smile: how strange is Thy procession, Lord; how quaint our human pride. There was Duma the hunter, striding free, carrying deadly weapons and a ladylike valise; Kibe the pilgrim, hides perched on his head, outthrust bottom wobbling under sweat-soaked white robes; and this Thy servant, vainly seeking to lull the babe who so enchants him. Grant him a lively mind and a humble spirit; grant him Thy precious gift of laughter.

Kibe fell into step beside him, and his mournful gaze sought out his own. 'No wedding now, Father, only a graveside service. You will not need an altar boy.'

'Nonsense! He must be baptised.' Kibe's face brightened under the pied burden.

'What shall he be called?'

The answer came without a moment's hesitation. 'We will christen him Leo, after the lion he vanquished.'

And all the way home, above the sound of forest doves and hungry squalling, the name rang like an anthem in Father Andrew's brain. Leo: Leo *Reid*.

4

BARE FEET RASPED on hard-baked dung, horny toenails glinted. Smoke rose, blurring a single lamp which hung from the sooty crossbeam. Its light touched hooded eyes and wizened necks, played on bulky bodies cloaked in monkey skin. Reeking of maize beer and old men's sweat, the elders squatted round Gitau's red hearth – like vultures, Duma thought, poised to rip the entrails from a wounded, weakened kid.

As chieftain, Gitau owned the largest hut and the choicest flock. Heavy-jowled and balding, he enjoyed authority, offspring from many wives and the sound of his own voice. Offering beer to age-mates, he preened in their approval for himself and his brew. They are united, Duma realised, while we two stand apart: a half-breed and an outcast Mission boy.

A brave outcast, Duma conceded, whose robes outshine the dimness, whose bearing yields to none. Ignoring the headman, Kibe's gaze sought the wellspring of true power – a slight, dark, silent figure who sat where the shadows joined and swung. Duma shivered and looked away. Only witless striplings challenge He Who Sits Alone.

The empty drinking horn flickered. Gitau scowled in condemnation. 'The huts abound in rumour,' he began, 'and there is doubt in our midst. Some say the priest brought forth spawn beneath a poison bush. Others speak of strange events and lions put to flight. We know this: Wanjui, whose birth was blighted, now gives suck to a son. A *white* son, round whom these rumours coil. The council wants to be rid of him. The council asks, who speaks for this child?'

'I do,' Kibe said, and Duma saw malice leap in Gitau's eye.

Kibe ignored it, speaking like a seasoned storyteller. 'It was morning in the forest. A newborn babe lay sleeping in green grass. There was sunshine and hot embers; and danger lurking in the shade.' His voice softened. Duma saw new interest in watchful, stony faces. 'A lion came,' breathed Kibe; 'its hunger stilled the glade.' Kibe's hands rose in the lamplight, their heels together, the fingers hooked. 'Its jaws,' he murmured, 'wide and bloody, hung above the pale flesh. The child cried out, the priest prayed: and that great beast turned tail and slunk away!'

He has won them, rejoiced Duma, as awed whispers mingled with the smoke. Then Kibe erred, by reminding them of who and what he was. 'This is a sacred child, a bearer of the living Word to lead us in God's way!'

'Do you swear it?' Gitau asked, deceptively humble.

'Yes!'

'Then you would take the oath?'

A sound stole from the shadows, like a slur of snakeskin on dry leaves: a sound of mirth and menace. Kibe whirled on it and thrust out a glint of gold and black. 'I give my oath on this, the Holy Bible!'

Words without weight, Duma knew, tokens of priestly interference. 'It is as we expected,' Gitau purred, 'a white man's foundling brought to spy; brought by a hutless Mission boy who dare not take the oath.'

'Your oaths are evil! I, Kibe, defecate upon them!'

Duma heard the collective gasp of outrage, shrank from righteous anger at his side. And flinched before that furthest shadow, from whence revenge would surely come.

A face emerged from the dimness, a hooked and hawklike face without expression. The flesh glowed smoothly, black and ageless. Yellow dik-dik horns enclosed the throat, a leather pouch on beaded thongs adorned the slim flat chest. The eyes held something old and red, something Duma didn't care to name. They were the eyes of Njau: Njau the Healer and giver of oaths, who walks and sits alone.

'I see you, Kibe,' he murmured, dangerously gentle. 'I hear your angry cry. Am I the evil of which you speak?'

The Mission boy steadied, holding the book like a small dark shield against his gleaming breast. 'You heal the sick, Njau, comfort the dying, bring peace to our disputes. For this, I honour you. It is God's work.'

'Then we have no quarrel, you and I.' Calm words; but Njau made them a threat.

'Your oaths *are* evil,' Kibe insisted. 'They feed like mould on darkness, bind us to eternal night and ancient, sinful arts!' He stood straight and held the Bible up. 'Here is joy and brightness, the Word of one true God! We have no quarrel, Njau. Some day we shall do battle for these poor, deluded souls!'

29

'Go to your Mission,' Njau advised, cold as mountain rain. 'Go and beg your meek, pale god that that day will never come.'

'It has begun,' breathed Kibe, 'in a fruitful prayer that turned a lion's lunge. You cannot withstand it!'

Njau was a scorpion, fierce and black and deadly. Kibe faced him, clothed in holy whiteness, erect and unafraid. This is the shape of wars to come, thought Duma. Neither will yield; their jealous gods could tear the tribe apart.

Gitau broke the deadlock, hawking phlegm, claiming the right of speech. 'Is our land not fair?' the headman demanded. 'Does it not please the senses and fatten the flocks?' He paused, his bald head dipping to the rumble of assent. 'Kibe has prattled of his god; now take heed of ours.'

Responding to him, the elders chanted '*Eeeh!*'

'Ngai gave us the sacred figs, where nine strong clans were spawned. He gave us plains to wander, sweet grass to feed our kine. What, then, is the greatest of his gifts?'

'Land,' they whispered, '*land!*' And even Duma joined them.

'Land,' agreed Gitau, smiling. Then, in sudden anger, 'Would you have us lose it? Have you forgotten Wa Kabiro's vision?' His tone hardened. Firelight etched disaster on his cheeks. 'Beware Red Strangers who ride an Iron Snake. They shall be among you like seeds on the wind. Where they settle, trees and flocks will die. There will be drought and famine; the clans will scatter. Then, when the land is empty, the Strangers will seize it for themselves!' His finger speared the gloom, aimed between Duma and Kibe. 'These fools would nurse such a stranger at our hearth!'

'Where is the famine?' cried Kibe. 'Where are the fleeing tribes? Here is the evil I spoke of! You would destroy this child, lest his power threatens your own!'

Gitau cupped a hand to his ear. 'Is this an elder's voice? Who is that noisy youth?' To a ripple of vengeful chuckles, he snapped, 'The council has heard you, Kibe. Leave us!'

We are divided, Duma realised. If Kibe disobeys, the child is forfeit. The law serves those who make it – fearful, cunning old men.

The fire flickered. Kibe's forlorn footfalls faded into the night outside. 'Now, hunter,' Gitau challenged, 'tell us of your catch.'

Duma's glance lifted to the hot gold lampglow seen through wisps of blue. I *am* a hunter, he thought. It is my one true talent, the thing that makes me a man. And this fat toad would mock it! He curbed his anger, and told the story simply, from his heart. 'First,' he said, 'this was no ordinary lion, being lame and near his natural end. He had drunk the blood of man; he had respect for nothing. Even fire held no terror for him. Without a white man's rifle, no force on earth could turn him.' He paused, tasting the tension he had created. 'Second, the babe lay as Kibe said, in the shadow of death. The lion's head went down, its fangs glistened. The child reached up and touched them, and frightened off a beast that knew no fear. Therefore, I say, the boy has magic powers and will grow up to grace our clan.' Seeing defeat in Gitau's sullen scowl, recalling the insult, he cried, 'He will be the greatest hunter in the tribe!'

'A hunter?' Gitau echoed. 'What use have we for *hunters*?' He rocked on his heels, sneering. 'Red Strangers, seeds on the wind.' His voice dropped, his eyes turned sly and sleepy. 'How fragile is new life,' he asked, 'how easily snuffed out? A careless moment at the river, a clumsy fall, a blanket draped across a sleeping face. Let the council answer: shall it be this way?'

Strange, thought Duma bitterly, how smoke can sting the eyes. Do they know the bleakness that will haunt Wanjui's eyes?

He heard the embers stutter and he blinked against sudden brightness. Njau stood lit by the smoulders, holding a small green gourd. 'Wait,' he said softly, 'will Duma eat the oath?'

Duma's breath quickened, his neck hair stood erect. He turned, unwilling, into that fearsome gaze – and caught his breath in wonder. The redness slumbered, laid to rest in depths of cool clear amber. These were *healing* eyes. Trust me, they said, for I can save the child. 'Yes!' said Duma. 'Gladly.'

Njau raised the gourd. His anklets jangled, his colobus-skin kirtle shone in pied splendour. 'The oath must be eaten and spoken seven times. *"If I have lied, may this oath scour my entrails, steal my sight and gnaw away my manhood. If I have lied, may this oath now destroy me."*'

Then Duma took the oath.

He tasted blood and brains, and something coldly caustic. The gourd felt smooth and harmless in his hands. At each swallow, he heard their solemn sighs. Each time he spoke, the truth within him hardened. He ate the oath and waited, unafraid.

'See,' breathed Njau, 'he lives! Duma the hunter stands before you proven in his truth!' The hut seethed with sound and movement. 'What does it mean?' Duma heard them ask. 'What shall befall the child?'

Njau cleared his throat, commanding instant silence. He moved as he spoke, in a silken sway of polished limbs. His voice took a subtle rhythm like the flowing of a stream. The planes in his face softened, redness returned to his eyes. He is using his powers, thought Duma, he is *making* them believe!

'Consider this meeting: a threat of gods at war, the council swayed by lowly men, a solemn, sacred oathing. And all because of this child. Is it not – *unusual?* Let the council answer!'

'*Eeeeh!*' growled Duma, nodding, blending his voice with the chorus.

'Consider the child himself,' Njau continued, 'who, in the very hour of birth, can lift a hand and quell a starving lion. From whence does his wondrous power spring? *Can* the council answer?'

The council couldn't. Heads shook, hands spread helplessly, deep frowns reappeared.

'*Duma* can answer!' cried Njau. '*Duma*, whose truth is proven, can answer one small question and put your minds at ease.'

So for a second time, Duma sought the healing glance and the sureness it bestowed. He found them both, and waited calmly.

'Tell the council, Duma: where was this child born?'

'In the tree.'

'The sacred fig tree?'

'The same.'

'So!' Njau swung round, black and white fur kirtle flying, teeth agleam. 'Do you not see? Red Strangers soiled a holy tree and Ngai sent a lion to kill them, to bless the clan with this, his favoured son! Consider one last omen: Wanjui has lately miscarried and is ripe to nourish and rear him. The god Ngai so wills it: let the council agree!'

Duma was swept up, embraced in furry arms and beery triumph. The lamp swung, the shadows stretched and shortened, until Njau hissed coldly and froze them where they stood.

'Wake the drummers,' he commanded, 'spread word throughout the tribe. Tell them this: the boy must grow to manhood and show us his great gifts. Njau the healer weaves a charm about him. Cursed shall be the living soul or beast that serves him ill!'

Duma paused at the threshold. Stars blazed high and silver, a nightwind soothed his skin. Wanjui's hut smelled warm and milky. Its musky welcome made his manhood stir.

I will wake them softly, he thought, so that the drums cause no alarm. I will breathe in these spicy embers, hear his healthy greed and watch the joy of suckling bloom upon Wanjui's face. He is *our* child now, held in sacred trust for all the tribe.

A *son*, he thought. A son to raise in love and duty, close to good green earth. He will learn the hunter's way: the speed of the hawk, the patience of the heron. He will know the spoor of bird and beast, the meanings in the wind. I, Duma, will teach him: teach him to dare the far free plains, to glory in the kill!

And the Mission shall not have him.

Earthly thunder stalked the night, rocking the floor Father Andrew knelt on, rocking his very faith. For the second time this long day his prayers were rudely shattered. Lord, he pleaded, must You so afflict me?

He quickened to the drums.

Their savage pulse inflamed him, waking a demon somewhere deep within. His brain conceived a lewd and livid image: naked figures writhing, firelight rich on high brown breasts and silky, swollen loins. His flesh crawled, his lips curled back in anguish. His eyes beseeched the wooden cross and the lamp which glowed above it. How feeble these thy tokens, how black this carnal spell!

He rose, retching, stumbling to the window; clutching the casement, he sucked great gouts of frigid, cleansing air. Furiously, tunelessly, he sought to drown the sound, by bellowing the first hymn that came to mind.

Rock of ages, cleft for me,
Let me hide myself in thee . . .

Slowly, the madness left him. It's just the drums, he thought, sending forth some superstitious nonsense. Something about Leo, probably.

Leo, he thought – so briefly held, so painfully surrendered. He is out there now, swaddled in sorcery, drifting away from God. *It must be stopped!* Tomorrow, I shall baptise him, deliver him from sin. He grinned, a clench of teeth without a hint of humour. Meanwhile – physician, heal thyself!

Father Andrew went to his knees beneath the cross, in the spirit of abasement and the scent of his own shame. 'Oh God, forgive this evil weakness. Grant me the soul of this child, make him Thy proud and spotless servant, that he may spread Thy pure sweet light on this benighted land!'

Only the drums answered, throbbing darkly, spreading Leo's legend throughout the listening tribe. A tale of death and birthing, a healer and his curse; a tale of myth and mystery, a lion and a boy.

5

HE CAME FROM THE west on a pale horse and a glitter of upthrown
dew. Only Duma heard the hoofbeats; only Duma saw him come.
He rode without haste, cleaving a straight dark furrow into the rain-
greened ridge. Sunlight flashed on his rifle and his round white hat.

The steady advance made Duma uneasy. The slight, slouched
khaki figure stirred a sleeping memory. Then, as the horse stumbled,
the hat tilted aside. Dark eyes blazed, a cry of anger echoed.

And Duma knew him.

Knew the face and voice, remembered the sallow cheeks and sulky
tone from a campfire in Samburu. The danger is upon us, he
thought, exactly as foretold.

The drums had rumbled, just three sunsets past. A Red Stranger
prowls the ridges, they said. Though heavily armed, he hunts
neither bird nor beast. No village can soothe his hunger. Beware,
warned the drums. He is not to be trusted.

'What does it mean?' Gitau had demanded, that night at the
council hearth. The question hung, unanswered, in the grey coiling
smoke.

Until Njau opened his leather pouch and cast the bones. In their
patterns, he could tell the future.

Time passed. Silence hung. The healer sat cross-legged and
unblinking. Only the shadows shifted, soft against his sleek black
skin. Slowly, the redness kindled in his eyes; his voice was harsh and
sure.

'He will come into a rising sun, borne on a great white ass. Greed
and fear ride with him, for he seeks to raise the dead.'

Njau's hand flexed and pounced. The bones chattered through his

34

fingers into their leather pouch. 'Guard the Lion Boy,' he whispered, 'lest the stranger does him harm.'

The mad memsahib lived again in Duma's mind; risen from the dead. He saw her clearly, stumbling through barren Samburu scrub, fleeing this stranger's greed and fear. Already, he thought, the word has become fact. If this much is true, Njau's whole vision will surely come to pass. Unless we prevent it.

A hush took the village, announcing the stranger's approach. Duma ran, up over dew-damp grass to the glaring whitewashed Mission wall. He turned the corner, unlatched the garden gate, and heard a sound which calmed his haste and made him grin with pleasure.

Leo was laughing.

It was a gurgle of innocent joy, a sound no villager could resist. When Leo laughed, the entire clan joined in. So they should, thought Duma. Throughout his four short seasons, the rains have been plentiful, the crops abundant, the herds fat and fruitful. And the boy has grown sturdy and clever.

This morning, while Wanjui tended forlorn blue flowers, Leo was testing the waters in a shallow, muddy pool. 'Churra!' he cried. 'See, Wanjui – Churra the frog!' He crouched and hopped, splashing noisily.

Duma's smile withered. Truth shone in the sunlight, a truth even Njau had overlooked. *Though we have raised and weaned him, taken him as our own, Leo is not born to the clan.* This same bright head will draw the stranger's gaze no matter how thick the crowd!

Somewhere within the building, Kibe's voice rose, anxiously calling the priest. Hoofsound and horse-smell eddied nearer. The secret plan faltered, an eyeblink from disaster. And Leo played on, untroubled, a child charmed by rainbow spray and flecked with rich brown mud.

Mud.

The word and the plan fused into Duma's brain. He lunged through the gate, falling to his knees beside his son and the blessed, cloudy pool.

'Father, the stranger is here!'

'*The* stranger, Kibe? Was he expected?'

'He is armed; he lingers near her grave.'

35

Next of kin, Father Andrew thought, someone to claim the dead. It was bound to happen, sooner or later; why, then, these evasions?

Childish laughter drifted in, distracting him further, bringing an involuntary smile to his lips. He stood up, pushing the half-written sermon aside. Leaning at the sunlit casement, ignoring Kibe's fidgets, he savoured the scene outside: Leo at play, romping and shimmering, Leo the golden one, the light of years to come. Enjoy these carefree moments, my son. Soon, you must learn the lessons, set out on the hard, long road to worthiness. The rod shall not be spared, for soldiers of God must be tempered early.

Kibe's hand was urgent at his sleeve. He looked down into a brown anguished gaze.

'*Please*, Father! This man means to steal the boy!'

'Nonsense! He has no right!'

But as he strode from the cool stone passage into brightness beyond, Father Andrew silently acknowledged the possibility. Next of kin might also claim the *living*. The fleeting happiness left him. Unkempt delphiniums proclaimed Wanjui's neglect; Duma's watery antics seemed merely irresponsible. Already, Leo's hair lay soiled and sodden. He could pass for a native boy.

'Take him inside,' Father Andrew snapped, 'clean the child! For heaven's sake, we have a visitor!'

And he wondered at Duma's knowing, sidelong glance.

The sun lifted, smouldering. Haze rippled on far green ridges. With doubt in his heart and Kibe at his heels, Father Andrew trudged towards an ancient Meru oak. Beneath it, he had raised a wooden cross to those who had bequeathed him a son. A monument, not a grave. The lion had left little to bury.

The great tree cast a deep shade. Within it, dimly, man and beast seemed one. The air smelled of blood and striving. Dark red spur gouges showed along pale, lathered flanks.

The horse snorted, acknowledging their approach. Its rider offered greeting. Aloft and faceless under the solar topee, he spoke softly and bitterly.

'My name is James Seton. I have travelled hard and far, and in vain. I had hoped to find Laura alive.'

'Console yourself,' Father Andrew murmured. 'She died swiftly and bravely.'

'You misunderstood, Father. She deserted us, turned our horses loose. *We* might have died, out in the scorching wastes. I came for a reckoning, not a valediction.' Seton dismounted, with a flicker of well-cut khaki, a creak of saddle leather. Tossing the reins at Kibe, he growled, 'Your nigger may water the beast.'

'His name is Kibe, sir. One day he will be a priest.'

'Bully for him.'

Bully, thought Father Andrew; very apt. He watched Seton pace the dewspread turf. He had cold, dark eyes, downcurled lips, an air of petulance. A spoilt young man, quick to vent displeasure, unused to opposition. His manicured hand rose, gesturing disdainfully at the cross.

'Laura was a slut, Father. For fifteen months, she dallied with a bearded oaf called Morgan. Come, don't look so naive. *What have you done with her child?*'

The drums, thought Father Andrew. The accursed drums have spread the rumour beyond the clan. He saw Kibe stiffen, with a furtive rustle of white robes. He felt the leap of his own pulse and sensed the onset of crisis. This is Leo's true kinsman, he thought, a preening bully bent on vengeance. Laura Howard had long since renounced him; must her son now be surrendered to his charge? He shall not, cried the soul of Andrew Reid. I cannot give him up.

Father Andrew straightened. 'You demanded truth, and received it. Now it is my turn. Where is your authority?'

Seton grinned, white and savage. Whirling, he drew the rifle from its scabbard. '*Here* is my authority. It demands sight of every child in the village.'

'Show him, Father. What have we to hide?' Kibe spoke evenly, in English.

''Pon my soul,' breathed Seton, 'a sensible, *civilised* nigger!'

There was ceremony, down among the huts. He could hear rhythmic footfalls, a rustle of cowhide kirtles. Oiled brown limbs swung in unison, trinkets blazed gold and scarlet and blue. The villagers filed past in family groups, gazing straight ahead. No one spoke. Even unweaned infants forbore to cry. It's so unlike them, Father Andrew mused, this silent discipline. Did they *know* we were coming?

'God's blood, they breed like vermin! How many more of these brats?' Seton was wilting in the heat. A livid flush suffused his cheeks; sweat stains crawled like spilled soup across his khaki shirt.

'You demanded *all* the children, Mr Seton.' Kibe spread his pale palms submissively.

'Move them along, damn you.'

It is immoral to deceive, Father Andrew thought. It is unchristian to relish another's discomfort. Yet, as the horse tugged uneasily at the reins and Seton's glower darkened, he was relishing it.

Until he saw Leo.

An impish grin and two unmistakable amber eyes glittered behind Wanjui's shoulder. She bore him Kikuyu-style, slung across her back. One chubby, mud-flecked leg dangled over her leather-clad hip. *He could pass for a native boy*, Father Andrew remembered. But *would* he? Seeing gold glint beneath the caked brown skull-cap, Father Andrew felt a sudden tightness in his chest. Dear God, he prayed, preserve us from discovery.

Suddenly Seton was moving, clutching the rifle in one hand, pawing Duma with the other. 'I know you! You were with Morgan at Samburu!' Duma checked, stared coldly at the splayed white fingers fast to his lean brown arm. Wanjui faltered, her eyes wide. Seton's face hovered, inches from Leo's head. He had only to turn a fraction.

But Seton had eyes for Duma alone. 'Ask him!' he ordered. 'Dare him to deny it!' Kibe placed himself at Duma's shoulder, shielding Wanjui and the child. The procession had halted, the hot air had turned sour. A glimmer of steel caught Father Andrew's attention; a warrior hefting a short, wicked spear. It was a tinder-box atmosphere; one rash act might set the spark. And Leo was still in the firing line.

Duma studied Seton dispassionately, from gleaming hat to polished boots. He spoke briefly in Kikuyu, mild words which defused the tension, forcing a grin to Father Andrew's dry lips. Muffled laughter spread; the young mothers giggled helplessly.

'What did he say?' snarled Seton. 'What did the bastard *say?*'

Kibe answered, his face tight with suppressed mirth. 'He said, "All white men look the same to me." '

'It's *him*, I tell you,' Seton raged, 'look at his bloody *teeth!*'

'Observe my people, Mr Seton,' Kibe murmured, 'it is the custom of this clan only.'

And Seton's flush turned crimson as he gazed at the circle of smiling, file-toothed warriors.

Wanjui had long since vanished with her precious burden. Duma shook off Seton's hand and loped away. The procession dissolved in a noisy hubbub. Even the horse, free at last, grazed gratefully.

38

Father Andrew let out a long sigh of relief. Meeting Kibe's eye, he opened his mouth to chide – and congratulate.

The report drowned his words, blasting across the ridges, creating instant stillness. Seton stood, wide-legged, the rifle angled skywards. Blue smoke hung above him; none of the watchers was smiling now.

'Come on then,' he goaded, and there was murder in his tone, 'let's see who laughs last! You're hiding something; I'll find it, if I have to ransack every stinking hovel!' He swaggered forward, the gun poised.

He emerged from the shade of Gitau's hut in a flutter of colobus skins and a clash of metal anklets, like a small pied jester on a village green. The young men parted before him, mouthing his name in a soft, collective sigh.

Njau.

His tone was quiet, sibilant, yet the words seemed to ring among the watching hills. 'Search the huts, stranger. If you find what you seek, you may go in peace. But if you fail, Njau's curse shall devour you. You will not leave this land alive.'

Again, the pent-up tension dissolved. The warriors relaxed, sheathing their weapons, watching Seton with a kind of pitying indifference.

'Don't translate,' Father Andrew warned Kibe, 'do not repeat this blasphemous curse!'

And Seton actually smiled. He swept off his hat, bowed to Njau, strode to his horse and slid the rifle into its scabbard.

'Let it not be said,' he muttered, 'that a Seton was *impolite*.' He set his hat jauntily, turned his palms upwards. 'See, Father, I am disarmed. I would like to speak to you – alone.'

Father Andrew hesitated only momentarily, conscious of Seton's almost girlish slightness, and of his own rawboned strength. Let us be done with each other, he thought.

'Come to the Mission,' he said.

The sanctum was blessedly cool. Muted light glowed on rough-hewn furniture and the hanging cross. Birdsong and soilscent rose from the garden outside.

Seton lounged at the casement, legs crossed, boots agleam, topee balanced on one slim, richly trousered knee. For a man who had suffered public defeat, he looked remarkably chipper.

'I need a document, Father. An official certificate of Laura's death.'

'You have it, man, in my report of her burial. Which, I assume, brought you here in the first place.'

'That, and certain – *rumours*.'

It is as I feared, Father Andrew thought. The drums have betrayed us. I must now surrender Leo, or continue this ungodly deceit.

Seton was already moving, utterly assured, to the desk. He selected a blank sheet, dipped the quill and wrote. He paused, frowned, bent once more. A whiff of cologne trailed him. The quill squeaked loudly. *He does not want Leo*, Father Andrew realised, in a moment of joyous insight. His belligerence faded at the first challenge. He was merely testing our resolve; acting, like everyone else. What, then, is his real purpose?

Seton turned, offered the paper and another dark, faintly malicious glance.

The vellum crackled in Father Andrew's hands. Fine calligraphy, a suitably ponderous tone.

I, Father Andrew Reid, resident priest of Kerinyagga Parish, do hereby certify the death of Laura Howard. She departed this life in February, 1894, victim of a savage beast. She died a spinster, without legal issue. I myself conducted her funeral service, and erected a monument to her memory, hard beside this Mission.

Given under my hand and the Mission Seal.

Seton had printed the date and left a space for the signature.

'A spinster,' Father Andrew noted, 'without legal issue.' An exact truth, to which a priest might testify without a qualm of conscience. Why, then, does my sight waver, why does my heart pound so?

Because there is a life at stake, a mysterious fusion of known blood, a soul cut loose from those who gave it being. Because this man looms over me, and I can almost taste the sourness of his need.

'It ends here, Father,' Seton vowed. 'Whatever lurks among the huts is safe from me for ever.' And Leo will be safe with *me*, Father Andrew thought: *for ever*.

So Father Andrew signed, relinquishing Leo's lineage; and recoiled from Seton's grin of fiendish triumph. 'Why?' he whispered. 'What is this to you?'

'*Wealth*, Father; a much improved inheritance. My parents died last year and left me a tidy sum. For some reason, Pater had a soft spot – made provision for Laura.' He smiled again, an evil, dark-skinned satyr. 'A lawyer chum explained it to me, after I'd read your report. If Laura *had* died, the money must be held in trust for her children.' He brandished the rolled paper. 'Laura did die. Noble Father Reid of Kerinyagga here proclaims it – and over the Mission seal. What court would question such credentials? *She died without issue*; her portion thus returns where it rightfully belongs – to me!' He paused in the doorway, doffed his hat once more. 'I wish you well, Father. May you and your – *foundling* – grow rich in the service of God!'

His boots clattered briskly along the passage. His laughter lingered, echoing, taunting. Presently, there came a hunter's halloo, a diminishing thunder of hooves.

Father Andrew slumped at his desk in the all-at-once sombre morning. It is easier, he reminded himself, for a camel to thread the eye of the needle than for the wealthy to enter the kingdom. Money cannot purchase happiness, nor love. Whosoever trusts in the Lord needs no worldly grandeur.

Oh Leo, what have I done?

A robber's judgement plagued Father Andrew deep into the night – *Laura was a slut*. Suppose it's true, he thought. She was Leo's mother. Would he too be tarnished by unseemly lust?

He let intuition guide him down the passage to the tiny storeroom where Laura's chattels lay. Setting the lamp down, he opened her valise. Her silks shimmered, green and pink and umber. How fine they were, how feminine, how delicately perfumed. Adornment for a lady – or the trappings of a whore?

His probing fingers touched something square and solid. He lifted it out, handling the dark brown leather binding gently, turning it to the light.

Laura Howard's diary.

It was a five-year journal, its pages edged in gold. He let it fall open at random. His scalp prickled. A single word erupted from the paper, composed of savage, black, inch-high strokes.

'WHY?'

He noted the date – May 1892 – rifled through the earlier months. Faint-ruled blank leaves, no clue to this shocking outburst. Then, in early June: 'I *know* why. I share his shame and understand his reasons. But, God, how I ache inside! That which was full is empty. That which should be emptied overflows!' A five-day gap, then another pain-racked entry. 'He who was so ardent now treats me with contempt: as if nothing has happened, as if I had no part in it. I am close to them yet distanced. I hunger yet cannot feed. And there is no end to it!'

What shame did she share, he wondered, for what did she hunger? There were shades of his own weakness here; passions veiled and sins concealed. He turned the pages faster, seeking her vindication. At the end of August, he came upon a clearer hand. 'James has invited me to safari in Africa, and cannot understand my dismay. I am resolved to leave and never to return. It is the best way, the only way. Part of me will always be here, *but I must go!*'

An unlikely whore, Father Andrew reasoned, who, consigned to the bush and able-bodied consorts, weeps for the 'part of her' that stays behind. He pulled the cassock tighter against night chill and read of evil in Samburu.

'James came to my tent tonight, inflamed and reeking of gin. The Hardys lurked behind him, smirking and swaggering, waiting their turn! They are filthy lechers, *and they know*! Don't struggle, they taunted, we will give you what you crave! I will not submit. Somehow, I will survive this nightmare!'

The last defiant sentence seemed to echo in the gloom. The lamp flared. Nightwind sighed. She was leaving him now, her character unblemished; leaving Seton branded thief – and liar. My judgement is restored, Father Andrew rejoiced. Praise God I didn't give the boy away!

The drums spoke abruptly, shaking cobwebbed walls. Pages lifted, wavered, settled. Father Andrew glanced down. 'Last night,' he read, 'I repaid Morgan's trust. I saw it, unspoken, in his moonlit eyes. *You are my woman, I will cherish and protect you.* I reared back across his thighs, his hardness deep inside me. Dear Lord, I pleaded, let me bear his child! His beard was silky at my breast. Our hot juices mingled. I melted to his hands, and all . . .'

Enough, he thought, replacing the diary, fighting pagan drum-rhythm and his own awakened manhood. He raised the lamp, closed and locked the door. I will not return here, he vowed. The dead shall keep their secrets. Rest in peace, Laura, prodigal daughter, worthy mother to my son.

BOOK II

LEO
1896–1918

6

BEYOND LUSH GREEN mangrove swamp, the Indian Ocean wallowed flat and oily blue. A Union Jack hung limp in the stifling afternoon sunshine. The entire white population had gathered underneath it.

The women sat in straight-backed chairs under gaily coloured parasols, wearing broad-sleeved, puff-shouldered floral prints, fanning powdered faces with pale, languid hands. Men stood ramrod stiff in starched dress-whites. Sword hilts glittered at their belts. Snowy solar topees hid their eyes. A phonograph played 'Rule, Britannia!' tinnily.

In May 1896, the English of Mombasa rallied to the flag.

Plagued by saddle-soreness, raw with prickly heat, James Seton glared down the hill and saw squalor behind the ceremony.

Snake-infested scrub still covered half the island. The dusty roads served both as drains and open sewers. Rats and buzzing blowflies swarmed the cemetery, where bleached bones jutted out from the shallow soil. The high-walled, cramped Arab bazaars oozed joss-scent and perspiration. Beggars with leprous stumps and suppurating bodies wriggled like black maggots through the refuse heaps.

And this was the Protectorate's main port.

Seton scratched his heat rash and spat, sizzling, on to baked brown earth.

The music stopped. Clipped orders were given. Men began to work: a dozen Indian coolies in yellow turbans and sweat-stained dhotis, two burly British navvies stripped to the waist. Sunlit muscles bunched and rippled. Sledgehammers made humming downward arcs. Sandalled feet crunched on gravel, timber sleepers thudded home, metal rang on metal. In minutes it was done. Two shiny steel rails lay firmly bedded, parallel, pointing north.

A tall white figure stepped forward, stroked his chestnut moustache and cleared his throat. He was Charles Whitehouse, Chief Engineer, Uganda Railway. 'Ladies and gentlemen,' he began, 'this is an historic moment! We are opening the hinterland to civilisation, and in due course will bear great riches out. East Africa will never be the same again. When this line is finished, the old darkness will be for ever gone. Long live the British Empire! God save the Queen!'

They rose as one and sang the Anthem, their voices strong, their faces fervent. Gentlemen huzzahed. Ladies applauded daintily.

Seton elbowed through the throng to Whitehouse's side. 'I say, what's all this tosh about riches?'

Whitehouse stiffened and peered haughtily down a long, straight nose. 'You have the advantage, sir. I don't believe we've been introduced.'

'Seton of Sussex. My taxes are paying for this madness! Where's the damn line going, anyway?'

'Westwards to Lake Victoria, northwards to Nairobi.'

'Nairobi? It's a soggy swamp full of wild beasts and wilder niggers, valueless as this place, only colder!'

Whitehouse's blue eyes took on a visionary glow. A half-smile lifted his moustache. 'Soon it will become a railhead. Within five years, I'll wager, you'll find a city thriving there.'

'And on what, pray, will it thrive?'

'Ivory,' breathed Whitehouse, 'hides from hunters, produce from the land.'

'Balderdash! I scoured the north for months three years ago, and never saw a single tusk. As for produce, the workers are savages dressed in skins, still using digging sticks. You are dreaming, and I must foot the bill!'

'Recoup some losses, Mr Seton. Be my guest for dinner at the club. There'll be another piece of history – ladies are to be allowed to stay after seven!'

Seton mumbled graceless assent, nonplussed by the gesture.

Whitehouse smiled consolingly. 'Men must always dream, so that realists like you may profit.' He moved away, leaving Seton unconvinced but outmanoeuvred.

As he stood scratching and sweating, someone touched his elbow. He turned to face a short lean man in bible black and a clerical collar, with dark straight centre-parted hair, hazel eyes and a soft Welsh lilt.

46

'Evans, I am, from the Mission. Mr Whitehouse got it back to front. The railway is for taking God's truth *in*. So many sins, so many souls to save.'

'Forget it,' Seton growled. 'You will never beat the juju men.'

'Have you seen their power, then?'

'I have watched armed warriors tremble at their word. They even tried to lay a curse on me!'

'And you survived? There's courage!'

Seton preened, and gave an exaggerated account of Njau's sorcery.

'You are an inspiration, sir.' Fingering his tight white collar, the Welshman flushed with heat and admiration. 'Where did you say it happened?'

'A long way north. Place called Kerinyagga.' The hazel eyes were all at once cool and assessing. Sensing danger, Seton cursed his own vanity.

'Kerinyagga, eh? Father Andrew's parish, is it?'

'What if it is?'

'Oh, nothing much. Just odd rumours drifting down – about crippled beasts and bewitched children. Leaving so soon, Mr Seton?'

'I'm invited to dinner. I must change.'

'Walk slower, I would, in this heat. I'll pray for you, sir!'

You do that, Seton thought, and I'll pray the boat leaves on time tomorrow.

And that no one asks damn fool questions at dinner.

Evening cool and talcum powder had soothed the irritation; well-cut evening clothes had raised morale. He left his pistol with many others at the Secretary's office and collected a complimentary glass of champagne. In the Mombasa club, for the first time in weeks, Seton began to feel at home.

The long verandah opened out a hundred feet above the ocean. Cool breezes carried palm-leaf rustle and the rhythm of the waves. The air smelled of salt, cigar smoke and French perfume.

The men were all well groomed and debonair, given extra grace and stature by evening suits. Snowy shirtfronts and velvet-black lapels complemented smooth tanned faces. They smiled and gestured broadly, toasting each other in champagne and cultured, confident voices.

Their ladies wore pastel silks that covered their shoulders and trailed along the floor. Their faces shone with pleasure. Even the plainest looked attractive.

Servants moved among them: soft-voiced, barefooted black men carrying silver trays. Each wore a long white kanzu, and a red fez balanced on dark curls. 'Bwana,' they whispered, 'memsahib.' They served drinks with white gloves, so that their black flesh should not soil the glasses.

'You see, Mr Seton?' Whitehouse challenged. 'The dream becomes reality. Lord Delamere passed through a while ago, full of energy and vision. There is a place up north, he says, fit for white man's country: hills for sheep to graze, plains where wheat will flourish. When he buys in next year, the rush will start. Then clubs like this will open through the land – and the railway will bring it all to pass!'

'And the savages?' Seton growled. 'Will they curb their warriors and give up the land?'

'Ah,' beamed Whitehouse, nodding at the men around him, 'that's where these fellows come in. They will establish districts, stamp out tribal war and heathen practices, and bring law and order to the hills.'

'Alone, against Masai spears and Kikuyu arrows? You're still dreaming, man!'

A lanky, earnest ginger youth called Hargreaves leaned forward. 'We shall recruit warriors to the Queen's colours. We will win tribal chieftains to our cause. It is our bounden duty to spread the Pax Britannica over godless lands!'

'Well said, Binky,' someone breathed, and patriotic fervour set all their eyes aglow.

'Besides,' Whitehouse added, 'they are not all savages. You can see how naturally they take to service. Now witness how well they may be trained. My houseboy has worked since sun-up on a menu worthy of the occasion. Ladies, gentlemen, dinner is served!'

He led them to the dining room and a single huge table set for forty. Silver cutlery and bone china sparkled beneath the chandeliers. Couples took their places in a hum of animated talk. Waiting in the doorway, Seton glanced back at the bar.

One man had stayed behind.

He was big, rawboned and grizzled, drinking whisky, not champagne. His bow tie was lopsided, his shirtfront dim with age, his dinner jacket green along the seams. As Seton stared, his craggy, weatherbeaten face creased into a yellow grin. One sea-green eye closed in a slow, sardonic wink.

He was like some unimpressed, indulgent father who had seen the children play this game before.

Then the queue moved forward. Whitehouse ushered Seton to his chair. The banquet began.

First came delicious clear turtle soup, followed by grilled fish that might have been best English lemon sole. From time to time, someone shouted 'Boy!' and a smiling middle-aged black waiter dispensed more crisp white wine.

'My dear!' exclaimed the horsey, florid girl at Seton's side. 'The natives are so lazy! Do you know my boy is demanding Sundays off?'

'It's those dreadful missionaries,' a plumper, straw-haired matron complained. 'Giving them ideas above their station. Equal in the sight of God, indeed; and me a judge's wife!'

'Such impudence,' snapped the horsey one, 'such ingratitude! Boy, more Chablis, chop-chop!'

'England is no better,' Seton commiserated. 'So hard to find reliable domestics.'

As the ladies expanded this lament, Seton heard a softer voice from his left. 'They're doing it all wrong, these office-wallahs. Shouldn't keep buck niggers in the house.' Turning, he confronted a portly type with a black toothbrush moustache and lank black hairstrands plastered across a receding forehead.

And a pair of hard shrewd grey eyes.

'Indeed?' he said. 'And how would you employ them?'

'There now, Mr Seton, I knew you were my kind. Employ, that's the word. They're *labour*, see, strong backs and feeble minds, exactly what we need to make this country grow. Teach 'em to value money, bring trinkets to buy for their women and they'll labour dawn to dusk. There'll be crops to plant and reap, roads to lay, houses to build. It's a goldmine, Mr Seton, once that railway gets through. A man like you should grab a piece right now. In ten years you could own a place like this, and have black men begging you to give them work!'

Perhaps it was the wine. Perhaps it was the elegance and luxury all around. Briefly, James Seton was disposed to share the dream.

Then Whitehouse stood and bellowed for attention. 'Cometh the hour, cometh the delicacy! Ladies and gentlemen, the moment you have been waiting for. Boy, bring the main dish!'

49

The double door swung inwards. An African entered, staggering under the weight of a vast salver covered by an equally enormous handled silver dome. He set it at the centre of the table, removed his fez, bowed and sidled out. Men and women craned forward eagerly. Even the shabby, solitary figure at the distant bar stood straight and stared.

'This is thrilling, Charlie,' a female voice cooed. 'Please don't keep us in suspense.'

'Come on, Wouse,' called Hargreaves. 'We're all agog!' And other watchers chorused their excitement.

'A great surprise,' Whitehouse crowed. 'You'll never see the like again!' With a showman's flourish, he reached across the table and lifted the great flashing dome away.

The main dish came to life.

There was a scuffling and scraping and a clicking of sharp pincers, a rasp of pointed feet on starched cloth. Cold eyes on long stalks glittered in the candlelight.

A hundred huge, long-legged, jet-black crabs marched out across the pure white damask.

Pandemonium.

Women were shrieking, weeping, jumping on to chairs and hauling up their skirts. Servants sagged, grey-faced, against the walls. Men were cursing, thrusting silver knives at shiny black carapaces. 'Damn you, Wouse!' someone bawled. 'My Mildred's having vapours!'

'My bloody cook,' wailed Whitehouse. 'I told him to *boil* them alive!'

'Thrash the bugger, teach him common sense!'

By this time, severed legs and claws were rattling like machine-gun fire upon the walls.

Seton crept away, bent double, holding a napkin to his face, and closed the doors behind him. In the suddenly silent bar, he met a brilliant, mirthful, sea-green gaze.

They guffawed together until they could hardly stand.

'Dear, oh lor',' the Craggy One finally spluttered, 'what a bunch of clowns! Building new England in ancient Africa, and none of them knows how to treat a wog. God-botherers bickering for his worthless soul, officials trying to make a little white man of him, money-men who'll break his back and throw the bits away.'

'The voice of experience,' Seton taunted, sobering. 'I suppose you do know how.'

'I'm a settler, working at it. You treat natives like the simpletons they are. Flog 'em when they're nasty, praise 'em when they're nice, let them help you tame the land. You have to prove you're tough. You have to keep a bit of magic back: how to mend a broken engine, how to make water run uphill. White man's magic, mind, things juju men in monkey skirts can't do.' He looked and sounded utterly certain. Impressed, Seton asked the question which had plagued him since the Welsh priest mentioned rumours.

Asked, indirectly, of the Lion Boy.

'What will happen to the whites, up north?'

'There will be war between the Masai and the Kyukes. God help any missionary who tries to stop it.' He wrapped a calloused paw around his whisky, downed it at a swallow and changed the subject. 'You staying at the club?'

'The hotel, near the harbour.'

'Take a rickshaw. Keep your pistol primed. It can be hairy on the streets at night.'

His doubts dispelled, his courage buoyed by drink, Seton took a patronising tone. 'Dark streets don't bother me. I've roamed the bush alone. I've taken quite a fancy to Africa.'

'You'll never be a pioneer. You haven't got the balls. Leave Africa to zealots – and to me.'

The dismissive, all-too-accurate assessment still rankled as Seton settled in the rickshaw. He longed to be a bwana, and make the settler eat his words.

At first the ride was pleasant, exhilarating: wheel-rumble on the dusty road, a cooling breeze, the patter of the boy's easy lope. In moonlight and velvet tropic air, even overripe, decaying scents seemed exotic.

Then they plunged into the cobbled Arab Quarter, and the dream became a waking nightmare.

First came low hunched shadows and eerie, wailing cries. The rickshaw boy's back stiffened. His body angled forward. His stride grew choppy, urgent.

The shadows thickened, narrowing the passage. The wails became angry howls. The boy swerved. The wheels whirred, struck soggy, unseen flesh, bounced and whirred again. Fumbling for the pistol, being flung from side to side, Seton glanced up into a brighter moonshaft – and a sight that chilled his soul.

Beggars blocked the way ahead.

They blotted out the cobbles, the halt, the blind, the maimed, their arms raised in entreaty, their heads flung back and baying in demand.

But the limbs they thrust towards him had neither toes nor fingers, only fraying grey-black stumps. And the faces in the moonlight had no features, only glistening teeth and eye-whites and ragged, gaping sores between. It was as if some catacomb had spewed up negro dross, the leprous, syphilitic, living dead.

The rickshaw boy faltered and gave a beseeching backward glance. Unnerved, Seton waved the pistol at him. 'Run, damn you, get me out of here!' The boy stood quivering like a spooked, two-legged horse. 'Bwana,' he whispered, '*bwana!*'

'Bwana,' the noseless, lipless creatures echoed, 'bwana, bwana, bwana!' The stench of rotting flesh was hideous. Stumps began to pound at the wheels. The rickshaw rocked. The slavering black mass croaked in triumph. Seton's courage cracked.

He pressed the trigger.

The muzzle-flash was blinding yellow. The report thundered in narrow confines. Something hot and viscous spattered nearby walls. Something tumbled, screaming in spine-chilling agony. Other things were humping, sliding, slithering into darkness, leaving slimy, snail-like trails of pus behind.

Leaving the street clear.

Suddenly, the rickshaw boy was bolting for dear life. He didn't stop until they reached the hotel.

Seton paced, naked in the dim, sultry room. A red heat rash had erupted around his groin and armpits. Leprous half-men still haunted his mind. Yet somewhere deep inside, a yearning lingered.

He had survived the bush and Mombasa horror. Even if Laura's bastard child existed, he would soon be consumed in tribal war. The secret and the inheritance were safe.

A dream of white man's country beckoned: fine food and wine in noble houses, meek uniformed black slaves speaking words that would be music to his ears.

Bwana Seton.

Then a coughing grunt outside raised short hairs at his nape and drew him, once more fearful, to the window.

A leopard padded from surrounding mangrove scrub and stood

poised and predatory, scenting the breeze. Moonlight struck cold gold fire in its eyes. Muscle bunched beneath its dappled, silvered pelt. Night birds and insects had fallen silent. No creature stirred, lest it should become prey. Seton shivered, conscious of his own pale puniness. This was the real Africa, he realised – beautiful, savage, never to be tamed.

In that awed, bright hush, James Seton knew a moment of prescience, remembering the instant when everything he'd learnt had come together.

It had happened as the railwayman raised the silver dome and black crabs had swarmed out over white damask.

This is how it must be, he thought, some day in the future. No matter that missionaries promise healing grace, that officials impose order and businessmen grow fat. No matter that tough settlers conjure foreign magic. One day the silver cage will lift, the black hordes will break free; and trample all the whiteness in their path.

He shivered, gazing at the tall, dim, ship-silhouette waiting in the harbour. That was all he longed for now.

He would go home and savour the inheritance, and be a white lord in a white man's land.

If a lion boy lived, he was more than welcome to black Africa.

7

LEO COULD MAKE pictures in his mind; he had been able to do it as long as he could remember. He never told anyone, not even Kibe, and especially not Father Andrew. It might be a sin, making pictures.

He scrambled on the orange bed cover, punching the pillow hard. 'Spect I deserve it, he admitted. I usually do, when Father Andrew beats me. I won't cry, though. I'm seven.

I wish he'd hurry, he thought. I wonder which slipper he'll use? One was cracked so it pinched, the other was flat and stung. Not much difference, really. Don't worry till it happens, Duma said.

I won't cry, he thought, and I won't worry. I'll lie here and make pictures where the whitewash is cracked, and Guy the gecko lives.

He did Kibe first, because it would be nice to have him here. Something had happened with Kibe, something Leo would never forget. Already, he could almost *taste* the way it was. And the pictures appeared, up there on the ceiling.

Sunday morning, cloudless and still, before the short rains came. Kibe was taking a special service at the river. Two new converts were to be baptised. It should have been done at the Mission, but Father Andrew was down with fever, and too weak to argue.

Secretly, Leo was pleased. If I were God, he thought, I'd rather live here than in some gloomy old church.

Leo loved the river, and this place best of all. Here, the current narrowed and came gurgling over a jumble of rocks into a slow, wide pool. Here, the trees almost touched overhead. The bush was thick on three sides, and creepers swept down like curtains.

Kibe was moving into deeper water. He had taken his robe off, and wore only a white loincloth. His skin is not much darker than mine, Leo thought, and wobbly like a girl's. The converts were hook-nosed and toothless, an old couple called Gatu and Mumbi. When they stood waist deep, the three joined hands and ducked beneath the surface. The flock began to clap and chant. The silver-green waters boiled and parted.

An imp of mischief lived in Leo's head. It woke now, and whispered slyly, 'Behold a pale hippo and a pair of old brown turtles!'

'Silence!' hissed his conscience. 'This is a place of worship!' Leo trembled with inner laughter, covered it with a sneeze. This was the most important time, he knew. Kibe, his wet face radiant, prepared to give his converts Christian names.

In that very moment, Leo heard louder, harsher laughter echo across the pool. Turning, he saw four broad dark figures leap from the creepers and plunge into the water. They surfaced, shouting and jostling in the shallows, then marched on to the sand beside him.

Warriors, he saw, led by Gitau's firstborn son, Maina, who was not fat like his father, but broad and tall and fierce. Maina, who could hold a yearling bull down, throw a spear beyond sight, outwrestle any man on the ridge. His wet muscles coiled like thick brown ropes; his eyes gleamed with malice. 'This is no church, Mission Boy. The river is open to all. We, the warriors, wish to swim.'

'That is true. So swim.' Kibe spoke quietly, placing one soft arm around each of the old people. He cannot protect them, Leo thought, he cannot stand against fighting men. Every time he tried to say the new names, one or other warrior swam past, whooping and kicking silvered spray into his face. He was slowly being driven to the bank. Leo could feel the fear of the converts, knowing that soon the little group would break and drift away. There would be no baptism. For the first time in his memory, the morning service would not be completed.

Leo's body shook with shame and despair. Tears prickled his eyes, his throat felt thick and dry. They wouldn't dare, he thought, if Father Andrew was here! But Kibe can't defeat them, and I am too small to try. Dear Lord, let me grow up hard and strong!

Kibe started to sing.

He sang in English, softly at first, as if unsure of the words.

Onward, Christian soldiers, marching as to war.
With the cross of Jesus going on before . . .

Then Leo saw his plump chest rise and fill, and heard Kibe sing as no man ever sang before. He stood to his knees in rippling water, eyes closed, head thrown back. He scorned the shouts and the spray which spattered his face, filling the dim green chamber with his anger and his joy.

Like a mighty army, leads against the foe,
Forward into battle, see his banners go!

His voice was a sound of living beauty, deep and full and pure. It soared above bright eddies and made the swimmers gape. The rhythm sent tingles down Leo's spine and lit fires in his blood. Poor, brave Kibe, you shall not stand alone! He ran, splashing through the shallows, hurling himself at Kibe's chest as the second verse rang out.

Kibe hardly faltered, sweeping him in, perching him upon a broad, slick shoulder. He clung there briefly, feeling the throb of Kibe's heart, drinking Kibe's courage. Then Leo sang, too: he pushed himself erect and sang with all the fury he could muster.

One by one, Kibe's flock moved into the river, humming a harmony, forming a line, standing against the current and the warriors. Kibe switched to Kikuyu, and the whole bedraggled congregation began to sing.

Not all the wetness on Kibe's face was spray, Leo saw. He was sobbing himself, between lines, in a kind of glorious rage.

They sang till the green leaves trembled, till the warriors tired and waded to the bank. When Maina came within inches and scowled, they shivered and sang on. He is helpless, thought Leo, singing, betrayed by his own words: *the river is open to all.* If he can swim, we can sing; no power on earth can stop us. They sang, hurling well-tuned defiance into the dark, sullen face. And after a while, Maina turned away!

They sang as the warriors swaggered off, spitting and sneering to ease their injured pride. They kept the chorus murmuring while Kibe named the converts, completed the service, and once more hoisted Leo to his shoulders. Then they marched in sunlit splendour to the Mission: Christian soldiers, going onward, singing.

It was the best morning service Leo ever knew.

Guy the gecko spoiled the picture, darting out, gobbling a sausage fly, and popping back into his crack. Leo frowned, reluctant to leave such a triumph. Yes, he thought, Kibe is my brother. The kind of big brother *I* would like to be, for Mwangi. If only he didn't taunt me so, if only he didn't tattle-tale to our father, Duma.

It was still light outside. He could hear cattle lowing, and the tinkle of goatbells. I ought to be out there, he thought, smelling the pasture, helping Duma with the herd. I love being with Duma. . . .

Duma gave Leo a bow.

He did it one day in the pasture, when the morning clouds were low and grey and the mountain was totally hidden.

'You are growing up,' he said. 'You must learn to shoot.' It was a beautiful bow. Its curved arms gleamed softly, its leather handgrip nestled snugly into Leo's fist.

'Duma,' he breathed, 'oh, *Duma*!' The string twanged sweetly; the tautness of it thrilled him to the core. Then Duna gave him a quiver of fine arrows, and his joy was complete.

'Can I try it? Watch me, Duma!' He set his feet wide, chose an arrow, notched it to the string. Duma's piebald ewe-goat grazed near by. He aimed just behind her. 'Now you will see,' he cried. 'Now I will give her a scare!'

The bow was torn from his fingers and the arrow slipped to the damp grass. He looked up in shock and anger, into Duma's lean, disdainful stare. 'Ow, that hurt! I was only playing!'

'It is a weapon, not a plaything! Never aim unless you mean to hit!'

Leo shuffled his feet, nursed his wrist, and watched a fork of lightning blurred by quickly welling tears. 'S'pose you think I'm too young. Keep it, then. Give it to Mwangi, when he's bigger.' A hand fell, not unkindly, on his shoulder, pushing him towards an old, gnarled stump. 'Sit with me, little hunter. Say your lessons. Then we shall see.'

Duma settled on the weathered wood, laid the bow across his knee. Leo sat at his feet, ignoring the wetness beneath, yearning. At least I still have the quiver, he thought. At least there is some hope.

'Tell me,' said Duma, 'tell me the reasons a man may use to kill.'

'Animals?' asked Leo slyly, 'or men?'

57

'Animals first.'

'For meat. For hides and horns and skins, to gain wealth. To save himself; to guard his huts or his flocks. He may kill when a beast is old and lame, from mercy. And to stop disease from spreading.'

'Correct.' Duma fingered the bow absently. 'Never on whim, as you might have done; never in anger; never, ever, for pleasure. Only thieves and leopards kill for pleasure. And since you are so clever,' Duma murmured, 'tell me when man may slay man.'

'In battle,' said Leo promptly, 'in wars or raids against his enemies. To save himself, or to win in fair combat. For vengeance in a bloodfeud; to protect his hearth and kin.'

'Yes. To protect hearth – or kin.' Leo glanced up, surprised at the weary tone. Duma sat slackly, his gaze distant and dim. Purple cloud loomed behind him, deep shadows haunted his face.

A flock of crows passed low, cawing. 'What birds are they?' snapped Duma. Leo told him.

'Come, Duma. Even Mwangi knows *that*.'

'Tell me in Masai.'

Leo gasped, appalled. 'How can I answer? You never taught me!'

'I should have. Tomorrow I will start. The Masai have ruled these ridges since time began. When they pass, men step aside and give them greeting, or taste the bitter sharpness of their steel. You will do well to learn their tongue.' Duma glanced down and seemed surprised at what he held in his hand. His face softened. He released the bow. 'It is a weapon,' he insisted, as the first fat drops pattered. 'Use it well. Remember today's lesson.'

'I will, Duma, I swear it!'

Rain struck Leo's bare skin, stinging him fiercely. He leapt up, brandishing the bow. 'See, Duma, I am the little hunter. Even in a downpour, a bright sun shines for me!' He saw, at last, his own grin returned, and knew he had somehow eased Duma's hurt.

Next day, the rains relented. Leo badgered Duma without pause, until, in the evening, the hunter gave in and took him down to the river.

There, where the thick bush dripped and swollen waters chuckled, Duma taught him archery – and Masai.

At first, his aim was poor and his tongue was clumsy. He could master neither the quick harsh sounds nor the slow strength of the bow.

Duma helped him patiently, repeating the words, guiding the line of his shoulders and the placement of his feet. Leo fumed and sweated, swallowed gnats, stung himself on nettles where his wayward arrows always seemed to fall. I'm useless, he mourned inwardly, even Mwangi could be better!

Then, quite suddenly, the language fitted his throat. '*Entasupai,*' he muttered – the warriors' greeting – '*Entasupai!*' And a few moments later, from fully fifteen yards, he placed all four arrows in or near the white slash Duma had cut for him from the bark of a podo tree. 'Ha!' he crowed. 'I am a true Masai bowman!'

'Eeh,' grunted Duma. '*Morani* use spears, not bows.'

'Can we hunt now?' Leo pleaded. 'Just back to the big pool?'

'Not this evening. You have made enough noise for that whole, tall nation. *Eeeeh*, all right. How can I refuse those golden Masai eyes?'

But though they spoke in whispers, bent low and treading light, they found not a trace of game.

Leo turned away from the reddening pool and looked up to give Duma his thanks. He saw the keen eyes narrow and sensed sudden tension. And he too heard, above the roar of the rapids, the beat of approaching wings.

A lone river duck, coming upstream fast and low; heading for calm waters, Leo thought, its plumage bright and burnished. It saw them, honked once, thrust out its dark neck and flew towards the swaying tree tops.

Leo saw it, then: the bowman's art in all its grace and glory. Duma unslung his bow, drew and nocked an arrow, set his feet, leaned wide and brought the string hard back. It seemed to happen in one sweet, rippling, brown movement; it happened in an eyeblink. There was the barest, slightest check – the instant of aim – then the bowstring thwanged and a second, leaner feathered form was streaking to the sky.

Leo watched, open-mouthed and breathless. He saw the gap between grow narrow, saw slim steel glint and wide wings hover. Then bird and arrow wheeled and tumbled, locked in a last embrace. And grey down drifted under faint stars to mark their silent meeting.

The picture was fading, the light had already gone. From beyond the window, Leo could hear frogcroak and a nightjar's churr. I saw what happened, he thought. I still see each swift, smooth movement clearly in my head. I will practise each day, until I, too, can do it. Until I am Leo the *big* hunter, and can use the bow like Duma.

As he contemplated this, Father Andrew marched into his mind: tall, dark-haired and rawboned, stern-eyed and firm-jawed. Father Andrew, priest and teacher, man of God and peace.

Just once, Leo had seen another Father Andrew . . .

Shade still covered half the garden, dew still glinted on the lawn. Cockcrow rose from the village. The air smelled sharp and clean.

Leo was enjoying a rare outdoor lesson. He sat with his back to the Mission wall, a drawing board propped against his flexed knees, the paper stretched and pinned tight. 'Watch the morning glory,' Father Andrew had said, 'see her petals open to the sun. Draw me a single bloom. Never mind the colours. Just get the shape right.' Then he had gone inside, to his daily meditations.

Leo had done his best, but it wouldn't come right. He couldn't get the frilly outer curves to join properly, or the deep purple folds near the stem. He frowned and rubbed out, hearing Mwangi's whimper and the lazy scrape of Wanjui's hoe.

The gate creaked. Leo heard a low, throaty growl. Duma often tested him like this: sneaking close and making some difficult sound. He, Leo, had to name the beast. 'Lioness,' he called, drawing. 'She's angry with her cubs.' The growl was repeated, which meant he must guess again. He nibbled his pencil, thinking.

Then Wanjui's scream shocked him into a waking nightmare.

The sun was in his eyes, his heart was pounding wildly. He saw only a dark, hunched, shambling figure and a blinding glitter of upraised steel. Mugo: once a famous warrior, soon to become an elder. Mugo, whom all respected, for whom the whole village had mourned when he had lost kin to a sickness – a wife, and three young sons. He stood, swaying, in the middle of the lawn. His red eyes flickered under a jutting brow, his broad shoulders were bunched. The simi gleamed and hissed. He was mumbling; saliva and a reek of spirits dribbled from his slack wet lips. This is not Mugo, thought Leo, trembling, this is no man I know. Grief and drink have ruined his mind. He will kill us now, without mercy, like a maddened ape. Leo's courage faltered, a sob welled in his throat. 'No,' he whispered, '*no!*'

'No indeed! Give me the knife, Mugo. You're drunk!' Father Andrew's voice, crisp and commanding. The priest came forward unhurriedly, his dark green cassock billowing. The creature Mugo lunged towards him with a slurred bellow of accusation and agony – '*Priest!*' The simi flashed round and down in a great, killing arc. Wanjui screeched, Leo flinched and covered his face.

He heard an angry grunt, a quick shuffle of feet. Peering between shaking fingers, he watched Father Andrew fight. He circled, swift and graceful, hands poised, chin lowered. He ducked one fierce lunge, swayed outside another; he stepped inside the third. His left arm blurred. There was a meaty thump. Mugo was lifted clean off his feet, thrown a yard backwards. He fell, rigid and senseless, in a flurry of rising dust.

Father Andrew flexed his left hand absently, picked up the simi and dragged the unconscious man into the shade. He bent, took his pulse and lifted one slack eyelid.

'He'll be all right. Let him sleep it off. He's had a rough time, poor chap. Pull yourself together, Wanjui. Let's see how you're getting on, Leo.'

Leo followed him, tranced. He couldn't seem to close his mouth. Father Andrew picked up the drawing and studied it thoughtfully. 'Hm. Not bad. Try to make this line smoother. Some shading here, perhaps. What are you gaping at, boy?'

'He had a knife. He was crazy. He might have killed you.' Leo gulped, still wonderstruck. 'Where did you learn to fight like that?'

'I boxed, when I was young.'

'Gosh, Father, you're a hero, like in the books!'

'It's nothing to be proud of. The man was almost incapable.' Father Andrew was intent on the drawing, his cheeks pink with embarrassment. 'As a matter of fact,' he muttered, 'it's not a good idea to fight an armed drunk. Bear it in mind, won't you?'

I've always loved him, Leo realised. On that day, I learned to honour and admire him. Today, I defied him, torturing a harmless frog to make my friends laugh. That's why he's making me wait, while night falls and the owls hoot: so that I can think about my sin, and accept my guilt, and vow to *myself* not to do it again.

As always, when he was lonely and miserable, Leo's thoughts turned to Wanjui. She will comfort me and give me courage to take what I deserve. I'll bring her here, in my mind, just for a little while, to make the waiting easier.

*

She sat at the hearth, nursing three-year-old Mwangi and stirring the maize porridge. The picture was blurry because of the smoke. It flickered because of the fireglow. It smelt of charcoal and warm beer, goat-grease and mothers' milk: the smells of home. 'Tell me the clan,' she would murmur, 'name our ancestors.'

'You are Wanjui, daughter of Kamau and Waithira.' He would reach back among great-great-grandparents, counting on his fingers, giving the age-grades, stretching his power of recall. She would nod, correcting him gently, making him start again until he got it right. Then she would smile, and croon a lullaby.

'It's like the Bible,' he'd grumbled, once, 'and all those blessed begats.' He had to explain. 'I know nothing of books,' she'd said. 'What you say is just another tribe, doing as we do: honouring the dead, remembering who they are and from whence they came.'

The shadows were kind to her, cloaking her plumpness, narrowing her face. She is not pretty, he thought; she has broad lips and a short, stubby nose. But when she smiles, the whole world looks brighter. There is beauty, deep in her eyes. There is beauty in her soul. She is my mother. I know.

He would envy Mwangi, then, who nestled darkly at her big, soft breasts. The warmest, safest place on earth, where all was peace and comfort and the slow throb of her heart. He understood the little boy's anger at having to share her with a white boy, and tried to soothe his distress. But Mwangi would not be soothed. Not by Leo, anyway.

'He is young,' Duma had said, 'he will get over it.'

But Mwangi never did get over it. He would steal choice meat which rightfully belonged to Leo. Chided, he would fly into a rage, wave his little fists and claim that Leo had stolen his. He is my brother, thought Leo sadly, I love him. Why does he hate me so? Come back, he beseeched Wanjui's fading image, don't leave me yet! Too late. For now, at last, he could hear firm footfalls in the passage outside.

Father Andrew closed the door behind him. In rising lamplight, his grey eyes glittered, and all the lines in his face curved down; he looked like a tall, sad eagle. He held a bedroom slipper in his hand. The left one, Leo saw, the one with the cracked sole. Oh my.

'Bend over.'

Leo obeyed, closing his eyes, clutching the cover.

The first stroke numbed him. Its sharp, flat, *crack* almost deafened him. The second pinched his flesh, as he'd known it would. After that, he stopped counting and simply endured, biting his lip, quivering, refusing to cry.

'That will do. Stand up.' Father Andrew's voice sounded raw, almost as if *he* had been beaten. 'You are truly sorry?'

'Yes.' Leo forced the answer between clenched teeth. The pain was growing, burning.

'You will not be cruel any more?'

'Never!'

'Then it is over. We shall not speak of it again. Go to bed, Leo.'

He curled himself into a ball, hugged the pillow and fought the tears. The lamp went out. 'No story tonight,' said Father Andrew. 'But I will stay a while, if you like.'

'Thank you, Father.'

For quite some time, Leo felt only the fire in his buttocks, spreading outwards and upwards, eating away his resolve. Slowly, it eased to an unpleasant tingle. I have won, he thought, I did not cry!

He opened his eyes cautiously, and began to hear again. There was nightwind, a chirp of crickets, and harsh, unsteady breathing. He shifted, wincing, until he could make out the lean silhouette near the window.

Father Andrew sat there, his head bowed, his hands hiding his face. The broad black shoulders shook. Father Andrew was weeping silently in the dark.

Why? thought Leo, in wonder. I sinned and was punished. Surely he doesn't think I won't love him when he beats me? That's how I know he does care, wants me to grow up pure and straight.

His own hurts faded. How can I help him, Leo wondered, how can I make him understand? Warmth crept over him, that lovely, floaty feeling just before sleep. He smiled to himself, saw the answer and found the words.

'Father Andrew?'

'What is it?'

'Will you teach me the left hook? The one that flattened Mugo?'

'Of course. When you are older.' Leo could hear the shaky relief, sense the sorrow lifting. Presently, he felt a hand at his brow, a rare, swift, furtive kiss on the cheek. 'You're a brave boy. Sleep now, and God bless.'

Leo sighed contentedly, his sore bottom forgotten. *There*, he thought. I knew I could make it right.

8

ELEVEN YEARS, THOUGHT Father Andrew watching Leo sleep. Eleven years of toil, and sixty converts made. I would forsake them, every one, to keep Leo near me; to see the bloom of manhood, to guide his soul towards God, to feed his boundless curiosity and wondrous swift intelligence. It is a joy to love him, a privilege to teach him. *But for how long?*

He has great freedom here, Father Andrew reminded himself. From Wanjui, he learns manners and deportment; from Kibe, moral courage and theology; from Duma, husbandry, natural history and the Masai tongue; and from me, the basics of a formal education. And it is not enough.

He has no one against whom to test his growing strength and knowledge. There is a wildness in him. He needs the discipline of a great school.

Father Andrew raised the lamp and watched gold shadows play on Leo's long, upcurved lashes, his finely sculpted lips and cheeks, a firm, straight nose, and hair the colour of burnished honey. And saw, in pride and sadness, a faint answering gleam from strands of down around the ungrown sex. He is so beautiful, Father Andrew thought, this half-tamed boy who hangs between childhood and adolescence. He sighed, stepped forward, drew the sheets up and tucked them in. Bending, he kissed the upturned brow. God bless you, and keep you through the night.

Back in his own room and unquiet darkness, he felt old and cold and fearful. Leo needs schooling, but I cannot let him go!

'You didn't *see*!' cried Mwangi. 'You didn't see me bring the goats home. You were watching Leo again!'

Duma started guiltily. He had been watching Leo: Leo running, his long legs flashing, his hair glinting, winning the herdboys' race by a long bowshot. When Leo ran, everyone watched – they simply couldn't help it. Which didn't help Mwangi at all.

'I saw you herd them together,' Duma muttered, 'and start towards the river. You are a much better herdsman than Leo.'

'*Eeh*, of course. But you like *hunters*, not herdsmen!'

Duma glanced down at his firstborn. Mwangi, too, was a handsome child, having Wanjui's fine, slightly slanted eyes and Duma's own sharp, clean features. But he was small and sickly, useless with bow and spear, and his forehead seemed forever bunched and clouded like a stormy sky.

'You are Mwangi,' Duma told him, not for the first time, 'the earliest fruit of my loins. I love you dearly.'

'Then why do you always favour Leo?'

'That is untrue. How do I so favour him?'

'Every two seasons, you give him a bow, each bigger and better than the last. You made only *one* bow for me!'

'Which you broke, Mwangi, inside ten days, and you lost all the arrows.'

'You take Leo hunting to the forest, you let him shoot duiker and eat wild honey!'

'Leo is older. You, too, shall do these things, when you are ready.'

'I'll *never* be ready! I'm only ready to stay in the pasture and tend the stupid goats! And you're *still* watching Leo!'

Duma turned his back on the wrestling bout, on Leo, who was throwing his rivals easily and smiling like a young, bronzed god. He gave his whole attention to Mwangi, whose thin shoulders quivered, whose angry eyes glinted with unshed tears in the late afternoon sun. Duma went down to his knees on the sweet-smelling pasture, and gathered the slight, reluctant boy to him. 'The goats are our wealth, son. You do us great service by tending them so well. Be easy now. Be calm and certain of our love.'

Presently, the sobs subsided. Mwangi pushed himself away and glanced up, sidelong and sly. 'There is *one* thing I can do, which Leo can never, ever match.' He thrust his chest forward, slapping it proudly. '*I* can help Njau make magic. He told me so, in secret. He says one day *I* could be the Healer!'

Duma stood up, impressed and somewhat uneasy.

'That is good,' he said, without much conviction. 'That is indeed a thing of pride.'

'*Eeeh!* Now I will go and tell Wanjui, before Leo comes to brag about the race.'

He swaggered off, round-shouldered and spindly, leaving Duma at once relieved and disturbed. The jealousy had always been one-sided. Leo bore it bravely, and never bragged. Mwangi had been spending time with Njau for two seasons, and the Healer seemed resigned to his hungry gaze and endless questions. Duma had not expected much to come of it.

He turned from the pasture and strolled towards the huts. The sky was turning pink; he could smell maize porridge. An ibis flapped to roost in a tall still gum, making its harsh evening sound: ha da *da*, ha da *da*.

It might be useful to have a Healer for a son, he thought. A man would gain much standing. But he still felt uneasy, remembering Mwangi's envy of the Lion Boy; remembering Njau's other, darker powers.

'Tell me again,' begged Leo, from campfire shadows. 'Show me how we tricked the khaki rider.' An oft-told tale, this always brought him pleasure. Duma shrugged off woodsmoke, cleared his throat. '*He came from the west on a pale horse . . .*'

'I was the muddy frog with yellow hair,' Leo chuckled, when it was done. 'Was the rider blind, or just too angry? Was my skin lighter then?' He thrust a bare tanned arm across the fireglow. 'Does it matter, that I am white?'

'Of course not.' Duma spoke too quickly, remembering Red Strangers and Njau's warning. One day, it might matter very much.

His sharpness broke the mood. Urgency appeared in Leo's firelit gaze. 'What about my father, Duma? What was Morgan like?'

'Tall and strong, like you. Unlike you, he didn't say a lot.' Too late for jokes. Flames and a night breeze fluttered. Leo's questions flowed like racing water.

'He was a marksman?'

'Yes.'

'A fine hunter?'

'Yes.'

'Was he kind to my mother?'

'Yes.'

'Did he treat you well?'

'Yes. It was long ago, Leo. Why do you ask?'

The fire crackled; unseen leaves rustled. When Leo spoke again, his tone was bitter. 'You sit there nodding, yes yes yes, and tell me nothing! Have you forgotten how an outcast feels? I need to know from whom and whence I came!'

For Duma, feud and fireside faded. He was once more newly circumcised, hiding from his age-mates in thick green bush beside the shimmering river. 'Spy!' they taunted. 'Traitor, son of a Masai cattle thief!'

The shame of it had haunted him for seasons, till Morgan himself appeared and praised young Duma's bushcraft. He took him for a tracker, awoke his self-respect and showed him that the past was dead and gone.

Duma kicked a bough on to the embers and settled snug inside his monkey-skin cloak. The sights and sounds and smells of Morgan's hunts came back to him. He told of them simply, hearing tree-frogs chunter, watching awe and sorrow cast soft shades on Leo's face. 'Morgan loved this land,' he said, at last. 'He kept faith with friends and died to save his kin. Be proud of your father, Leo. He was a man.'

'I am sorry for the rudeness, Duma. Henceforth, may I do honour to his name.'

Perhaps there were tears in Leo's eyes. Surely there was tribute in his words. Yet something in the tone made Duma wary; a hint of sorrow undeclared and doubts not yet at rest.

He arrived unannounced, while Father Andrew took the morning air and golden weavers bickered in the gum tree. Green eyes glittered underneath his hatbrim. Sunlight streaked his chestnut beard, blued the barrel of his muzzle-loader. His name was Kobus Coetze; he filled the Mission garden with brooding, buckskinned menace. 'Tell them, menheer,' he growled, 'tell them we want our kettle back.'

'Kettle?' Father Andrew echoed. 'I assure you it's not here.'

'*Them*, not it. A bullock and two heifers gone this week.'

'Oh, you mean cattle!'

'So: you find my accent amusing.' A prickly character, this spokesman for the Boers who'd come to farm across the river. Father Andrew sought to make amends. 'Wait, I didn't . . .'

'No, man, *you* wait, before you dare to mock us! We trekked here, through suffering and danger. Crosses for our loved ones mark every mile along the Tsavo plain.' Coetze pointed at the distant ridge, where toylike cattle grazed. 'We carried more than half the stock along: scrawny, rack-ribbed beasts already three parts dead. They should be fattening now, on this good grass. Instead, they disappear, taken by those you call your flock.'

'You're guessing, Coetze,' Father Andrew snapped, in priestly loyalty. 'Can you show me proof?'

'Hell, they *eat* the proof!'

'Then what do you expect of me?'

'Leadership, man. Don't you teach the Commandments?'

'If you came to church, you wouldn't ask!'

Coetze gaped, genuinely outraged. 'And share God's house with thieving kaffirs?'

'You are a small and isolated group. Beware, lest *thieving kaffirs* turn against you.'

Suddenly, Coetze was moving, with speed and grace quite alien to his stolid build. The gun came smoothly to his shoulder, levelled, and belched orange fire and blue-black smoke. The report crashed around the garden walls. From a towering eucalyptus tree a hundred yards away, a tiny yellow-feathered corpse spiralled to the grass. Coetze's beard parted in a gleaming, wolfish grin. 'Turn on us? Let them try, menheer, by all means *let them try*!'

The smile and the tone softened. He was staring out above the wooded river, where whitewashed mud and wattle homesteads shimmered in the sun. 'There, that's where we raise our children and our cattle. We'll kill whoever threatens one or both.'

'By what right?' cried Father Andrew. 'In whose name?'

'For those we lost, along the way. For Him who bade us follow, through stormy seas and trackless desert.' Kobus Coetze's face was radiant, utterly assured. 'We claim this land in *God*'s name.'

Golden feathers fluttered into Father Andrew's vision. Bloody slaughter terrorised his mind; carnage, wrought by quiet men in buckskin, armed with marksmen's rifles and this same serenely murderous faith. He shivered, hearing Coetze's demand once more. *'Tell them we want our cattle back.'*

'I'll tell them,' Father Andrew promised.

They wouldn't listen.

For an hour in Gitau's hut and oily lamplight, Father Andrew had harangued the elders. They each knew the rustler – he felt their knowledge coiling in the smoke that stung his eyes and writhing in

68

the beer fumes that made his stomach heave. They sat in dancing shadow, with hooded eyes and sly half-smiles and no words at all. More than once, his resolution faltered; Kibe's white-robed presence reinforced his self-control. 'It doesn't matter who took them,' he insisted. 'Just get them across the river and they'll find their own way home.'

'Hide and horns,' Gitau murmured. 'Only hide and horns.'

Instantly, the elders erupted, howling with laughter, spilling beer, clapping one another's fur-clad shoulders. 'A joke,' Kibe whispered. 'He means only hide and horns are left.'

The headman squatted near the hearth, maintaining dignity and a plump poker face. But there was subtle defiance in his posture, a glint of guilty triumph in his eyes.

'It was him,' Father Andrew breathed. '*Gitau* is the thief!'

'Probably: though he will never admit it.' Kibe sounded rueful but resigned.

Father Andrew's long-tried patience finally expired. 'Fools!' he snarled. 'You call the Masai robbers, yet laugh when neighbours' stock is taken. Will you not observe your own laws? Is cattle theft not a grievous crime?'

'Only within clan and tribe,' Gitau retorted, 'not from *your* friends, the greedy Boers!'

Such is the peacemaker's lot, Father Andrew mused. Spurned for housing 'kaffirs', mistrusted for 'befriending' the Boers. 'Indeed? And how long d'you think they'll supply livestock for your *jokes*?'

'They need not. They need not even stay here.'

'Didn't you listen, Gitau? Nothing but wholesale war will move them!'

'*Eeeeh.*' A sound of heavy satisfaction. Gitau rose and ambled to the middle of the hut. In broader light, his grey hair glittered. The monkey-skin cloak barely met across his belly. Yet his gaze was sharp and his step was sprightly, as if alcohol and argument could somehow keep him young. 'How many times?' he pleaded, with a sweep of the arms and a flash of beaded wristlets. 'How many times did I, your headman, preach the danger and the prophecy? *Red Strangers!* Already they ring us around, using our water, tilling our ground!'

'They draw water far below the village,' Kibe corrected, 'and that has never been our land.'

Gitau went on blithely, immune to inconvenient facts. 'Now they would blame and harry us, whenever their stock strays. They are seeds no longer, but pale weeds grown among us. They suck the goodness from our soil and dull the bloom of youth!' The elders were nodding, rumbling, stamping their feet. The lamp swung, the fire flared dull yellow. Gitau showed the whites of his eyes, punching his palm for emphasis. 'The Father says they want war – then let us *give* them war!'

The elders' chant became a fully-fledged war cry, bringing Father Andrew close to tears of sheer frustration. Standing aloof, Kibe caught his eye and mouthed, 'Wait. It is not finished.' Following his gaze, Father Andrew glimpsed movement in a deeply shadowed corner; he heard metallic jangles and watched Njau's spare black figure drift into the light.

And marvelled at the sudden, instant hush.

How does he do it? Father Andrew wondered. What is so compelling about this frail old spindle-shanks? He should be a figure of fun, in bells and beads and a baggy piebald kirtle; yet he keeps the elders wholly in his thrall. There *is* a certain presence, a curious coppery sheen about his eyes. There *is* a sinuous grace to every gesture, a faint, hypnotic slur within his voice. Father Andrew started. *That's* how it's done, he realised, and summoned godly images against the Healer's force.

'You should heed this priest,' Njau was saying, slow and sibilant. 'Though misguided, he is honest when he speaks of small birds slain from far away. It is done with noise and fire in the blink of white men's eyes: and you would make *war* against them?' He sent Gitau a weary, withering glance. 'Curb your bloodlust, chief, lest you would see our clansblood stain the pasture. Some day, the tribe may rise against Red Strangers. This is not the time or place. War is not the way.' He seemed to be diminishing, merging with the shadows. Only his words remained, swathed in smoke beneath the sooty rafters. 'Observe the law, respect your neighbours. *And give the cattle back.*'

Outside there was a welcome breeze and freshness, a glint of stars, and the Mission, pale and ghostly on the hill. Darkness was welcome too, hiding the shameful flush on priestly cheeks.

'It was the right choice,' Kibe declared. 'They would not have made it if you hadn't forced them.'

'You are kind and loyal, Kibe; and sadly mistaken. It was total defeat, public humiliation. Njau's hold is as strong as ever. And I thought we were making progress!'

'Oh, but we are!'

The yellow hutlight dwindled behind them; loud slurred elders' voices faded. As they trod the dew-damp grasses, Kibe prattled brightly of success: converts among the middle-aged, a recent rash of baptisms, two of his own age-mates who might be brought to God. Father Andrew scarcely listened. It all seemed so trifling, compared to Njau's effortless command.

9

WHEN LEO WAS FOURTEEN he asked about the *thingira*. He asked Thuo, who was a year older, two inches shorter, as black, sturdy and ugly as Duma's yearling bullock, and as staunch a friend as anyone could wish for. Thuo was distant kin to Gitau, and natural leader of the age-group. But Leo had beaten him at wrestling, and had thereby earned his unswerving loyalty.

The *thingira* was a hut which stood apart, in a quiet glade near the river. Leo had seen young men and women going there eagerly, walking close together, whispering and giggling. Something still puzzled him, that he had heard from Wanjui. 'Unwed women are not allowed to get with child. Warriors cannot become fathers. So what happens, at the *thingira*?'

'*Ngweko.*'

'And what, Thuo the wise, is *ngweko*?'

'Relief,' said Thuo simply. Seeing Leo's puzzled frown, he continued, 'The maiden must tie her apron tight between her legs. Neither may touch the other's private parts with hands or lips. They may fondle and *play* sex. They must not mate. Where are you going?'

Leo was on his feet, stepping into the sunlight. There was a strange heaviness in his blood and an urgent curiosity in his mind. 'I saw Maina, on his way there with a girl. I want to see; I want to know.' Thuo stared up, pop-eyed and aghast. 'You cannot! It is tabu, you are not circumcised!'

Leo sidled away, grinning, moving towards a glint of water between green boughs. Presently, he heard Thuo's wary, heavy footfalls at his back.

It is as well, Leo thought, loosening another handful of thatch, that the leaves sigh loudly to the wind and the river babbles so bravely. Thuo is like a clumsy elephant in the bush, and my climb up here was hardly silent. Perhaps *ngweko* makes people deaf.

He lay spreadeagled along a stout roofpole. The sun warmed his back and the thatch tickled his thighs; it tickled something between his thighs, as well. He enlarged the hole stealthily and peered into the gloom below.

At first, he could see little more than rhythmic, shadowy movement. Sounds reached him, faint but growing stronger: high-pitched moans, deeper, harsher grunts.

He glanced down. Thuo stood in mottled shade, gazing upwards. From this angle, his head looked huge, his body short and thin, like a stranded black tadpole.

'What are they doing?' he whispered.

'Dying, I think.'

Leo stretched cautiously and pushed his face into the space above. Slowly, his vision cleared.

Maina sprawled beneath him on a raised liana couch. His head rolled backwards, his eyes were clenched, his teeth shone in a grimace of pure agony. He was gripping the wooden crosspiece fiercely. Veins writhed in his biceps and under the dark, sweat-slick sheen of his neck.

A slimmer, lighter figure knelt across his wide-flung thighs. Each time she bent forward, her hips seemed to thrust straight into Leo's face: Firm, round, almond-coloured moons, wondrously curved and silky. Each time she paused, the thin leather thongs which rose from beneath drew taut in the cleft of her buttocks. The shaded pouch below and between loomed in Leo's vision, like a mysterious, inviting cavern. Then she would rise, her back arched and sinuous, her breasts outthrust and gleaming. These were not Wanjui's breasts, bulbous and broadnosed; these were tight and upswept, their points as long and curved and sharp as blackthorns. The tingle at Leo's groin was spreading, growing hard and heavy.

The girl leaned forward again, pressing herself to Maina's chest.

'She *is* killing him,' Leo breathed. 'She's stabbing him with her teats!' And indeed, Maina now looked and sounded beyond help, gasping like a beached fish.

The movements and the noises quickened. Suddenly, the girl stiffened, cried 'No!' and rolled sideways in a tumble of limbs on to the dim green grass. She huddled there, her head lolling, her hands fluttering like wounded birds over the dampened pouch.

73

And no wonder. 'My *God*,' hissed Leo, unaware and unheeding of his blasphemy. 'He has a war-club, there between his legs! It's monstrous, Thuo, she could not survive it. But wait! He erupts! Oh, his body arcs like a bowstring, his weapon spurts white blood!'

Leo's own weapon leaped and quivered, his senses wavered. He shifted, grabbed vainly at the roofpole – and tumbled headlong through the yielding thatch.

He fell like a cat, arched and twisting, landing with outstretched feet and fingertips at either side of the supine girl. His arms and knees buckled at the impact. He crumpled across her belly, his face nestling into her moist, hot pouch. Musk and languor drowned him. His groin pulsed sweetly. This is heaven, he mused, whatever Father Andrew says.

But not for long. The softness beneath tensed and quivered. A shriek skewered his eardrums. 'The woodsprite! Ngai, save me, the woodsprite devours me!' Leo was hurled aside. The girl leapt up and bolted in ungainly female panic: breasts jouncing, knees akimbo, buttocks flashing amber in the sun. He still hadn't seen her face.

He saw Maina's face, though, saw it swell and darken in rage and recognition. As Maina rose, his thick-veined war-club wilted; and heaven paled before his hellish wrath. 'Owl-turd!' he roared. 'Slinking, prying hyena! I will geld you for this!'

Leo ran for dear life and newfound manhood, out of the hut, across the glade and into the bright green bush. He broke out on to the river bank, plunged in, and splashed his way across. He paused briefly on the further shingle, swept up a handful of pebbles and heard the thrash of pursuit drawing nearer. Squinting across the glitter, he saw deliverance hanging from a low, moss-furred bough – a wild bees' hive.

He threw, missed narrowly, threw again. The hive kicked upwards, swung wildly. And Maina blundered, fanged and vengeful, into the swarm's buzzing rage.

Maina hopped. Maina danced. Maina bellowed in pain, lurched in circles, and hurled himself into the water. Three times he reared up in glittering gouts of spray. Three times the bees found him and drove him under again.

Leo sat on a warm round rock and laughed until he cried. He laughed harder when the warrior finally staggered away, bent double, clutching his once-proud manhood. Even from here, Leo could see angry welts rise from Maina's thorn-raked haunches; he could picture the new, painful knots upon that shrivelled war-club.

But after a while, the mirth turned sour. There would be a reckoning, he knew: welts raised on his own backside by Father Andrew's slipper.

'Beat me,' Leo begged, 'burn my bow and arrows, take away the poems! I will study twice as hard. *Please* don't do this!'

Father Andrew towered in Leo's bedroom doorway. He wore the eagle face again, sad, stony and unyielding. 'You know the law, Leo. You flouted tabu, damaged communal property, taunted and injured a warrior. The matter must be settled between his father and yours. You have left Duma at the mercy of Gitau, whom he despises, to whom he must now surrender both pride and cattle in recompense. Very well, let Duma punish you. And let Mwangi revel in your downfall. Don't gawp at me, son. I am neither so blind nor so unworldly as you think.'

'I will do whatever Duma wishes,' muttered Leo. 'I am used to Mwangi's hatred. This, I can survive. But *you* would send me away! I don't want to go! I want to be like the others in my age-group. I want to be circumcised!'

Father Andrew stood up, tall and green against the orange curtains. There was pain in his face, and a kind of angry sadness. 'So now you would be a naked young buck, and dally with the maidens in *ngweko*. Do you know what it means, this circumcision? To squat all night in an icy stream, chanting a pagan hymn; to sit, splay-legged, unflinching and unresisting, while an evil old man with a rusty knife saws away your foreskin; to staunch the wound with dirty leaves and pray it does not fester. And this crude ritual will make you a *man*?'

'I am not afraid,' mumbled Leo, who suddenly was. 'I do not fear pain, nor Njau's knife.' Father Andrew strode to the bed, knelt and took Leo's hand. 'You do not fear the knife, you say; you *do* fear English schooling. Very well: grasp the nettle and conquer the greater fear – let us never more dispute your manhood! Do this for me: do this for yourself.'

A strand of moonlight slid between Leo's curtains, rested cool and bright on Leo's hand. The hand Father Andrew had released and then shaken: *man to man*.

'I will write to England tonight,' he had promised, 'and to Mission Headquarters for the scholarship. With luck, we shall find

75

you a place by September.' His tone had deepened and faltered. 'Mine is the punishment, son. I dare not think how it will be, without you.'

Six months, thought Leo, closer to tears than he'd been since he was seven. Six months to hunt with Duma, wrestle with Thuo, honour Wanjui and try to win Mwangi's affection.

The moonshaft rested on his childish books, long unopened – the ones Father Andrew used to read, full of adventure and derring-do.

I must do something heroic, Leo thought, like the sturdy, blue-eyed lads in those books. They don't send heroes away to school – do they?

10

ONE EVENING IN JUNE, Leo let Thuo win a wrestling bout. He did it in the pasture, while goatbells clanked and eager age-mates cheered him on. It was hard, because he'd seen Thuo's throw coming, and he could have countered it easily. It was harder still, with damp grass beneath his back and Thuo's grin of unearned triumph blazing, to feign defeat, to hear the stunned silence, to know that the news would travel faster than even he could run. He did it with a rueful smile and an aching heart, so that the age-group would have a respected, circumcised leader; and he wept inside, all the way back to the Mission.

After supper, he butchered a Latin unseen, and endured a stern, lamplit reproach from Father Andrew. 'You will not always have a private tutor, Leo. Concentrate: set a good foundation, lest you wear the dunce's cap!'

That night, he lay in darkness under crisp, coarse sheets, pining for Wanjui's gentle smile, mourning the injustice. I *have* been heroic, he thought, and no one will ever know. That night, he cried himself to sleep; the bitterest tears of his boyhood.

He woke at first light to a damp pillow and a lingering sense of loss. He slipped away from the Mission, seeking solitude, a high place, a vision to cherish through the coming exile. He climbed the hill and prowled the forest fringe, and saw the morning quicken.

I *will* return, vowed Leo. This is my home, these are the visions which call me back. The distant, pure white peak, the rolling, windswept plains; a pall of blue-grey smoke above the northern ridge, the slow, olive-green curve of the river; a scatter of goats in the pasture, kite-wings glinting rufous, and sunlight pale on the Mission walls. I will go down now, accept Thuo's rule and Mwangi's jibes and Father Andrew's lessons, and dream of my return.

He lingered, troubled by one of his images, something he had never noticed before.

Smoke, on the northern ridge.

Too much smoke, too thick and too dark, billowing over the neighbouring village. What are they burning, Leo wondered; surely the sickness hasn't come back? He shielded his eyes. Presently, he saw movement on the ridge.

Cattle, he thought, moving quickly. Among and around them, he glimpsed a flicker of steel. His mind was racing, remembering tales of raiding, along the northern boundary. Then, behind and to the left of the moving beasts, he saw men: men who carried oval shields of red and white and grey.

He ran, past the silent trees, over the crest, towards the waking huts. He ran with all the speed he could muster, to alert the clan and raise the alarm; to tell them the Masai were coming.

'If I get my algebra right, can I join the battle?'

'It's not a joking matter, Leo. Eat your porridge. And save a little of that sugar for my tea.'

'I'm not joking, Father. Duma plans an ambush. He's taking Thuo and the others.'

'Indeed? How do you know?'

'Duma came to my window, at dawn. He was like a brown ghost, in the mist. The warriors need help, he said. Herdboys shall be bowmen.'

'A foolish brown ghost! I must have words with Duma!'

'But Father, I am the best archer. They *need* me!'

'Elbows off the table, son. Manners maketh man.'

Father Andrew set his cup down. An early sunslant burnished the willow-pattern plate and made a halo of Leo's hair. The boy was ablaze with warlike fervour. 'It's not a game,' Father Andrew warned him. 'Men will die, today. Finish your breakfast, go about your studies. This is not your fight.'

Leo completed a dozen problems in half an hour. Wonderful, he thought: the clan arms for battle and the Lion Boy does *sums*.

It was hotter now, and brighter. The air seemed to throb with tension. He pictured the warriors, greasing their bodies and grinning to mask their nerves. He pictured Duma, stealing along the upper pasture, placing his young bowmen, praising them quietly to build their courage. He pictured Thuo, moonfaced and fearless, testing his bow and pining for action. For the first time, he hated this gift of pictures.

Sounds reached him, dribbling down the passage from the sanctum: Kibe's voice, quick and anxious, Father Andrew's deeper, crisper tones. Leo tiptoed closer, through yellow sunpools cast on the cool pale stone.

'The women won't come here,' Kibe was complaining. 'Victory is certain, they say. The raiders will not even reach the huts.'

'Indeed?' growled Father Andrew. 'By which all-seeing prophet is this known? Don't tell me – Njau!'

'It doesn't change, Father. His power rules them yet.'

'It *must* change, Kibe! By sunset, they may see the error of their ways.'

Leo heard thoughtful footfalls, the rustle of Father Andrew's cassock. 'What about Wanjui and her brood?'

'I trust Ngai, she said, who lives on Kerinyagga. I will not hide among those unblessed stones.'

'And you forsook her? I want her safe, man! Must I do everything myself?'

Silence.

A sigh, a note of priestly regret. 'Forgive me, Kibe, I am ill-humoured today. I snapped at Leo, too.'

'No, you are right, Father. I will go back and try again.'

She will not come, thought Leo. She is gentle but stubborn, and constant to the only god she knows.

'Pray for me,' said Kibe, and Father Andrew's answer sent Leo scuttling away.

'I will pray for us all, while Leo is still at his books.'

The sanctum door creaked. Kibe's leather sandals slap-slapped down the passage into the garden beyond. Leo stood poised in his doorway, beset by silence, opportunity and the heavy surge of his own pulse.

Honour thy father and thy mother, he thought. What if, in honouring one, a boy must defy the other? Duma, too, is my father. Can I defy him command of my sure, swift arrows? I did not promise to stay, he remembered. I promised to do my duty. *And Wanjui will not come!*

He took his bow and his quiver, and sidled again along the dappled stone. He paused just once, safe and undetected beyond the sanctum door. Forgive me, Father, for you know not what I do. You have forced me to choose: I choose to do my duty by Wanjui. You will be proud of me, today.

Then Leo slipped into the blazing morning, and warrior's fire kindled in his blood.

On the way to the huts, he met Duma's group and had to explain himself. 'Wanjui and the children are safely hidden in the forest,' Duma told him.

You must go back, said Leo's conscience. He hesitated in the sunshine, lusting for combat, trammelled by his vow. Thuo's eyes beseeched him. Come, they said, we need your strength and speed. Then Duma spoke the magic word, and set him free. 'We are under attack, Leo. It is a duty.' So Leo silenced his conscience, and went with them.

From a sheltered hollow on the upper pasture, Duma gave his orders. 'Spread out, stay low. There is the target − the flat place between the river and the huts. Aim upwards, let your arrows bring death from above. Hurry. They draw nearer.' He touched Leo's shoulder as the others slipped away. 'Stay close. Do as I do.'

Leo crawled through the yellowing grass, strung his bow and breathed peppery dust. He crawled and crouched and waited, and watched the Masai come.

They came in formation, over a rise and through a rippling haze. Leo counted two dozen − eight ranks, three abreast; long, hard, ochred men with ostrich feathers in their hair, great pied plumes which made them even taller. At each stride, they flicked their upright spears aloft. Wide steel spun and glistened rhythmically. At each stride, they chanted: ay-*yah*, ay-*yah*! They march as if they own the earth, Leo thought, as if no living force can stand against them.

'*Now!*' breathed Duma, rising taut against his bow's hard arc. Leo obeyed, gauging the distance, launching arrows as fast as he could nock them. The air hummed around him. The sky was cleft by slim shafts; climbing, levelling, curving down. 'Kikuyu bees,' cried Leo. 'See them swoop and sting!'

'You crow too soon,' Duma warned. 'Watch.'

As he spoke, oval shields were lifting above proud, feathered heads; others were tilted forward, others still lay flat along the flanks. The column advanced, armoured on all sides in grey and white and scarlet, like a huge, painted tortoise. Arrows rattled on toughened hide, cartwheeled uselessly away.

Gitau's war-horn bellowed, brave and bullish, restoring Leo's spirits and unleashing the Kikuyu warriors. They swarmed from the huts, their greased limbs flashing amber, their stabbing spears poised. The Masai formation shifted, and formed a single line. All the shields faced forward. Leo flinched from the rending crash of impact. He was edging down the slope, breathing fast, itching to fight.

He heard the ring of spear on spear, a roar of rage, a scream of pain. Dust flew and eddied. The air was ripe with gore and sweat. And the Masai line swept slowly forward.

He saw a lean moran check, pluck a spear from his shoulder and drive savagely on. He saw a clansman stagger back, slump to the grass, clutch his riven belly where purple entrails slithered through the redness. 'Kill them!' he screamed. 'Make them burn and bleed!'

Duma grasped his arm and shook him roughly. 'Calm yourself, boy! You are too young to join the warriors. Seize the moment, make each arrow count. *Think!*' Leo breathed deeply, dashed the angry tears away. He shut out the heat and the dust and the sounds of dying, and looked to the heart of the fight where Duma pointed.

The Masai lines had altered yet again. Now they formed an arrowhead, aimed directly towards the huts; and at its tip was the tallest man of all.

Even from here, Leo could see the fierce joy in his hawk-nosed, ochre-tinted face. Even as the man lunged and thrust and scattered the clan before him, Leo could not but admire his warlike grace and boldness. '*That* is the one,' breathed Duma. 'That is their leader. If he falls, they will retreat. It is their way. Maina knows it. See how Maina strives to reach him.'

Maina, the dark-browed bully of the baptism; Maina, the clown of *thingira*, the hapless butt of bees, Leo had always despised him. But he could not despise this sturdy, blood-smeared warrior, this wounded bull besieged by sharp black storks. The bobbing plumes were closing round him, the steel sang ever nearer to his chest. The Masai leader loomed above him, grinning. Maina fought on, defying the odds, seeking to rally the clan. In vain. One by one, the warriors were cut down or driven back. The pasture was turning red; Maina was in danger of total isolation. Still, he snarled and hacked, and kept them from the huts.

Leo's mind steadied and he recalled another image: of Kibe at the river, singing, displaying the same strength, the same courage. *It must not stand alone.*

So Leo ran.

He ran as only he could run, swift and free as the wind. He ran in certain knowledge, with truth and power surging through his veins. 'The Lion Boy,' he shouted, 'follow the Lion Boy!' Bending in full stride, he swept up a fallen simi and raced towards Maina. As he passed, he sensed his fleeing kinsmen's horror, heard them check, heard their new resolve – 'The Masai shall not have him!' Ahead, the clash of weapons beckoned. Then he was in the thick of it, weaving, dodging, swinging the simi, relishing the jar of blade on bone. He was drinking the scent of blood and combat, inches from death, more alive than ever before. And his brain was icy clear.

It happened exactly as he had foreseen. The Masai were tall, and taken by surprise. Their spearthrusts hissed harmlessly above him, and his reddened simi made them hop and howl.

Until he reached Maina's side, and stood beneath the shadow of the Masai leader's spear. He looked along a dazzle of steel to the cold, black eyes behind. He thought he saw respect there, a fighting man's acknowledgement; but he saw no mercy and no doubt. He did see the high black shoulder tense, and he brought his own blade up defiantly. It is done, he thought. I can hear the clan regrouping, feel the tide of battle turning. The Lion Boy will die a hero.

The arrowhead glinted once, plunged into the Masai leader's neck, burst through throat and flesh and out the other side. Blood spurted, bright and crimson. The slim body seemed to melt, bowing at the waist, folding into the dust. Pied feathers trailed, fluttered weakly, and lay still. *Duma*, thought Leo. Only Duma would venture such a shot, only Duma could strike such a slender target. Maina roared his triumph. The war-horn thundered. The Masai line faltered, wavered and broke. The battle was over, reduced to a series of skirmishes and tall, plumed figures fleeing.

I wonder if Father Andrew will beat me, Leo thought.

He never saw the blow that felled him. He felt a sudden, blinding pain, and heard a clang like a hundred Mission bells in his head. He was spinning, floating, falling. The blood-slick pasture rose and hit him in the back. Dimly, he saw a vengeful Masai face above him, a raw wound gaping in coal-black flesh. 'Leave me alone,' he mumbled, 'I'm tired.'

The sky was turning red. It is my own redness, Leo realised, I am dying after all. It didn't seem to matter very much. There was no pain, only a curious lifting sensation. He felt light and life leaving him, and he couldn't keep his hold on either. I *am* a hero, he thought. They won't forget the Lion Boy.

And I never did go to school.

I I

'A LION BOY,' SNARLED His Excellency above the rhythmic clop of hooves, 'foisted on me by His Grace the bloody bishop! As if I don't get grief enough from you!'

'Me, sir?' Hugo Berkeley murmured, as the official carriage jolted through deep ruts.

The Governor slapped the reins on shiny chestnut withers. Morning sunlight glinted in his bloodshot blue eyes, setting his rufous sidewhiskers aflame. 'Take young Hugo to the colony, your pater pleaded, make a man of him. Should've known better, seeing those languid airs, that milksop complexion. I trusted you; how am I rewarded?' A red-furred finger stabbed at Hugo's chest. 'Overdue accounts at Lola's Funhouse. Drunken revels at the club. Gambling debts, unredeemed; tailor's bills, unpaid. You sir, are a toper, a wastrel and a fop!'

A bit thick, Hugo thought, coming from a man who favoured native trollops and was seldom sober after dusk. He thought it, but said nothing. His slender, almost girlish good looks demanded frequent reassertions of manhood. The Governor's fiefdom oozed patronage and sloth; Hugo was trusted only to minute trivial grievances from clod-hopping settlers.

He daren't cross H.E., who revelled in authority and wielded fearsome influence at home. A word from him, my lad, and Pater will surely cut you off. Apologise, smile sweetly, take your wigging like the thick-skinned toady H.E. would have you be.

'Sorry,' Hugo grunted.

The Governor mellowed somewhat, reining back the pony, wearing a foxy grin that boded someone ill. 'Sorry?' he echoed. 'Can't pay dues with "sorry". As penance you shall take the bishop's pawn in hand.'

'But sir, I know nothing about him!'

'Listen, then, and learn. D'you think I brought you for the ride? He's a legend to both Masai and Kyuke, and a thundering embarrassment to the Church. Born in superstition, it seems, brought up in a mission, cross between a savage and a saint. Hasn't been to school, probably illiterate. Rough clay for you to mould.'

'Is that an order?' Hugo enquired weakly.

'Damn right it is! It'll keep you out of mischief, cut your debts to size. Then maybe I can send Pater a *balanced* account, what?'

Hugo sagged against the red plush leather and watched the town roll past. Dear God, he thought, how I hate Nairobi; the grubby, unmade streets and ugly redbrick buildings, the stench of spice and native sweat, the hot fierce light and garish colours. How I long for soft green meadows, clothes that fit and plumbing that works, a decent book, an intelligent conversation; and cool white scented flesh in bed, instead of reeking, raucous, Nubian whores. Even that worldly pleasure would now be forfeit while he wet-nursed a mission-born yahoo who would doubtless combine the worst of both worlds – prissy church morality and native witlessness.

By the time they reached the station, Hugo was disposed to loathe the Lion Boy on sight.

The Governor checked the carriage under a Nandi flame tree in a quiet corner of the station yard.

'He may not see us,' Hugo pointed out. 'Shouldn't we go closer?'

'And have the whole town think he's something special? Where's your pride, man? He must come to us!'

A stickler for protocol, was H.E. He lounged and fanned himself with his white cockaded hat as if he were merely resting the horse.

Presently the up-country train clanked in, smelling of oil and sulphur, painting grey smokeswirls on the clear blue sky. The platform bustled with activity – modish gentlefolk under multi-coloured parasols; weatherbeaten settlers with baggy shorts and pistols at their hips; Indians wearing pure white robes and yellow turbans, squawking like crested cockatoos; black rickshaw boys naked but for grubby loincloths, raising dust and clamouring for trade. There was hullooing and hoorahing, a piercing whistle, and a final blast of steam that made Hugo flinch.

It cleared around a strapping youth with silver in his hair.

'That's him,' H.E. muttered, with a taunting grin. 'Seventeen, and twice the man you'll ever be.'

He was over six feet tall, broad-shouldered, deeply suntanned. A pale scar at the left temple saved him from too–perfect handsomeness. The outmoded, ill-cut, dung-brown suit could not disguise his natural grace. There *was* something special about him, some inner force which gave him presence way beyond his years.

'Come,' said Hugo miserably. 'Better get it over.' H.E.'s hard hand clamped his arm.

'Wait. No doubt by now you'd be crying for your mama. Let's see how he performs.'

He performed admirably, ignoring amused whispers and pitying stares from white onlookers until the crowd dispersed. Alone, he showed no sign of anxiety: he stood poised yet patient, studying his surroundings.

This is what he would do in the bush, Hugo realised, watching the blond head lift and seeing the finely sculpted nostrils flare. There is a primitive within him, who trusts senses city men have never known.

Then his glance fell on the carriage, and he moved.

He came forward in an easy, feline lope, swinging the big brown battered suitcase effortlessly. Consumed with envy, Hugo hunched lower in the seat, and heard his well-modulated, oddly archaic introduction. 'Leo Reid. I am pleased to make your acquaintance and will serve you faithfully.'

The carriage creaked. The Governor stood, resplendent in dress-whites and gold epaulettes, peering down his nose. 'Sir!' he snapped. 'Now and henceforth, you will address me as "sir".'

'Your pardon – sir.' A faint ironic undertone made Hugo's ears prick. 'I mean no discourtesy. In my tribe, you see, a man must *earn* respect.'

Oh, *priceless*, Hugo exulted, hugging himself in secret joy, watching the Governor's cheeks turn puce. The biter so politely bitten, lending new brightness to the day!

He looked up for the first time into an innocent amber gaze and a physique he would gladly die for. What mating had forged such manly beauty, he wondered, what heroism had earned the scar, what sorrow had set silver in the tawny mane? Envy yielded to admiration.

Reid offered a muscular paw and an engaging, boyish grin. 'I'm glad you came. In Kikuyuland it is considered rude to stare.' The handshake tightened. 'Friends call me Leo,' he added.

It was only a formal clasp of flesh under orange and green foliage to the cry of hawkers and the flight of birds. Even as it happened, Hugo felt his heart leap, felt the order of things changing and knew he would remember this moment all his life. Leo Reid is everything I'm not, he thought, a natural warrior, a throwback to earlier, nobler days. Yet he too feels the force between us, a sudden sense of futures intertwined. We are opposites attracted, minds and spirits merging down the years. I will teach him subtlety, he will give me strength. And *what* a swathe we'll cut together through Nairobi females!

Aloud, demurely, as became the senior partner, he murmured, 'Welcome to Government, Leo.'

H.E.'s voice held no such warmth. 'Get billeted with Berkeley, and be back at Government House by six sharp. Having a soirée and a little pow-wow on the Masai. You do possess a D. J., I assume?' He was in command again, relishing Leo's sudden confusion. 'There'll be two evils you will have to face – sundowners and bloody Delamere. You'll oblige me by calling him "my lord".'

For the second time, Hugo met Leo's eye. Again, unspoken communion was complete. With straight faces and only a hint of laughter in their voices, they chorused 'Yes, *sir!*'

'Berkeley's Billet' was a timbered, two-bedroomed cottage set among emerald lawns and clipped yew hedges. The Ngong Hills rose behind it, dappled by small cloud shadows, arced and knobbly as a pi-dog's spine. While Leo washed travel grime away, Hugo issued explanations.

'Sundowners are evening cocktails. Lord Delamere is chief spokesman for the settlers, lifelong champion of the Masai. No one wields more local power. No one challenges officialdom more frequently – and wins. Don't fret about a dinner jacket; H.E.'s little joke. He'll be at it again when we get there. Listen, smile – and obey.'

H.E. was at it again, herding them through the twilit residence. 'You're a new boy, Reid. Mingle. Keep your wits about you, and your piggy little snout out of the gintrough. Come, Berkeley, we have groundwork to prepare.'

The soirée was already in full swing. Sunset played on crystal glasses and real jewellery; genteel conversation eddied on the breeze.

Left alone on the verandah among more white folk than he'd ever seen before, Leo felt anticipation stirring. This was the ordered elegance Father Andrew wanted for him. He was ready to be part of it.

Then the ladies of Nairobi flocked to greet him.

They wore long, rich-coloured dresses that rustled as they moved. Their artful coiffures and naked shoulders shimmered. Their eyes were bright with curiosity.

'So you're the famous Lion Boy,' a horsey, handsome creature in gold taffeta exclaimed. 'A wonder you have grown so well among the heathens.'

'They have their own gods,' Leo demurred,' and are faithful to them.'

'You should tell the missionaries,' a thinner, silver-haired matron interrupted. 'Would you believe they're trying to bring servants to *our* church?'

'My adoptive father is a missionary,' Leo said. 'His congregation is all Kikuyu.'

'My dears,' mourned Gold Taffeta, 'can you imagine the *smell*? You must have found it so distressing, Mr Reid.'

Leo wrinkled his nose at the heady whiff of gin and musky perfume. 'It is a natural scent,' he said. 'It reminds me of my mother. And I was raised by warriors, not servants.'

'How awful,' Silver Hair consoled him. 'I understand they're totally promiscuous.'

'You are mistaken, ma'am. A warrior is constant to his wives.'

'*Wives?*' Gold Taffeta echoed. 'You mean they have more than one?'

'They do so to avoid promiscuity.'

'Young man, that is a contradiction in terms!'

'When a wife gives birth,' Leo explained patiently, 'a warrior must wait two years before lying with her again. In the meantime, he may wed another.'

'Disgraceful!' Gold Taffeta snorted. 'Have they no self-control? Why, pray, should they wait so long?'

'It is the law,' said Leo. 'Twenty-four moons must wax and wane before the menstrual flow is cleansed.' Misinterpreting the abrupt, goggle-eyed hush, he warmed to his theme. 'In courtship, maidens must remain completely chaste. Circumcised boys find relief at the doodling bush. They compete there. He who doodles best is much prized as a husband.'

'Doodling?' breathed Silver Hair faintly. 'What on earth do you mean?'

Leo wagged his head, astounded at such ignorance. 'I suppose you would call it masturbation.'

'*Well!*' gasped Gold Taffeta, flushing scarlet. 'Well I do declare!' And, with a toss of her head and a twitch of her broad rump, she led the outraged, twittering flock away.

Leo was left baffled, and staring into Berkeley's appalled face.

'For God's sake, Leo, they might have swooned on the spot!'

'They asked me,' Leo protested. 'I only told the truth.'

'Oh my,' grinned Berkeley wanly, 'have you got things to learn! *Never* speak like that to ladies.'

'Introduce me, then. What about those fellows over there?' He pointed to a group of rough-hewn men in dusty clothes guffawing near the bar.

'Steer clear of them. They're settlers.' Hugo made it sound like a disease; and stiffened as H.E. called his name. 'Hang it, I'm in trouble.' He dragged Leo over to a lanky figure in white uniform. 'Binky Hargreaves, Leo Reid. You two have mutual interests. I must fly!'

Hargreaves had flame-red hair, freckles and supercilious blue eyes. 'Hoped we'd meet,' he drawled. 'Done ten years at the coast, just been promoted. Going north to spread the King's peace. Good huntin' up there, I'm told. How do the native chappies go about it?'

'They dig a pit and set sharp stakes at the bottom. When a rhino or a buffalo is impaled, they slaughter it with simis.'

'Good God, boy, I said huntin', not butchery! Don't any of them have the guts to do it single-handed?'

'A few, Mr Hargreaves. Those archers who are bravest and best.'

Leo was aware of other uniformed men gathering, and of Hargreaves's narrow, disdainful glare. 'So that is how you earned fame, Mr Reid. Doubtless *you* used a gun.'

'I am proficient with a rifle. But arrows are quieter, and just as deadly.'

'Indeed? And how does one kill buffalo with arrows?'

'I told you, Mr Hargreaves, only the best archers can. You must be sure to strike an eye.'

'I say, you chaps,' sneered Hargreaves, 'this Lion Boy thinks he's Will the Conqueror!'

Their mocking laughter fanned Leo's anger, the anger which had once spurred him into mortal combat. He drew himself up, feeling hot blood pounding at his temples.

'Are you calling me a liar, sir?'

Hargreaves licked his dry lips. Freckles blazed against his sudden pallor. 'I do not doubt your word,' he blustered, 'I deplore your attitude. Englishmen don't trumpet their achievements!' He turned to his cronies. 'Come, gentlemen, a drink to wash the taste away.'

For a second time, Leo was left adrift in Father Andrew's bright white world, to ponder on half-naked ladies who blenched at natural facts, and to wonder at officials who were blind to truth and who treated settlers like enemies.

He was still pondering when a servant approached, a wizened little brown man in a white kanzu and a crimson cummerbund. There was pleasure in his eyes and awe in his voice. 'You are the special one, born in a sacred tree. Come. I have maize beer.'

It was a great relief, then, to slip into the shadows and speak Kikuyu words, to gossip with the old one about crops and seasons and mutual friends. The beer was warm and yeasty. Party noises seemed to come from far away.

For a while, it was like being home again.

So that when they were discovered, he could smile at Hugo's consternation.

'Leo, you will be the death of me! If H.E. catches you skulking with the servants there will be hell to pay!'

'Not servants, Hugo, kinsmen. You too have things to learn.'

'All right, but not now; Lord Delamere is waiting!'

Poor Hugo, Leo thought, scurrying like a lapdog to do H.E.'s bidding. Why is he so afraid?

No time to ask. The 'pow-wow' had assembled in a dim, quiet room. H.E. drew Leo to one side. 'Ears and eyes open, mouth shut. If I want your wisdom, I'll ask, clear?'

Darkness drew in. The Governor downed gin in vast amounts, his colour growing ever more livid against immaculate dress-whites. Silent servants drifted through and lit the lamps. Moths committed sizzling suicide in the flames. The night fell quieter, leaving only insect hum and a lonely dog, howling.

Delamere sat, small, auburn, tight-knit, in a batwing rattan chair, while a man called Eric Stuart took the floor. A bristling, rawboned figure, he wore standard settler garb – a baggy, long-sleeved white shirt, knee-length khaki shorts, olive-green puttees and sensible brown brogues.

'I give ye the Masai,' he began, lifting an amber glass into the lampglow, revealing a broad, Scottish burr, 'more worthy of his salt than all the rest.'

'In his place, sir,' the Governor grunted. 'Only in his place.'

'Oh aye? And where might that be?'

'Show him, Berkeley,' H.E. snapped; adding, just loud enough to be heard, 'As if he doesn't know.'

Hugo cleared the table and unrolled a map, weighting the corners with crystal tumblers which splintered lamplight into yellow shards. He looked elegant and assured, his black hair a shining helmet around pale, even features, the navy sweater and moleskin trousers outlining his compact frame. 'The 1904 agreement created two reserves. Ever since, Masai paramount chiefs have complained about controlling such distantly separate units. Meanwhile, we have driven the railway through here, and encouraged white settlement in these highlands. As you see, the siting of the northern reserve poses direct dangers.'

'To whom?' Delamere enquired softly. 'Us – or the Masai?'

'A settler was killed, D,' the Governor interrupted, aiming a thick forefinger at Delamere's shaded corner. 'He was the sort of chap you're crying out for more of. Solution's obvious. A single, larger, southern reserve, along the border with German East Africa. Face facts, man. You can't trust the Masai any more.'

'There's no other black man'll look ye square in the eye, and give his word, and keep it!' Stuart thumped a bony fist on to the map. ''Tis better to deal with yon moran than with treacherous Kyukes who'll no doubt take their place!'

It was a gratuitous insult, which drove H.E.'s orders and Hugo's warning clean out of Leo's mind. He came boldly to Kikuyu defence.

'The people you speak of, sir, are honourable and trustworthy. I have lived with them all my life!'

'I thought we were speaking of the Masai.'

'An arrogant race,' Leo retorted, 'who care more for cows than people.'

'Ye're quite the wee expert, laddie! How long have ye lived with *them*?'

'Two years,' said Leo quietly, seeing delight on Hugo's face and triumph in the Governor's bloodshot gaze. 'I learned their language and many of their customs. Do *you* speak Masai, Mr Stuart?'

H.E. crossed to the drinks tray, casting a long shadow, making the boards creak. Lead glass tinkled prettily, a waft of gin rode the warm still air. 'Nothing to say, Eric?' he taunted.

The Scot shook his head, pale at the lips and gills.

'Ready to charge your glass, then, and drink to relocation?'

'Not quite,' objected Delamere; and tension coiled once more through dwindling lampglow. 'Let us now be clear. You propose voluntary relocation, in the mutual interest of settler and Masai. If, however, there should be the barest hint of force – why, then I'd be obliged to muster forces of my own.'

From deep within the shadows, his eyes blazed pale blue fire. Clearly, his was not an idle threat. Then he was up, brisk, flame-headed and rather ugly in the brightness, bidding H.E. a civil good evening, towing Eric Stuart along by sheer force of personality.

Hugo Berkeley drifted close to Leo, his pointed, faun-like face alight with joy. 'A brilliant ambush, my lad! That hairy-kneed halfwit blundered straight in. H.E. is ecstatic. He so rarely puts one over on his Lordship.'

'It wasn't intended as a trap,' Leo confessed.

'Don't you dare disillusion H.E.! I'd better take you away, before you say something silly and spoil it all.'

'Where can we go, at this time of night hour?'

Hugo smiled indulgently. 'Lola's, of course. Where else?'

The lamps in Lola's place burned low and red. Thick-piled russet carpets absorbed noise. The furniture was ornate, upholstered in scarlet velvet, cushioned and trimmed in gold. The air smelled of crushed roses, mellow wine, and something headier than both; something deeply female which stirred the blood and made the senses swim. Lola must be very rich, Leo mused, to keep a house like this and entertain so many friends.

They were so *very* friendly, these lightly clothed ladies who jostled prettily in eagerness to greet him, and vied among themselves to offer him the most adoring glance.

One in particular took his eye, standing forlornly apart from the rest.

She curtsied, demure and dulcet. 'Do you like me, sir? My name is Elsie.'

'I think you're absolutely charming!'

A small, surprisingly strong hand grasped his own. Knowing fingers caressed his wrist and forearm. 'Alone at last, dearie. How much d'you want, for how long?'

He stared down in astonishment at the brittle, sensuous creature at his side, at the small, sharp, artfully displayed bosom, the pink tongue between pouted lips, the calculating blue stare from which all innocence had drained.

'I'm sorry,' he mumbled, 'there's been a mistake.'

'Your loss, dearie. Plenty more fish in this sea!' She swept away, tossing her head, twitching her turquoise rump.

Leo went after Berkeley.

He found him sprawling on an overstuffed chaise-longue, his sleek head almost buried between huge, black, gleaming Nubian breasts.

'You didn't tell me,' Leo raged. 'You didn't say it was a whore-house!'

'What did you expect, old chap?' Berkeley enquired dreamily, fingering a nipple the exact size, shape and colour of a ripe damson. '*I* left Sunday school years ago.'

The Nubian girl was purring like a big contented cat. The chaise-longue creaked to each convulsion of her hips. Berkeley sat up, grinning vacantly, unbuckling his belt. 'You're being a bore, Leo, bothering the clientele. You don't have to watch: I know the way.'

Leo turned on his heel, stormed past the simpering, giggling girls towards the fresh clean air outside. As he reached the door, Hugo's grateful bellow shook the rafters.

'Tally ho-o-o-o-o!'

Leo made his way to the courtyard, where the rickshaw boy was waiting. The wooden shaft gleamed faintly on his shoulders and his breathing sounded regular and soft. He stood there in the starlight, bolt upright, fast asleep.

It seemed pointless to disturb him. There was no great hurry, no moon to waken bitter memories. Leo strolled away from lights and laughter and tinkling pianola sounds, through dimness and the scent of frangipani. It was good to be alone, to draw breath, to seek a sane perspective on this long, eventful day.

First impressions: a sprawling, seedy township, full of muddy streets and ugly buildings; a governor who drinks too much and trusts too little, yet could be a forceful ally against the Masai; a first, intoxicating whiff of real power, a glimpse of the Delamere dynamo in action. I don't think I shall like Nairobi, he thought, but I won't be bored.

Sudden, urgent footfalls overtook him. He turned and saw a slight, silken figure, who made an anxious plea.

'Come quick, dearie, your mate's in big trouble.'

Elsie.

'I won't come back in there, whatever story you dream up.' He allowed himself a faint, rueful smile. 'Besides, I haven't any money.'

'You stupid great ninny, I told you I had other fish. It's Hugo, for Christ's sake! Can't you bleedin' well listen?'

Leo leaned forward, cupping his ear. Faintly, he thought he heard unladylike shrieks, a crash of broken glass, and a man's voice raised in pain and supplication. Steady on, he thought, running, you'll wake the rickshaw boy.

Lola was fair and fat – and fuming. 'How old are you? Eighteen? Twenty? What use is a stripling like you against Big Flynn?' The ceiling shuddered. Flakes of plaster spiralled down. 'Oh my Gawd, I'm ruined!'

'You'll get no sense from 'er,' sniffed Elsie. 'Come on. I'll show you.'

She led him upstairs, chattering compulsively over her shoulder. 'Flynn's a railway man, a Friday regular, always has Bertha – you know, the Nubian cow. Well, he's a day early, mean Irish drunk, and caught her with Mr Berkeley.' There was another rending crash, and a high-pitched, eerie moan. Elsie blanched, and pointed. 'In there.'

Leo took a deep breath, opened the panelled door – and stepped into bedlam.

Bertha cowered in a corner, the whites of her eyes huge with terror, her naked flesh as quivery as chocolate blancmange. The moaning came from the plum-black, thickly muscled Negro who shambled across the smoke-blue carpet clutching his shaven head in shovel-like hands. 'That's Reuben,' Elsie whispered breathily, 'the bouncer'.

Flynn sat at the hub of the chaos, his vast, grubbily underclothed haunches overflowing both sides of a Queen Anne chair. Thick black fur covered his barrel chest and belly and blue stubble shadowed his jowls. One meaty paw contained a flask of whisky; in the other, he held Hugo.

He held a fistful of Hugo's navy sweater; of Hugo's trousers, Leo saw no trace. After each vast swallow, Flynn would swing Hugo off his feet and shake him in time to a bouncy curiously melodic chant. 'Thou shalt not steal Old Uncle Flynn's fat-chested little blackbird.'

Hugo's eyes crossed, Hugo's teeth chattered. The navy sweater ruckered upwards. Hugo's pale and flaccid sex waggled weakly. 'Poor Mr Berkeley,' crooned Elsie, 'he was quite a big man once.' The gross indignity of it spurred Leo to action. 'Enough, Mr Flynn,' he said. 'Isn't it time you went home?'

The room was suddenly still, but for Reuben's whimpers and Elsie drawing in her breath. Flynn lifted his great head, focusing his pink piggy squint. His breath seethed with raw spirits, bringing moisture to Leo's eyes. 'And what's it to you, me fine blond-headed bucko? Away to your bed and your mama!'

'You have hold of my friend there. I can't leave without him.'

'Is that so? Well now, perhaps there's more sport to be had with the likes of you, for he's a feeble fellow, to be sure.' Flynn leered slyly. 'Would ye be after taking his place?'

Leo frowned, feigning doubt and indecision. 'Well . . . If you'll let me cleanse you and say a grace my priestly Father taught me.'

'`Tis ready I am, for prayers with any man. Step a little closer, boy.'

'One moment. First, the grace.' Leo placed his hands together, fashioned a pious gaze. 'Close your eyes and repeat after me: for what we are to receive.'

Flynn obeyed. Leo took one swift stride forward, pivoted, and threw every ounce of weight and strength into the left hook Father Andrew had taught him, so many years ago. It landed, flush on the point of Flynn's jaw. The impact jarred Leo right down to his heels.

Flynn's eyes opened, widened. He spoke in tones of wonder, touching his bestubbled jowl in awe. 'Bejasus, 'tis a powerful prayer; I felt an angel's kiss!' He grinned savagely, started to rise, his grip on Hugo's sweater undiminished. Leo backed off, swallowing hard, steeling himself for a losing battle. Then Flynn slid gently sideways off the chair, rolling on to his back, aiming glassy smiles and blissful snores at the ceiling.

Released, brimming with admiration and gratitude, Hugo was preserving token modesty with one hand and slapping Leo's shoulder with the other. Elsie leered up at him, thrust herself against him in feline abandon. Bertha advanced, tall and proud, the promise of her award for valour quivering on every shiny, nude, magnificent ounce. From the stairwell came the chatter of eager women – eager, no doubt, to render separate but similar tributes.

So Leo ran.

He bounded down the stairs, avoiding clutching hands and amorous glances. He ran through the sultry red light out into the scented darkness beyond. He fled in horror of disease, in fear for his mortal soul, out beneath the gum trees, past the still-dozing rickshaw boy under the spangled sky. He burrowed into a bougainvillaea bush, heedless of the prickles, and cowered there till Hugo's now fully clothed silhouette appeared. 'Can I come out?' he whispered anxiously. 'Is it safe?' And he couldn't understand why Hugo laughed so much.

Wheels whirled and clattered over unseen ruts. The rickshaw swayed, the boy's footfalls pattered. The Ngong Hills loomed black and lumpy against the midnight blue.

'The Lion Boy,' breathed Hugo. 'No wonder they call you that.'

'You don't understand.' Leo found it easier, in the rattling, scented dark, to speak of his birthing in a tree and the parents he had never known. 'It must be nice,' he added, 'to know who you are and where you're bound.'

'I would forfeit my heritage,' Hugo told him, 'for a quarter of your courage. My eldest brother will inherit, the middle one is Captain of Hussars, and I must face the fact that I'm a coward. You saw it, tonight. I let that drunken oaf humiliate me! What's the secret, Leo? How can one so young be so unafraid?'

Behind the bantering tone, Leo sensed a desperate urgency. He searched his memory and gave a simple, honest answer. 'I think you must find something you are prepared to die for.'

'And you already have?'

'Oh yes,' breathed Leo, consciously changing the tense. 'I did.'

Hugo's curiosity was almost tangible. 'Did it happen while the Masai held you?' But by now the rickshaw boy was slowing. The moon and painful images were rising and the lights of Berkeley's Billet gleamed ahead. In the flurry of payment and disembarkation,

Leo deflected the inquisition, pleaded exhaustion and escaped to bed.

But there, in an unfamiliar room, the pictures formed unbidden, drawing backwards into the bitter, windswept past.

And two years with the Masai.

It was hours before the pictures let him sleep.

12

'A FINE START!' H.E. SNAPPED, as Hugo and Leo sat sheepishly on hard chairs before his polished walnut desk. 'Brawling over harlots, vandalising property, assaulting members of the public. You are dragging this office through the mire! Don't sneer, Berkeley, I know what you're thinking: the kettle and the pot. Wrong. *I* don't whore in public.'

'It was my fault . . .' Leo began, and H.E. rounded on him.

'Hold your tongue, boy, and learn the first law of officialdom – be discreet about your indiscretions!' He eyed Berkeley slyly, a faint grin lurking under ginger whiskers. 'Care to represent me at a wedding?'

'Rather!' Hugo breathed, scarcely believing his luck.

'My, such zeal! It's not what you expect. All-African affair at Kerinyagga Mission. Interesting, what?'

'Fascinating,' Hugo muttered faintly, imagining snakes and saddle-sores and sleeping in the loathsome great outdoors. 'On second thoughts, I'm not awfully enamoured.'

'Prefer a one-way trip to Pater, would you, with a note from me explaining why you failed?'

The desk gleamed. Sunrays splintered on the water jug, highlighting broken veins on H.E.'s nose. He looked utterly implacable.

'Well,' Hugo mumbled, 'if you put it that way . . .'

'It must be Kibe's wedding,' Leo interjected. 'He's like a brother to me. I'll go, with pleasure.'

'Damn it, boy, you've only just arrived!'

Leo sat straighter, handsome, bronzed, refusing to kow-tow. 'I would be a fitting envoy at the wedding. Hugo is more useful here. You are being spiteful; that's inefficient management.'

'What the hell do you know of management? White men earn respect by taking up a burden they would rather others bear! Or will you, too, take a failure letter home?'

There was a cold sheen to Leo's eyes, a glimpse of that inner force Hugo hoped he'd never have to face. Then his wide shoulders relaxed, his blond head nodded briefly, once. 'I have vowed to serve you – sir.'

'Start now,' the Governor ordered. 'Get your nose into the files, discover how I manage, before you dare to speak of it again.'

'After the wedding,' H.E. continued, as the door closed on Leo, 'you'll take a little march on Kinangop. As I said last night, the Masai killed a settler up there. Caught him rustling cattle, slung a great big spear clean through him. Justified, perhaps, but bad for morale.' Hugo shuddered. H.E. grinned. 'They'll have to go. Can't have 'em using whites for pincushions. Their chieftain's called Leshinga. Sound him out – find out what it'll take to shift 'em.' H.E. paused, his bushy red eyebrows aloft.

Hugo asked the obvious question. 'Any connection, between the Mission and the Masai?'

'Course there is. That's why Reid can't go. Leshinga's laddies captured him, took him to their noble black bosoms for nigh on two years. Find out why they think so highly of him. Tap Father Andrew for young Reid's strengths and flaws. We need to know how best he can be used.' The Governor's grin widened, sly and snaggle-toothed. 'See the country, toughen up a bit. Call it duty, shall we? You do know what it means?' He sat straighter, shrugging off bonhomie like a coat no longer needed. 'On your way, Berkeley. If you get it wrong, don't bother to come back.'

On the first night out, they camped a few miles north of Thika River. Hugo woke next morning to dim light through canvas, crisp chill air and the crackle and whiff of bacon frying over an open fire. Presently, the cook brought tea and breakfast with a broad, snowy grin. '*Jambo, bwana. Habari yako leo?*'

'*Mzuri, asante.* Thank you, I am well.' A brief exchange of life's courtesies in a language which was beginning to make sense and roll easily off Hugo's tongue. He pulled on a heavy, olive-drab sweater, warmed his hands on the tea mug, opened the tent flaps and stepped outside.

99

The camp was coming to life. An axe rang clean on timber, throwing up a white arc of chippings. Horses tramped and snorted, gunmetal gleamed, orders were shouted and obeyed. Then, as Hugo strolled, the morning greyness lifted, and sunshine blazed on Kerinyagga.

He stood in splendour, under the great, green, ice-capped mountain, with birdsong in his ears, fern-sweet breezes in his face, the joy of living vibrant in his blood – and a stunning revelation in his mind.

My oath, a man could grow to like this land!

The sanctum throbbed with mothball-scented brilliance. A snowy surplice covered the purple cassock, the silken pallium glinted red and gold. This was Father Andrew's long-neglected finery, which clothed but could not counter deep unease. Why hasn't Njau tried to stop us?

This wedding offers him a public challenge, strikes deeply at the heart of tribal lore. So why does Njau turn his back, squatting on his high green knoll and gazing at the sky? His stillness is more menacing than action.

The bells stopped pealing, the floor ceased to quiver underfoot. Father Andrew paced the sunlit passage. From outside rose the sounds of clans amassed – laughter, gossip, greetings called and answered. Two villages gather today, he realised. Does the Healer simply crave a larger audience? I wish Leo were here to ward off evil. O Lord, send blessings on this service, that those who watch shall learn to praise Thy name.

He paused, his plea unheard, his faith uncertain; then he squared his shoulders, crossed the vestry and strode into the church.

Every pew was taken. Standing villagers lined the aisle, darkened the walls, dimmed the open doorway. Dust shimmered upwards, tiger-striped by sunshafts through thin windows – shafts which dappled on row on watchful row of almond eyes and taut brown faces, on vivid, twinkling beads and cowhide kirtles. Berkeley, the Governor's man, sat erect and elegant in crisply pressed khaki. Kibe waited, patient as ever, dazzlingly robed. The air seemed charged with strange, conflicting currents – there was too much curiosity, and precious little reverence. Father Andrew shivered, at prey to chill misgiving, incapable of grace.

Children were cheering, maidens' voices rose in ululation. Watchers in the doorway parted, letting Esther pass.

The long white gown constrained her stride and emphasised her plumpness. Behind the lacy veil, perspiration beaded lines of tension down her homely face.

Then Esther saw Kibe, and smiled.

It was a smile that spoke devotion beyond the power of words; that lent her lambent beauty and brought Kibe proud and eager to her side. They stood before the altar, arrayed in mutual joy and blazing whiteness. Radiance flowed between them, filling the nave, touching high, arched rafters, shining from the faces of the spell-bound congregation. Holy light, Father Andrew realised. Only the pure in heart can shed such brightness, however black the flesh wherein they dwell.

'Dearly beloved,' he began, 'we are gathered together in the sight of God and this congregation . . .'

The sense of oneness deepened. He was binding two people together, fashioning an historic day, giving well-worn phrases Kikuyu force and freshness. 'If anyone here present knows just cause and impediment why these two shall not be joined in holy matrimony, ye are now to declare it.' He glanced up, allowing the obligatory pause; then turned the page and opened his mouth to continue. Pied movement caught his eye. Coldness settled on his soul. He heard a faint, familiar metal jangle, a savage sibilance of accusation.

'She is unclean!'

'Who speaks?' cried Father Andrew, into the rising babble, past Kibe's puzzled frown and Esther's plainness suddenly reborn. 'Who speaks?' he called again, fearing the answer, dreading yet another confrontation. 'On what grounds can this union be denied?'

The voice climbed, high and fluting, above disordered dust. 'No woman may take a husband without first being properly cleansed. It is the law! This woman is uncircumcised, *unclean*!'

Assenting *eehs* rumbled. Someone prowled the dimness in mid-aisle, someone clad in black and white, wearing iron anklets, bearing eerie likeness to Njau. Sunlight split the shadows, shifted, settled, fused – and struck gold-tinted fury deep in Mwangi's narrowed eyes.

One day, Father Andrew vowed, I shall weep for this child: Leo's closest kin suborned, inveigled into witchcraft. Now, there is no time. He was conscious of growing division, Berkeley's foolish, fishlike gape, Kibe's reassuring arm on Esther's shoulder. Her wondrous smile was dying.

'Speak not of female circumcision here!' he thundered. 'It is itself unclean! Begone, boy, or risk the Lord's dark wrath!'

Mwangi sneered, spat contempt upon the red stone floor. '*That* for your toothless God whose anger injures neither man nor beast. Listen, priest. Hear the rage which falls on those who dare defy *real* gods!'

Evil shimmered round him, more profound than even Njau's aura. Crouching, his arm and finger aimed at Esther, he looked like some malevolent, coiled, black snake. 'Until the knife shall bless you, be barren as the moon. May Kibe's seed devour you, strip away the richness from your womb. *Unless* the knife shall bless you, never bear a son to any man!'

The congregation huddled, wide-eyed and subdued. Bride and groom were gazing at each other, the space between them broadened and laden with despair. No tribal marriage could survive this cruellest of all *thahus* – the curse of childnessness.

But Esther would *not* be childless.

Father Andrew knew this, as surely as he knew the way to save her and understood which tribal tale would reaffirm her faith. 'Though there be no sons, you *shall* be fertile. Remember Mumbi, mother of the tribe, whose every daughter founded a great clan? You, too, shall bear such healthy girls. They shall spread His teachings through the land!' The Word within him burned like living fire. God was upon him as never before, filling his voice with fiery exaltation. 'You will be the *modern* Mumbi-Christian mother to the whole Kikuyu nation!' He touched Kibe's shoulder gently and whispered a single word. 'Sing.'

And Kibe sang. He smiled, took Esther's hand, and made an inspired choice.

Love divine, all loves excelling . . .

Standing so close, Father Andrew saw the brief physical thrill which tautened Esther's body and watched wonder bloom again upon her face. Then she sang too, her marvellously rich contralto in poignant counterpoint to Kibe's tenor.

They stood together at the sunlit altar, their white robes intermingled, their broad brown faces luminous with joy. Their voices swelled and soared, bearing the great hymn up through golden light and dusty shade, aweing the congregation, sending chills of ecstasy down Father Andrew's spine. Presently, converts took up the refrain, smiling, clapping softly to the rhythm. Life and love and beauty filled the church, pouring out upon the greenery beyond.

Ignored and outmanoeuvred in the aisleway, Mwangi seemed visibly to shrink. Hate still soured his eyes and bowed his slightness; but menace had deserted him, overcome by cheerfulness and song. Suddenly, he was just a spiteful little black boy in a piebald kirtle quite a lot too large.

The last notes faded. The couple waited hand in hand. Esther's goodness was reaching out once more, making more than half the watchers smile. It *will* happen, Father Andrew realised, in heartfelt gratitude and relief. In years to come, we shall look back and say – this was the beginning, our first and greatest triumph over wizardry.

He opened the book, smiling forgiveness on the outrageous hate. 'Who giveth this woman?'

The response rang bold and clear. The service gathered dignity and power. When Mwangi turned and slunk away, his vengeful parting glower merely made the victory sweeter.

'Isn't it a trifle hard,' enquired Hugo, 'to lose your only son a second time?' And smiled, to mollify the sting.

Divested of drama and ceremonial splendour, Father Andrew seemed a lot less saintly. Slightly stooped and greying, robed in dingy green, he looked careworn, ascetic – and distinctly unamused. 'I lost him to hunting before the Masai came.'

'All alone, in darkest A? Was he not of somewhat tender years?'

'Duma was with him.'

'Ah, Duma. Doubtless that explains everything.'

Outside the sanctum there was birdsong and brightness. The priest ignored both, withdrawing to the shadows near his desk, toying with an exquisite grey quill. His reticence was painful to behold. 'It hasn't been easy, raising an orphan in this place. Duma has helped; he became his tribal father.'

'A reliable chap, I assume?'

'Totally.'

Father Andrew had a way of halting conversation in its tracks. The silence lengthened. Hugo felt impelled to explanations of his own. 'It's H.E., d'you see. He asked me to find out about Leo and the Masai.'

Father Andrew caught the implication and reacted sharply. 'He

103

was deprived of love and freedom for two years. He won't discuss it with me, let alone a stranger.'

Time for conciliation, Hugo thought, before the tropic air between us freezes solid. 'I enjoyed the performance this morning, Father,' he said. 'A telling addition to the service.'

'Performance?'

'The morality play, right against wrong, black against white. The little boy in magpie clothes made a most convincing witch. Did he leave on a broomstick?'

'You choose to joke, sir, about an issue which is absolutely crucial!' Suddenly the priest was formidable again, risen to his full height, his grey eyes blazing.

Not, Hugo conceded inwardly, the smoothest start to a career in diplomacy. 'Forgive me,' he murmured, 'I am unfamiliar with the dialect. What issue?'

'Circumcision. The Church condemns it; tribal law forbids a girl to wed without it.'

'You mean they circumcise their *women*?'

Father Andrew's lean face writhed in disgust. 'The custom has a certain crude logic. It reduces sexual feeling, making women less inclined to infidelity. The clitoris and upper labial lips are excised in one swift stroke.'

Hugo's stomach lurched. He felt the blood draining from his face.

'Quite, Mr Berkeley,' Father Andrew said. 'It's sheer barbarity, mutilation for its own sake. That is why today's events are so important – hard-won steps from darkness towards our Saviour's grace!'

'Be assured, Father, H.E. shall hear of it.' Hugo paused, putting entreaty into his voice. 'Can't you tell me a little about Leo after he escaped from the Masai?' Father Andrew's grey eyes softened. Hugo sensed his resistance falter, sensed him reaching back through time and space for painful memories . . .

Sounds of celebration drifted in; ululation, soft, insistent drumming. The air smelled of pasture and festive cooking, as it had when Leo returned. Father Andrew savoured remembrances, passed them on to this small, slim, elegant official who so clearly longed to be Leo's friend.

To Father Andrew, Leo's escape from Masai bondage was a miracle long prayed for and fervently enjoyed. To the clan, it was joyous, irrefutable proof of Leo's mystic powers.

There was a week of daylight rejoicing, of drums and firelight dancing deep into the night; a week of getting used to a larger presence in the Mission. Once, in the still small hours, Father Andrew had tiptoed back through time along the moonlit passage; slipped into Leo's room, knelt and kissed the scarred forehead; and stayed awhile, glorying in the older, bolder, still-golden aura that hovered around his sleeping son.

It was a month before the trouble started, before the hour after morning prayers became known as 'problem time'.

Thuo complained first. 'When he's near, the age-group just won't listen. They know he can still outrun me, could throw me with one hand behind his back. Let him lead us, Father – or keep him from our sight!'

Given this choice, Leo hid the hurt as best he could – a flicker of amber-eyed sorrow, the careful walk of one who bleeds inside – and ventured across the river where youngsters of another ilk and colour played.

Five days later, Kobus Coetze called.

His glare was narrow, level, icy-green. 'Keep your son at home, menheer. It's better for us – and him.'

Challenged, Coetze counted sins and sources on calloused fingers. 'The van Zyls are outraged – they saw him nearly naked on the Sabbath. Ouma Hendricks worries for her daughter's chastity. Boettie Claasen's back was nearly broken in a friendly wrestling bout. He is everything we Boers had hoped to leave behind – half English, half savage, wholly heathen. *Keep him away from us!*'

Coetze's eyes had taken on a pale, fanatic glaze, inclining Father Andrew to tartness and the better part of valour. 'I'm sure he would rather stay home than cause you such *distress*.'

Father Andrew's respite lasted a week, until one morning after meditation, when Maina waylaid him in a sunlit corridor.

'His bow is now more deadly than even that of Duma. He uses the white man's rifle as if it were part of him. And he makes me afraid!' He stood in the yellow light, his broad pink palms outspread. 'My warriors are only men. They will die, trying to be like him. Father, what shall I do?'

'All *right*!' Leo had snapped, that evening. 'I am trying very hard to please you, Father. What else do you want of me?'

'Lessons,' Father Andrew had suggested. 'Study the theory of music. When Kibe returns from his "honeymoon", he can help with the practice. Meanwhile, delve among the scriptures, find yourself a pathway back to God.'

Not, he had privately to acknowledge, the most tempting of prospects to place before a vigorous sixteen-year-old. Meanwhile, the village headman was demanding audience.

Gitau's presence seemed to fill the sanctum – portly, beaded, smelling of old age and mealie beer. He began as custom demanded, with protracted pleasantries. The rains were overdue; he hoped they would soon start. Father Andrew's Ryeland sheep had bred up well; the Boers were using something called 'terracing' to grow maize higher up the ridges. Red Strangers, Gitau conceded, might bring benefits as well as problems.

Then his manner grew knowing and confidential. 'Let Leo be circumcised and take his rightful place among the warriors. Let him wed a good Kikuyu girl, and keep his powers safe within the clan. Thus shall my people know your God, and lift their hearts towards Him: though He takes us from our customs, He gives us back our Lion Boy.'

A Kikuyu girl would make Leo an excellent wife, Father Andrew thought. She would tend his crops, give unquestioning obedience, bear him many sturdy children. She would stand, faithful, at his side, wearing soft-cured hide and cheap glass beads, smelling of hut and hearth, smiling in that sweet, simple, slightly vacuous Kikuyu maidenly way.

The vision quickly faded, freezing, chilled by an inner truth that made him squirm in self-disgust.

This is not what I want for my son.

He didn't have to say it. Gitau was already turning away, hunched and domed and wrinkled, like a disappointed tortoise. 'You want to have our souls, yet cannot bear the colour of our bodies.'

'We had a fearful row that night,' Father Andrew confessed. 'Gitau had shamed me. Leo rejected me and turned away from God. It was mostly my fault, and I had to make amends. Alone, by candlelight, I wrote to the bishop and asked him to give Leo a purpose. Does Leo have a purpose, Mr Berkeley? Will he make his way in Government?' There was anguish in the bony face, aching, unabashed paternal love.

'We are much impressed by him,' Hugo soothed. 'H.E. already has him firmly in hand.'

'Take my prayers to him,' Father Andrew implored. 'Help him be a better man than I!'

Hugo carried a precious gift from Kerinyagga Mission: the knowledge that at least one man had faith in him.

It rained in Masailand.

It was not the usual flash and rumble African deluge, more a steady silvered seepage, driven slantwise by the ceaseless wind. Whichever way he rode, the slant seemed always aimed at Hugo's eyes.

There was no horizon, and precious little colour to the grass. They crossed the soughing, desolate plain below Kinangop, moving ever upward through shifting veils of cloud. One day, the manyatta simply loomed into their path − so many glistening, mushroom-shaped dwellings, cow-dung coloured, leaking pale blue smoke.

The greetings were terse and perfunctory. Hugo deployed the troops in plain view, their rifles well to the fore, and ducked into the headman's hut.

Charcoal fumes stung his eyes. The air reeked of sheepfat, honey-beer and human perspiration. Chief Leshinga lounged beside the fire, prickly, bloodshot, pot-bellied, like an overweight, overhung porcupine. The interpreter fawned around him, seedy and dull-skinned in elderly, ill-matched European clothes. Simel the warrior-prince stood guard across the entrance. His pied ostrich plumes drooped wetly; a single fat bright raindrop hung quivering from his hawklike beak. The moran lounged in rank and file beyond him, their spears angled up across their shoulders. They looked morose, bedraggled, ineffectual, like thin black chimney sweeps in London fog.

'*Move?*' Leshinga echoed, through the sly interpreter. 'Why should we move from these, our sacred grounds?' His red-rimmed eyes were suddenly baleful and belligerent. Beware, they seemed to warn. We have already despatched one feeble white man with impunity; why not another?

Simel shifted, pursing his lips, running a lean dark finger across the glitter of his spear-edge. Outside, his warriors looked all at once eager and alert.

Hugo felt an old familiar tremor in his stomach, sensing incipient panic among the soldiers behind. The interpreter was sidling, grey-faced, to the door. *What will it take to shift them?* H.E. had demanded.

Better to survive and give the answer: a stronger leader and more resolute troops. 'I will tell the Governor,' Hugo muttered, with much relief and little dignity. And left the hut, and led the sodden retreat towards Nairobi.

Later, he crouched in damp, chill blankets within the lamplit tents beside the dripping forest. His body ached, his spirit sagged, his mind fled back across the years to England: to a sleepy Wealdland village and the confrontation which began his long, slow slide from grace.

An April morning, a bruised sky, rooks abicker in the elms and a wind like edged flint. Hugo was ten years old, free as air, with silver jingling in his knickerbocker pocket.

An urchin sidled from a narrow doorway, dark of brow and tooth, with a grubby face and jersey. 'Give us a penny, else I'll break yer crown!'

'Indeed?' drawled Hugo, very lordly, who had played these games with his older brothers. 'You and whose army?' He sauntered forward, into a knobby fist which cracked against his cheekbone and froze him to the spot. For the first time in his life, he saw viciousness in another human face: the will to hit and hurt and humiliate. Shock and sheer malevolence paralysed him.

The urchin moved in, taunting, stabbing Hugo's brown velveteen jacket with a hard, hurtful finger. 'Put yer mits up, nancy boy. Fight, why don't yer!' Hugo stumbled back, his hands rigid at his sides, the hot tears spurting. Until, with a mouldering wall against his back and terror in his heart, he flung the coins on to glinting cobbles, turned and fled, sobbing, for home.

Pater hauled him up the stairs and whaled him with a carpet slipper. 'Afraid? I'll make you more afraid of me! Go back and face the little lout!' But though his buttocks burned like fire, nothing could make him brave those fists again. Mother saved him. She was small and fine, like Hugo, weeping even harder than he. 'He's only a baby, Edward. For goodness' sake, show mercy!'

Pater threw the slipper down and stamped away. 'Damn it, Sarah, you've bred me a poltroon!'

So began the blight on Hugo's childhood, which Pater soon transferred to his two older brothers. Like Pater, they were burly and rawboned, black-haired and heavy-handed, afraid of neither man nor beast. They made him play their manly rough-house games and swore that they would make him tough. But the more they joshed and jostled, the more timid he became.

And the more Pater sneered.

In school, he was thought 'promising' at rugger, being fleet-footed, quick-witted and well-balanced. But whenever some skinny, wasp-jerseyed boy came charging through, he would flinch from gritted teeth and thrusting, mud-stained knees, waver in the tackle and be swept aside. 'He has little stomach for physical contact,' the disappointed gamesmaster wrote.

Pater snarled, and burned the school report.

At fifteen, Hugo discovered horses, and took to the saddle as if he had been born there. He rode fearlessly and fast, taking the steepest, sternest fences without a tremor, and rode point-to-point amongst grown men – and won. Mother cheered, and kissed him. 'Must have been a damned brave horse,' said Pater.

When the two elder Berkeleys won renown at bloodsports and joined decent regiments, Hugo became Mother's favourite. She taught him courtliness and gallantry, and the intricacies of the waltz. Meanwhile, he captained the school debating team, and played Henry the Fifth in the end-of-term production. 'A bold and convincing portrayal,' the local *Gazette* reported. 'Precocious prowess in the Thespian art.' 'Of course it was,' growled Pater. 'He was *acting* the hero!'

It is just tolerable, Hugo thought, to be despised for one's faults. It is heartbreaking to be derided for one's virtues.

Because, in spite of everything, he honoured and admired his father, and longed to be valued in return. Pater was wealthy, popular and respected. He had fought the Mahdi's hordes in the Sudan, the Boers at Ladysmith and Mafeking. He had medals to prove his courage: and withering contempt for his youngest son.

Hugo made one final effort to prove himself in Pater's eyes. In desperation and his final term at school, he turned to boxing. Secret roadwork down misty, rustic lanes, sweaty sessions with the unforgiving, massive leather punch bag, trunk-curls in the dusty golden sunslants through the wall-bars. His determination impressed the heroes of the upper sixth. Pooling their skills and muscle, they showed him how to shuffle, weave and hook. Speed, footwork and a lurking reservoir of pure fright carried him unscathed through the house contests and won him selection at welterweight for the grudge match against a nearby agricultural college. Pater received the news with open disbelief, consenting to attend only after seeing Hugo's name in the programme.

He knew a moment of triumph, then, in the packed gymnasium that smelled of resin and expectation; he danced lightly on squeaky canvas, kneaded the shiny brown gloves together and saw Pater's proud smile gleam within the ringside gloom.

Then the bell rang.

He came out in the classic upright stance, his mouth dry, adrenalin surging through his blood; and, for the first time, took stock of his opponent.

He might have been that very same urchin, grown to the full bloom of warring manhood: he had the same tight, menacing crouch, the same dark, destroying glower, the same intent to bruise and batter. All Hugo's hard-earned skills deserted him. He rushed forward, flailing wildly, and ran plumb into a straight left that split his lips and brought the moisture, scalding, to his eyes. He stumbled to the ropes, felt rough hemp bite into his back, cowered, covered up, let unresisted blows rain upon his arms and brow and shoulders. He hung on, clinching and clutching at wiry, pumping arms, tasting his own coppery blood, sobbing in misery and terror.

Halfway through the first round, the referee stopped the fight; disqualified Hugo for persistent holding. Slumped in his corner while the agricultural urchin preened and pranced, Hugo heard only the raucous catcalls of his schoolmates, saw only the empty ringside seat and Pater's rigid, outraged, retreating back. 'It was brave of you to try, dear,' Mother soothed, dabbing at his riven, swollen lips with pine-scented disinfectant. Pater said nothing at all. His single, sidelong glance of loathing was more wounding than a thousand blows.

A week later, he was called to Pater's study and given another dose of tight-lipped contempt – and his marching orders. 'Thankfully, I have connections in the colonies. The arrangements are made. I have ceded you a living allowance. Stay out of my sight until you are a man, until I need not squirm to think you are a Berkeley!'

Hugo sighed, in chilly shadow, under the dripping canvas. Three years and half a world away, and nothing much has changed. Leshinga and Simel had sensed the weakness in him, browbeaten him with polished, ochred muscle, naked steel and undisguised hostility. If only I didn't have to stand alone, he thought. If only there was someone brave and strong to buoy my spirits, some spark of steadfast courage at my side. Then perhaps, the worm might turn. Then I might gain honour and respect, some accolade to carry home to Pater.

13

AFTERNOON SUN AND RARE benevolence filled the Governor's office. Hugo had been given coffee and a quizzical sidelong glance. 'Taking the vows, Berkeley? Shamed into your duty by Chief Leshinga's brush-off?'

Hugo nodded, blushing; an uncomfortably accurate assessment.

'Time for the ABC then. Who runs this Protectorate?'

'You do, sir.'

'Wrong, Westminster does. But Westminster bows to Whitehall, and Treasury rules both. It's economics, first and last.' H.E. eyed Hugo over the bone china. 'Treasury says the railway must make a profit. Means more settlement, new land opened up. *Masai* land. *Ergo*, Masai must move. An external imperative, d'you see, over which we have no control.' He set his cup down musically and developed the thesis. 'Powerful chap, Lord Delamere – the settlers think he's God. Has a blind spot though, treats Masai like the chosen race. So here's your local imperative. Shift the Masai without upsetting D. Inside the month, if you please.'

'I say, that's a bit steep!'

'Agreement in four weeks or off to Pater. Call it a *personal* imperative, shall we?'

A shower spattered the window, driven by a sudden, savage gust. The Governor's grin glittered in the gloom. No wonder, Hugo thought. If the scheme succeeds, H.E. takes the credit. Failure will be laid at Berkeley's door. Observe the art of politics, my lad. Foresee the danger, delegate the risks, get your blow in first. And when the reckoning comes, make sure that you're the one keeping score.

But H.E.'s demonstration hadn't ended. 'Don't get too chummy with young Reid. Pick his brains, make sure he's told you all he knows about Leshinga. Then get rid of him.'

'Ah – why should I do that, sir?'

'Use your noddle, man! God and Government just don't mix. Can't have little church mice spying at our altar!'

'How shall I explain things to the bishop?'

H.E.'s narrow shoulders shifted, making his starched white shirt creak softly. He slid a buff file across dark polished wood. 'Reid's natural father. Found him in the archives. Real bad egg, it seems. Enough dirt there to see off twenty bishops.'

Divide and rule, Hugo thought grimly. What price friendship in the Governor's domain?

Later, in his dingy alcove, Hugo closed the file distastefully. Feeling cold and sick inside, he remembered Leo's wistful words. 'Nice to know who you are and where you're bound.' Not if your father turns out to be a 'real bad egg', and a would-be friend is too cowardly to tell you to your face.

Leo had spent a miserable week. Incessant rain had dampened his spirits and prevented him from exploring the town. Berkeley's Billet had proved lonely and isolated. He received no visitors, no invitations. H.E. ignored him. Fellow officials gave him apprehensive glances, as if he were some half-tamed house pet.

He had orders to study policy, and access to a lumber room. Today, as every other day, he perched on a hard stool beneath the single fanlight. Mouldering black cabin trunks cluttered the dusty boards. A suspiciously gold-eyed stuffed owl watched him from a cracked glass case.

It looked about as wise as the policy, which seemed to consist of thwarting missionaries and antagonising settlers.

So, when Hugo sidled in, Leo greeted him with genuine delight. 'How was the wedding? Did you meet Leshinga? Are my people up there in good heart?'

'They miss you. They pray for you; which is more than I can say for Leshinga!'

'Sit down, Hugo. Tell me all about it!'

Berkeley avoided his eye, shuffled his feet and pushed a folder on to the dilapidated desk. 'You'd better see this first. I'm going to the Billet for a bath and a good stiff drink.'

He left, abrupt and hangdog. Sunrays flickered through the dust he'd raised, tracing blue inscriptions on the matt buff cover.

'Jethro E. Morgan, Lieutenant. R.N.'

The Royal Navy, Leo thought, in pride and wonder. My father was an officer and a gentleman! He sat quite still, seeing the sun strike tawny owl feathers, feeling the past and present fuse within. Now, at last, I shall know who I am.

Morgan was an exemplary sailor, [he read] commissioned from the ranks by dint of hard work, good character and expertise in gunnery.

Recently, however, he voiced concern about certain long established traditions: to whit, the punishment of malefactory ratings.

While his ship neared Mombasa, a well-known malingerer was caught in flagrant breech of regulations. As duty officer, Morgan was obliged to supervise the flogging. He refused, saying the punishment was needlessly brutal. He was confined to his quarters, in order to reflect upon his dereliction and come to his senses.

When the ship berthed at Mombasa, Morgan overpowered his guard, took a muzzle-loader from the armoury and escaped.

The purpose of this document is threefold.

1. To appraise Your Excellency of Morgan's presence somewhere in the hinterland.

2. To request your co-operation in bringing him to book.

3. To advise caution in the pursuit. Morgan is an expert marksman; has already shown himself capable of assault, theft and desertion. From these infractions, it is but a short step to the greatest crime of all. I trust you can forestall this step without fatal consequences.

10 November 1891

Leo sat rigid beneath the yellowed fanlight, watching scarlet gather in the palm of his left hand. It welled from four deep crescents carved by his own fingernails. Small tears blurred his vision; he tried to still his grief, and recoiled from the bloodsmears dark and sticky on the desk.

Bad blood . . .

Leo Morgan, son of a deserter.

The knowledge drove him on to Nairobi streets at eventide. Dust and sunset washed the sky deep orange. Hawkers and horsemen filled the air with trade cries and slow hoofbeats. He drifted among the crowds and coolies, meeting no one's eye.

Leo Morgan, offspring of a thief.

Would *they* care? he wondered, watching beaded natives crouch near a blue-flamed brazier, smelling corn fresh-roasted in the flames. Twilight came and went within a twinkling. Night descended; moonless, spicy, warm. He was following some fundamental instinct, not yet knowing where it led.

Leo Morgan, born with violence burning in his veins.

Was this the secret Father Andrew guarded, down the years? It would explain a lot – the mystery of Laura's diary, the doomed attempt to keep a boy from warfare, the constant exhortations to redemption, love and peace. And priestly footwear stinging youthful buttocks. Perhaps he'd tried to beat the badness out.

Leo's mind was drifting back to Kerinyagga and the conflicts which had so swiftly soured his escape from Masailand. They had erupted the day Chief Gitau complained to Father Andrew. . . .

Leo had left the Mission with thunder and Kibe's tonic solfa resounding, a glimpse of Gitau sidling into the sanctum, and a weary question risen in his mind: what have I done *this* time?

Mwangi appeared outside the garden gate, his face as dark and sullen as the sky. 'My mother was unwell, while you were gone. She couldn't dig. I am going now to hoe her mealie field, before the rains come.' His tone forbade any further discourse; his posture begged for company and guidance. Leo chose a wistful air, conciliatory words. 'Though you could easily do the job alone, I would like to help – to show honour and respect for Wanjui.'

'Come then.' Mwangi glanced up, unable to hide his satisfaction, masking it within a graceless growl. 'We have no time for idle talk.'

There came a time that afternoon, when Wanjui's maize patch seemed to be the only place on earth. A single, steadfast sunshaft kept it green and gold, while purple storms and great grey rain-shrouds swallowed up the landscape all around.

Mwangi edged nearer. Presently, speaking as if deeply ashamed from the downturned corner of his mouth, he asked, 'Are you still a Christian?'

Leo paused, wiping his brow with his forearm. 'I don't know.'

The answer clearly troubled Mwangi. 'When the Masai took you,' he whispered, 'Duma went away for many moons, scouting their encampments. Everybody prayed; some to Ngai, some in church. I mocked the Christians, Leo, told them they should trust in Njau's power. Now you have returned, and I feel that power shrivelling inside me.'

Mwangi lifted his hoe and swung it in a vicious, glittering arc. Avoiding Leo's eye, he couldn't keep the fear out of his voice. 'Did I choose the wrong god? Do *you* think I did wrong?'

Here was the real Mwangi at last, crouching in this windswept field, blinking into this unlikely sunshine: a small, confused boy craving reassurance from an older brother he had so long, so secretly admired.

'You were wrong, Mwangi,' he murmured. 'Not for setting Ngai over God, but because you tried to force the choice on others. A man may worship many gods, or none. First, before and above all, he must be true to himself.'

'*Leo,*' Mwangi breathed, his small face taut with longing. 'How pure and brave you look, saying it. Did Father Andrew teach you this belief?'

The question brought Leo back to earth. The answer made him shake his head in wonder. 'The man who taught me this will teach you too. You only have to watch and listen. He is always near when needed – he is our father, Duma!'

He actually felt Mwangi's questing spirit clench and curl in upon itself, saw agony contort the small brown face. Then Mwangi was upright, hurling the hoe aside, marching blindly over broken soil.

'*What?*' cried Leo, in anguish. 'What is it?'

Mwangi checked and turned. Before him lay love and light and laughter, a brotherhood of choice as long as he might claim it. Behind was only windtossed space and rainswept pasture. His head went back, his spindly body arced and stiffened. Teartracks glistened on his cheeks. '*My* father, not yours! And he is *never* here when needed!' Then Mwangi whirled around and chose the darkness; stumbled, lone and lost, into the storm.

The sunshaft was fading, the first fat drops of rain began to fall. So ends enchantment, Leo mourned, here lies the Healer's broken charm.

We shall never be as close again.

That night, the bedside lantern guttered low and blue, as did Leo's spirit. His room, like the bed on which he lay, seemed narrow and diminished. I don't belong here any more, he thought, but this time there is nowhere else to go. Outside, the night is wet and frigid, offering neither comfort nor escape.

The row had begun at supper, when Father Andrew came down from the sanctum. He looked dreadful, his skin stretched grey and parchment-thin across his cheekbones, his lips leeched bone-white, his eyes aflame – as if he'd been dealt some mortal blow.

'It's time you cut your hair, put aside those ugly weapons and put proper clothes on. You must raise yourself above these ill-starred natives! You were born the noblest of God's creatures, a white, Christian gentleman. It's time for you to act and dress like one!'

Leo sneered, pushed his plate aside. 'How shall I, with no one here I can emulate?'

'Do you dare to offer insolence? Go to your room, at once: or else, even though you're now full grown, I shall give you the thrashing you seem hell-bent to earn!'

Only if I let you, Leo thought, seeing the suddenly stooped and skinny frame, knowing that the balance of strength had long since shifted. But in the end, he couldn't raise a hand against this strange, severe, tormented 'father'.

In the end, he had come to bed.

For nearly two years, he thought, I have lived among the Masai, whom many white men seem to revere. I found them haughty and callous, and could not escape quickly enough.

Now, back in the valley, among people and places I love, I am restless and uneasy.

Where do I belong?

The Masai called me Ojuju. To the villagers, I am still the Lion Boy. Kibe would make me a priestly musician, Father Andrew wants me to be a gentleman.

Who am I?

His memory stirred, focusing on a dusty passage and a locked door, and something Kibe had said many years ago. 'That is forbidden territory, little brother. That is where Laura Howard's possessions lie.'

Perhaps it is forbidden because the answers are there, he thought. It is worth exploring, anyway.

She was waiting, he knew it as soon as he closed the door behind him. No one he could see, no one he could ever know. Though his scalp prickled and his nape-hair rose, he felt no fear. Her presence was passive, gentle, benign. But she was there.

He opened her trunk, and her perfume flooded the dim, crowded air. Something clear and astringent and citrusy, underlain with sadness and decay. He fingered her silks, wondering at the texture and the colours. So many shades of green, he thought. They would look good with red hair.

Did you have red hair?

He burrowed among her clothing and lifted her diary into the ruddy light. But before he could even begin to read, the door was flung open. Father Andrew towered in the passage, his voice heavy with disgust. 'Already, you have upset this whole valley. Now you violate the sanctum, steal my keys and trespass here.' He waved Leo's denial away. 'You must leave this place, go where God and white men govern, and raise young men to honour!' He closed Laura's trunk. Anger swirled around him like a living force. 'Have you no decency? Must you rummage in her past?'

'It is my past too.' Leo spoke with cold intensity. 'You have no right to deny me. You are not my father!'

Father Andrew's body seemed to shrink and hunch and withdraw upon itself. He will look like this, Leo thought, when he is old: gaunt and grey, as if the flesh of his face has grown too tight for the bones it contains. I am not sorry, for him or myself. It is a truth. It had to be told. . . .

Leo prowled Nairobi dimness, feeling more alone than ever before: ashamed of his heritage, alienated from those who claimed to love him. He was only half aware of stealthy movement behind; until the sounds drew too close to ignore, until shadows loomed up all around him – until it was too late.

Light straggled weakly outwards from the station bar, touching tight black curls and sallow faces, showing malice flaring in cold black eyes, glinting slyly on a golden gypsy ear-ring. A chain hummed darkly, cleaving the air an inch from Leo's face. Three knife blades flickered, curved and steely. The ring of shadows narrowed, reeking of cheap gin and open drains. 'Give us your purse, then. Give us something valuable.'

A spark rekindled. Deep within, the Lion Boy awoke and flexed his claws. Leo straightened, slipped out of his jacket, furled it round his arm and turned at bay.

Surprise lent him fleeting advantage. His first left-handed swing struck blubbery gut-flesh. One of the footpads grunted, buckled, hissed and fell. The others closed in, cursing.

Leo held them off, whirling and flailing, ducking under kicked-up dust and glittering knife arcs, unable to set himself and launch a counter-strike. They forced him deeper into the gloom, where thrusts came at him out of almost total darkness. Bright steel slashed his jacket and scored his skin. The thrumming chain clipped his shoulder. Pain deadened his arm. He was breathing hard, blinking salt sweat away, scenting his own blood and their rank excitement.

The winded one, now recovered, came slinking in again. They were splitting, two by two, aiming to surround him; he had neither speed nor strength left to prevent them.

Half-forgotten battle instincts stirred, warning him of movement at his back. There were more of them, he realised grimly, feeling hot breath at his nape, flinching from the treachery behind him.

'Look to your front, me bucko,' a genial Irish voice advised. 'Yer Uncle Flynn will mount the rearguard action!'

Relief took Leo like a Healer's potion, restoring will and vigour. He lunged forward, seized the nearest knife arm and improvised a fierce cross-buttock throw. The robber's spinning outline flew up across the light, the trapped arm came straight, checked only briefly by the elbow's hinge. The joint collapsed, with a noise like splintered matchwood. The body tumbled, screaming, to the dust. Leo was suddenly alone in failing lampglow, hearing sounds of lesser pain and fleeing footfalls.

He turned and watched his rescuer at work.

Six feet four was Flynn, built like the giant Meru oak that shaded Laura's grave. He stood to his full height, silhouetted against yellow lampglow. Footpads dangled from each high-brandished fist.

Flynn was teaching them manners.

He brought his fists smartly together, making the curly black heads clash like cymbals. 'The station is Flynn's patch. Trespassers will be marmalised!' He opened his hands, let his captures fall and wagged a sausage-like finger before two pairs of vacant black eyes. 'The joke's over, me lads. Next toime I see yer ugly faces hereabouts, I'll be bound to do ye harm!'

He stepped across the shapeless, groaning huddle, faced the light and draped a bulky arm over Leo's shoulders. A puglike, gap-toothed grin split his blue jowls; his dark, button eyes twinkled. 'There now,

Mr Reid, I'd say that makes us even. Ye saved me a broth of trouble, I'm hearing, out at Lola's lately.' He massaged his jaw, making a sound like sandpaper. ''Tis a powerful wallop ye pack, for a little feller. Come. I'll stand you a toddy at yonder trough, and drink to eternal friendship.' And he ushered Leo away, without so much as a backward glance at the carnage.

A single rough-hewn plank formed the station bar, balanced on a pair of empty oildrums, sheltered by a smoke-stained wooden shack. Multicoloured bottles lined the shelves. A tarnished brass lamp cast unsteady brightness upon the clientele. Native waifs and strays, thought Leo, noting dull brown skin, threadbare blankets and lethargic, bloodshot stares. Amongst them, Flynn seemed larger than life – clad in smart railway blue serge and bright tin buttons, flushed with exertion, triumph and rude good health.

'Rum, Ali,' he told a thin black barman with a china eye. ''Tis toime to splice the mainbrace.' Leo cleared his throat, but his polite refusal was waved away. 'Grand stuff, Mr Reid. I came to know its powers with the eastbound fleet.'

'Indeed?' said Leo cautiously, mistrusting the coincidence. 'What was a railway expert doing in the Navy?'

'A nodding acquaintanceship,' said Flynn airily. 'Dozed off in a Cork alley, awoke halfway across the Irish Sea.'

'I thought they outlawed press gangs years ago.'

'Right ye are, me bucko.' Flynn cupped a vast palm around his tumbler and rocked the tarry liquid absently. 'In me cups, I must have been persuaded. T'would be the divil's task, to force the Flynn.'

Leo sipped rum, wincing at its pungent, sugary bite, and framed his next, crucial question delicately. 'I suppose you bought yourself out, at Mombasa?'

Flynn produced his gargoyle grin again. His whole face wrinkled, his eyes all but disappeared. 'Bless ye, boy, what with – shirt buttons? And didn't I do what any man of spunk would? Sure, I jumped ship.'

'You're a deserter,' Leo breathed, unable to hold the words back. He started as Flynn's great booming laugh rocked the shelves and set the bottles jingling.

'Will ye look at the boy, sitting there all solemn and big-eyed, as if meself had broken wind in church! You've been listening to po-faced admirals who'd have ye think the likes of me a coward.' His dark eyes narrowed, his humour turned belligerent. 'Would *you* be thinking Flynn a coward, Mr Reid?'

'How can I,' Leo asked, 'after what I saw outside?'

'There ye are then. Truth is, the Navy's run by sadists, bloodless English gentry half-pickled in port wine. No one who calls himself a man would stay in half a day.'

Somewhere outside, a train whistle sounded, two-toned and mournful. Flynn's puglike face twisted in dismay. 'Here's me talking like a sea lawyer, and a nightshift to oversee.' He drained his glass in a single swallow, smacked his lips and gave Leo's shoulder an affectionate, meaty thump. 'Away home with you now, Mr Reid, you'll not be troubled further. Ye have Flynn's protection on you, this and every night.' Then he was gone, swiftly and silently, into the dusty, dusky world he ruled.

Hugo was waiting on the verandah at Ngong, smelling of whisky, looking at once sheepish and determined. 'I know I should have told you about Morgan: I couldn't summon enough pluck. Listen, now, before you pass judgement on me or him: there's something you should know.' Suddenly, despite his unsteady gait, the elegant cream shirt and dandyish breeches, there was unusual authority about him: an air of command that made Leo pay attention.

'My pater bought the fastest passage for me, aboard a Lascar man o' war. I saw a naval flogging – something I've been trying to forget.' He stood straighter, his brown eyes narrow and inward-looking. 'There was a roll of planking underfoot, and tropic sunshine overhead; wave-swash and the clank of dull steel leg-irons; a whiff of salt and fear, and something much worse – the gloating smell of men who savour other people's pain.

'I saw the lash curl, black and snaky against pure blue sky, and I saw it nuzzle into naked flesh. The man's whole body quivered at the shock. I heard the whine of breath each stroke was driving from his lungs. Soon, his back lay split by crimson furrows: I remember the mangled sinews, exposed rib-bones glinting through the mush. The lash rose, spattering blood to the sky, and fell again savagely. When it was over, the man's chained legs wouldn't hold him. The cords stood out like wires in his neck. And he still made no sound.

'So they filled their oak buckets and hurled salt water on his gaping wounds.' Hugo paused, rigid as a guardsman, pallid as a corpse. 'Sometimes I wake in a cold sweat, with that man's howling in my ears. *No one* deserves such treatment, whatever he has done. Honour your father, Leo. He held fast to his beliefs, stood alone against barbarity. That's true courage: the legacy he has bequeathed to you.' He paused, gave a half-choked sob and said in an envious whisper, 'You don't know how lucky you are!' And he stumbled into the darkened cottage.

Leo lingered uneasily in starlight, breathing frangipani scent, hearing crickets whirr. Though Morgan's ghost had mustered two eloquent advocates, neither was a pillar of moral rectitude; and Hugo had himself confessed to cowardice. For the moment, Leo mused, I must continue to be Mr Reid. I have lived eighteen years in doubt about my parents. It will not hurt to doubt a little longer.

The moon rose, horned and silver, reviving ugly memories, reminding him of a more immediate matter.

The Masai must be moved.

14

HE WAS TALL AND BLACK and coltish, very recently circumcised, little more than a boy. He was called Segi, and he was the brand-new laibon – paramount leader of the Masai tribe. Standing in Ngong's dim and cobwebbed Mission Hall, flanked by portly 'uncles' who would shape his adult rule, he spoke to the assembled chiefs and elders. They listened, high-cheeked, scarred and haughty, with storklike stance, and their glittering spearblades still, giving Segi total silence and respect.

'Let the People and the government make peace. Let treaties be observed on either side. Let the northern Masai leave that high cold place, to dwell in strength and wisdom with the southern clans!'

Leo shivered in his shadowy corner, beneath a wide-brimmed hat and ragged, off-white robes. He was here, disguised, at Hugo's request, to monitor translations during the meeting. Already guttural language and a reek of sheepfat had made his hackles rise. The law endures: its power must be broken.

Berkeley rose, in trimly cut khaki, before a bright, broad chart. His pointer sketched extended southern borders, shown as a bold red block among the buff environs. 'For what you have to give up, we offer half as much again: not one but two permanent rivers.' His pointer traced an oval touched by thin blue threads. 'Here, between the Mara and the Uaso Nyiro, lies the richest, greenest grazing in the land.'

Wearing stained grey trousers, a tattered army greatcoat and his usual unctuous grin, the interpreter conveyed a harsher message. 'He claims this land is better. But see, the only watered place is where his long stick rests.'

Copper armlets glittered, and Leshinga took the floor. 'How often will the white man seek to move us? Must this warrior nation dance to his command? What of the treaty Segi's father won?' The interpreter gave the sense but not the tone, turned Leshinga's challenge into a request.

The treaty would be honoured, Hugo said. No one could force the northerners to move.

The interpreter's stained teeth glistened. Leo saw the swift, sly glance he sent Leshinga's way. 'If you do not move,' he murmured, 'Ojuju's guns will force you.' The lies were like slow poison, killing off the trust between two races, setting clan on clan.

Leshinga spoke again, his jowl bristling silver. 'Will you take our circumcision grounds? Will you also steal the Kinangop?'

This time, Hugo needed no translation. His pointer angled northwards over tight black contours. 'Your customs are acknowledged, your access guaranteed. This passage shall be yours for all time.'

'He shows the way to nowhere.' The interpreter's voice oozed sarcasm. 'When white men take the highlands, that path will cease to be.'

Dark intuitions clouded Leo's mind: he saw a troubled time, the tribe split, its laibon fresh and vulnerable, all because of a northern chief's ambition, an interpreter's deceit. The shape of treason gathered, shimmered, held. The crowd parted. Weak sunshine slid across a scarred black shoulder, framed a hawklike profile that towered half a head above the rest.

Simel's profile.

Simel the destroyer, whose fighting force could bring the whole benighted scheme to pass. One glimpse was enough to raise all Leo's ghosts: to bear him, raging, from this crowded hall back through the years to the barren Masai hut where he'd lain dying from his fearsome battle wound.

He remembered a dream of pain and sickness; a fire raging in his head, something hard and sticky sealing his eyes and clawing at his cheek. There came a time, then, when it would have been so easy to let go. The inner spark guttered, things outside lost all sense and shape. The pain was easing, fading.

Smoke revived him, stinging him awake. It was thinner and more bitter than Kikuyu smoke, and smelled of beef, not goat. He was in a hut, he could tell by the echoes and the quality of dimness through his gummed lids. Duma's lessons paid off: he could understand one of the voices. 'He is young. If he decides to live, the wound will heal. But Simel's blow was fearful. I am worried for this boy's sight. Let him rest, now.' Leo heard their footfalls pad away.

Simel, he thought. He must be the one who carried me. I would like to see him.

I would like to *see*.

He lifted his hand, brought it towards his eyes, let it drop away. I am afraid to feel, and know that I am blind. If I am blind, he vowed, I'll let the fever take me.

Her touch was gentle, like Wanjui's, but her fingers were slimmer and younger. Because the water had been warmed, she knew it would hurt, yet she kept the hurt small. Only a woman could do it this way: her touch was like moth's wings, brushing, soothing. He knew it was a woman because of the scent: delicate as forest flowers, yet bearing a hint of something rich and secret.

He lay, breathless and rigid, while the stickiness on his face softened and slid away. At last, he sensed that it was done, and sensed that she, too, was taut and fearful.

Leo opened his eyes.

Oh God, he prayed, let it be night, for I have never known such darkness! She moved, let in a shaft of moonlight, and showed him he could see: dimly at first, blurred by the moisture, then sharply and distinctly – black and grey and silver, and muted redness where his head had lain. He sensed her unseen smile within the shadows, and knew that *she* knew and was rejoicing with him. Neither said a word.

She moved again, and showed him her smile by moonlight; showed him a face to light a thousand dreams.

Her eyes were deep and slanted, under long, curved lashes. Her nose was slim and straight, her cheekbones wide and high. She had a regal face and the snowy smile of a coal-black eastern goddess, like a mask recovered from a Pharaoh's tomb. Except that this mask lived and breathed and spoke.

'Get well, Ojuju; for I, Linde, would like to know you better.'

Then the fever stole upon him, racking his limbs, dulling his new-found vision. If I live a hundred years and never see her again, hers will be the beauty that I take beyond the grave. Why does she call me Ojuju?

He woke once more, much later, to a bleak, grey hostile dawn. His face felt tight and bloated, his head ached vilely. He shivered, feeling the fever gather for one final, fierce assault.

He could see clearly now: the curved, spare gloom of the unfamiliar hut, a treeless, windswept plain beyond the doorway. I am a prisoner, he thought, held by a savage people in this savage place. I must lie and bear the pain, retreat from endless darkness, wait until the fever's passed. For Duma and Wanjui, for Father Andrew and Kibe; for evenings by the river and mornings with the bow; for all the days of life ahead, which I will not forsake.

And for a Masai girl called Linde.

The fever broke, one morning, and Leo came back from the edge. Back to a cheerless, fireless, low-ceilinged hut, to a cowhide pallet rank with his own sweat and sickness; back to a raging thirst and the Masai Healer's steady dispassionate gaze.

The Healer moved to the doorway, beckoning, making washing gestures. Yes, thought Leo, wrinkling his nose, I smell like a long-dead goat.

He dogged the Healer's footfalls through a gap in the blackthorn fence, following a path which curved downhill into a wooded ravine under branches draped in Spanish moss, through birdsong and a whiff of mouldered leaves; until, at last, sunshafts bounced and sparkled below, and Leo heard the stream trickling. He went to his knees in yellow silt beside a slow, dark pool. The surface was a gently shifting mirror. Then he shrank before the stranger kneeling there; shrank before his own deformed reflection. The eyes burned pink and pained from skull-like sockets. Cheekbones jutted under waxen flesh. A jagged red weal crawled from the left temple to the shaven crown. Small wonder Linde never returned, he thought, if she saw me in daylight.

Touching the scar, speaking Masai slowly and clearly, he asked, 'Which person must I thank for this?'

'How can this be?' the Healer muttered. 'Ojuju knows the People's tongue!'

Leo said nothing, raising his eyebrows, touching the weal again. 'It is I you must thank,' the Healer declared, 'though I have tended and cured many worse.'

'I meant the cause,' Leo murmured, 'not the cure.'

'Ho, then that is Simel, who is now the moran leader, who could have slain you, but brought you here instead. Soon he will sit with the elders, to decide your future.'

Walking back, hearing the crackle of leaves underfoot, Leo enquired, 'Did you not have help, in curing me? Did I dream a woman called Linde?'

The Healer glanced down, bright with malice. 'Linde is a girl, and already betrothed. When she is a woman, she will be Simel's wife.'

Leo saw him in the distance, as evening shadow dimmed the wind-swept kraal: a lone, lean figure etched in charcoal on the umber plain. He was tall, even for a Masai. He had a warrior's easy, rippling gait. As he drew near, the People thronged to greet him, clapping and chanting his name.

Simel.

He paused inside the blackthorn fence, his ochred muscles glinting, his hawk face fierce and proud; he thrust his great broad spearblade two feet into the soil, leaving the tall haft quivering.

Simel softened to the People. He had handshakes for the elders, caresses for the wives, a gentle touch for every single child. Briefly, he was just a man at peace with living, coming home. It will be like this for me, Leo thought, some day in Kerinyagga. The crowd parted. Leo's stomach clenched. He knew what must happen now. From the doorway of his lonely, barren hut, he watched Linde welcome her betrothed.

She moved, as he had known she would, with slender, lilting grace, making him remember the pleasures of *thingira*. She is even lovelier than my daydreams, he thought bitterly, and must soon become the moran leader's bride.

Then as Simel bent to kiss her, she shivered and turned her face away.

It might have been shyness, a maidenly rejection of public display. It might have been obedience to the People's law.

But it gave Leo sudden, flaring hope.

A hope that would sustain him through the elders' meetings.

I do not trust this chief Leshinga, Leo thought. I do not like the sly amusement in his sidelong glance. He is plumper than all his tribe, sleek-skinned, grey-jowled, pot-bellied. He reminds me of Gitau.

'Behold!' Leshinga bade the assembled elders. 'Behold Ojuju, the Pale One. He is short and scarred and ill-favoured, without ancestry or name. Must the People support him?'

'I am Leo Reid of Kerinyagga! I am the Lion Boy!'

'Silence! Only he who brought you here may speak on your behalf!'

Simel moved unhurriedly to the hub of the elders' circle. He squatted there, his long bare thighs glinting.

'You have seen him,' Simel said. 'You have heard him speak our tongue. Is this not a strange thing, a white Kikuyu who speaks Masai? "I am the Lion Boy", he says. What does he mean? What do the Kikuyu know of lions? I, who dragged him from the battlefield, say this boy is charmed. Let me have him, let me use his secrets to make the People prosper.'

'We have not seen your courage,' Leshinga said, speaking directly to Leo for the second time, 'nor the gifts that Simel says you own. To us, you are just another Kikuyu orphan, worthy only to herd cows.' He glanced up, wearing Gitau's sneer again. 'If you want to win respect, you must do what every Masai herdboy does: you must go and slay a lion.'

Leo drew himself up, conscious of the evening sun on his scar, remembering the image he had cast on the water. 'I am Leo Reid,' he said, 'of Kerinyagga. Find me the lion you would have me kill.'

There, he thought, it is done. I hope Linde was watching.

Masai warriors rose on either side of the stream, like thin black saplings bursting from the turf. They came leaping and whooping down the moorland valley, their great spears poised and flashing.

Leo braced Simel's shield more snugly along his forearm. The lower point rested on the ground, the upper curve almost touched his chin. The lion slunk from thick green marsh grass, sixty yards away. He came out on his belly, his ears and mane flattened, his tail lashing, his head turned towards the din behind. Leo set his feet wider, waiting to be seen – and charged. The lion had turned completely, and was slinking tailfirst towards him.

Of course, he realised, the wind is in my face. The stupid beast hasn't scented me! He stepped from behind the shield, stamped his foot, screamed a Kikuyu oath. The lion ignored him, one small voice among so many others.

He let the shield fall, leaving it rocking gently, belly down. He went forward through the bedlam, counting the paces in his head. There was nothing in his mind but this counting, the precise distance he would have to cover, coming back, and a clean, cool, certainty.

I can do it.

Twenty-five paces. He actually saw fleas hop through the lion's golden, sunshot fur. He was vaguely aware of its snarling, the sudden hush among the warriors. He stooped and wrenched the lion's tail. He saw the blunt head swing round, and saw fear in yellow eyes turn to fury. Then he sprinted, counting, towards the downturned shield; twenty-five paces, ten of my swiftest, longest running strides.

At the count of eight, he dived, with hot breath at his heels and a growl of savage triumph in his ears. He dived and skidded on his side, still measuring, still calculating. He thrust his right arm through the braces and swept the shield up and over.

He curled tight in the darkness, laughing in sheer exultation, hearing the rasp of fang on touched cowskin, watching one ivory-coloured claw hook and rake at the wooden frame, breathing the feral reek of angry cat.

Until the warriors came to spear it. The sounds changed, the snarls turned to sobbing, coughing grunts, and bright blood came gouting through punctured hide to pool beside his head.

Simel lifted the shield, and stared down in awe and disbelief.

'You are insane, Ojuju!'

'I am alive, Simel. And my name is Leo.'

Women and children waited, inside the blackthorn fence, where embers flickered and roast beef scented the air. They clicked their tongues and clapped their hands at Leo's tawny cloak. Their smiles flashed white. Excitement bubbled in the smoky dusk.

Linde was there, hanging back, smiling for Simel alone. But once, as the moran leader praised his courage, Leo won a single, doe-eyed glance. *I would like to know you better.*

Ole Leshinga stepped from the shadows, portly and disdainful. 'So, Ojuju,' he murmured, 'you have won the warriors' favour with a foolish prank. Take off that cloak! Only moran have the right to wear it.'

'You said I would be a moran, when the lion was killed!'

'Simel said that, not I, nor any elder.' Leshinga's grizzled jowls shook in disgust. 'You have proved yourself worthy, that is all. At sunrise you shall start to tend my cows.'

I shouldn't have trusted them, Leo thought, letting the lionskin drop, hoping that darkness would hide the tears of humiliation. I should have followed my instincts and played the sickly herdboy, waiting a chance to escape.

He woke when a pale, perfect triangle of moonlight silvered the open doorway, when his many dreams of vengeance had burned themselves to ashes. He woke with his mind as bright and icy as the night itself, seeing at last how foolish they had been, marvelling at the gift they had bequeathed him.

Simel must go back to the manyatta, he thought, with the warriors; and Linde must stay here with me.

He had to wait four months, while the short rains raged across the upland plains. Four months of herding and milking Leshinga's cows, while icy rain and scything wind flayed his body, younger herdboys tried to break his spirit and memories of hearth and home occupied his mind.

Until a roving storyteller called, and the People of the five kraals gathered around the fire, watching the flames leap and crackle, and watching their lean, rubber-limbed jester perform.

And Leo watched Linde, watching him.

As the first laughter ripple spread, she rose and backed into the dimness between the domed huts. She made no sound, attracted no attention. Her glance teased and beckoned. Leo followed, joyous but stealthy.

She faced him, only a little shorter, poised and graceful as a gazelle. Moonlight played on her perfect cheekbones, shaded high sweet curves beneath her cloak. Her beauty blooms by night, he thought, and smells of forest flowers.

'I see you, Linde,' he whispered. 'I have dreamed of you like this.'

'And I, of you.' She was staring frankly upwards. Leo remembered the scar, raised a self-conscious, shielding hand. 'It is healing well,' she whispered. 'Soon, no one will notice – except for the hair.'

'What do you mean?'

'The hair around your scar is growing silver. It looks very fine, silver in the gold. No one will ever mistake you.' She sighed, soft and pleasured, stirring his blood.

'Come closer, Lion Boy. I do not like this cruel, pale light.'

'Yet it becomes you so,' he told her, drawing near, breathing her sweet green fragrance.

'It becomes no one!' He halted, stunned by her bitterness. 'I'm sorry,' she murmured, 'you do not know the legend. You do not understand.'

'Then tell me, so I may comfort you!'

Her face was in his shadow. He thought he saw the glimmer of a smile. 'I would enjoy that, I think. So be it, Leo: for you alone.'

She kept quite still, letting her voice bring depth and colour to the tale. 'One day, a girl-child died in the ancestor Le-eyo's camp. The people mourned, and begged Le-eyo to restore her. "I cannot," he said, "I will ask Ngai."

'That night, he carried the body beyond the kraal and laid it on the grass. He called Ngai, and told him the people's wish. "Wait until the moon rises," Ngai said. "Look her in the face and say, 'Girl die and be reborn; moon die, and never live again'."

'Owls screeched, hyenas chuckled slyly. Le-eyo grew afraid, beside this cold body he did not know or love. How terrible, he thought, if the dark must always be so black, and Mistress Moon must never, ever shine. So, when the first glint of silver touched the sky, he cried, "Girl die and never live again; moon die, and be reborn." And he fled back to the kraal.'

Linde's voice had fallen to a whisper, barely heard above the gusty wind.

'When Le-eyo returned, his own beloved daughter lay dead. He snatched her up, bellowed his grief to Ngai and the lightening sky. "Moon die and never live again. *Girl die and be reborn!*"

'And the moon rose higher, smiling coldly. And the daughter hung lifeless in his arms.

'Then Ngai said, "You defied me, manthing. Henceforth, no human shall return from death. The moon will always die and rise anew!"'

She threw the last words upwards, her beauty blind with tears. 'To this day, the People do not mourn the dead, do not even say their names. The bodies are left beyond the kraals, for hyenas and carrion birds. And the moon smiles and rises! I hate to see her, watching and waiting! I don't want to die, and be forgotten!'

He went to her then, across the smoky, shadowed night, drawn to a depth of feeling she alone among the people had revealed. Her body quivered in his arms, vibrant with sobs.

'Look at me, Linde. *Hear my truth by moonlight.* This is the first time we have talked. Even if it's the last, I will never forget you.'

Her eyes sought his, softened, closed. Peace and a kind of blurred

131

radiance returned to her face. 'Comfort me, Lion Boy,' she whispered.

Teardrops dewed her long, upcurled lashes. Her lips parted. Her breath was soft and sweet and needy.

He kissed her.

The sheer pleasure made his senses swim, tingled deep along his spine. She shifted, nestling, a tearful girl no longer: a woman, now. 'Waken me,' she murmured, 'Lion Man.' And kissed him in return.

Her breasts swelled, high and taunting, into his chest. Her thighs burned fierily beneath her cloak. Her scent grew stronger, richer. His manhood woke, pulsing, brushing her lean, flat belly. Embarrassed and confused, he half-turned aside. Her hand moved to the small of his back, gentle but insistent, pressing him close.

'Don't be ashamed,' she whispered, 'that is how it must be, between man and woman. I like it. I want it.'

He laid her down upon the soft, tanned cloak, let his kirtle fall and feasted on her splendour: firm peaked breasts, a sweeping flare of waist and hip, a lean clean curve of inner thigh. The risen moon caressed her, laying smoky, silvered tints across her flesh. He crouched between her knees, felt her heated moisture at the tip of his manhood, eased her trembling haunches upwards. 'I will be gentle, Linde.'

Her eyes widened, her thighs hardened. 'No,' she whispered. '*No!*'

Steely fingers twined into his hair. He was lifted and hurled aside, his own knee smashing against his temple. He lay winded, gazing blankly at the whirling stars. Vaguely, he heard angry voices; he struggled to breathe, to rise again, and see.

'You must not harm him,' she cried. 'I love him!'

'Then it is finished,' Simel said.

Simel!

The words and the deadly tone brought Leo to his feet – too late, too far away.

He saw her stand, her slim arms outspread in naked appeal, and heard her beseech a moran's mercy. '*Please*, Simel, spare him!'

He saw Simel's arm coil back and whip forward, saw the great spear flash and leap; he saw it bite between her breasts, stealing her grace away, bearing her downwards into the blackening grass.

There was a terrible noise in his head.

He knelt beside her and held her limp, outflung hand. Her eyes were open, but glazed and sightless. He watched the life and beauty in them dwindle until only his tear-blurred reflection lingered. Perhaps she spoke his name. He never knew.

Because the sound was not only in his head. It filled the whole shadowed kraal, an animal howl of pain and grief. He leaned back, arced and rigid, and hurled her name at the high, pale, sneering moon.

'*Lind-e-e-e!*'

He turned on Simel, kicking, cursing, biting. 'Kill me too,' he sobbed. '*Me too!*' But Simel was a moran, full grown and battle hardened. He hit back, long clubbing blows, driving Leo to his knees. 'Come, Ojuju,' he snapped. 'You will answer for this at the council.'

The wind had never blown so bitter, the kraal had never loomed so dark and chill. Physically battered, emotionally numb, Leo stood at sunrise before the council, under a bloodied sky.

'She was naked,' he cried, 'defenceless and pleading for forgiveness – and *this* noble moran struck her dead. In the name of God, redeem her, make him pay the price!'

Leshinga stirred, cold-eyed, hard-jowled. His plump finger stabbed at Leo's belly 'Speak only when you are asked, Ojuju. One more word, a single mention of her name, and you will go under guard to your hut. Is that clear?' He nodded to Simel, bidding the moran leader speak.

'She shamed me,' Simel told him. 'She sinned, and now can sin no more.' His dark eyes glittered, his tall spear glinted pink. 'Should I, your greatest warrior, wed a herdsboy's leavings?'

A weapon, Lord, prayed Leo, as the red veil dimmed his thoughts once more. Give me a weapon, a moonless night, and this moran leader.

The voice of Linde's father brought him back: a voice of greed, not grief. 'She was comely, Simel, and much admired. Not all are as proud as you. She might yet have won a fair price. Let us hear Ojuju's tale; perhaps it was he who sinned.'

'He is a foundling,' Simel snapped, 'who was not taught these laws!'

'Even so,' said Leshinga, softly and surprisingly, 'the council will hear him.'

In the sudden hush, Leo sensed her living presence, deep within where she would always be. He stood straight and gave them more than truth: he gave them an elegy for Linde.

'She healed my sight and left me with a vision, a love not one of you shall ever see. She was the best of all your tribe, and you have let a jealous man destroy her, who will not even speak her name aloud!' They were muttering, shaking their heads, old cold men beyond the reach of feeling. He gazed up to the empty, tear-blurred sky, making sure the council heard his final tribute. 'I loved a girl called Linde – and Linde loved me!'

There, he thought, sobbing, now they will remember.

'Take him away,' Leshinga snapped, 'take him to his hut.'

'Let him stay,' said Simel. 'Let him learn our custom and her value.'

The council murmured assent. Leshinga shrugged. Linde's father turned the talk to business. 'Bride-price was set at forty head,' he observed. 'The boy is clearly more than half to blame. I will take twenty.'

'Don't insult me, man,' Simel warned, 'I do not count her worth a single bullock!'

Leo heard and was sickened as he heard Linde's father haggle with her killer, heard them set the terms and seal the trade.

Five cows.

There is no God, thought Leo. There cannot be, when it has happened exactly as she feared. The carrion will have her broken beauty, the moon will leer above her ravaged corpse. Lovely, loving Linde, forsaken and despoiled, her value set at five sway-backed cows.

It shall not be, he vowed, as the elders strolled contentedly away. I shall not let it be. Some day, I shall *make* Simel remember. Somehow, I shall make the whole tribe pay.

This resolution, and Linde's inward image, sustained him through another year of bitter, loveless captivity, until the day he led the herd towards the forest, over the hill, almost beyond sight of the kraal.

The clouds were rolling down the horizon, the sky above blazed empty blue. Are You there? he wondered, gazing upwards, do You nurse her soul with gentle hands? The sun sneered, the grass rustled slyly. Leo blinked and sighed – and saw the arrow's flight.

It rose above the forest path where Linde's body lay. It climbed in a lazy, languid arc, levelled and gleamed, then began the downward plunge. His spirit soared to meet it, his mind fled back across the years between: back to the sunset river, to the lean black archer locked in faultless stance. Only one man, he thought, as the point bit and the shaft thrummed upright just beyond arms' reach, only one man could venture such a distance, hold the aim so true.

Duma.

Suddenly, Leo was running.

He sprinted downhill, where forest shadow stretched to greet him. Already, he could hear Simel's voice, rousing the moran to pursuit. Duma's answer flickered swiftly overhead – four Kikuyu arrows fired as one, climbing the slope, hanging briefly, homing on the Masai like a stoop of long, bright hawks. And the Masai had no shields!

Duma rose, dark against dark leaves, thirty yards ahead.

'Greetings, son,' he called. 'I've made you a new bow.' Then Leo was at his side, clasping his hand, seeing the joy in his eyes. He took the bow, nocked an arrow, took aim and launched the next wave of fine-tuned, feathered death.

'Fall back,' said Duma. 'Let us take them to the forest and teach them some new tricks.'

Three figures were loping down the path ahead: Maina, and two more familiar warriors. Duma halted, drew his simi and pointed upwards. A taut yellow liana glinted among the heavy foliage. 'Wait,' breathed Duma, 'watch.'

The pound and crackle of pursuit drew nearer. Metal gleamed at the curve of the track. Duma's simi flashed. The liana thwanged and parted – and half the forest seemed to stir. It was a huge tree trunk, Leo realised, eight feet long by three feet round, suspended fore and aft on thicker creepers, held in check by the single strand Duma had just severed. Freed, it swung downwards with silent, deadly force.

The first two moran rounded the corner and slithered to a halt. The weight of numbers pushed them forward. Duma's battering ram struck square and true. Leo heard the crunch of shattered ribs, a single shriek of pain, and Simel's anger, surging through the gloom.

'There are two less,' said Duma, 'and we must move on.'

They passed the Healer's pool where Leo had seen his scar. A dim green cavern opened, fifty yards before them: a broader path, a higher, thinner canopy. As they neared its mid-point, Duma ushered Leo to the left. 'Keep close to the bush,' he ordered, 'step carefully.'

The Masai came warily into the open. Sweat and ochre streaked their faces.

Simel alone hung back, perhaps sensing the trap. The others leaped forward, their spears poised and gleaming.

The first three crashed through false forest floor on to the vicious, white-tipped stakes below. The white tips soon shone crimson, while hardened moran writhed and sobbed and died. *That* is why I had to tread carefully, Leo realised. This is Duma's last and best trick.

Hissing with fury at the edge of the pit, a young moran drew back his spear. Duma's arrow took him cleanly through the heart. He fell, limp and gory, among his gutted friends.

The reek of sudden death filled Leo's nostrils. The lust for vengeance smouldered in his blood. It would have been very easy, then, to shoot Simel down.

Too easy. Simel's death should not be quick and clean.

He lowered the bow, freed the arrow, spat on the ground.

'Go home, Simel, as I am going home.'

'A mistake, Ojuju. You will live to regret it.' Simel was as tall and proud as ever, shepherding his two survivors away.

'Tell the People,' Leo shouted, at his lean, retreating back. 'Tell them I have not forgotten *her*; nor have I done with them!'

That is what I am prepared to die for, Leo thought, back in the present and Ngong Mission Hall. I will die gladly to avenge Linde, to bring the People's power to an end.

And now is the time to start. He straightened up in the shadows and used the people's tongue. 'Beware, Segi!' He pointed at the interpreter. 'This man yearns to lead the entire nation. He twists your words, making liars of the white man and yourself!'

Segi drew himself up, lean and proud. His flesh shone with youth and rich red ochre. 'Who makes this charge?'

'I do!' Leo was striding forward, elbowing full-grown moran aside. He tossed the hat away and stepped before a window, letting the setting sun strike full upon his face. 'I am that Ojuju who speaks the Masai tongue. See where moonbeams touch my hair, and Simel's deathstroke scarred my forehead. I am not of the People, yet every one among you knows my name!'

They were shrinking away, these mighty warriors, fearful of the legend this wounded white Kikuyu had left behind. 'I am the one who taunted Simel's moran, led them to the forest and slew them by the score. I am the one they call the Lion Boy!' Power was welling up within him. He turned on Leshinga. 'Will you dare contest this accusation?' Sullen silence, downcast red-rimmed eyes, a guilty slouch more eloquent than any words. Leo swung on Simel, looking only slightly upwards into hook-nosed hatred. 'Did you not come to back Leshinga's greed? Have you no voice – *woman-killer*!'

Simel's spear arm quivered, as Leo had seen it quiver in a thousand bloodied dreams. This time, Leo's hand was quicker, seizing the hard black wrist, meeting force with greater, truer force. The broad bright blade locked upright, poised between two faces: one white, one darkly savage.

'Enough!' The laibon's youthful voice held total authority. There was a swift movement, shifting shadows, a narrow ring of lionskin cloaks and naked steel. Segi's guard had closed around them, hard men whose steady eyes showed neither fear nor favour. 'Will you shame the People?' the boy chief demanded. 'Curb your anger, Simel! Fight your private battle when our business here is done!' Leo sensed resistance fading, let his own hand drop and let the guardsmen usher him towards the coloured map.

'I have heard of you, Ojuju.' The laibon spoke respectfully, as to an equal. 'Your words today impress me. Will no one from the north deny them?'

The interpreter quavered, refusing to meet his gaze. Leshinga shuffled, mumbled, shook his head. And Simel stood erect and unforgiving, locked within some silent, inward rage.

'So be it,' Segi murmured. 'Later, Leshinga shall answer to the council. Meanwhile this Lion Boy who knows our language shall speak for either side.'

Then, under Hugo Berkeley's wondering stare, as evening shadows deepened and nightbirds sang outside, Leo touched the map and explained the treaty. One by one, he silenced the objections, pledged them entry to their sacred heights, and made them feel the lure of the south. Piece by piece, he stripped their power from them, and never let them see his soaring joy.

When he had finished, Hugo set the document out and opened up the ink pad. The chiefs filed by and smeared the ink on ageing, calloused thumbs, leaving wavery blue smudges on the creamy vellum.

Leshinga came, the last of all. 'It was the interpreter's idea,' he told Segi. 'I only want the best for the five kraals.' His sly, bloodshot gaze flickered Leo's way. 'This Ojuju explains the treaty so well. It would sit much better on my people, if he could come north and do what he has done today.'

Leo saw Segi hesitate, understanding the young laibon's dilemma. Such a gesture would be good statesmanship and might help to heal the rift. 'We have arranged to meet in Rumuruti, before this moon wanes,' Leshinga added, fawning outrageously. 'We would be honoured by his presence.' His thumb hovered over the treaty – the final mark which would make it law.

'I will go,' Leo sighed, noting Segi's ill-concealed relief and Leshinga's wolfish grin. The thumb moved, pressed down, lifted.

Hugo sprinkled french chalk on still-damp ink and folded the document hastily. 'Come away,' he breathed, 'before they change their minds!' He went, striding briskly, a hunched khaki figure in the falling twilight. Leo lingered, savouring the moment, laying ghosts to rest.

A tall, lean shadow sidled closer. Simel's angry whisper cut the gloom. 'It is not over, Ojuju. I will be waiting, at Rumuruti.'

'Wait in fear, Simel,' said Leo. 'May Ngai speed the day!'

15

Hooves drummed and sputtered, wooden shafts thocked upon each other, players' voices echoed crisp and harsh. Wheeling fleet and catlike from the mêlée, the big bay gelding struck a regal gallop and came thundering along the open flank. Wide black nostrils chuntered rhythmically; up-tossed chunks of greenness cartwheeled into bright blue sky.

The rider nestled to his saddle as if born there, his polo mallet poised and tilted like a yellow softwood lance. Regimental grey and scarlet fluttered from his back. Graceful as a picador, swift as a stooping hawk, he leaned far out and swept the mallet down. There was a sweet, clean click, a high, slow arc, and the white ball floated easily between the slender poles. 'A six-goal man,' an admiring female watcher said. 'Wouldn't it be great to play like that?' Leo could only nod in wistful assent. It would be great to *play*.

The subaltern reined in, turned his mount and tipped his solar topee to the ecstatic, parasoled, pastel-tinted ladies of Nairobi. Cantering back, he wove between the ill-kempt nags and faded khaki blousons of H.E.'s hastily mustered 'government team'. His jodhpurs gleamed, his brown knee boots glittered. A smug smile split the shadow underneath his hatbrim.

'Bravo!' his colonel drawled, brandishing a blue-tinged gin and tonic, relishing the score. 'Four nil to us.' He sat in pasha-like aloofness, mopping florid cheeks and walrus moustachios with a cerise kerchief, importuning Leo for more drink at shorter intervals, snarling at those who moved between him and the field.

And trampling roughshod over H.E.'s pride.

'We're *bound* to be superior,' he was crowing, as horsemen reared and lunged and pounded round the ball. 'Workin' beasts, d'you see, have to be maintained in tip-top trim. Hulloo, you chaps! Look sharp, the blighter's got away!'

Hugo Berkeley's wiry grey had indeed run clear. Briefly, only empty, sunstruck greensward and the loose white ball lay between him and the distant soldiers' goal. The ladies screeched, H.E. rose, the Colonel's moustache quivered nervously.

The subaltern's bay came smoothly to the rescue, its sweat-streaked quarters rippling like oiled, old-gold silk. Berkeley was ridden down, the ball was poached, and siege was laid to H.E.'s goal once more. This time, packed defence and unkind bounces kept the tally down.

'Must say, H.E.' smirked the Colonel, his condescension instantly restored, 'your chaps don't look frightfully fit. Comes from ridin' desks no doubt.' One black, bleary, monocled eye fastened on Leo as if seeing him for the very first time. 'You, boy! Surely you'd rather play than serve liquor?'

Ignoring H.E.'s hot blue glare, Leo answered truthfully, 'Indeed I would!'

'Then why are you here?'

'For one thing, I have no horse.'

'Borrow one of ours! Well-set lad like you might turn the scales.' The Colonel gave the Governor a conciliatory leer. 'Don't much care for easy victories. Takes all the fun away.' A patently hollow gesture. With only one chukka left, his bet was safe. Even a six-goal man couldn't make that much difference.

'I can't oblige you, Colonel,' Leo admitted, 'I don't ride.'

The Colonel's moustache bristled. The monocle tumbled, glittering, from a suddenly widened eye. An angry bellow, laced with gin, made the canvas walls resound. 'God's blood, what is the Empire coming to? Hear that, H.E.? This able-bodied puppy tells me he doesn't ride!' He made it sound depraved, leaving Leo trapped in awkward hush and pitying female glances.

Smarting from his team's annihilation, H.E. leaned forward, cold-eyed and flame-whiskered, making every word cut to the bone. 'Not all of us, Colonel, inherit wealth or rank. Young Reid has neither, being orphaned shortly after birth. Look at him, sir! See the pain your hasty judgement causes, by forcing me to make his circumstances public. Be thankful you live in civilised times. In my day, a man might call you out for less.'

Leo was squirming, feeling the flush burn livid on his cheeks.

'Twas said for love of sport, and not from mischief,' the Colonel growled. He was choking on the words, swallowing bloated pride. It must be many years, Leo thought, since he's apologised; he never has, to one as young as me. Glancing up, Leo glimpsed raw malice in his close-set muddy eyes, and knew H.E. had endowed him with a lifelong enemy. He didn't even know the Colonel's name.

The bell rang, the chukka ended. Tension ebbed away in hasty movement and overloud conversation. The ladies were twittering, drifting with studied, false indifference towards the paddock, where natives decked in grey and scarlet groomed the steaming horses, and hungry-eyed subalterns offered old-world gallantry. Leo was briefly enveloped in a cloud of lavender. A small hand grasped his, offered a sharp-edged card, withdrew. The crowd passed on. Not a single lady raised her head and met his eye.

He set the silver drinks tray down, strolled out of the marquee and shielded the card with his body. On one side, engraved in gold, a long, grand name: 'The Countess Tharasina Gunhilde von Heidel Hesselring.' On the other, five neatly printed words: 'I will teach you riding.'

He found Hugo squatting in a blue gum's shade, nursing the grey's front fetlock, murmuring endearments, probing with a marlin-spike along one steely shoe. The air smelled of horses and exertion. Listening, Hugo looked excited and intrigued. 'They say she's very rich, and an excellent horsewoman. Do it, Leo.' He nodded at the empty, sunlit green. 'This is sport for princes, even if you lose.'

'Perhaps,' Leo conceded. 'First, we must sport with the Masai.'

Masai drums were rumbling, deep-throated in the dark. A dozen campfires burned below, on Rumuruti plain. Spearblades glinted, lean black matchstick figures whirled and leaped: Leshinga's legions, chanting warlike fervour at the stars.

'There must be several hundred,' Hugo breathed, his face a yellow oval near the embers, 'and you behave as if it were a game!'

'Their rule is ending,' Leo told him. 'Soon they will be gone.'

Hugo huddled to the warmth. Leo heard the shiver in his voice. 'You're actually looking forward to it!'

'They owe me a life. At sunrise, I shall take it.'

'How can you be sure?'

Because my gift of pictures has returned, Leo thought, because I am once more the Lion Boy. The Healer's charm surrounds me, unbroken, steady, sure. He didn't say these things. Neither Hugo nor any white man would understand. Instead, he spoke as to a fretful child. 'Rest now; trust me.'

Berkeley's pale, slim silhouette moved quickly to the tent, up between the sentries whose teeth and rifles gleamed, along the picket line where unseen horses whickered. The embers popped and gave off small blue flames. Leo let his pictures coil amongst them: the issues which had brought him to this time and place. . . .

H.E. stood before the largest office window, his ginger whiskers burnished, his white tunic agleam. Beneath the habitual tetchiness, Leo sensed concern. 'The Colonel can spare only two dozen men and a native NCO. Situation's altered. Secret communication from young Segi: council decision. Leshinga is forgiven his treachery, and welcome to join them in the south. Conditionally.'

Hugo had stiffened, his eyes dark and suspicious. 'What are the conditions, sir?'

'Perfectly reasonable, really.' H.E. muttered. 'Can't blame them, in the circumstances. I mean, the fat clown tried a coup!'

'Sir,' breathed Hugo, 'what is it?'

'No warriors,' snapped H.E. 'No weapons. Perfectly straight-forward – explain the treaty, disarm the moran.'

'Disarm?' Hugo's voice rose and quivered. 'You send a score of native troops to disarm Leshinga's clan? Is that an order, sir?'

H.E. turned, fanged and fiery in the sunlight. 'Lost your nerve, Berkeley? What happened to all that dedication and purpose? Going home to Pater, are we, soon as things get tough?'

'It's all right,' Leo said softly. 'We're just a bit surprised.' Excitement tingled in his veins, a plan began to gather in his mind.

A reckoning was very close at hand.

'We'll do our best, sir,' Leo promised, fixing Hugo with a glare that forbade disagreement. 'Won't we, Berkeley?'

Hugo blanched, swallowed, nodded, clearly not trusting himself to speak.

H.E. came briskly to the desk, settling above his own reflection in the glowing walnut grain, eyeing Leo narrowly. 'Been hearing things about you, boy. Interesting things. Quite a feather in your cap, if you pull this off.'

'It's nothing to smirk about,' Hugo hissed, later. 'Did you hear the way he said *if*?'

*

142

The fires on the plain flared brighter crimson. The war dance reached new heights of frenzy. Behind him, Leo heard sentries changing watch – muffled boot-tramp, handslap on wooden rifle stock, a password told in deep, melodious Swahili. A horse whinnied. Leo touched his own haunches gingerly. After one precarious, painful day in the saddle, he had returned to Shanks's pony, slowing progress and adding to the troopers' apprehension. Soon I must see this countess, he vowed. I must learn to ride with style, like Hugo.

Meanwhile, more pictures were forming . . .

An eagle soared, buff and stubby-winged, against the cloudless blue. Zebra cropped distant emerald slopes, their black and white striped plumpness quivering in the haze. The moran campsite smelled of curdled milk and ashes. The reception group wore ochre, cowhide, and no friendliness at all. Simel, dark and deceptively languid, leaned on his planted spear; Leshinga, pot-bellied and grey-jowled, curled his lip at Leo's challenge.

'I come to claim a bloodfeud with this warrior,' Leo began, 'and settle it according to your law.'

Simel straightened, waving a contemptuous black hand at Hugo's troopers, whose rifles gleamed in afternoon sunlight. 'Do you take me for a fool, Ojuju? Should I stand against the white man's guns?'

'I carry no gun,' snapped Leo. 'Single combat to the finish, armed with only stabbing swords. Your law, Simel. The Lion Boy will use it to defeat you.' Leo spoke slowly and scornfully, saw awed recognition on watching moran faces, and saw a shade of doubt in Simel's stare. He added a final goad. 'Surely such a warrior is not *afraid* to fight?'

'*Now!*' hissed Simel, grey with fury. 'Let us do it now!'

'Calm yourself,' Leshinga snapped. 'Be patient till the people are all here.' He turned to Leo, erect and commanding. 'You shall meet on this plain, when the next sun touches that hill.'

In the evening, the plain was alive with movement, with Masai streaming in from every corner like thin black lines of soldier ants. Camped in a copse on an eastern ridge, Swahili troopers huddled round the fire, keeping their rifles primed and cocked. While nightwind rustled overhanging leaves, Hugo learned some facts of Masai life.

'They don't want war,' Leo explained. 'Ages back, their prophets warned them: if they fight the white man, their tribe will rot away.'

'Then why are they dancing? Why do they sound those accursed drums?'

'To rouse their battle gods, and claim his strength for Simel in the morning.'

Leo outlined the People's law of combat. 'They have but one weakness – total faith in their moran leader. If he dies, they break and scatter, no matter how great their numbers, how near the victory. Now do you understand?'

'I'm an office-wallah, Leo, afraid and far from home. Words of one syllable please.'

'When Simel falls, the warriors will be leaderless. Leshinga will be unable to resist. In that moment, you ride out, shielded by modern firearms and an ancient belief.' Clearly sensing Hugo's reservations, Leo added, 'I will be beside you, the white boy who has brought their champion down. They fear me already, and credit me with supernatural power.'

'Very comforting,' Hugo grunted, feeling anything but comfortable. 'I hate to say it, Leo, but it could be you who falls. Then what shall I do?'

'Shoot Simel.'

He makes it sound easy, Hugo thought, sleepless in the drumming dark. He knows my inner weakness, yet treats me as if I were as brave as him.

Dear Lord, don't let me disappoint him.

Drums and Masai war chants dwindled into silence. Down on the plain, red-eyed embers winked and guttered out. Leo lay back on the dew-damp grass, seeing midnight blue between the ragged leaflines, and a lean, horned moon take flight and sneer.

Hugo is right, he realised. Even Lion Boys can't tell the future; I might never see another moon. Coldness touched his soul. At last, the long-forbidden picture gathered in his mind: spear flight in a wink of cruel stars, lithe and lovely nakedness cut down. He fought the sorrow, curbed the rage, forged himself a warrior's inner peace.

Whatever happens, dawn will bring release. I shall avenge my first and fiercest love; or join her in some sunlit place where nothing else can hurt us.

16

Smoky dampness billowed over Rumuruti plain, chilling Leo's spirit, muffling the dawn. Beside him, Hugo's placid mount came swashing through tall grass; two score shivering soldiers kept reluctant step. On either flank, Leshinga's warriors waited, looming in the greyness like charred and silent ghosts. No one spoke, no bird sang. Leo's moonlit certainties dissolved.

Then the sun rose, casting bloodstains on the sky, peeling back the mist above the killing field. Yellowed wisps coiled round lean black shoulders, thinned and slid away, revealing the northern clans in their painted splendour.

They formed twin lines, face to face, a hundred feet apart. Their eyes shone in fiery expectation, their oval shields blazed crimson, white and grey. Between them, dewspread grass lay green and empty; empty but for Simel, the fiercest of them all.

An early breeze disturbed his ostrich head-dress, making the tall pied plumage gleam and toss. The watching tribe awoke and bayed his name.

The war cry made the cool earth shudder, rousing uneasy images in Leo's mind: Simel, slicing through Maina's warriors, spilling purple entrails, ablaze with hawk-faced joy. He felt the dread in men and beast behind him, sensing the moment when they would turn and flee. Then the inward picture altered. Linde's loveliness restored him. He thought he heard her whisper one last plea. *Remember me.*

'Stand firm,' he ordered Hugo. 'Hold your station and your fire.'

He stripped, discarding white man's clothes and custom, and stood in a simple breechclout; he touched the scalp-scar where he knew the hair grew silver, showing them that the Lion Boy was in their midst once more.

Simel circled, lean and greased and sinuous. The chant grew measured, certain. Leo saw the broad blade flicker and threw himself aside. Simel's sword hissed by, raking his rib-flesh like a thousand bee stings. He glimpsed a scarlet trickle, and whirled in time to clamp Simel's upflung wrist – and have his own thrust similarly halted.

They strained together, chests touching, arms and swords locked overhead. Simel's strength was harsh and wiry, Leo's strength was leaking from his side. 'Ojuju bleeds!' he heard the watchers shouting. 'See, Ojuju bleeds!' Wrenching free, giving ground, he feigned a stumble. This time, he drove his own blade across the glittering arc of Simel's downstroke. Impact juddered through him. Steel clash set his teeth on edge. Simel's sword went spinning outwards on to the reddened grass.

The chant dwindled. Simel scowled in disbelief at the limp black fingers which had so betrayed him.

Leo let his sword fall, and heard amazement hum among the watchers, heard Hugo Berkeley's partly stifled mutter of alarm. 'We are not yet done,' he told Simel. 'I come to claim bloodprice for Linde's death.'

Simel's glance dwelt on Leo's wound. Hope and cunning bloomed anew within his dark, cold gaze. 'Should I know this name? I don't recall it.'

'Then I shall remind you.' Leo pitched the insult high enough for everyone to hear. 'Linde chose a half-grown white boy who was more a man than you!'

Simel was upon him, all caution gone, all fighting sense forgotten: snarling, tearing at the open gash. Retreating, Leo parried blows, forcing taloned fingers away. Though blood still seeped, he felt his power stirring: a Healer's charm, a dying lover's blessing. Sidestepping the next lunge, he drove a left hook under flailing arms, sending the moran leader face-first to the grass; he dropped his knees into the broad black back, linked his fingers under Simel's chin, and hauled up until his shoulders creaked. Spittle slimed his palms, the flesh beneath him cringed. In a moment of savage, vaulting triumph, he threw his whole weight backwards and bellowed Linde's name.

Simel's neck cracked, sharp as rifleshot. His dying spasms juddered under Leo's knees. Then he was upright, trampling Simel's head-dress, pouring out his rage upon the People. 'Your laibon bids you southward, humble and unarmed. Set your shields and spears down, beside your champion's corpse!' Whirling, he seized Leshinga's spear, raised it in two hands, snapped the shaft across his knee.

'Order it,' he snarled, 'or face Ojuju's wrath!'

In a corner of his vision, he saw Hugo's rifle glimmer, heard other breechbolts clicking into place. 'Slope arms,' he cried, 'stand easy. The People are prepared to go in peace!'

Leshinga was watching him, sullen and bestubbled. 'Ah, Ojuju,' he muttered, 'I should have killed you when I had the chance. What have you done to the People?'

'I have made them remember Linde!'

Leshinga wagged his head, scornful but strangely dignified. 'No. You have made them remember you.'

They filed like silent mourners past Hugo's tall roan horse, their faces turned away from Simel's body. One by one, they let their weapons fall, piling the splendid, multicoloured shields together. Discarded spearblades mirrored pale blue sky; the shield stack teetered high above the plain.

Then Leo bent and set the spark.

Hugo watched the red flame kindle, saw white and grey hide frazzle, saw oval frames and spear shafts warp and crack and buckle. Heat rolled out across the springy turf. The moran huddled like lost black sheep among the rolling haze.

They were sobbing, these hard, once haughty men: bowed and bereft on Rumuruti pasture, wringing their hands, watching Leo's flame devour their glory, and weeping for a way of life they'd never know again.

Leo drew near, his face still taut with vengeful fury. 'Wait here,' he snapped. 'Make them watch until the embers cool.' And he turned on his heel, and strode away.

The Lion Boy, thought Hugo, who stood alone against an entire Masai clan, challenged their chieftain, observed their law – and won. What had he said? *Find something you are prepared to die for.*

And for which you are prepared to kill.

He shuddered, glancing at Simel's sprawled, spreadeagled form, hearing again that final crack and Leo's primeval victory shout.

If this is courage, I am not sure I want it.

Gradually, he became aware of grateful admiring glances from the troopers. A spark of pride lit somewhere deep inside him, in honour of this morning's work.

I held the line, he thought, did Leo's bidding boldly and unflinching. In my own small, timid way, I helped move the Masai.

The morning was suddenly brighter. His spirits rose, his heart felt strong and light. There's hope for you yet, Hugo. One day the worm may turn, after all.

Leo walked upwards and eastwards, away from the crackling flame and the reek of scorched hide, back to the copse where they had camped. There, alone beneath green swaying leaves, he gazed once more across the plain and witnessed the tart, dark fruit of his ambitions.

Simel's body sprawled where he had left it, naked, abandoned, devoid of dignity, according to the law.

Simel the butcher, slain by these bare hands.

The moran huddled near the fading fire, beside the ashes of their warlike dream.

The power of the People is no more.

Smoke rose, slim and straight and black as any Masai. The death-pall of the northern clans, ringed about by gliding kites and vultures.

A funeral pyre for Linde, to be seen throughout the land.

His eyes stung, his outer vision wavered. She lived once more within his mind, smiling, lithe and lovely. *This is my image, burned on the inner eye.* Your murder is avenged, he breathed, your spirit is set free.

Go in peace, my love.

Chandeliers and silverware sparkled in the candlelight. A hint of Dijon mustard spiced the air. A saffron-robed servant cleared the dinner debris, his broad brown fingers reverent on the Delft plates. Settling back, savouring prime stilton, Hugo took stock of his fellow guests.

Colonel Elliot, of recent polo notoriety, sported regimental scarlet with campaign ribbons. He hunched over his dessert dish, monocled, florid and still munching. Leo, broad-shouldered, flaxen-headed, looked dashing but uneasy in a brand-new dinner jacket. An ill-matched pair, Hugo thought, diverse in age and influence, having but a single common interest.

Their hostess.

The Countess had scandalised Nairobi, holding parties such as this while her husband was away, unchaperoned, with single eligible men. Nothing indelicate, the gossips grudgingly conceded, but *so* unladylike. Mad about her horses, they continued, much too free with natives, often seen in jodhpurs and mistaken for a man!

Her jet-black hair was unfashionably fringed and bobbed, her features were handsome rather than pretty: a strong, straight nose, a wide, firm mouth. But soft female fires lit her violet gaze, and the deep V of her gentian-blue gown revealed sweet *décolletage*. Tonight, mused Hugo, only a sightless eunuch might misconstrue her gender.

'Colonel,' she began, pronouncing it *cole-o-nell* in a husky continental drawl, 'why do you stop this boy to have lessons?'

'Not I, ma'am. He's not in my command.' God help him if he was, the tone said clearly.

The Countess turned reproachfully on Leo. 'Then why do you not come? You had my card months ago.' She smiled, mischievous and beguiling. 'Am I so old, so ugly?'

Leo sat in his finery, crimson with embarrassment, fingering his starched white collar, mumbling about recent heavy rains. The Colonel grinned coldly, relishing the moment.

Hugo allowed himself some spiteful satisfaction. Social warfare, this, conducted in formal clothing over damask-shrouded battle-fields. The weapons are wit and word, the wounds unseen and carved upon the psyche. Such a *civilised* form of conflict, in which no one dies and only the steaks are bloodied. And poor Leo's courage is no help at all.

He shook himself, forsook unworthy pleasure and came belatedly to Leo's rescue. 'He was busy, milady, before the rains. Modesty forbids him to broadcast his part in last year's Masai skirmish. It was heroic, be assured.'

'So. Now he is busy no more.'

Leo found his tongue and made a fervent promise. 'Next week, Countess. Nothing shall keep me away!'

'Good. Please to call me Tara; everybody does.' She clapped sharply, once. The manservant reappeared, setting a silver drinks tray down. Candles flickered, striking ruby shards through crystal glass. 'Port,' announced the Countess, as the yellow robes rustled away. 'But I will not go to powder the nose. Instead, we drink together. Yes?' She laughed, her throat rippling, her lips moist and very red. There was an earthy vibrancy about her that stirred Hugo's blood, setting strong currents flowing through the room: mutual warmth between Leo and the Countess, Elliot's hot-eyed envy of the younger man.

Perhaps sensing this, Tara danced attention on the Colonel, flattering him shamelessly. 'You are King's African Rifles, no? Always, I argue my husband, tell him K.A.R. is best, because they have brave officers like you.'

The Colonel puffed out his scarlet tunic, fingered the slim, multicoloured medal ribbons. 'Clever of you to notice, m'dear. Some of us were heroes in *real* war.' Hugo sipped mellow port, concealing a smile, watching the full implication of her words take hold. The Colonel's porcine features darkened, his monocle glinted bright and blank. 'Argue? Who does your husband think is best?'

'The Schutzetruppe, in German East Africa, natives of the old warrior tribes. He says they are better trained and disciplined.'

'Huns,' Elliot snarled, 'who flog their niggers into obedience. That is slavery, madam, not discipline!'

Tara shrugged her graceful creamy shoulders. 'The Count says this, not me – that they are masters of bush fighting.'

The Colonel slammed his glass down, slopping port across the tablecloth like bloodstains in snow. Furiously, he detailed battalion strengths, armaments and field pieces, forthcoming manoeuvres and soaring morale. Hugo's attention wandered. Leo was gazing heavenward, through the flickering chandelier. Tara alone retained the appearance of interest, eyeing Elliot over the rim of her glass as if he were the only man on earth.

'But of course,' she murmured, when it was over. 'I have French blood, and little liking for the Boche.' She leaned forward, her eyes huge and dark, her bosom swelling above the deep blue fabric. 'The Count is Swiss and very neutral. He takes rich people from Europe and America, for the big game hunting. Ah, at last you smile! Are you, too, a hunter?'

The Colonel was preening again, polishing his monocle. 'Tigers, in Inja, don't you know. Past it now, but I always send the chaps on leave out huntin'. Improves their eye, brushes up their horsemanship.'

Leo interrupted, his tanned face dangerous above the gleaming shirtfront. 'You let them kill, from horseback?'

The Colonel shot him a glance of loathing. 'Of course. What do you know about it?'

'I have been hungry in the bush,' murmured Leo.

'Not the same, boy! I'm talkin' about sport, battle-weary soldiers havin' fun!'

'Only thieves and leopards kill for pleasure.'

Spoken softly, almost dreamily, Leo's words provoked more military fury. A deep red flush suffused the Colonel's cheeks. His voice shook with drink and outrage. 'God's blood, I won't have that! Insult to the whole damned regiment!'

'If the cap fits,' Leo advised him, 'wear it.' He had the Rumuruti stillness about him: a quiet, yellow-eyed warrior in a dinner suit. Briefly, violence stalked the rich, dim room. Hugo's stomach churned in grim anticipation.

Then Tara spoke, as if to errant schoolboys. 'Gentlemen!' Her accent made it sound like *shenellmen*. 'Will you brawl like peasants at my table? Come, shake hands, be peaceful; let us end as we began, in friendship!'

They obeyed without warmth or conviction; it was a mere suspension of hostilities. Conversation dangled, stuttered, ceased. 'Time to go,' Hugo murmured, and won a grateful, violet-tinted glance.

Outside, the night smelled of fresh-turned earth. Insects whirred around a softly gleaming lamp. Beneath it, Leo held Tara's hand and made a courtly, golden-headed bow. Hugo, watching, saw the yearning take her pale, strong face; and the Colonel's silent, ruddy, vengeful snarl. Beware, Leo, he thought. You stir emotions just as sharp as any Masai spear.

Before his lesson, Leo watched Tara's gelding terrorise the native groom, ears back, eye-whites rolling madly, yellow-bladed teeth agape and snapping. Then Tara came and caressed his quivering flanks. The great beast started like a guilty child, pricked its ears and laid loving, velvet nostrils in her hair. 'I call him Tonneur,' she said, 'because of the sound his hooves make, because he is big and black and stormy.' Tonneur meant thunder, she explained, swinging into the saddle, murmuring the name as softly as early morning breeze – making Leo wonder that gentleness could tame such savagery.

It was one of several contradictions she had shown him, like the big revolving pistol strapped to her thigh, which looked much too heavy for her slender hands. She wore a plain white shirt and fawn jodhpurs which ought to make her mannish; instead, they showed the outline of her ripe and rounded body. Every inch a woman, she curbed the gelding's vivid force without apparent effort. And the grey mare she had lent him posed a greater riddle still: how to ride in comfort.

She was broad-beamed and forgiving, sweet-tempered, eager to please. But for two long depressing hours, she had jolted and jounced him down the length of Count Gustav's ranch, beneath the high blue humps of the Ngong Hills. The rhythm of her swaying walk escaped him. No matter how he flexed his knees and braced his back for comfort, the saddle seemed to dip and slide away. Whenever he relaxed it rose and thumped him, bruised his buttocks, drove the breath out of his lungs. All the while, the Countess rode beside him, as if she were a living part of Tonneur's sleek black back.

Cresting a rise, reining in, she turned her horse towards him and read ill-concealed discomfort on his face. 'Patience! It will ease, with practice. I have brought you here to see how it can be. Look!'

The ground swept down below her proud, extended arm. A stream shone like quicksilver in the mid-afternoon sunlight, rippling through rushes and grey boulders. The glen on either side lay flat and green, and echoed to the chatter of the water. The air was warm and still and smelled of clover. 'Pretty,' he conceded, 'but I'm too sore to enjoy it.'

'Silly boy; I'm showing you the jumps!'

It was cleverly done, easy to mistake the underlying purpose. The obstacles had been placed at irregular intervals on the downward slope: a rustic gate, a pile of rotting logs, a length of moss-fringed, dry-stone wall where the gradient levelled out. 'Go there, beside the wall,' Tara told him, 'give the mare a drink. Then watch, and learn what one day you shall do.'

Leo obeyed, dismounted gratefully and let the mare sup and paddle, then turned uphill and saw the Countess start her run.

First there was only a muffled drumming, as a single centaur creature spanned the brown-barred gate, fast and far away. He watched her gather for the next, hands and reins thrust high up on the mane, her face a pale oval beside the dark, arched neck. They seemed to take the logs with scarcely a break in stride. Then Tonneur proved his name, struck thunder from the greensward, and came at a breakneck gallop to the wall.

Leo saw his white fetlocks lift and tuck, saw his great black silken quarters coil and bunch and spring. There was a sudden, eerie silence. Horse and rider hung in space above. Tara sat upright, her face blooming with triumph, one hand outflung and pointing at the sky. Tonneur seemed to blaze with force and beauty, poised between midleap and full extension, etched in living ebony against the bare blue sky. Then they were down, still galloping, lashing the stream up into high and silvered spray; slowing, cantering up the opposite slope and whirling in their tracks. '*Fantastique!*' cried Tara, standing in the stirrups, pounding Tonneur's neck. 'The nearest thing to flying! Hola, we go again!'

The horse reared, nostrils flared, huge dark eyes aglitter. This time, Leo shared the excitement and cheered them on, feeling his heart grow light as they approached. And this time, it went dreadfully wrong.

Perhaps the water hobbled Tonneur's stride, maybe Tara misjudged height and distance. The horse was suddenly hard below the wall, arching backwards, scrabbling awkwardly into the air. His ironshod hooves struck sparks from the cold grey stone. The impact wrenched the partnership asunder. Tara was flung a dozen yards across the wall, falling heavily, lying sprawled and still. Tonneur cartwheeled, legs awhirl, and landed with a crash that shook the earth; he whinnied, snorted, scrambled to his feet.

Leo ran towards her, cold with fear beneath the careless sun.

She lay stunned, spreadeagled, her dark hair spilling on the green, her breathing quick and shallow. He knelt, removed and folded his shirt, eased it under her head, and stroked her pale, smooth brow. Her long black lashes flickered. Her eyes opened, widened and searched his anxious face. She gave a dreamy smile, a smoky violet gaze. 'To wake among such fair gods, I should fall more often!' Then, weakly, 'Water, if you please.'

Light-headed with relief and her flattery, he went down to the dappled stream where the mare browsed peacefully. Watching iridescent blue dragonflies hover, he let cool bright water trickle into the canteen, and bore it carefully across the slope.

She sat erect and ashen, her small face gaunt with pain.

'What is it?' he breathed. 'Where do you hurt?'

'Not I: him.'

Tonneur stood aquiver, his midnight flanks heaving and lather-flecked. He stood brokenly, on three unsteady legs. His nearside fetlock dangled, misshapen and unhinged.

'For him, it is finished,' she whispered. 'Let it be quick and clean.' She rose shakily, fumbling at the brown leather holster. He saw the anguish take her and offered her a measure of release.

'Let me do it, Tara. He does not know me.' She rounded on him, hissing like a lovely, angry cat, 'That is why it must be me!'

She talked to her crippled horse in the careless sunshine, tugged his ears, kissed his soft dark nose. '*Couche, mon brave, mon chéri*; ah Tonneur, please lie down!' Slowly, awkwardly, Tonneur knelt and sighed, and rolled on his flank in the grass. She sat beside him, couching his proud black head in her lap, soothing, murmuring. He saw a simple, childlike trust fill Tonneur's wounded eyes, and he sensed abiding love between the woman and the beast. The pistol rose, ugly, steely grey, resting softly against his white-blazed forehead. Leo watched her pale slim finger tighten on the trigger, saw the rigour take her, flinched and turned away.

The report echoed, dull and muffled, up and down the glen. The mare started, whinnied, pawed the turf. Suddenly, the day was sharp with cordite smoke and coppery bloodshed.

She came towards him, her shirt smeared scarlet, the pistol hanging from her slackened fingers. She moved slowly, as if each step caused her torture, as if the hurt inside would never heal. He went to her, and took her in his arms.

She surrendered then, to Leo and her grief, clinging and sobbing helplessly. He felt the piteous tremors in her body, felt the hot tears trickle down his chest. 'There,' he mumbled, stroking her fine, damp hair. 'There, there.'

Gradually, her movements slowed and softened. Her fists opened, her palms explored his back. She stared up at him, her eyes dark swimming purple, her face flushed and stark with longing. 'He is gone, but we are still alive. Hold me, Leo. Comfort me!'

The words and the expression struck deep into his soul, lighting long-lost force and fire in his loins. His legs grew weak and heavy. He eased her down among the gold and green.

Her breathing was warm and wanting, her lips hungered softly at his neck. Somehow, clothing slid away between them. They were naked, flesh on flesh and springy turf. Spicy female musk inflamed him, tempering the reek of new-shed blood. He entered her, in one long steely swoop, goaded by the scents of sudden death and urgent life.

Beneath him, she was pale and pink and eager, her breasts firm yet yielding in his grasp, her thighs wide and warm about his waist. She drew him to the moist and fiery depths, moaning in abandon, meeting his thrusts with joyful, silken strength. Pleasure surged, white-hot, along his veins, driving his head up and back, tightening his buttocks, arching his spine – and exploded, at the exact, pulsing

154

centre where their bodies met and joined and clove together. He felt her spasms sucking at his hardness, drawing his essence far within; he heard her fierce cry rise and hang in descant to his own. Then he was lost, in limbo, drifting towards a sensual swoon.

He shifted, withdrew gently, easing his weight aside, and laid his cheek between her breasts. Sunshine and knowing fingers warmed his flank. Her heartbeat rumbled, rapid, in his ear. Along his chest, her flesh lay slick and springy, smelling of meadowsweet and satisfaction.

He had never felt such languor, never shared the glowing aftermath. With her flushed and tender beauty, she was everything he'd ever want: the lover he had lost, the mother he had never known. He breathed her name, nuzzled her fragrant skin, held her very close.

Somewhere far inside, the ice was melting, setting free his frozen, locked-in pain. Tears welled up, squeezed between closed lids, and slid across his skin and on to hers. He was weeping for Laura, for Linde, for all the empty, loveless years between.

This time, Tara offered strength and comfort, a soothing touch, a sympathetic tone. 'Don't grieve, Leo. He was only a horse.'

17

He loomed at Hugo's office window, his rufous whiskers gleaming above a crisp white shirt.

H.E. had come to claim his pound of flesh.

'I want a minute on my desk directly. You rid us of the Masai: now get rid of Leo Reid.'

'*Leo* moved the Masai. With what should he be charged?'

'Dalliance, with our noble riding teacher. Call it adultery, shall we?'

'People in glass houses,' Hugo muttered, 'should be sure they're fully clothed.'

'My,' breathed the Governor, showing his fangs, 'such defiance from such a craven soul. Don't threaten *me*, man, use the dirt in Morgan's file!'

It was the first real test since Rumuruti, long awaited, carefully anticipated. Hugo swallowed hard and took his stand. 'I'm sorry, sir, I know of no such file.'

'You will deny you had it?'

'I will.'

'You would lie on oath, for Leo Reid?'

'No man need answer for his father's sins; now nobody can hold them against him.'

H.E. stiffened, his pale blue glare incredulous. 'You destroyed official documents? You put your own neck on the block?'

Hugo allowed himself a gentle smile. 'I checked the archive, sir. *You* drew Morgan's file. Yours is the last signature on record.'

'I'll be damned!' H.E. prowled the office, rumbling like a caged ginger bear. 'The worm turns, eh? Never thought you had it in you.' His voice softened, took on a wheedling tone. 'Just between the two of us, what really happened to the file?'

'I think I must have . . .' Hugo paused, sensing the trap. 'I think *you* must have burnt it, sir.'

Suddenly, H.E. was laughing, ringing peals that made the window rattle. ''Pon my soul, Berkeley, we'll make a civil servant of you yet! Hoist on me own petard, what, hamstrung by my own bureaucracy. All right, keep your half-tamed playmate, but for God's sake teach him how to be discreet!'

He was given little time to bask in triumph. Hardly had H.E.'s footfalls faded than a larger shadow fell across his desk. Familiar Irish cadences brought his hackles up.

'Ahoy there, brother Berkeley, I've a bone to pick with you!' Tin buttons glittered on tightly stretched blue serge. Flynn's bullet-headed bulk threatened to engulf him. 'You're trespassing, me bucko, trifling with my favourite blackbird again!' Boldness wavered before dark-jowled truculence.

Time for diplomacy, Hugo realised. Inspired, he found exactly the right blend of resistance and conciliation. 'We're two of a kind, sharing a taste in women and a hankering for sport. Come: I'll toss you for her.'

Flynn glowered, wagged his shiny dome.

''Tis many a fancy coin-trick I've seen played by gentlefolk.'

'Here then, take the shilling, do the deed yourself. Heads I win, tails she's yours alone.' And as Flynn hesitated, fingering the silver reluctantly, Hugo added, 'Surely lovely Bertha's worth the risk?'

Flynn snorted, and flicked a stubby thumb. The coin arced high, tinkled on to the desk, wobbled drunkenly. Flynn watched, breathless and intent.

The shilling settled, head-side upwards.

'There,' said Hugo contentedly, riding his luck, guying the Irish accent. 'She's ours to share, 'tis written in the stars.' Flynn gaped forlornly at King Edward's head, slumped and swaying like a baited bull. 'For goodness' sake,' grinned Hugo, 'it's no great tragedy. I'll not intrude upon your Friday sessions.'

'You don't understand, Mr Berkeley.' Flynn's button eyes were suddenly abject. ''Tis mad I am for Bertha, and set to wean her from the wayward life. It sickens me to see her with another man.'

Touched by brute force so reduced, tiring of the game, Hugo sighed and let him have his way. 'You should have said so, man. Very well, next time I'll ask for Elsie.'

Flynn's great shoulders straightened. His great paw shot out and mangled Hugo's hand. 'You're a true prince, Mr Berkeley, and Flynn will be forever in your debt. Bless you, sir, you'll not regret this day!'

Amazing, Hugo thought, as the second set of footfalls dwindled down the corridor. A little bit of backbone, a little bit of tact, and even the most formidable foes are overcome.

Perhaps I *will* make a civil servant.

A phantom haunted Leo for almost eighteen months: a phantom called Count Gustav von Hesselring. He never met the man. Tara kept no likeness in the ranch-house.

'I was so young,' she told Leo one evening at the hearth, while fireglow made a poem of her body through sheer silk. 'My family had fallen on hard times. He was powerful, gallant and very rich. A marriage was – how do you say – arranged? He gave me fine clothes and good living, called me his pretty little bird.' She shivered, picking nervously at the sheepskin rug. 'He has always kept racing pigeons. He has them now, in a loft outside. Winners he treats like clever children; he kisses them, gives them special food. Then sometimes, a strangeness overcomes him. He goes and wrings the neck of every loser, plucks the bodies, bakes a pigeon pie. Don't you see? They, too, are pretty birds!' Her violet eyes beseeched him, beneath the fine dark fringe. 'He has such hard, cold hands. His touch is not gentle like yours.' She led Leo's fingers to her breast. 'Touch me, Leo. Hold the darkness back!' Her flesh burned, her nipple nuzzled at his palm. Silk whispered. Her thighs parted, sending a deep, slow thrill along his spine. Her essence brought him to instant hardness and drew him down upon her and the creamy rug. He rode her honeyed smoothness, thrusting the phantom briefly from his mind.

'Leave him,' Leo murmured later, as the logs glowed black and orange, and pine smoke mingled with the scents of love. 'I can give you all the tenderness you need.'

She stroked his hair, laying light fingertips along the scar. 'Some day I might be free, for Gustav is much older. Till then, I am bound by the Church that joined us, and to my people who survive on his largesse. Till then, be happy, *chéri*, be glad he is away.'

It was an honest answer; one no Christian gentleman could contest.

But whenever the Count returned, Leo was banished from the

ranch, consigned to jealous misery and his room beneath the Ngong Hills. There, when Hugo caroused at Lola's, he would lie alone and listen to the nightwind, and let his pictures roam among the dark brown beams above his bed. There, using fragments Tara had revealed, Leo turned the phantom into flesh.

He conjured up a shiny, shaven pate, pallid jowls, a ragged duelling scar; ice-blue eyes, broad, Teutonic features, a stocky body clad in hunting drab.

How marvellous it would be, Leo sometimes mused – and how fitting – if one morning as the Count went to garotte more hapless birds, the whole flock should erupt in hissing fury. Whirring wings would smash him supine into pale, stale droppings. Needle-pointed beaks would put his eyes out, slash at his exposed face till his own blood filled his mouth. He would gurgle, drum his heels, and then lie still.

But somehow, Leo's pictures could never make this scene work.

The daydream always faded, the phantom never died. A day or a week later, the familiar engraved card would appear on Leo's desk, carrying a familiar message: '*He is gone, and I am needing comfort!*'

She would be waiting in her boudoir, where evening sunrays squeezed between drawn curtains, slanting warm on ivory-tinted bedsheets, and laying a peach-like bloom upon her nakedness. She would smile in welcome; sensuous, heavy-lidded, purring like a great gold and pink cat.

Once, he had smelled stale cigar-smoke, and stared in horror at purple, hand-shaped bruises on her hip. 'How dare he!' Leo hissed. 'How can you let him use you so?'

She rose, in a swift, sinuous movement, knelt before him and laid her sleek dark head against his belly. 'Do not permit him to hurt you, too! I cannot deny him what is his by right. I must not give him any cause for anger.' He couldn't move, couldn't bring himself to touch her; he stood unsteady, fighting rage and nausea. Her hands were busy at his belt, her breathing hot along his thighs, her lips soft but greedy at his groin. Again she brought the pleasure surging through him, steered him over and into her, banishing all his doubts with her great need.

She never seemed to tire of his body, nor he of hers. She was pale where Linde had been so dark, full and yielding where Linde had been so lean, wanton where Linde had been so shy. Linde had brought him to the end of boyhood; Tara made him a man.

A change, he soon discovered, which hadn't passed unnoticed.

'I should have known better,' Hugo had confessed, when the affair was still quite young. He lounged on the verandah, sipping pink gin while ring-doves crooned and sunset draped mauve shadows over the Ngong Hills. 'I took you for a prig, because you wouldn't come to Lola's. And all the time, you had your own grass widow!' His brown eyes twinkled. 'Don't look so pained, you can't keep secrets in Nairobi. Servants talk.' He finished his drink and stretched his trim, white-shirted frame against the twilight sky. 'Meanwhile, we poor mortals must powder and curl – and pay for our pleasure!'

But as the months passed, the relationship surpassed mere beds and bodies. Tara blossomed under his attentions and found subtle ways of reflecting them; she delighted in his knowledge of birds and flowers, learning simple Kikuyu words of endearment, treating his inept horsemanship with sunny patience. Many a day ended in the privacy of her dining room, where she served him choice tit-bits and noble wines, asking eagerly about his work, sharing visions of a future somewhere, together. And recently, she had begun to test his past.

'When you came with the cochon Elliot, your friend 'Ugo spoke about the Masai. Come, *mon chéri*, tell me how it happened.' She gave him a glance of violet adoration; he could refuse her nothing.

He told the tale sparingly, leaving Linde out, making light of Simel's death.

'*Mon Dieu,*' she breathed, '*c'est magnifique!*' Her small, handsome face clouded in the candlelight. 'But he is a monster, this Colonel! How could he send you against the hordes with only twenty men?'

'There are more pressing duties. You know, strategic things.'

'*Oh là là,* strategic!' She smiled, beguiling and impish. 'What can be more pressing than the safety of my Leo?'

'The safety of the railway, actually.'

' Rusty trucks and smelly engines? Pouf, ridiculous!'

He took a silver fork and made indentations in the snowy damask. 'Here's the Mombasa line, which carries all supplies. Here's the border with German East. For more than a hundred miles they run parallel, and less than fifty miles apart.'

'And what has this to do with duty?'

'The track must be defended. That is what soldiers are for.'

'But the Germans have their own Northern Railway! Attend me, *chéri*. Soldiers live only so that men may play at war.' Her tone

160

softened, her gaze burned deepest purple. '*Alors*, are we ready for the next engagement?'

Leo was. He carried her to her boudoir, locked the world outside and fell willingly once more beneath her perfumed spell. Hugo was wrong, he thought, as sense gave way to passion. We do this in joy, with no reward except the mutual pleasure that it brings us . . .

Even so, the phantom would not leave him. Twice, on quiet afternoons at Government House, Leo had searched the archives for Count Gustav's provenance: in vain. He found only passing mention in official files. The man was wealthy and successful: he knew that already.

I am rising twenty, Leo thought, trusted by the Governor, respected by my friends, feared by warring tribes – and sinning against every god I know. Tara is ten years older, immeasurably richer, another man's wife.

And I want her for my own.

Why do I, the Lion Boy, fear a Swiss I have never met? Must I kill him, as I killed Simel, in order to become a Lion Man? Is there, after all, a darker phantom hidden in my own past?

Soon I must go back to the Mission, talk to Father Andrew and draw from him much more of Morgan's truth.

But first, I need more riding lessons.

Duma stood on Njau's knoll, above the sunlit village. Beyond the river, fields of yellow wheat had replaced pasture. Coetze's sleek brown cattle grazed the distant ridge. The clansfolk, too, had prospered. Maize stands and broad-leaved banana plants now reached down to the water's edge. The bush was disappearing. Even in the forest, it was hard to find much game.

A man grows older, Duma thought, and change comes on him slyly, like a leopard in the dusk.

The change that troubled him most had brought him up here, with Wanjui bent and stumbling at his side. In the two years since the Masai were defeated, a sickness had possessed her. It took her often and severely, stealing the gladness from her living and the plumpness from her face. She didn't sing, she couldn't work.

She needed a Healer.

Njau came from his hut, in jingling anklets and pied colobus skins. He touched Wanjui's shrunken, shrivelled belly and murmured gentle questions. 'She has an evil spirit, deep within,' he said at last.

'Support your woman, Duma. Dig a hole between her feet while I prepare a charm.'

Duma obeyed, trying to force his love into her failing flesh. 'Be brave,' he urged, 'let the magic cure you.'

Njau returned, shook grey powder from his leather pouch into a gourd, and handed her the sloshing mixture. 'Drink. Let the badness bubble, spit it into the hole and send it back to dirt and darkness whence it came.'

Wanjui's body arched and clenched, with a force Duma could hardly contain. She folded at the waist, her mouth agape, the tendons in her neck taut and trembling. Duma felt her stomach heave, saw scarlet gush and spatter into cold black earth.

'Bury it,' Njau commanded. 'Bring her, follow me!'

Duma bore her in Njau's footsteps, through evening cooking smells under a reddened sky; he laid her down and covered her, and watched Njau complete the ceremony. He swept the hut with tangy herbs, doused the fire, brought new kindling, lit fresh yellow flame. 'It is done,' he said. 'Her soul will brighten this fire. Soon she will sing again.'

But Wanjui's soul did not brighten. Though Mwangi came and prayed and sang every charm he knew, an ashy greyness settled on her skin, and lines of pain cut deeper across her once-smooth face. By day, she lay beneath the blanket, glassy-eyed and moaning. By night, she tossed and whimpered and cried out in her sleep. When embers faltered and cruel nightwind stirred the thatch, Duma held her weakened body, smelled the rank corruption in her vomit, and was desperately afraid.

Then, one lonely anxious night, he heard the name she mumbled and understood a fundamental truth. Wanjui's sickness had begun before the Masai left. It began the day Leo had walked out of the valley.

There is one last hope, he thought. I must make the Lion Boy return.

The reins that sawed at Leo's hands were slippery with sweat. The road bucked underneath him like a swollen, dull, red stream. Hot wind and flying insects flayed his face. Drumming hooves resounded through his body; Father Andrew's written words resounded in his mind.

'Come quickly. Wanjui sickens, and calls your name at night.'

'Go at first light,' Hugo had urged him. 'Leave the note with me. I will make the Governor grant you leave.'

'Of course you must take the mare!' Tara had exclaimed, her small face tight with sympathy, her breath pluming in the chill grey dawn. 'Godspeed, *chéri*. I will pray for you – and her.' He had mounted gratefully, clattered through the misted, drowsing streets, and set the mare upon the Nyeri road.

Some time on that blazing, northbound dash, somewhere between Thika and Fort Hall, Leo's undertrained and overburdened riding muscles seized. He slumped in the saddle, slackened the reins and gave the mare her head. Her gallop struck a fire in his bones, jolting him from crown to aching coccyx. Sun and wind grew stronger, miles and hours passed, bitter orange dust rasped at his throat. He hung on, in heat and pain and desperation, begging gods he didn't trust to spare Wanjui's life.

She calls my name at night.

At eventide, in the deepening purple shadow of Nyeri Hill, he turned westward and started up the ridge. The mare was blowing, slowing. Leo's pain receded, setting his senses free. He heard the river's babble, saw sunlight sparkle on white mission walls, breathed the roasting-goatflesh scent of home. He heard again the lullaby she'd sung him and remembered the gentle, plump brown flesh that kept him from the cold. Don't die, he begged, when I have come so close.

He spurred across the last steep rise, into a sound that chilled his blood and stopped him in his tracks: the high, keen ululation of Kikuyu grief.

Perhaps the drums had spoken, perhaps the herdboys saw him, outlined against the pinkened sky. As he dismounted stiffly, the keening stopped. He led the mare down past empty huts, his body numb, his spirit bleeding. This time, no one cheered. This time, villagers stood in silent, sad-eyed lines that led him up beyond the Mission to the ancient, shady Meru Oak. There, alongside Laura's weathered cross, the mounded earth lay dark and raw. There, the dimness moved and hissed, taking on Mwangi's furious, stricken form.

'I stayed with her, I did her work and soothed her sickness; yet she died with your name on her lips! Is there nothing you won't steal from me?'

Then Duma came – a greyer, colder Duma – letting Leo see the teartracks on his haggard hunter's face. For the first time ever, he turned his back on Leo, and gently coaxed his younger son away.

Leo pressed his forehead to the grey mare's lathered flank, breathed heated horse and cold dead soil, and wept for the loss of loved ones still alive: he wept for both his mothers taken early to their rest.

Later, he took supper at the Mission. Lamplight stung his eyes. The food might have been ashes in his mouth. 'Kibe and Esther are spreading the Word along the ridges,' Father Andrew declared. 'They have become the messengers of God.' Beneath the pride, Leo sensed conflicts lurking, ill-concealed censure and deep wounds as yet unhealed. He mumbled something dutiful and pushed his plate aside. Grief and guilt oppressed him. Mwangi's charge had carried much uncomfortable truth.

He slept in his own room, under whitewashed walls, orange curtains, books of boyish derring-do. Poignant childhood memories ruled his dreams. He woke, and longed for Tara's warm smooth body, hungering for the living when he should only mourn the dead.

At sunrise, he climbed the forest edge through silvered dew and early birdsong, and gazed on the high grey mountain peak where Wanjui's spirit now dwelt. I will not forget you, he vowed. You who took me in and suckled me, gave me love and laughter, and deep Kikuyu roots.

You called my name; I have already answered, driven the Masai from this valley. Henceforth, smile down on greenness, peace and plenty.

His vision blurred. Duma's gaunt, accusing face took shape within his mind. Have I also lost a father?

Cloud shadow darkened Kerinyagga's brow. Kree the kite shrilled overhead, his rufous wings ablaze. Omens beckoned, waking his inner power, showing him hidden purpose in Wanjui's death: a chance to uncover his true parentage. Here it all began. I stand above the Mission where the mystery abides. I will go and outface priestly anger, unearth the man whose stigma I must bear.

'You must pray for Wanjui's soul, and seek forgiveness for your own transgressions.' Father Andrew blocked the chapel doorway. He was shorter now than Leo, stooped and silver-haired in drab green robes. But his voice still held a preacher's power and his grey-eyed glare still commanded respect.

'I have made peace with Wanjui's spirit,' Leo murmured. 'From which transgression must I be redeemed?'

'Don't wriggle, boy! These days, gossip travels fast. You came on a valuable horse. It bears a Spanish leather saddle, a blanket with "Tara" embroidered in gold thread.' Father Andrew's pale lips writhed in disgust. 'You were taken by the Governor at my request, recommended by the Bishop himself. How dare you flaunt carnality before good Christian folk!'

Leo struck back, spurred by injured pride and unhealed grief. 'What did you expect? You, who smothered me in godliness, who tried to beat the taint of sin away? You knew Morgan's crimes: you never told me!'

'He was a hunter and a vagabond. Even I do not call those crimes.'

'The naval record disagrees. He was accused of desertion, theft and assault.'

'I swear I did not know!'

'Why, then, have you hoarded Laura's papers all these years? If there is nothing to hide, give me the key!'

Father Andrew scowled and retreated into incense-smelling sanctuary behind. 'You're wrong, Leo. She, at least, was full of goodness. Let her rest in peace.'

Leo stepped forward, thrust out his hand. 'Must I wreck the Mission? Must I break down doors?'

Smooth cold metal dropped into his palm. The chapel door shut. Father Andrew's voice pursued him, strained and querulous. 'On your head be it. No good will come of this.'

Dust and cobwebs dimmed the inner chamber. The silks had lost their colours and felt brittle in his hands. But soon, through fading words on crumbling yellow pages, he met a vibrant woman whose love and pain had once burned bright.

He wondered at her early desolation, wondered what precious loss had caused such bitterness. He suffered with her through that first long-ago safari, fixing the names of her tormentors in his brain. The Hardy boys and James Seton: some day, somewhere, there would be a reckoning.

He read of Morgan's hunting skills, his calmness and his strength. There was nothing in her diaries about his naval background, no hint of cowardice. The doubt endures, thought Leo. The mystery may lie forever hidden in my blood.

Unless my deeds can somehow exorcise it.

Presently, he came upon a lyrical passage. 'Sometimes I only want to sit with him by starlight, touch his fine strong hand and see a loving future in his eyes. Land of our own, a house beside the river, our children playing in the bright sun.' Laura's dream, he thought, his vision misting. She lost it to a lion, and bore the Lion Boy. 'Sometimes,' she continued, 'I yearn for those hands at my breast, those same eyes hot with passion, that wondrous thick-veined hardness pleasuring my flesh.'

Does Tara yearn for me like this? Leo wondered. I must ask her, while I pleasure *her* flesh.

As erotic daydreams flowered in Leo's mind, Father Andrew burst in, his anger now turned to quivering excitement.

'News from Nairobi: you must go back at once. The Empire is at war with Germany!'

'I haven't finished, Father. No doubt the war will last another day without me.'

'Leo, Leo, don't you understand? Morgan's past is meaningless now.' Father Andrew stood among the cobwebs, his face flushed, his grey eyes pleading. 'The greatest honour any man can ask – to bear arms for his country and his God! In one brief hour on the battlefield, you can wipe out anything that may have gone before. Come to the chapel. Pray with me, for courage and safe passage!' There was something poignantly familiar in this posture, another echo out of bygone years: the awkward, clumsy, fatherly affection he had always found so hard to show. 'Come,' he urged, 'your horse awaits. Put that sad old book away.'

Obeying, so making things right once more, Leo glimpsed Laura's neat handwriting inside the flyleaf. 'Laura Howard, care of Priory Manor, near Lewes, Sussex, England.' Some day, he vowed, I will go there.

After the war.

He left an hour later, his fingers tingling from Father Andrew's handshake, and his 'Godspeed!' ringing in his ears. Wanjui's hut, he noticed, had already been burnt down, according to the custom. Ashes and a circular blackened scorch mark were all that remained of a place that he had loved so well. Duma and Mwangi, he was told, had gone side by side into the forest. Dying, Wanjui had achieved her life's ambition: she had brought together man and natural son.

It is fitting, Leo told himself. Why should it hurt me so?

Because, he realised far too late, Duma was more my father than any other man. And now I must leave, and go to war, without even saying goodbye.

Leo turned in the saddle, stared up the sleepy, smoky valley to the dark green trees, and willed two heartfelt words across the space between.

Thank you.

He camped on a wooded slope beside a swift clear stream some fifteen miles south. At nightfall, by low blue firelight, he tried to make sense of his fractured feelings.

He was restored to Father Andrew's grace, yet he had lost Wanjui, deepened Mwangi's loathing, forfeited Duma's valued trust. This time, he mused, Tara will have to comfort *me*. He slept, and dreamt of her pale, soft, pliant limbs.

He woke to eerie rustling, and chill bright stars and nameless dread. The fire flickered, low and fitful, casting grotesque shadows through the trees. The rustling came again, bringing his nape-hairs up; it was a sound no beast he knew could ever make. His mind was dulled with dreaming and he felt cowed by death. The hobbled mare stood ghostly at the corner of his vision. His rifle glinted in her saddle sheath. Fanged faces seemed to dance among the dark bushes, hyena sniggers seemed to hover in the grey mist above the stream. Gauging the distance across failing embers, he set himself to spring towards the gun.

Hard fingers trapped his shoulder, freezing him to the spot. 'Be calm, oh foolish warrior,' Duma said.

He moved into the ember-glow, letting Leo see the old affection shining in his eyes. 'Wanjui's ghost would haunt me if I let you go alone.'

18

'I HAVE NAE SEEN SUCH sport for years,' Eric Stuart grinned, watching his Fighting Horse Brigade lay siege to Lola's Funhouse. Bearded, bandoliered, wearing pistols in their belts, they unclothed Lola's lovelies where they stood and bore giggling, pinkly jiggling, very willing captives up the dim red stairs.

'Mother Nature's remedy for war-nerves,' Stuart said, 'I'll take one more wee dram while we're waiting.'

The fourth wee dram, actually. Hugo paid, wrinkling his nose at cheap Scotch and Scottish cheapness, trying to recall which day it was.

Patriotic white men had descended on Nairobi, carrying bizarre weapons, wearing feathers in their hats. Denied entry to the K.A.R., they mustered private armies like Stuart's Fighting Horse Brigade. By day, they did desultory drill; by night, they drank and fought among themselves. H.E. smiled his foxy smile and put Hugo in charge of Irregular Deployment.

For a week, Hugo ran ragged. Chaos ruled his working hours, rumour wrecked his leisure. Already this evening, a K.A.R. subaltern had roared up on a motor cycle, warned of an approaching German aircraft, and departed in a volley of back-fires and the whinnying tramp of Stuart's panicked horses. Making his way through bearded leers and bouncing, perfumed nipples, Hugo strove to make the danger clear. 'Take cover, dim the lamps!'

'Spoilsport,' Lola chided. 'The girls charge double when the lights are on!'

'There could be bombs,' growled Hugo. A passing trooper winked and stroked his lovely's gleaming rump. 'What a way to go!'

It might be sport for settlers, Hugo reflected; for officials, war is hell.

'They're bonny lads,' drawled Stuart, getting maudlin. 'They'll give the Hun a thrashing, before the campaign's through.'

'Indeed,' said Hugo drily, as the sound of thumps and female squawking filtered down. 'Provided they survive the fornication.'

The noises swelled, ominously familiar – meaty thwacks, falling bodies, a tuneful deep-voiced roar. Recognition jolted whisky into Hugo's windpipe. 'Dear God,' he gasped, 'it's Friday!'

He hurried to the hallway, through falling plaster dust and Lola's rising wail. 'Oh my gawd, he's gone berserk again!'

Flynn bestrode the stairhead, a massive hairy ape in wrinkled drawers. Bertha lolled behind him, her nude brown thighs akimbo, her hard brown breasts upcocked. And Stuart's Fighting Horse surged up towards her promised land.

Each time a trooper came in range, Flynn knocked him silly. Each time a victim staggered back, a sprawling mob of beards and buttocks tumbled down the stairs.

'Avast, me buckos!' Flynn would urge. 'Put on your breeches, give a man a foight!'

'Who is he?' Stuart breathed, at Hugo's elbow. 'Who is the bold Horatio?' At which point, the banisters collapsed, spewing white wood splinters out across the rug. Flynn pranced, victorious, his paws clasped overhead. Bertha pouted, lovelies cheered, Lola's bereaved howling reached new heights. 'Me chandeliers, mind me chandeliers!'

'You there,' bellowed Stuart, quelling the riot, setting the precious chandeliers ajingle, 'how d'ye like to fight the Hun?'

'Bless ye, sorr, where is he? I'll foight any man!'

'Stand to, then. Show a soldierly bearing.'

Flynn obeyed, his matted barrel chest outthrust, his fingers neatly aligned to the sideseams of his drawers.

'Sir?' called one of Stuart's younger members, from the open, darkened doorway. 'There's something you should know.'

'Silence! Can't ye recognise a solemn moment? Tenshun, the Fighting Horse. Prepare to meet your sergeant major!'

'That's what I mean,' the pimply trooper whined. 'There ain't no horses. That bleedin' motor cycle made 'em bolt!'

A lovely giggled. Flynn's belly sagged above the waistline of his drawers. The 'solemn moment' teetered towards farce.

'What the hell,' grinned Stuart. 'Welcome, Sarn't Major, to Stuart's Fighting *Foot*.'

'Disgraceful!' Elliot fumed, as Hugo opened the weekly war council with the story. Sitting crimson-cheeked between Hugo and Leo, the Colonel gave his outrage full rein. 'Breakin' up bordellos, tear-arsin' after non-existent aircraft; damnfool rabble ought to be disbanded!'

'The Germans use irregulars,' Leo pointed out. 'The Schutze-truppe depends on them.'

Elliot's lip writhed in scorn. 'Took German prisoners, lately, tryin' to blow the Tsavo bridge. Rescued 'em near Voi, half dead of thirst and thirty miles adrift.' His heavy palm thumped H.E.'s polished desk. '*That's* your famous Schutzetruppe! Missed the target, couldn't take the heat, couldn't even find their own way home!'

'Cocked it up, did they?' H.E. enquired, with the vulgar matiness Hugo so mistrusted.

'Got lost,' Elliot grunted. '*Amateurs!*'

'Not lost,' H.E. corrected, 'led astray. They were using an official British military map – inaccurate, fortunately. Clearly, they have breached our security. Go ye and do likewise.'

'You're talkin' cloak and dagger,' objected Elliot, 'dirty tricks behind the lines.'

'I'm speaking of intelligence – access to enemy intentions and de-ployment.'

Elliot rose abruptly to attention, glared above H.E.'s head and his own khaki image in dark veneer. 'I want no part of it. I'm a soldier, not a spy.' He paused in the doorway, pompous, portly, oddly dignified. 'Gentlemen do not make war this way!'

His heavy footfalls faded. H.E. picked up the threads as if there had been no interruption. 'The new Masai reserve straddles the border; it's a perfect area to gather information. We need chaps who know the people and their language.' He was gazing straight at Leo; he could scarcely have made his purpose plainer.

There was a long, expectant pause. From outside came the ever-present sounds of men at drill: shouted orders, jingling metal, marching boots. Presently, Leo sighed. 'I'd like to volunteer, sir.'

'Good man! I'll send word to the Masai laibon!'

'You misunderstand. I'd like to join the front-line troops.'

'Didn't you hear me, boy?' H.E.'s tone was dangerously quiet. 'Didn't you take my meaning?'

'I took the Colonel's meaning. I, too, have pressing reasons for a gentlemanly war.'

'I have better reasons to keep you here!'

'You refuse permission, sir?'

'I do.'

There was only a minute's shift in Leo's posture, only a brief, cold yellow flicker in his eyes: suddenly, there was a shade of Rumuruti in the sunlit office. The Governor didn't see or didn't care.

'Very well,' said Leo, pointedly polite. 'My resignation will be on your desk by noon. I have enjoyed working for you.'

The Governor's jaw sagged. 'Where the *hell* d'you think you're going?'

He stood poised in H.E.'s open doorway: golden-haired, broad-shouldered and full of warlike grace. 'I'm going to sign on with Stuart's Foot.'

The door closed. H.E. fixed Hugo with a brooding, ice-blue stare. 'Better go after him.'

'I doubt that I can change his mind.'

'Course not. To Stuart's Foot, I meant.'

'Join up? *Me*, sir?'

'*You*, sir. You convinced me of his value. Now you must go and keep an eye on him.'

'Do I have a choice?'

'Certainly. Volunteer, or take a white feather home to Pater.'

H.E. leaned back stroking his red whiskers complacently. This time, there was no gainsaying him. Leaving, Hugo hid a bitter smile, savouring the implied, back-handed compliment: H.E. thinks I can protect the Lion Boy. I must be making progress, he reflected. I would rather face the Schutzetruppe than confess to cowardice.

Remounted, Stuart led them south through steely scrub and stinging yellow dust. Noonday sunshine lit his tartan bonnet and glittered on the claymore at his waist. 'Some hoary kinsman blooded it on Sassenachs at Flodden,' he had claimed. 'Time to let the Junkers feel its bite.' Duma loped ahead and quartered the horizon, a bow and quiver bobbing on his lean brown back. Then came Hugo, in a trim white shirt and moleskin trews, high-strung as the roan polo-pony that bore him. Next came Flynn, a bulky serge blue sack on Stuart's mule. Sweat coursed down his stubbled jowls beneath his fawn felt terai. His tuneful tenor echoed; troopers grinned and trotted on and bellowed the refrain.

Hurrah, Hurrah, we're off to G.E.A.,
Hurrah, Hurrah, the squareheads we will slay.
So we sing this lusty song
Upon this dusty day
While we go marching to glory.

Leo brought up the rear, humming, nursing Tara's mare along and peering through yellowed haze at their distant shimmering objective.

Longido.

Longido Hill stood on German territory, ninety miles south of Nairobi, thirty miles north-west of Mount Kilimanjaro. Rising conical and steep-sided, it commanded vital, blistering plains between the border and the railway. There, said Colonel Elliot, General von Lettow had holed up with his Schutzetruppe.

'Naval blockade's workin',' Elliot growled, at the final briefing. 'German reinforcements can't land; one boatload of ours already here from Inja. Second due to disembark and chase the Hun from Tanga Port directly.' He waddled, khaki and self-important, to the map, set his monocle firmly, took a pointer and struck the tight-drawn parchment salutary blows. 'Injun Company C march down from Nairobi, approach Longido here.' Thwack. 'Injun Company B take Tanga, entrain north to Kilimanjaro, march on Longido from the opposite flank, here.' Thwack. His muddy, unglassed eye gleamed spitefully at Leo. 'Stuart's Horse will cut off the retreat here.' Thwack. 'Classic three-way pincer, gentlemen. Hello Longido, goodbye Schutzetruppe. Thank you and good huntin'.'

The bush ahead erupted, driving every picture out of Leo's mind. Orange muzzle flashes set the horses plunging. The mules laid back their ears and skittered sideways, the song stopped dead in mid verse. A second thunderous volley threatened total disarray. Beside him, Leo noted Berkeley's fearful, frozen gape. Someone shouted, 'Ambush, run for cover!' and every instinct urged him to obey. Then amidst black powder-smoke and rising panic, Leo watched a Christian gentleman make war.

Stuart wheeled his gelding, drew the claymore and trained it like a short, bright lance along the chestnut flank. 'Sound the charge!' he bellowed. 'Follow on!' And galloped out against the levelled guns.

Raw courage and a bugle blast lit fires in Leo's blood. One short familiar sentence urged him into Stuart's dust.

He shall not ride alone.

Hot wind flayed his face. Bullets snapped about him. He unsheathed his carbine, holding it like a club. A dozen bearded horsemen came whooping at his side.

Cordite-tainted smoke dispersed, revealing a score of kneeling men in khaki tunics: brown faces, wide eye-whites, an imperial German eagle glinting gold on khaki caps, the blue-grey gleam of Mauser rifles. They flinched beneath the flashing claymore, scattered from the chestnut's flailing hooves. 'They fear cold steel,' cried Stuart. 'Spread out and ride 'em down!'

Leo tried. The mare did her utmost. But the rifle was too cumbersome to wield one-handed, the scrub was too dense, the enemy too agile.

Recall sounded. Stuart sheathed the claymore, gave the tartan hat a rakish tilt. 'I've heard tell native troops are prone to fire high,' he drawled. 'Nice to see it proven.' In the middle distance, dust-palls marked the Schutzetruppe foot patrol in full retreat.

It was only a minor skirmish, Leo mused. We shed no blood and caused no losses. But we held firm under fire, ventured and survived. With one mad gallop, Stuart has raised the Fighting Horse Brigade's morale to the skies.

Duma alone voiced small misgivings, grim-faced in the declining heat. 'I saw strange birds,' he murmured. 'They flew like doves but showed unusual colours: white and iron-grey.'

'Tend your arrows,' Leo urged him. 'Make sure Kikuyu bees are fit to sting.' He can't escape the omens, Leo thought. He is uneasy in this white man's war.

They camped beyond Longido's steep black slope, beneath a stand of slender fever trees. Stars shone cool and silver; embers glowed dull pink; the night air smelled of gun-oil, smoke and cocoa. Cicadas hissed, the horses grazed and whickered. Somewhere in the dark someone played a mouth-organ, picking out the strains of 'Saudie Marie'. It was usually a marching tune, bellowed by Boers to bolster flagging spirits. Whoever played it now had something else in mind; played it high and haunting, slow and true, making it sweet and soft as any love-lilt.

Leo lay back on wiry grass, letting the music take him, letting his pictures form between thin feathered leaflets against the deep blue sky; letting them frame the image of his love.

On that last night, she wore a low-cut gown of creamy silk; she fed him fresh asparagus and venison by candlelight, toasting swift re-union in sparkling pink champagne. Afterwards she took his hand and made her parting gift. 'You must have the mare. Remember me when you are firm astride her. Daydream of our rhythms as you ride.' Gratitude and grief almost unmanned him. He bowed his head, barely able to breathe her name.

She came and nestled in his lap, laying one sweetly swelling breast against his cheek and beseeching him with swimming violet eyes. 'Tell me where you go and what you do, so my prayers may find you, and keep you from harm's way.'

So he told her of Stuart's Horse-cum-Foot, of mighty Flynn's recruitment, of Elliot's three-way pincer on Longido which would start and end the war. He told her lightly, guying Elliot's pomp and Stuart's accent, trying to drive the shadows from her face and dam the sorrow welling up inside him. Presently, she laughed, as he intended, feline and full-throated. Her mouth was moist and red and welcoming. She kissed him, lingering, hungering; she unclothed him and herself before the fire, quickened and aroused him to her need.

She had never burned so bright before him, never taken him so far within, never surged so long and strong beneath him. When at last their shared and shuddering violence broke, she seemed to melt around him, moaning, drawing him even deeper as if she could not bear the smallest space between. When the thunder in his own blood ceased to blind him, when pleasure's silken spasms set him free, he felt not merely in her but a living part of her.

Later, in musky languor, she shifted, turned him, settled softly across him, sighed and slept, content in his embrace. She was supple, spicy, pliant; tender, yielding, warm. For the first time in my life, he thought, I have found a home, and one person to whom I truly, totally belong.

Until the grey dawn broke and called him, shivering, from her side.

Scarcely awake, she stirred and stretched and mumbled. '*Mon Dieu*, make this war short, send my man back safe to me.' He stood there, cold and sad and yearning, gazed down on smooth-thighed, pink-tipped splendour still ablush with love.

The tune had long since faded, the fire had long since died. Night-wind swayed the thin acacia branches, blowing Tara's naked loveliness away. A horse neighed, a man coughed harshly. Half a mile westward, Longido's cone loomed against the starlight, silent and forbidding, still in German hands.

Until tomorrow.

Tomorrow will not be some outback tribal skirmish. We engage in open combat, bound by formal codes. Tomorrow I shall drive the Schutzetruppe from Longido, atone for Morgan's dereliction, become an English hero in a gentlemanly war.

And prove that I am worthy of a Countess.

Early sunlight settled on Longido, burnishing grey rock and umber grasses. Indian troops stormed the northern foothills, their royal-blue pennants fluttering, their turbans bobbing white. From the vortex of a growing yellow dustcloud to the south, Hugo saw a heliograph wink blurred belligerence. *'B company reporting. We'll beat you to the top!'* Stuart brought the Fighting Horse to station and line abreast in shadow beneath the eastern slopes. The morning smelt of fading dew and rising expectation.

The opening volley burst from dense green scrub below the crest. Thick black smoke rolled down, enveloping the assault. Bugles blared, the upward movement faltered. Harsh thin screams set Hugo's roan aquiver.

In half an hour, the Indians made no progress and were harried into cover around the slope, pinned where they lay by withering fusillades. The southern dustcloud dawdled. Stalemate ruled the hill. Then, from deep within the smoke-shrouded confusion, C company's heliograph began to flash. *'We are outflanked. Send horsemen to relieve us. Hold the southern incline until B group arrives.'*

Stuart set the tartan bonnet squarely on his head and urged the chestnut to a restrained trot. 'Those with horses, ride along with me,' he ordered. 'Muleteers bide here with Sergeant Major. Follow when we seize the higher ground.'

He led them up a rocky gully, through growing heat towards battlesounds. Leaving, Hugo caught a glimpse of Duma's downcast scowl and heard Flynn's disappointed bellow. 'Ye highland vandal, save the Hun for me!'

'My stomach quakes,' breathed Hugo, 'my throat is parched. Yesterday the bullets cowed me. Today I am afraid of only fear.'

175

'Ride with me,' urged Leo. 'Remember Rumuruti. You stood firm there. Now go forward and rejoice.' A warrior's aura surrounded him. He looked golden, cruel, inviolate. The Lion Boy, thought Hugo. Perhaps I am prepared to die for him.

The gully opened on to gently rising, sere brown grass; and the now familiar half-circle of kneeling, khaki-coated Schutzetruppe riflemen. Again, they fired early, high and wide. Again they broke and scattered under Stuart's scything blade.

The Boers roared out their warsong, lauded Saudie Marie, drove on like bearded dervishes through blinding, acrid smoke. Hugo let collective bloodlust take him, spurred to Leo's side and swooped up across a rocky outcrop on to even barer, flatter ground. At breakneck pace, he sensed a shift in balance, watched fleeing khaki figures go to earth and recognised the long low curve of man-made cover.

From a hidden nest among the sandbags, the Schutzetruppe laid machine-gun fire down.

Perhaps sheer speed deceived them; perhaps the glittering clay-more spoiled their aim. For a few brief, blazing seconds, the glory of the charge endured. Stuart's chestnut raging forward under bare, bright steel; Boers in bandoliers and awesome, tuneful voice; Leo, broad and upright in the saddle, noble as some ancient English knight. They thundered on, through upkicked yellow dust and humming bullets, undaunted, undeterred. And Hugo galloped with them, in savage, pounding joy. I was here, his inner voice exulted. No one can ever take this moment from me.

Then the German gunner found the range, and cut the Fighting Horse to shreds.

Leo heard the sickening whump of bullets striking flesh, saw the chestnut rear up, gashing scarlet, throwing Stuart to the dust. The Boers were tumbling right and left, their song reduced to moans of mortal pain. Horses stumbled, riderless into the murderous hail, white-eyed and squealing at the sudden reek of blood. And Hugo was suddenly missing from his side.

A dull red fighting haze took Leo's brain, shutting out the dead and dying, and launching him on a wide diagonal drive towards the sandbags. The mare felt strong and sinewy beneath him, her ears laid back, her grey mane whipping at his face. He'd never jumped before; she did it for him, bearing down in one swift stretch above the chattering gun. In that soaring, airborne instant, he gazed down on an open-mouthed *white* face, swung the rifle and felt the stock splinter against the machine-gun barrel. He gloried in abrupt, eerie silence. He sawed the reins, dragged the mare's head round, and hurled his shattered rifle at the gaping khaki hordes; then he veered left beyond the outer sandbags and headed down the hill.

The madness faded into desolation, leaving his senses numbed yet diamond-clear. He saw the hot wind ruffle beards on blank-eyed slack-jawed corpses, smelled the exposed entrails of a stricken horse he couldn't even shoot – and heard a rasping, pain-dulled Scottish whisper. 'By Christ, laddie, that was a bonny ride! I'll thank ye for a lift.'

Stuart huddled underneath a threadbare thornbush, his claymore still to hand, his left shin shot to bloody splinters. Ignoring sporadic rifle-fire behind, Leo hoisted the settler to the saddle, walked the mare back over the rise to the flimsy, baking shelter of the rock outcrop.

They gathered there, the wordless, stunned survivors: five troopers without mounts or comprehension; Duma and Flynn, who'd disobeyed orders too belatedly to join the charge; and Hugo Berkeley, pale and furious, mourning the slaughter of his gallant roan. Duma muttered plaintively about his ill-starred birds. Even Flynn seemed disinclined to venture out.

'The Fighting Foot,' growled Stuart, in a doomed attempt at humour. A burst of firing made him wince, as it whined viciously among the rocks. He gripped his wounded leg, bared his teeth and gave them brutal news. 'Lying there, I watched the southern group advance. Someone blundered. They're Germans, not Indians. Very soon, they'll take us from the rear.' He turned to Leo, gaunt with pain and urgency. 'Ye have to get us off this blasted hill!'

Deep in Leo's heart, a treasured dream lay bleeding. Elliot's noble war had lasted two short shimmering days, had ended here in ambush and deception. Now, white Christian gentlemen must bow and leave the stage. The Lion Boy must wake once more, invoke the charm, confound the foe and fashion the survival.

Somehow, he found the contemptuous words and a hectoring demeanour. Somehow, he goaded them to discipline and order. With Duma scouting out each meagre scrap of cover, with Flynn carrying Stuart's now unconscious, fevered body, with Hugo coaxing Tara's lathered mare along, they slunk like hunted jackals down Longido's sun-browned side. Twice, while Duma's arrows hissed above his head, Leo knelt in plain view and laid covering fire with a borrowed carbine while Hugo led the others boldly over open ground. Once, when a Schutzetruppe foot patrol surprised them in thick bush, he had taken Stuart's claymore, spurred the grey to one last lonely gallop, defied more flying bullets and carved a passage through. Each time, he killed coldly, without pleasure, hearing carefully chosen shots thump home, slicing at brown flesh with silver steel, letting the bright red blood drip down the blade and spatter on his breeches.

Until, as sunset glowed, and routed Indian soldiers came fleeing down the slope, he brought the Flying Foot back to the place they had started. There, while German victory songs inflamed the dusk above, half a dozen awestruck muleteers made game-meat stew, tended wounds and mumbled foolish questions. One by one, they came to gaze at Tara's mare and glance wonderingly at Leo's bloodied clothing. 'He's a hero,' someone whispered, 'he's bound to get a gong.'

Then Stuart, lying haggard but aware beside the fire, leaned up on his elbow and voiced a soldier's truth. 'He has nae a hope. No army offers medals to men who lead retreats.'

No one sang that night around the campfire. Apart from Stuart's whimpers and incessant insect hum, there was hardly a sound. Men withdrew to exhausted sleep or private mourning, blanket-shrouded islands in the sombre, deep blue night.

Words, not pictures, haunted Leo's mind: H.E.'s cold-eyed dictum on intelligence. *'We must know the enemy intentions and deployments.'* The Schutzetruppe had known more – precise details of the pincer movement, C group's recognition code, the timing of the Indian assault; had know early enough to intercept the southern column and organise a large-scale decoy unit. Who had told them? How had information been relayed? The plan had been revealed mere days ago, and only to a trusted few at Elliot's final briefing.

Elliot's final briefing.

Elliot's orders echoed in Leo's brain. 'Stuart's horse to cross the border, cut off the retreat here!' Orders delivered with a thwack of wood on paper, with a monocled glare that bespoke cunning vengeance. Had the Colonel known, even then, what Stuart would encounter? What Leo, whom he hated, would encounter?

Absurd, said a logical voice in Leo's head. Elliot is too senior and too stupid for such subtleties. Wait, the Lion Boy insisted. If I were choosing someone to spy on British soldiers, who better than the pompous, blimpish, tiger-hunting Colonel Elliot?

He saddled up, scribbled a note to Hugo, slipped off northwards into the sultry dark. He had travelled several miles, dozing, lulled by the grey mare's easy stride, before more pleasant memories stirred. *'Daydream to our rhythms as you ride.'*

Soon, I shall be with Tara again.

19

'COLONEL *ELLIOT*?' H.E. RUMBLED, from the shaded wing of the
Government House verandah. 'Never heard such tosh in all me life!'
For an hour, while Tara's lathered mare champed trim green lawns
below, he had tolerated Leo's tale of carnage and deception. Now he
rose and paced, and scowled his scorn. 'You're overwrought, pur-
suing a personal vendetta. Elliot, indeed. Face facts, boy!'

'Sir, I have considered nothing else!'

'Nonsense!' A whiskered profile against the fading day, H.E. took
a gentler tone. 'Fact is, we have obtained a list of Schutzetruppe
intelligence staff, including the officer in charge. His name is Gustav
von Hesselring.'

'He's not here!' Leo's protest erupted without thought or volition.
'He hasn't been near Nairobi for months!'

'Quite.' H.E.'s veiled blue gaze invited speculation. Leo dismissed
it angrily. 'He couldn't know Longido codes in time to lay the
ambush. We didn't know ourselves, three days before!'

'He's the spy, not Elliot. *Someone* must have told him.' H.E.
glanced down. Tara's mare whisked her tail, set flies abuzz against
the pale pink sky.

'Nice horse,' H.E. murmured. 'Faithful, is she, to both her master
and her mistress? Go away, Reid. Work it out yourself.'

No urchins cheered, no maidens blew him demure kisses. The
streets were solemn, shorn of soldiers, muted by defeat at Longido
and the coast. The mare's tired hoofbeats rang flatly from brown
walls. H.E.'s 'fact' appalled him. The 'mistress' innuendo woke
unwelcome pictures in his mind.

Tara, glorious in gentian blue, intent on Elliot's drink-flushed face across the candlelight. That night, the Colonel laid the K.A.R.'s cupboard bare and told her the railway was unguarded.

Tara, pouting prettily in sheer flesh-tinted silk, watching Leo's silver fork inscribe the crucial zone, learning the strategic role of Tsavo Bridge.

Lastly, very lately: Tara, nestled in his lap, her breast soft and scented at his cheek. *'Tell me where you go and what you do.'* And his own unguarded answers, giving details of the pincer on the hill.

Face facts, boy. Tara knew.

It doesn't matter, a stubborn inner voice maintained. No one could inform the Count so swiftly. He plodded on, his spirit bowed, his certainties dissolving.

Blue gums whispered, either side of Ngong road. Frogs churred, mosquitoes whined, a borer bee droned past. Doves clattered overhead, circled, went to roost. Sunset burnished slate-grey wings and snowy coverts. Too big for doves, Leo realised, their plumage is too bright. And he remembered Duma's vision of ill omen. *'They flew like doves but showed unusual colours.'*

Suddenly, sickeningly, Leo saw how it was done, saw secrets fly like feathered arrows south across the land. Daybreak on Longido, evening at Ngong, time and distance conquered by these self-same birds. Pigeons, not doves.

Count Gustav's homing pigeons.

The mare was pulling, spurred by well-known scents. Leo jounced in the saddle, relived that blazing charge, and heard again the soggy thump of bullets driving home. I'm back, Tara, with ghosts at my shoulder and dread in my heart. Only you can heal me, only you can break this bitter logic.

Tell me it isn't true!

He swung into the driveway, through bougainvillaea arches and a whiff of rambling rose. The pigeon loft was empty, the unhinged door hung creaking in the breeze. Some birds have flown, thought Leo. Who and what remains?

The mare halted, bridling at the quietness ahead. Usually, yellow lamplight glowed on greensward, welcoming whickers issued from the yard. Tonight the buildings loomed in deepening shadow: silent, unlit, seemingly deserted. He dismounted, freed the skittish mare, and used Tara's key to enter the brooding dimness.

He trod the thick-pile carpet to her boudoir, saw opened drawers and scattered clothing, and sensed violation on the sultry air. Her lavender perfume lingered, overlain by stale tobacco smoke. The Count has been here, Leo realised. *It's happening again.* He waited, tense with foreboding. Moonlight scaled the window, crept across the room, probed tumbled, rumpled bedclothes in the furthest corner and blazed whitely on an object that protruded from beneath.

A woman's upcurled, outflung hand.

His flesh crawled, his stomach heaved, a tightness took his chest. Horror numbed his feelings, cold reason tolled his guilt. Of course the Count would come here, to burn the papers, free the birds, and silence an unfaithful wife. Again, you have provoked a jealous man; again the one you love has paid the price.

Forgive me, Tara. I could not keep you from the dark.

He stumbled forward, steeled himself for butchered beauty, bent and eased the cool slick silk aside; and wondered at the force of self-deception.

Touched Tara's white, discarded glove in awe and disbelief.

Even as his heart rejoiced, his mind contrived fresh doubts. She lives, and yet has gone with him; was she, after all, his willing helper? Then, from clouded depths within, a bitter insight gleamed.

I would rather mourn her death than suffer her betrayal.

Anger and disgust possessed him. He read the signs of urgent, joint departure, shrank from the bed where he had known such joy. Did they plan it all together? Had she lain with him tonight? Were they laughing as they stole away?

The darkness seemed to rock with laughter round him. Curtains swayed and sniggered, rafters groaned in mirth, nightwind sneered beneath the timbered eaves. 'You're overwrought,' H.E. had snapped rightly, as Leo named the Colonel. Were these charges also mere figments of a greater loss?

Then, as he strove to master rogue emotions, he heard a board creak and a distinct, stealthy footfall.

He moved as Duma had taught him in the forest and went noiselessly through shadowed rooms that once held light and warmth.

The kitchen door stood open, the curtain hung askew. The moon struck scattered rice grains and painted broad white flour splashes on dull, polished boards. There was malice in the chequered shade, an angry alien shimmer in the air. His senses quickened, raised his hackles and set a copper taste upon his tongue. He entered, poised and craning.

The door eased to behind him. He whirled, into a cowering figure with flickering eye-whites and levelled silver steel. Long-pent rage welled up within him. He grabbed the knife hand, forged a wrestler's lock against the joint, smashed his attacker bodily to the moonlit wall. And stared into the gibbering face of Tara's Kikuyu servant. 'Have mercy, Lion Boy! I thought you were the Count come back to beat me!'

A household candle lit the fresh-swept kitchen – gleaming boards, a glowing stove, a plain wooden table. Leo perched on an upright chair, letting hot sweet tea restore him, pressing Tara's servant for the truth. 'I meant no harm, bwana. I only wanted flour and rice.'

He hunched at the table, his yellow robe torn and stained, his brown hands still trembling around the white enamel mug. 'Is that why the Count beat you?' Leo demanded. 'For stealing food?'

'He beat me when tea spilled, when the fire smoked, for singing at my work.'

'Why, then, did you stay?'

'The mistress was kind, and paid well. I need money for goats, to go back home . . .'

Leo cut this familiar story brusquely short. 'When did the Count come back?'

'Sometimes at night, after you had gone. He beat her then, I heard the blows and cries. I couldn't stop it, bwana! He is fierce and strong, like you!'

Leo uncurled his fists, curbed his fury; settled in his seat. '*Not* like me. When did they leave?'

'Two days past, at sunrise. He came like a great wind, roaring and laughing. She struggled in his arms. He threw her on a horse and made her go.'

She is innocent, Leo thought, in weary relief; swiftly tempered by a searing sense of loss. He has taken her far behind the lines; perhaps for ever beyond reach. 'Take your rice and flour,' he growled. 'Go home and tend your goats. Tell no one what happened here tonight.'

The servant moved so fast that the candle guttered. 'Ngai reward you, bwana. May fortune travel with the Lion Boy.'

'How do you know?' Leo asked. 'Who told you my name?'

'I am Kikuyu. Everybody knows . . .'

He couldn't bring himself to leave, could not yet relinquish claim to her. He carried the candle to her boudoir, sank down on the unmade, perfumed bed, struggled for some semblance of composure. Questions coiled around him in the ghostly yellow light. How often did the Count lurk and leer while we made love? When did she discover he was a German spy? How had she been forced to spy for him?

Easily, said a bitter voice in Leo's mind. The Count would lay a strangled pigeon on Tara's breakfast plate and watch the terror bleed her face bone-white. He would step behind her, encircling her slender throat in huge, hooked hands. His scar would twitch, his voice would be as soft as morning breeze. 'See, *leibling*, how it goes with losers. Be kind to Mr Reid, who works for the Governor and knows all English secrets. Tell me the sweet nothings he whispers in your ear. Then you can be a winner, and fly free.'

It is as it was with Linde and Simel, he realised. Once again, a cruel cold man denies me. But Tara lives and the war provides a reason for her pursuit. I will go back, revive the Fighting Horse, endure Elliot's incompetence, and hound the Schutzetruppe until I find some trace of her.

Somewhere, somehow, my pretty bird shall fly free.

They sent Stuart northwards in an unsprung ox-cart, a whimpering, sweat-soaked ghost whose leg already reeked of gangrene. Coetze followed, mourning Boer losses and British foolishness. Flynn was called away to mend the damaged railway. Within five days, the Fighting Horse had ceased to be.

Then Leo returned.

He came tight-lipped to Hugo's fireside, while the nearby K.A.R. detatchment lay low and licked its wounds. There, in flickering ember-glow and the smell of roasting buck, he told his story and confirmed his vow.

'We'll scout for Elliot,' he declared. 'Duma and I have been hungry in the bush before.' And, seeing the apprehension Hugo couldn't quite conceal, he added, 'Go back to Nairobi, Hugo. It isn't your fight any more.'

But later, as stars rose and Leo slept exhausted beside his tribal father, memories and conscience stole Hugo's sleep. He remembered Rumuruti, and the glory of the doomed Longido charge. He felt the strength and resolution deep inside him, he knew fear would never unman him again.

And knew he owed his courage to Leo.

He remembered the suppressed anger in Leo's voice, the fearless, frightening yellow fire in his eyes. And knew Duma could not temper it with prudence.

Someone will have to go with them, he thought, someone whose mind is not devoured by passion, someone who can curb their recklessness.

It might as well be me.

20

Duma crouched on parched brown soil a hundred miles behind the lines. Parting steely thornstrands, he squinted down on green acacia trees, a sluggish stream and an isolated German fort. Its high white walls were jagged, like a mouth with missing teeth. Through the gaps, he glimpsed uniforms and a glitter of gunmetal. There were thirty men inside, he knew, more than twice the strength of Leo's patrol. But they were planners, not front-line troops, unaware they stood between the Lion Boy and what he wanted most.

The heat-haze blurred. A go-away bird hooted. Dust eddies tickled Duma's nose. Waiting, he let his mind slip back across the two-year hunt that was about to end here.

They formed the patrol in the bitterness of defeat at Longido Hill – Leo, Duma, a handful of trusted warriors, and Berkeley. He comes to test his new-found boldness, Duma thought. He will not endure long.

But on the very first sortie, Berkeley had proved him wrong.

They had stumbled on a large Schutzetruppe detatchment, laid an ambush and slipped away into the night. One of the tribesmen was wounded; Leo would not leave him. Slowed by clinging scrub and the sick man's pain, their canteens almost empty, they'd fled through starlit darkness to the sound and scent of ever nearer pursuit.

Duma found a waterhole at daybreak, where a small herd of impala milled and drank.

'Kill them,' Berkeley whispered, at his elbow; and Duma looked enquiringly at Leo.

'There is no time,' he said, 'we don't need meat.'

'Do it,' Leo snapped.

Duma sent three arrows hissing across the still, chill air. Three red-flanked buck kicked weakly and died. 'Fill your canteens,' Berkeley ordered. As the tribesmen obeyed, Berkeley sealed the arrow wounds with dust, laid the carcasses along the water's edge. Then he cut white wood flashes from dusty, stunted thorn trees, and drew 'Poison' signs in charcoal. When Leo led the rest away, Berkeley lay at Duma's side in growing heat and gathering fly-hum, and watched the Schutzetruppe come.

They came three hours later, their uniforms stained by dust and gunsmoke, their eyes lighting up at the sight of water.

Then as the native troopers surged across the mud, their white officer barked a warning. Duma saw his broad, sun-baked face crease in disgust, saw him kick the poison sign in anger, watched him call his men away from perfectly good water; and give up the chase.

Beside him, Berkeley smiled in quiet satisfaction.

After that, they hunted only at night, dodging lions they dared not shoot for fear of noise, eating sun-dried meat they dared not cook lest the flame betray them. Always outnumbered and outgunned, they relied on sudden action, fast retreat – and one another. Duma's arrows slew men and beasts in silence. Leo's courage won them many a rearguard action. Berkeley's cunning kept them clear of Schutzetruppe ambush. Soon, the bonds between them went far beyond mere friendship. They fought and trekked and thirsted as one.

And once, cut off by a sudden shift in battle, their canteens bumping hollow against their sweat-sheened chests, they had been forced to drink each other's strained urine. Duma had watched Berkeley's handsome, narrow face contort, watched him close his eyes and swallow – and ask for more.

Then he knew that the once-pale office boy had become a fighting man.

But no matter how far they ranged, they had found no trace of Leo's woman.

And no matter how hard the scouting units worked, fat, red-faced Elliot continued to lose the war. He is like a Masai chief, Duma often thought. He wants great battles on the burnt, brown plains. The Schutzetruppers are more like the Kikuyu. They snipe and harry, and slip into the night. When Elliot's heavy-footed troopers follow, they stagger into ambush and heavy losses. Doesn't he know the Masai were beaten by a Kikuyu Lion Boy?

'That's his problem,' Leo snapped, prowling base camp after a furious argument with Elliot. 'Rest a while; then we must go out again.'

The woman has become a madness in him, Duma thought. She rules his waking hours, he calls her name in dreams. Even here, while Berkeley drinks and lies with willing harlots as any soldier should, Leo reads despatches, searches paper for the evil Count who took the brightness from his life.

At base camp, Leo questioned prisoners – another thing that puzzled Duma sorely. Elliot treated Germans like brothers, not enemies – he gave them food and wine and shelter, salutes and courtesy. He could see they wouldn't answer Leo, and watched them shrug and smile and turn away.

'Beat them,' Duma urged, when Leo came back long-faced and defeated. 'Make them tell the truth!'

'It is not our custom,' Berkeley told him, in precise Swahili. 'It is forbidden by our law.'

But not by mine, thought Duma.

He had to wait until the rains had come and gone; until, on yet another searing, far-flung patrol, they came unseen within gunshot of a larger Schutzetruppe force. Then, at white-hot noon, while Leo and Berkeley dozed beneath hanging orange rock, Duma slipped silently away.

He found what he sought on damper ground, pale pink flowers nodding to the breeze. The roots were plump and fibrous. He pressed them between two pebbles and stiffened the yellow sap with soil and ash. Turning his head from the bitter reek, he placed a tiny pinch of paste at his left wrist; then he drew the simi and opened a cut on his forearm. Blood welled down and touched the paste. Purple stained the scarlet, leaping up towards the wound. He wiped it away quickly. The mixture was too potent. He added more soil, tested once more. The purple stain climbed slowly. He smeared the paste along the simi blade and watched it thicken and dry; he sheathed the tainted weapon and went cautiously towards the enemy camp. Presently, he came upon a broad red path, leading away from the tents. He knelt, sifting dust through his fingers.

The man had passed earlier, free-striding and light-footed: a soldier from this gathering, moving into the bush. Sooner or later, he would return.

The sun inched westwards, the shadows slanted east. Birds fell silent, even cicadas ceased to hum. Footfalls approached. Duma rose and stepped into the path. The Schutztruppe native askari was tall, straight-nosed and thin-lipped; he wore khaki shorts and an arrogant scowl. He checked in midstride, his long spear poised and glinting. Cool, upslanted eyes weighed up Duma, then narrowed in contempt.

'You are not a soldier. Remove yourself from my sight!'

Duma spat and said nothing. The spear rose, the throwing arm quivered. 'Be warned, short one! Step side, let this warrior pass!'

'I see no warrior,' Duma taunted, 'cast your useless plaything, herdboy!' He used the word 'uncircumcised', saw the insult bite, hurled himself forward and under the singing spearflight. Rolling, thrusting upwards, he saw the doctored simi slice deep into ochred flank.

The askari swayed, touching the wound in wonder. 'So,' he hissed, 'the jackal knows our tongue and drinks a soldier's blood.' He drew a stabbing spear from its sheath along his calf. 'Prepare to die, jackal!'

The first lunge was swift and savage. Duma barely evaded it. The second faltered, wide and slow. The askari stumbled, sank to his knees. The stabbing spear slid from his grasp.

Duma knelt and opened his canteen. The poison melted muscles, he knew, leaving the brain clear. It also made men crave water.

The askari slumped, his gaze blank and unbelieving. Duma squatted beside him, tilting the canteen, watching silvered droplets star the dust. 'You are dying, warrior,' he said, 'bested by the jackal in fair combat. Answer me, and I will ease your passing.'

The upturned eyes blazed defiance. 'I am poisoned. This is not fair combat!'

'You threw. You had the first chance, and the last.' Duma shook the canteen, made the water gurgle. 'Will you die like a sulky girl?'

'I am a soldier.' The hoarse whisper throbbed with pride. 'Ease my thirst and I will speak.'

'Answer!' Duma hissed. 'Answers first, water later.' He let the canteen trickle, saw yearning in the slack, stricken face.

'What is your question, jackal?'

'There is a noble white man in your command. He guides your efforts, tells you when to strike. And keeps a dark-haired woman at his side. Where does he stay?'

'A strange strong man, for whom the birds bring messages. He stays at the fort: Kondoa Irangi, far to the south-west . . .'

Duma leaned closer, demanding facts and figures, printing hard-won truths into his brain. The voice dwindled, the lean chest fluttered. Duma issued water, stood up and prepared to leave. The askari shuddered, made a final plea. 'Give me a warrior's death!'

And this law, Duma understood.

He struck hard and true, felt the simi bite, watched the dark eyes glaze and empty; he wiped the blade and loped away, smiling – picturing Leo's face when he heard the news.

Leo's face loomed above him through the haze, his yellow eyes alight with expectation. 'All is ready, Father. I will watch till nightfall, till the attack begins!' Duma nodded, and sidled over the sandy rise to where Berkeley and the patrol lay in wait. I have done a father's duty, he thought. I have found the hiding place, led them here across the blazing desert. Now the Lion Boy can set his woman free.

The sun waned coppery, towards low western hills. The fort gates creaked ajar. Half a dozen white men strolled towards the shaded stream. They wore weathered khaki fatigues: hatless, young, athletic men, some fair, some dark, one mousey. No one was hunched or domed. There was no sign of the Count. Leo saw them pause and turn, sensing, even at this distance, their collective admiration.

A single, slighter figure came through the shadowed arch, with sleek dark hair, a sea-green skirt, an easy, lilting stride. Leo adjusted his fieldglasses with eager, trembling hands. Against the background glitter of slow water, Tara's face formed sharp and clear.

With her full red lips, deep violet eyes, she had a beauty that made his pulses race and woke urgent tingles at his groin.

Which faded even as his hunger grew. This was no unwilling captive. This was a free and vibrant woman, smiling as she used to smile for him.

Stunned, he watched the group diverge, and saw her move towards the tall blond man who stood alone beside the stream. There was bold intelligence in his Aryan profile, unashamed desire in his pale blue eyes. She spoke softly to him, her body language subtle but alluring.

And suddenly, Leo understood.

The Count was dead, a victim of the war. Released from bondage,

Tara sought the only comfort she could find – from someone who reminded her of Leo.

He set the glasses down, measuring the distance between the couple and the group, feeling power coil inside him. Wait, my love, he breathed. You no longer need a substitute.

He ghosted down the hillside like a leopard on the prowl, using every scrap of cover until he crouched beneath green acacia fronds mere yards from where she stood. He breathed her lavender perfume; he saw the tall, broad silhouette reach for her; he heard her teasing, unconvincing protest. 'You mustn't – not here, not now.'

'Not now,' Leo growled, 'not ever!' And launched himself across dappled shade. Briefly, he met vigorous resistance, sensing a tough, unyielding spirit ranged against him. But the German had no warning and no wrestling skill; and Leo was fighting for his love.

It was over in one swift, savage wrist-and-shoulder throw: the German somersaulted into risen dust, the breath forced from him in one painful, gusty whoosh. Bending, reaching for the unprotected throat, Leo heard a sharp, metallic click. Glancing up, he saw sunset touch grey gunmetal – the pistol Tara always carried. 'Don't shoot,' he hissed, 'the noise will betray us. Go up the hill, where men and horses wait. I will kill him silently, and follow!'

'Let him be, you stupid, *stupid* boy!'

Leo straightened slowly, unbelieving, and looked into ice-cold violet eyes and loveliness drawn pale and taut with anger.

'Are you still unwitting, Leo? Have you not grasped why the pigeons flew and what messages they bore?'

It is guilt that haunts her, Leo realised in relief. She thinks I have come to take revenge. 'Don't torture yourself, Tara,' he soothed. 'I know you were forced to treachery.'

Her red lips parted in a peal of mocking laughter. White tendons rippled at her throat. The gun muzzle aimed, unwavering, at Leo's chest. 'Treachery? I am German. It was my idea!'

The blond man scrambled to his feet, grinning in pained triumph. Leo set himself to strike again. Tara thrust the pistol forward. 'Stand to attention, boy, close your foolish mouth! You are in the presence of nobility. Allow me to present my husband – Count Gustav von Hesselring!'

'Go home, my secret little source,' the Count advised, in perfect English. 'There is nothing for you here. Pass my compliments to those who gave you trust.'

No need for pistols now. Leo stood incapable of thought or action, facing the enormity of his own folly. The Count slipped his arm round Tara's shoulders, and led her, laughing, back towards the fort.

In Leo's stricken mind, the last illusion crumbled. *This* was the man she'd pined for, love-flushed, naked, only half aware. '*Send him back safe to me,*' she had pleaded, as he, Leo, left for the battlefields. Her frightened servant had told an exact truth. '*The Count is tall and strong – like you!*'

She used her body to command my brain, enslave my feelings, corrupt the precious gift of pictures. That is why I couldn't see her husband clearly. There never was a scar-faced pigeon-strangler, only a cunning woman and a blind, besotted boy.

A boy who betrayed the secrets of Longido, and led the Fighting Horse into a German trap.

Madness took him then, redder than the rage that ruled Longido, blacker than the fury which had broken Simel's neck. He reared up, with vengeance in his heart and an incoherent war-howl on his lips.

He ran as only the Lion Boy could run, towards the couple who had dishonoured him, across the cooling, rattling scree, between the clutching thorns. Ran on while the white men shouted warnings and scuttled to the fort; ran on while orange powder flashes blossomed on white walls; ran on until the first fierce blow broke his stride and the second spun him round in spraying scarlet, smashing him flat upon the harsh earth. He lay there watching the sky turn black, smelling peppery dust, hearing his life-blood drip and gurgle.

As sense and feeling dwindled, he thought he saw a crippled lion tense and crouch and spring.

As Duma heard him howl and saw him fall, he felt as if the bullets had pierced his own flesh. The pain was deep and deadly, holding him bowed and rigid beneath the cooling sun. He was dimly aware of the tribesmen's awed whispers, their air of hopelessness; of Berkeley's bone-white stare and urgent whisper. 'We must bring him in: who goes with me?' Dark, dull silence. 'Then I will go alone!'

He went out into twilight beneath the bristling fort, ignoring the muzzle flashes and the bullets which whined and kicked up dust around him. Presently, perhaps in honour of his courage, the shooting stopped. Duma's own numbed courage woke. He goaded the tribesmen out to help. Tenderly, tearfully, they eased Leo's bleeding, barely breathing body on to a wooden litter. Berkeley ripped up his own shirt, plugged two ragged bullet holes high in Leo's breast, and led the bitter, beaten retreat.

They marched all night, taking turns to bear the litter, ignoring the cold, keeping pace with Berkeley's horse. No one spoke. Leo's still, empty face gleamed chalky in the moonlight. His laboured breathing sounded louder than the clop of hooves. Duma held his limp hand and beseeched Ngai's blessing every step of the way.

At dawn and base camp, white officers and native troopers stood around the medical tent, joined in awe and sorrow. 'He mustn't die,' Duma heard a young Kikuyu warrior whisper. 'He is the Lion Boy.'

Then the army doctor came out, mopping sweat from his brow. 'Nairobi,' he snapped. 'At once.'

Berkeley commandeered the Colonel's staff car. He did it with a cold force that left Elliot gaping like some red-faced, one-eyed fish. The engine clattered fiercely, the springs lurched and creaked, the hot air inside reeked of petrol. Duma scarcely noticed, bracing Leo's limpness against the worst jolts, moistening his pale lips with cold water.

Be strong my son, he pleaded.

He waited in the shade outside the hospital, squatting like a beggar against the warm red wall, begging every god he knew for mercy. Much later, Berkeley came out alone, bloodshot, staggering with weariness. 'He must go to England, where there may be skills to save him. If he lasts the journey, there is hope.' His face softened. 'Go home, Duma. For you this thing is finished.'

Not quite, Duma thought. There is one more thing I can do.

He shook Berkeley's offered hand warmly, letting respect and affection show. 'I think it is over for you, too.'

'Not for me. I am going back to war.'

Duma walked. He walked for three days and nights, eating little, sleeping less. He walked straight to Kerinyagga, through the sleeping village, past the dim pale Mission up to Njau's knoll. When grey dawn broke, he woke the Healer and asked his single, urgent question. 'Can Leo live, now Germans have stolen his great power?'

Njau coughed. He touched the leather pouch around his neck, making the unseen bones rattle. 'How many times must I tell you? The Lion Boy cannot be killed by bullets, or by man. You should pray for Mwangi, whose spirit I still cannot make clean for healing.'

But Mwangi's eyes held only scorn and envy. I have but one son, Duma thought.

So, every morning, Duma prayed to Ngai on the shining, white-topped mountain. Every evening, he climbed the sloping pasture, watched the sky grow pink, and gazed southwards down the red road to Nairobi.

From whence, one day, the Lion Boy would come.

Late in 1918, pursued by superior British forces, the Schutzetruppe retreated into Portuguese East Africa. They surrendered, undefeated, when the European Front collapsed. Tara and the Count were stripped of their possessions and forbidden entry to German East, which became British Mandated Territory. Strange, mused Hugo, hearing this, that even in defeat, the Lion Boy is triumphant. His own war ended, Hugo received an honourable discharge and a campaign medal.

Back in Nairobi, he heard that Leo had come through two operations, and was convalescing somewhere in the southern shires.

One evening at the billet, Hugo lounged on the verandah and eyed his medal pensively: a bronze, beribboned token to successful soldiering, allowing him to face Pater and his brothers on equal terms.

Now I can claim my rightful place among the family, he thought. Now I can go home.

The sky was turning purple. Stars gleamed along the lumpy ridge of the Ngong Hills. Kites wheeled in the dimness, catching insects on the wing. The air smelled of peppery dust and frangipani. It was very quiet at the billet, without Leo.

And very beautiful.

Sipping whisky, fanning mosquitoes away, Hugo fell to memories and dusk-dreams. Rowdy nights at Lola's; the clash of wit and will with H.E.; the day his courage stirred before ochred Masai moran at Rumuruti; the pleasures of the polo-field; the bright, brief glory of Longido's charge; Flynn's forbidding fury and unlikely tenderness; Duma's faithfulness through so many harsh patrols; the Last Post, heard too often for too many fallen comrades; the slant of sun on Mount Kenya's snowy peak.

I have made my life here, he thought. In fighting for this land, I've learned to love it.

My oath, I am already home!

*

Leo drifted on a pain-tossed sea that had neither shoreline nor horizon. For a while there had been real sea: swashing movement, gull-mew and salt-sharp air. Later came a jolting journey along a pale, dim tunnel, a room that smelt of death and disinfectant. Grey-gowned figures gathered round him, probed his wounds and wagged their heads. Clammy rubber sealed his mouth. The sickly reek of ether took him down.

Awareness returned, with a smaller pain: a sense that, given time, his fleshly hurts would heal. But the unseen wounds had cut much deeper. Grief and guilt laid siege to his soul. Longido ghosts re-proached him: brave men he had betrayed. Tara's wanton image rose to taunt him, and bitter memories of Morgan's crime. So, when the image of the crippled lion that had killed his parents came to stalk him, he was ready to surrender. Take me, he invited. I am no longer worthy of my name.

Then voices from the living world stole in.

'Still here, Rebecca? You should have been off duty hours ago.'

'It's all right. I'm not tired.'

'Come away, dear. Can't you see he's dying?'

'Not if I can help it!'

He heard the door click shut. Starched clothing rustled at his side. Warm fingers rested on his unwounded shoulder. 'You're supposed to be a soldier. For God's sake *fight*!'

He glimpsed wide grey eyes, a generous mouth, unruly ash-blonde hair. A face he'd never seen before, yet which seemed hauntingly familiar: a face which woke his gift of pictures. Suddenly, he was back in the lamplit Mission storeroom, touching faded feminine silks, reading of an ill-starred love from yellowed diary pages.

Who is she? he wondered; why does her nearness soothe me so?

Her name seemed to echo in his waking dream. Without good reason or the smallest doubt, he knew that she could help to solve the riddle of his past. A spark of courage kindled, fanned by the mystery she inspired. Presently, his drugged mind found some answers.

Her vibrant tenderness reminds me of Linde. Her loveliness drives Tara from my mind. And, like Laura Howard, she shields me in the moment of my dying, and makes the crippled lion turn away. In her, there is a part of every woman I have loved.

I *will* fight, he decided. I will conquer pain and guilt, recover strength and purpose and search England for the truth about my mother. And about Rebecca: someone who might be worth *living* for . . .

But by the time the pain released him, Rebecca had disappeared.

'There's a war on,' the harassed, bloodshot hospital administrator snapped. 'We don't keep records of voluntary staff.'

'Sussex, I think,' a plump, blue-cloaked Sister said. 'Somewhere near the sea. Isn't it awful? I don't even know her surname!'

Even so, another piece of the puzzle fell into place. Sussex, Leo mused, where Laura Howard lived when she was young. The search must start somewhere near the sea.

BOOK III

REBECCA

1919–1929

21

GLORIOUS JUNE, IN 1919. The whump of tennis balls on tight-strung catgut, a heady scent of strawberries and wine. Swallows darted underneath the oak-boughs, velvety brown bees prowled pink rose petals. While midday sunshine warmed her naked shoulders, striking heavy through her ankle-length blue cotton dress, Rebecca played hostess to gilded youth. And longed for evening, when they would be gone.

His appearance caused the tennis girls to preen and flutter. He stood half a head taller than the other men, wearing a travel-stained white shirt and khaki battledress slacks. An unkempt tawny mane obscured his features. He looked weary yet exotic, out of time and place.

Another of James's lame ducks, Rebecca concluded, and kept a prudent distance. He had that wounded, questing air: of a man seeking something he knew might be for ever beyond reach. She saw him speak to James, saw her brother flinch as if he had been struck.

She drifted closer, mildly curious. The stranger saw her, stiffened, cut James dead, came prowling across the daisy-speckled lawn towards her. Briefly, his size and speed alarmed her, conveying a sense of power tightly reined, of looming feline grace. Then he smiled at her, like sunrise on golden Sussex corn.

There was a sudden catch in her throat, a tremor in her pulse as if she knew him from some bolder life long, long ago. Somewhere in her mind, a mirror began to crack.

'Rebecca,' he whispered. 'I thought you were lost!'

She was not in the least surprised he knew her name, not in the least disturbed by the familiarity. She felt an answering smile on her own lips, an inner joy she hadn't known since she was ten years old.

'You should have coal-black hair,' she said, 'a mighty warhorse and a silver bugle.'

'Then you, milady, ought to pine before enchanted glass.'

He knew the poem, of course he did, just as she knew so many things about him – saw them shimmer in his bold bronzed face. He had been hurt in soul and body, ill-used by love and war. Now, like her, he faltered on the threshold of redemption.

'We are cousins,' he announced, 'though I did not expect to find you here. I came looking for your aunt, who was my mother.'

'She died when I was very young. I know nothing of her.' She met his admiring glance levelly. 'You'll have to settle for me.'

'Are you always so forward, milady?'

'I prefer to say – honest.'

'Don't ever lie to me, Rebecca!' The pain was sudden upon him again, a yellow flicker deep within his eyes. She remembered the last white lie she'd told, the scarlet letters screaming from a sick-room wall – and gave him only truths.

'I am twenty-six years old, and have never pleased a man.'

'Then please one now: walk with me.'

'There is work to do here,' she protested, conscious of the gawping watchers. 'I cannot leave the others.'

His warming smile returned, installing her at the centre of his world. 'What others?'

They moved beneath the sheltering oaks, away from prurient stares and wagging tongues.

'How did you know me?' she demanded.

He named the hospital, gave the dates. 'You held my hand and kept my ghosts at bay. You made me want to live, when I was dying.'

'I don't remember you,' she murmured, shivering in the summer shade. 'If it wasn't for Aunt Laura, we might not have met again.' He smiled; he had a scarred yet boyish beauty that made her senses swim. 'Fair ladies should not notice bandaged knights. It seemed as if I'd always known you. I would have found you, somehow.'

'Tell me who you are,' she said.

African mystery clothed him, under the English trees. He made her see his dream of a farm among the rippling plains and purple ridges, sleek brown cattle, endless, open skies. And children growing, fearless, in the sun.

'It was my mother's dream,' he admitted.

Which, perhaps, she thought, is why we share it. Then, aloud, in wonder: 'I don't even know your name!'

'Leo. They call me the Lion Boy.' And he explained that, too. Listening, she felt the sense of oneness growing, of common pasts and futures intertwined. She sensed the strength within him, and a tender wellspring far too long untapped. 'Rebecca,' he murmured, like a prayer. 'Cousins may be married. Shall we go and tell them?' She took his hand in quiet joy and walked beside him through blue twilight towards the dim, grey-towered house.

Lazy dew was falling as they crossed the shadowed lawns, approaching the ghostly ramparts of Shalott. The party had ended. James waited alone, a portly glowering outline in the yellowed doorway. 'He is an upstart, Rebecca, Laura Howard's bastard son!'

There was a movement, swift and fierce beside her, Leo's hidden power surging free. James was lifted bodily and thrust against the wall.

'You tormented my mother when she was helpless and alone!'

'A mistake, a misunderstanding! She chose the bush, and a bearded wanderer! I never saw her again!' James's flush had whitened. He writhed feebly in Leo's casual grasp. 'You have no business here. Your priestly Father saw to that!'

She saw Leo's anger falter, sensed mystery upon him. Released, pressing his unexpected advantage, James spoke of confrontation under an African sun: of thatched huts and sullen tribesmen, and whitewashed mission walls, a Healer's curse, a green-robed priest's deception. 'He was the stubbornest of all. Father Andrew wouldn't even own to your existence.'

'Father Andrew!' Leo echoed, like a man betrayed.

'The inheritance is *ours*,' James crowed, 'I have documents to prove it!'

'I didn't come for wealth,' Leo said wearily. 'I only want your sister.'

'You mean to marry?' A greedy smile split James's jowls. 'My dear chap, you must stay until the ceremony!' He strode, restored and chuckling, into the dim house, and Rebecca understood why he had tried so long and hard to wed her off.

So that the Seton riches would be his alone.

Leo understood it too, and she saw the knowledge weigh him down. 'It will take years of work before I can match this comfort. I'm sorry, Rebecca. I shouldn't have come.'

'Fool!' she snapped. 'Do you think I give a tinker's curse for James's money?'

Nightwind rustled in the ivy. Swallows swooped across the misted lawn. His eyes met hers, seemed to gaze deep into her soul. He smiled.

'Then perhaps I'll stay,' he said.

He came to her by moonlight as she prepared for bed, filling her quiet room with his silvered strength. Shy and apprehensive, she hugged the green silk nightgown to her body, afraid she might in some way disappoint him.

At first, he simply held her, a modest, almost brotherly embrace; he stroked her hair, told her she would always be his lady. She heard his steady heartbeat through the thin white shirt, breathed his clean male fragrance. We are cousins, she thought, we share a dream. That is why it seems so safe, so right.

His mouth moved tenderly along her cheek, sought the quickening pulse within her neck. She sighed and nestled closer, slid her arms around his waist, felt the curl of supple skin through crisp, thin fabric. He kissed her lips and took her breath away. His hand moved softly down her arm and up beneath her rising, swelling breast. Small waves of pleasure rippled outwards from its hardened peak. She felt her body stirring, opening like a flower to his gentle heat.

The scent of him was changing, growing sweet and musky. Sudden heavy thickness at his groin made her light-headed. Through half-closed eyes she saw the passion light his face, making it harsh and pure and beautiful. The bed was but a step away. She wanted only to lie and draw him down upon her, take him in and satisfy his need.

Then, above the drumming of her heartbeat, she heard a furtive movement through the wall, and knew it could not begin like this.

'Don't be afraid,' he whispered, sensing her disquiet.

'I'll never be afraid again.' She gazed into his blazing golden hunger, honouring her vow. 'I want you, now; but not while James is listening next door. Let it be in private, with God's blessing. Humour me until our wedding night.'

He only had to draw her close again: she could see he knew it, too. She saw him check, breathe deeply, and rein his power in. Carefully, ceremonially, he bent and kissed the cleft between her breasts. 'My lady, I am yours to command.'

All doubts dissolved, the lonely years might not have been. From this moment onward she would be *his* to command, so long as they both might live.

She woke to small-hour darkness, with an empty space beside her in the double bed, and a sense of some encroaching evil half-perceived in sleep. Unfamiliar insects rasped and muttered. Nightwind slithered slyly through the thatch. Be calm, she warned herself. You are Rebecca Reid now, freshly married to a pioneer. No use having vapours the first time you are left alone.

'I'll be back tomorrow,' Leo had promised. 'I'll get a bank loan, choose some cattle, order what is needed for the house.'

'Don't rush,' she had retorted. 'We're three months wed; I'm weary of your company.'

He gave her a flashing, gold-eyed glance, kissed her soundly, heedless of the grinning tribesmen, made her blush with embarrassment and pride.

That had been while sunrise greened the pasture, and singing native woman hoed the rich brown soil. Now the night breathed menace, and Leo was away.

Starlight probed the narrow window, touched the charcoal stove, gleamed faintly on the hard-baked mud floor. She'd lived a week within this daub and wattle shack. Long enough, she reckoned. Soon, they'd build a proper place, give substance to the dream they shared. The knowledge soothed her. Drowsiness crept back.

A sound splintered the night, cutting like icy lightning down her spine: a harsh, primeval shriek which made the walls and rafters quiver. Her nape-hairs rose. Gooseflesh crawled along her arms. She sat erect, clutching the rough blanket, remembering brother James's threat. 'You are going to a heathen land, where whites are driven mad by sorcery!'

The sound died. Her fear grew curved batwings and filled the gloom. Fear of the unknown, she told herself. Be bold, get up and face it!

She slipped out of bed, drew Leo's greatcoat on, taking comfort from his clean male essence.

Outside, the forest stretched and creaked against cold, steely stars. The tribesmen's conelike huts stood silent as abandoned witches' hats. No drooling demon lurked here, no ravenous creature pounced. Nothing could explain the dreadful cry.

Which rose again, closer, making the cold earth tremble underfoot, driving her down the slope towards a whiff of woodsmoke and feeble ember-glow. A hooded figure prowled among the huts, growing red-flecked eyes and pale filed fangs. She stumbled back, her mind aghast, her courage stretched to breaking point.

Firm hands gripped her shoulders. The screaming wavered, gargled, died away. Duma pushed the blanket from his forehead and offered her reassuring Swahili words. It was a small animal, he was saying, who lives within the forest and only wants his mate. 'Me too,' she breathed, in English, fighting off hysteria. '*Me too!*'

Fresh flame flared on watching brown faces. She sensed mocking male amusement all around. Duma spoke again, offering to go with her and guard against the night. She felt demeaned and foolish, desperately ashamed. 'I'm all right now,' she snapped, striving for dignity despite her shivers and the clownlike coat. 'I'm sorry I disturbed you.' And marched up towards the sneering forest, and the empty, hateful, *hideous* little hut.

Oh Leo, why did you leave me in this awful place?

Around him, grins were glinting, maize-beered breath made grey mist feathers in the night. Men chuckled and clicked their tongues at such childish fear. 'Be silent,' Duma chided. 'Go to your hearths, show her some respect.' But he couldn't really blame them. What kind of wife was this, to shudder like a birthing ewe because the hyrax called? A meek and harmless beast, as every Kikuyu knew, whose mating call sounds like a man in mortal pain.

Why do white men prize such females so? Duma wondered. She had cowered like a wide-eyed doe, her pale, boyish flanks agleam beneath the big brown coat. How could such a woman produce sturdy sons, and help a man to labour on the land?

He settled, grumpy, at his embers, tugged the blanket over his head and blew a gust of orange warmth from the black, smoky ashes. I brought him from mewly whelp to full-grown manhood. Must I now play wet nurse to his wife?

Only a week ago, Duma had blessed Njau's name, and gloried with the villagers in Leo's long-awaited return. Now we can roam again, he had thought. Now we can share again the fierceness of the hunt.

Leo had asked for land, and built a hut, and left this skinny woman-child among them. Why, Duma wondered again, why does he behave like a Boer settler? He is the Lion Boy, who can never be a humble tiller of the soil.

It must be her idea. Soon, no doubt, she'll weary of it, and go back where she came from. If a hyrax call can cow her, she will not endure real hardship.

Then a memory stirred – of Morgan's woman, all those years ago. She, too, had started as a comely burden, had in the end proved braver than she looked. Had, in the end, borne Leo.

Morgan loved his Laura, Duma remembered, whom this Rebecca is so like. And whom Leo clearly loves. Wait and see, then. Time alone will tell.

Duma sighed, breathed ashes, sneezed. How much simpler life would be, he thought, if Leo had wed a strong, plump village girl.

Rebecca curled under scratchy blankets on the crackling fern-filled mattress, appalled at her own stupidity. How shall I face those leering heathens in the morning? How shall I face Leo when he comes?

She stared into the darkness, lonely and afraid, remembering other endless, empty nights . . .

The house rose like a short grey tower from the seaward slope of Sussex Downs. Sometimes, sunshine made the distant blue waves sparkle. More often, smoky drizzle hid them, and turned the hills and copses gloomy green.

Downstairs was always warm and cosy, where godlike grown-up brother James played host to college friends. Becky's room stood at the highest, chilliest corner. There, while laughter echoed from below, Nanny read her fairy tales at bedtime.

Nanny was big and old and Scottish, with a stern voice and twinkly blue eyes. She wore a starched white cap and apron and thick black stockings, and had downy hairs on her upper lip. When Nanny tucked her in, Becky squirmed with pleasure at the love which tingled from each fingertip.

Daddy's goodnight touch always pleased her too, though his whiskers prickled, and the smell of bay rum made her sneeze. 'Sleep well, princess. May flights of angels sing you to your rest.'

But she was never sure if Mummy would come.

Mummy was fair and slim and scented, everything a little girl could wish to be. On Sundays at the village church, she smiled at those who praised Becky's yellow ringlets and perfect manners. But she seldom smiled for Becky, or came into her room. Children, Mummy sometimes said, should be neither seen nor heard.

So Becky would lie in the dull brown-panelled room and watch the night-light flicker on the drab ottoman, and hug the one-eyed teddy bear which once belonged to James.

And wonder why Mummy hadn't come to say goodnight.

The nursery lay opposite the lumber room. One morning, while rare sunshine lit the windows, and Nanny hummed and changed the bed, Becky crossed the narrow corridor and went exploring among the bric-à-brac.

Presently, in a dim and dusty corner, she came upon a special treasure.

It was a small oval picture in a silver frame: of a fine-boned fair-haired person who was no longer a girl nor yet a full-grown lady. She looked a lot like Mummy, and even more like someone Becky knew well but couldn't quite remember.

She turned the picture this way and that, puzzling. Of course, she realised suddenly, it's me! I will look like this when I grow up. It gave her a funny feeling, holding this picture of herself-to-be.

She heard a footfall, smelt Mummy's lavender perfume, turned to share her pleasure and her pride. 'Look, Mummy, isn't she pretty!'

Mummy's slim body went tight and stiff under the fawn, wide-shouldered dress. Her nose wrinkled, her eyes gleamed like wet grey pebbles on the beach. Suddenly, despite the sun, it felt frosty in the lumber room.

Something was terribly wrong.

The picture was torn from Becky's fingers, flung face-down on dusty boards. The tinkle of breaking glass seemed very loud. A cold hand clamped round Becky's wrist.

'Come back where you belong, child!'

Two short, angry strides for Mummy, four dragging steps for Becky; and Nanny got a ticking off.

'Ah Becky,' sighed Nanny, 'you'll be getting me the sack.'

'Who is she, Nanny? Who is the lady in the picture?'

She had to explain. Nanny's eyes went soft and dim. 'That would be your Aunt Laura. Long gone, poor wee soul.'

'Gone where?'

'To foreign parts, they say, and never to be heard of again.'

'But why was Mummy so cross?'

There was another funny, tingly hush. Nanny went pink, and rushed her to the bathroom. 'Come now, let's play sailors – and no more questions!'

So she asked Daddy, when he came to say goodnight, 'Why did Aunt Laura have to go away?' She sensed the same cold stiffness in him, felt him draw away. 'Hush, princess, don't even say her name. It's long ago, and you're too young to understand.' He was glancing like a robber at the open doorway, as if afraid Mummy might come and scold him too.

But Mummy didn't come.

So Becky plucked up courage and tiptoed to the lumber room, groped carefully among the scattered glass-shards, and carried Aunt Laura's picture into the light.

This time, the tingling was sharp and nasty, like ghostly fingers down her spine.

Where Aunt Laura's eyes had been, were two round dark holes. A thick red crayon had slashed across the fine young face.

Shuddering, feeling sick inside, Becky put the picture back and burrowed into crisp, fresh sheets.

Aunt Laura must have done something very bad, she thought. I was bad, too, for showing her to Mummy. Tomorrow I'll be good, and make Mummy smile for me.

But no matter how hard she tried, Mummy wouldn't smile for her; and she never came to say goodnight again.

There came a day that summer, when she was five years old, when thunder rumbled round the Downs and set the floorboards jiggling. Her parents had gone to Norfolk on a boating holiday; James was staying with a college friend. A smell of baking drifted from the kitchen, where Cook and Nanny gossiped over morning tea.

Downstairs is always empty, Becky thought wistfully, when I'm allowed to play.

Hearing a bell tinkling outside, she pressed her nose to cool, rain-pimpled glass. The postman pedalled by, hunched in blue against the wet. Funny. The postman never calls at morning teatime.

Nanny came slowly through the kitchen doorway, her big hands cupped round bone-white cheeks. 'There's been a dreadful accident,' she whispered. 'Your mummy and daddy have been drowned.'

The whole house seemed to crouch and listen. Wind gusts

thumped the window, water gurgled down the pipes. Becky felt that nasty tingly pain again, and was suddenly lonely, guilty and afraid. 'Was it my fault?' she asked. 'Was it because I found Aunt Laura's picture?' Nanny swept her up and clutched her to the crinkly white apron. 'Of course not, my dove! The good Lord took them early. They are with the angels now.'

Clinging to Nanny's shoulder, feeling the force of Nanny's love, Becky saw the sense in this. That's why Mummy couldn't love me, she thought. She knew she would be going to the angels, who are cold and fair and far away like her. That is why her going doesn't hurt me – because she never gave me any warmth.

It will be all right, she thought, as long as Nanny stays here. I needn't worry about Aunt Laura's picture any more.

James had been away again.

Like Aunt Laura, he had been to foreign parts – Africa, Cook said importantly. He arrived one afternoon beneath a low grey sky, told the hansom cab driver to wait and marched Becky upstairs to the nursery. 'Stay here,' he said. 'Be brave. I have things to settle down below.'

She heard raised voices and the slamming of doors. Whinnying drew her to the window. Unbelieving, she watched Cook help Nanny into the cab.

The pain in Becky's heart was so bad she couldn't cry. 'Why?' she beseeched James. 'Why did she have to go? She didn't even kiss me goodbye!'

James, she suddenly noticed, had a face as red as his waistcoat and greasy tousled hair. He smelled rich and fruity, and couldn't say his words properly.

'She was slow and ugly, and getting much too old. You shall have a young, pretty nanny.'

'No! I want *my* nanny back!' He ignored her, grinning like the big bad wolf, moving unsteadily up the front steps.

'Blood is thicker than water – you stick by your old brother James. Don't cry, little Becky. We're rich!'

He bought a grown-up gilt-rimmed mirror for her bedroom wall, and frilly frocks to wear to church on Sundays, but he never went with her, and never read her stories. He seemed to think presents could ease her loneliness.

No one will ever buy my love, she vowed.

Nannies came and went like passing seasons. They taught her the ABC and tables, dull dates and boring battles. Each nanny was young and pretty. None of them had loving fingertips. They seemed to be more interested in James than in Becky's lessons.

They were supposed to sleep with Cook, in the basement. Sometimes, while Teddy's one eye glimmered on her pillow, Becky heard soft footfalls on the lower landing, and the mousey squeak of James's bedroom door. Presently, strange noises would trickle up the stairway – low moans, bedcreak and high-pitched giggles. What can they be doing? she wondered. What can James learn from a nanny, so late at night, so often?

'Don't be nosy,' James snapped, 'or I'll lock your bedroom door.'

When she was eleven, a nanny brought her treasure – a poem called *The Lady of Shalott*.

Her sweet low voice made pictures bloom in Becky's mind. Tirra lirra sang the knight beside the river, clop and clatter went the horse. Moonlight shimmered ghostly on the dying lady's shroud. The magic voice turned tender and breathed the final verses like a prayer.

> But Launcelot mused a little space;
> He said, 'She has a lovely face;
> God in his mercy lend her grace,
> The Lady of Shalott.'

The beauty of it lingered. Becky rose and set the mirror on the blank wall over her desk, opposite the one high, narrow window, and gazed above her own reflection at the dim, back-to-front world beyond. There, when the strange sounds sidled up the stairway and owls swooped over windswept, moonlit cornfields, she spoke the poem softly and dreamed the night away.

Somewhere my gold knight is waiting. When I am grown to Aunt Laura's beauty, he will ride into the morning meadow and make the mirror crack from side to side. I will not die, like that sad lady. I will ride behind him, singing, to far-off, sunlit Camelot . . .

James held a party for her on her eighteenth birthday.

She wore a bright red ballgown, cut low, with thin lace straps, which pinched her waist and pushed her bosom up.

At twilight, sleek black motor cars crunched the gravel underneath her window. Bell-shaped headlamps sent white beams across the soft blue dusk. She heard the rising hum of conversation, the miaow of a violin being tuned. Excitement lit a bright-eyed, ash-blonde beauty in her mirror; perhaps her knight would enter, from a petrol-burning steed.

At eight o'clock she swept downstairs, savouring the hush she had created, and the surreptitious envy on other girlish faces.

'By God!' breathed James, 'you are so like her!'

'Like whom?' Briefly, his pallor and confusion awoke old mysteries. He shook his head, turned away. The moment passed, as starched white shirts surrounded her. Her card was quickly filled. The band struck up. She moved in joy and expectation into the dance.

They had receding chins and haw-haw voices, these would-be suitors. Clumsy patent leather shoes barked her shins; clammy paws crushed her dress and made her skin crawl. The powdered, giggly girls could talk only of fashion, and cocked their noses at her ignorance. By eleven, the guests had paired among themselves. Becky was left to haunt the empty balcony, and gaze, alone and sadly disillusioned, on the distant silvered sea.

So began a drawn-out, two-year charade. James invited every eligible male in England's southern shires, paraded 'choice blood-stock' for her inspection. Most were vain and callow, seeking only meekness and a compliant body in which to plant their seed. 'How will you love me,' she would enquire, 'when you save so much affection for yourself?'

Hearties wooed her, ruddy giants of the manly sports. They held her gingerly, and breathed stale beer into her face.

'Do you know *Morte d'Arthur*?' she once asked.

'Who does he play for, old thing?'

Then there were the poets, aspiring scribes who cast hungry gazes on her upthrust bosom whilst laying earnest claim to her soul.

'I need someone to find me whenever I am lost,' breathed one. 'Someone to recharge my failing spirits.'

'How about a nice St Bernard bitch?' she suggested sweetly.

'Don't you know men distrust wit?' James snarled. 'I would never wed a woman cleverer than myself!'

'Then you will no doubt stay a bachelor!'

This one tart exchange taught her yet another lesson.

Even James could not force her to make a choice.

It took war to release her, and a fiery sermon from a Sussex priest. On a February Sunday in 1915, he prowled the oaken pulpit and punched the frigid air, leaving little smoke-like puffs after every urgent word. Above his chalky surplice, his hot dark glare seemed focused directly on Rebecca. 'How dare you sit in comfort while this great conflict rages, and English yeomen bleed for God and King! Go forth, seek Christly blessing, and find some task to speed the victory!'

Rebecca knew exactly what she had to do.

'London?' echoed James contemptuously. 'Who will keep you, who will pay the fare?'

'You will make me an allowance, starting today.' And as James grinned in bloodshot disbelief, she added, 'I will walk the streets if I must. When they arrest me, I'll tell them where I learned my trade – outside the great James Seton's bedroom door!'

Why didn't I challenge him before, she wondered, while James fumed and blustered – and wrote a cheque.

For thirty months, amid the stench of bile and gangrene, she stitched wounds, soothed nightmares, held palsied hands. She wept inside for mutilated bodies. She wept openly for those who howled and drooled and hammered on the walls.

Each night, she returned to a dingy flat which smelt of boiled cabbage, drew the walls of Shalott tightly around her, and prayed that her knight might survive; that he would some day ride into her golden mirror, his manliness untainted by the war.

And one day, he rode into her life on a hospital trolley.

He had chestnut locks and clearly sculpted features almost too beautiful for manhood. His eyes were calm and navy blue. His bare chest gleamed like classically carved marble. 'You are the loveliest thing I have ever seen,' he told her. 'Now I know I shall get well.'

She helped to place him in a private room, beside the window. He looked longingly at the mare's-tail blue outside.

'That's the future,' he whispered. 'You should see the aircraft gliding there, safe and free above the shot and shell. I'm going to be a flier!'

'First,' she warned, 'we've got to cut the German bullets out.'

'West Indies,' he said, 'or some Pacific Island. Sunshine and coconut palms, and our children laughing in the spray.' He took her hand, a tender, yearning touch. 'Say you'll come! Say you'll be my lady!' It was absurd, she knew, but his confidence moved her deeply. For the first time in her life, maleness stirred her.

She assisted at his operation. 'Someone steady,' the surgeon had insisted. 'Someone not too squeamish.'

She stood white-masked and rubber-gloved within the reek of ether. Blue-Eyes lay faceless and grey-shrouded on the table. Someone eased the shroud aside. A ragged, black-lipped chasm gaped, high inside the sturdy, blue-veined thigh. She caught her breath, swallowed, went to work.

'Scalpel.' A wink of skilfully wielded brightness.

'Swab.' Soft lint turning red.

'Sutures.' A hiss of catgut through taut drawn flesh.

Slowly, the void filled and came together. She sensed the surgeon's satisfaction, heard Blue-Eyes's rhythmic breathing. It's happening, she thought. He will recover.

The surgeon raised the grey material a little higher and made her senses reel. The scalpel swooped past his limp pink manhood, sliced into the grossly swollen bag below. She swabbed dark pus-filled ooze away, saw the two purplish, gristly lumps with grey steel shards embedded and glittering coldly.

'Shrapnel,' growled the surgeon. 'Too much of it, too deep.' He thrust a kidney-shaped metal bowl into her hands. The scalpel glinted, poised above a twisting yellowish cord.

'What are you doing?' she breathed.

'Castrating him, of course. Hold *still*, woman!'

Someone will have to tell him, she thought. Someone will have to be there when he wakes.

So as the day dwindled and sickness filled her own soul, she sat in the private room beside his bed, rehearsing the lines she must use.

You may learn to fly. We may find an island paradise.

But we will never raise your children.

At last, the blue eyes fluttered, swum and steadied. 'Hello, my love. How am I?' She sensed the hope within, the courage it had taken just to ask; and couldn't say the words. Let him grow a little stronger, she pleaded to herself. Let him live, before he learns of living death.

'You will get better,' she whispered shakily. 'Rest now. I will come back soon.'

'How soon?'

'This evening, when it's quiet and we can talk.'

'Don't be late. I'll dream of you.'

She nodded and slipped away, unable to endure doomed beauty any longer.

She never knew how far she walked through the mean grey twilit streets, how much she cried, how often she railed against her heedless God.

Or how she found the strength to keep her promise.

She only knew that this time, he *must* be told. She was sobbing 'I'm so sorry' as she eased the door ajar – and stepped into a waking nightmare.

The sheets had been hurled back. The marbled thighs lay wide and pallid. The wound had been wrenched open. A crimson lake drowned the space between. The beautiful face shone gaunt and still, its lips for ever set in bitter scorn. Deep blue eyes glared, sightless, at the wall.

A dim white wall, streaked with sudden scarlet. Two words, scrawled in blood and fury, a final condemnation she would carry to her grave: *You lied.*

Past and present fused inside her mind. The scream which had woken her carried exact echoes of Blue-Eyes's agony. Surely no small animal could make such a hideous cry? Did *Duma* lie, she wondered, had these file-toothed savages performed some bloody ritual in the dark? African night coiled, sinister, around her. Small-hour fears came sidling back.

Leo didn't tell me about the sly rustling thatch, the thin grey moon, the grunts and whoops that filter from the forest. He didn't tell me about Nairobi's snooty whites, who treat him like a pasha, and me like a useless ornament. He didn't tell me about the tribesmen, with whom he shares so many jokes that I can't understand. He didn't warn me of Duma's ill-concealed contempt, or of unearthly shrieking in the night. The dream which had sustained her wouldn't focus. Shalott was closing in on her again.

For goodness' sake do something, she urged herself. You didn't come to Africa to cower in the dark, to whimper like an orphan, frightened and alone.

Presently, she got up and lit the lamp, closed her mind to mocking nightsounds, and began to sweep the floor.

22

By daybreak, the whole hut smelled of beeswax. Rebecca's need for action lingered on. She donned walking shoes and a long white cotton dress, stacked washing in a metal pail, and ventured out. She trod the grey-gold, dewspread meadows to the river's edge, avoiding the huts, unwilling to face Duma and the tribesmen. Their mockery still rankled; eerie shrieks still echoed in her mind.

She scrubbed and rinsed, beside the singing waters. There was budding warmth and birdsong, sunsparkle on her skin, a chime of goatbells close behind. She could hear the women chanting in the village maize-patch; she could smell tart eucalyptus sap and fresh-turned soil.

Normality restored her. The morning broadened, blue-skied and benign.

And when night returned, Leo would be home.

A shadow fell across her as she folded the last shirt. Glancing up, she saw a stocky, buckskinned figure propped against an ancient rifle, and a ripe-lipped sneer above a sunbleached beard.

'Be warned, mevrouw. Keep your goats away from us. My name is Kobus Coetze. I speak for all the Boers.' The strident accent grated. Unprovoked aggression brought her hackles up.

'In the first place, these are not my goats. Secondly, you're standing on our land!'

'Then tell your husband. Tell the famous Lion Boy, whose heroism cost us good Boer blood.'

'Tell him yourself if you dare. He will be back by sundown.'

A mistake, she realised at once. She was acutely conscious of isolation, of damp, semi-transparent cotton clinging to her flesh. While Coetze's voice rose to near-religious fervour, his hungry green gaze feasted on her body. 'Goats are the Lord's abomination, visited upon these pagan tribes. They do not graze: they ravage, root and branch. They make dustbowls of green pasture, bring pestilence among our healthy kine. At our side of the water, we shoot them down on sight.'

Rebecca drew herself up, blushing furiously, folding protective arms across her breasts. 'Then stick to your side, Mr Coetze. You may be sure that we will stay on ours!'

She spun away from his devouring leer, stormed to the hut, hauled the wet dress off and covered herself with thick blue serge. She felt used and grubby, as if she had been touched by slimy paws.

Kobus Coetze, she thought: another ugly creature Leo forgot to mention: the new day was blighted.

Starlit shame returned to haunt her. She recalled a scathing comment overheard in Nairobi, from a stately dowager in floral print. 'Poor little thing, fresh from Blighty, banished to the outback. The Kikuyu will run rings round her.'

No they won't, she thought. Oh no they won't!

This time, she strode directly to the smoke-swathed huts, where tribesmen lounged and Duma ate maize porridge from a round green gourd. She found a crude Swahili phrase and spoke it forcefully.

'You must go to work!'

Duma took a mouthful of disgusting off-white goo, licked his lean brown fingers, gave her a leisurely sidelong glance. 'What would memsahib have us do?'

'There is a house to build. We need timber.'

'Where shall we find timber?'

She gestured briskly at the great dark green canopy above them. 'Up there, of course!'

'The trees are too thick. Our blades are too small.'

'Give me a simi,' she demanded. 'I'll do it.'

'Wait till Leo brings the axe,' Duma grunted. 'This is man's work.'

She thrust out an imperious hand. Duma shrugged and passed her the weapon. It felt rough and unwieldy.

'I will come,' he sighed. 'There is danger, in the forest.'

'Sit down. Stay, till your precious axe arrives!'

She went, high-headed, up the hill. Warm breezes ruffled her hair. Pied goats shied from her advance. She didn't look back, not

215

once. Let them watch and sneer. Let them see what a *white* woman can do.

She wouldn't let the forest overwhelm her, refused to bow before its mystery and mould. I won't be afraid, she vowed. I will make them respect me. And swung the simi fiercely at the nearest smooth straight trunk.

The impact shuddered through her. Small red spots danced before her eyes. She had barely marked the greyish, iron-hard bark.

She found a thinner sapling, bared her teeth and gripped the handle tighter; she hacked until the spasms shook her arm. Sweat stung her eyes. Pain flared in her palm. She sensed a yield, heard a groaning rustle, saw the slim bole yaw and lurch and fall. They will have timber, she exulted, even if it's just one roofing pole! Bending, wincing at the bite of bark on blistered flesh, she flexed her knees and pulled.

She couldn't move her roofing pole one inch.

Muttering soldiers' language, she marched to the leafy end and tried again. Branches caught in tangled undergrowth. The thicker section still refused to budge.

Strength and courage dwindled. She sagged on crackling dead leaves beside the sap-dulled blade. Tears slid through her bloodied palm, forming a small pink pool on faded greenery.

Dimly, she sensed another human presence, and looked up into Duma's cool, dark stare. 'Come,' he said. She followed, too exhausted to resist.

He took her, wordless, to a brook, bathed her wound in icy brilliance, laid aromatic leaves upon the sores. The pain eased. She felt like a foolish schoolgirl.

She trailed his narrow, stiff, brown back to the forest edge and pitiless blue sky. He checked and pointed down the slope.

Kikuyu women plodded, bald-pated, towards the village, chirruping under vast loads of firewood. Each bore a dozen logs across her cowhide-covered back. Each log was twice as thick as the roofing pole. They are so strong and vital, she thought miserably, and I am so puny. And Duma stands here stony-faced, forcing me to wallow in more humiliation.

Oh Leo, I have let you down again!

Then Duma leaned towards her, touching her reddened hand gently. 'It is a good place, memsahib. Go down and rest. I will tell them that the Lion Boy has found a worthy wife.'

She didn't see filed fangs any more, scarcely noticed the smell of smoke and goat-grease. He was just an older, wiser man, sighing for her, hurting for her. Through sudden, grateful tears, she watched him turn and lope away.

Descending, reprieved, she overlooked the distant blue-green ridge, the thatched and drowsy village to her right, and Leo's pleasant pastures that swept down to the silvered river. It *is* a good place, she thought, and Duma will help to build the dream.

Hoofbeats broke her reverie, making her heart race – Leo, home much earlier than expected! Squinting into the noonday glare, she saw a smaller horse, a slimmer, more accomplished rider. He wore a khaki sweater, moleskin trousers and polished riding boots. Dismounting, he doffed his topee and gave her a sweeping bow. 'Hugo Berkeley, at your service; and you must be Rebecca. Trust Leo to pick himself a beauty!'

The compliment annoyed her, implying prior claim to Leo and an all-male bond she couldn't share. She mistrusted his languid air, the cultured drawl, the soulful dark eyes. She had met too many like him, in the southern shires – spoilt sons of near-nobility. He was 'desolated' because he'd missed the wedding, and had been unable to visit earlier. 'Pressure of work,' he explained. 'They've made me District Commissioner, Nyeri. At least we shall be neighbours.' He eyed the hut distastefully.

'You must let me give you dinner, take a break from pioneering.'

'It's what I came for, Mr Berkeley. I'll tell Leo you called.'

'Please do. There is stock theft on the northern ridges. I need his knowledge of the country and his grasp of tribal law.' He smiled, taking it for granted. More patronage, another implication of female unimportance.

'We are building a life here, Mr Berkeley.' She smiled sweetly. 'For once, you'll have to get along without him.'

Berkeley flushed to the roots of his sleek dark hair; replaced his topee, mounted, wheeled the chestnut brusquely. He glanced down, his brown eyes bright with disappointment and reproach.

'I hope we can be friends, Rebecca. You see – I love him, too.'

Leo returned at sunset, riding his grey mare along the river, bold and golden-headed, the very essence of Sir Lancelot. So long as he is near, she thought, the dream protects us. I must cling to it whenever he's away.

217

From the doorway of the hut, she watched the village go to greet him, chattering and chanting through smoke-stained, sunshot dust. From the women, he won soft, admiring glances; from the men, wide grins and cheerful waves. *Everybody* loves him, she saw with poignant insight, they want him to notice and respond in kind. It will not be so easy, living with a legend.

Ah Leo, don't give all your love away.

Going home, Leo had detoured to the Mission, avoiding the village, loth to create a stir. He rode up in the hush of evening with growing anger in his heart, towards the pinkened walls which seemed diminished by the passing years.

Kibe met him, with a tremulous embrace and a smile whose brilliance needed no mere words. Then Leo asked his single urgent question: 'Where is Father Andrew?'

Kibe's broad brown face turned sombre. He drew a letter from his snowy robes. 'He has gone to be a prison chaplain in the Northern Frontiers. Read this somewhere quiet by yourself. We prayed for your deliverance and hoped to reopen the Mission when you returned.'

'I'm sorry,' Leo grunted, 'I have a more worldly mission of my own.' He turned away from Kibe's hurt, and a God he had long since ceased to trust.

Instinct took him to the ancient Meru oak and three silent weathered crosses where a father and two mothers lay. There, while evening deepened, he spread the crisp cream paper and read the neat black script, making a grey-haired, green-robed picture of the writer.

'Now you know. You have met James Seton, learned how I deceived him long ago, for the pleasure of a son I couldn't sire. You gave me more than pleasure, more pride than any man deserves; but my falsehood will haunt me to the grave. I signed your heritage away.'

Mine and Rebecca's, Leo thought bitterly. And you didn't even have the courage to face us.

It doesn't matter, he realised, hearing the river babble, watching the hutsmoke rise, smelling dewfall on familiar pastures. This is all the wealth we'll ever need. Somehow, Rebecca knew it from the start.

'Before I left,' the priestly voice continued, 'I burned Laura's papers. Be assured, they held no hint of crime, his or hers. Meanwhile, I go to harsher climes and harder battles: the last chance to atone.'

In Leo's mind, the final mystery yielded. It was *Father Andrew*'s guilt that lingered among perfumed clothing, cast gaunt shadow upon the growing Lion Boy. All those years, he kept her papers from me, in case I should discover *his* dark secret.

'If you can,' the letter ended, 'forgive me my great trespass. If you will, remember me with love. Go forward with God's blessing and with mine.

'There is nothing in the past to cause you shame.'

In the fading sunshine, the graveside seemed to bloom with light and truth. Rest in peace at last, you who gave me life; and Wanjui, who took the foundling in. The mare snickered gently. Facing northwards, Leo let one final picture form – a stooped, green-robed martyr, facing harder battles, bringing hardened criminals to his Bible and his God.

Farewell, you who tried so hard to be my father, and left me the gift of inner peace. Now I can return to my Rebecca, raise the children we long for, bring the dream to life.

There is nothing in the past to cause us shame.

He had only been away for a thirty-six-hour span: to see her was like being born again.

She turned the hut into a castle with her brightness: her slender, upright beauty, luminous grey eyes, the elfin look which made her seem so vulnerable.

And twilight radiant in her ash-blonde hair.

He saw at once the damaged hand she tried hard to hide, sensed her troubled spirit, marvelled anew at the bonds between them, that went far beyond mere wedding vows and blood ties.

'Duma will protect you,' he soothed, 'Hugo is my friend. You will learn to love the forest and tolerate the Boers.'

Later in lamplight and shy pride, she showed him her splendour and her need, took him down and in, brought him to a tender release. And curled within his arms like a wounded, silken bird.

Then as she slept and familiar night sounds rustled, a tiny nagging doubt kept him from rest. It had plagued him through their salt-fresh shipboard honeymoon, now made him squirm with self-disgust.

She had not yet aroused his passions to the heights that Tara had reached.

Hugo stood in starlight on a sheltered slope in Mount Kenya's southern foothills. Nightwind chilled his face and probed his great coat. Owlhoot and frogcroak drifted from the wooded shadows behind. The air smelled of woodsmoke and cattle dung. Beside him, tribal policemen waited, their rifles primed and glinting, their curly-headed outlines tense and still. Below, in the steep ravine, the stock-thieves' campfire embers flickered orange, throwing sleeping, blanketed figures into dim relief.

A far cry, this, from the fear of Rumuruti, the belly-twisting tortures of Longido Hill. These were neither fearless Masai nor battle-tempered Schutzetruppe; just renegade Kikuyu youths whose raids had provoked much wrath among the settlers. He had tracked them for a week through wild and rocky country, using the stealth and skill he'd learned from Duma. Now they were trapped, out-numbered, and powerless beneath the guns. He felt no bloodlust, only the weight of duty on his shoulders and the need to keep casualties low.

'Spread out,' he whispered. 'Don't strike until the circle is complete. No shooting, if it can be avoided.'

They moved like wraiths downhill, with only the hiss of boots on damp grass and the creak of leather belts to mark their passage. Hugo slipped towards the mouth of the ravine, where the walls were widest and a narrow stream gurgled, blocking the most obvious escape route.

He heard the harsh-voiced challenge, the click of breech bolts, the sudden, single warning shot. Firelight flared, fanned by flailing movement. A rifle butt thumped meatily on naked flesh, a man cried out in pain and protest. Straightening, parting dew-damp branches, he peered in satisfaction at the outcome of a perfect ambush.

The youths stood in a shivering, cowhide-kilted knot, their hands raised, their eyes dulled by sleep and shock. Grinning troopers herded them together, crowed boastfully, and began to bring the stolen cattle out of the shadows.

He had just a fleeting premonition of danger, a flicker in the corner of his eye, a rustle in the undergrowth ahead. The stocky, fleeing figure smashed into his midriff, drove him down and back-wards to the rocks beside the stream. Stunned and winded, half-blind with tears of pain, he could make out only a dark-skinned, round-faced silhouette above him. A reek of goat-grease made him retch. Strong, slippery fingers clawed his throat, bony knees trapped his arms. Briefly, his vision cleared. He gazed dully up at a pale, fresh-risen quarter moon – and a glittering upflung spear.

What a feeble, futile way to die, he thought. Five yards away from firelight and safety, and armed troopers too busy celebrating to notice.

The spear quivered, and begun its sharp, swift plunge.

In that same instant, he sensed a softening of the strength that trapped him, heard a curious whimper of dismay. The blade swerved, flashed across his face, bit deeply into the soft soil beside his ear.

'I cannot kill you,' a Kikuyu voice complained. 'You are Berkeley, who rode beside the Lion Boy!'

The fear will come later, Hugo decided, astonished at his own composure.

'I am Thuo,' the voice continued, 'who was Leo's friend.'

'You will not kill,' croaked Hugo, 'yet you steal cattle and live like an animal in the bush. *Why?*'

'Would you have me tend goats, like an uncircumcised herdboy? Should I hoe the fields like a useless woman? I was trained to be a warrior, to win honour on the war grounds and keep my people safe.'

Hugo could actually feel frustration flowing through Thuo's body, thrusting him deeper into the soggy earth. I won't even recognise him again, he realised. I will only know the voice.

Now, at last, other voices intruded, calling his name anxiously. The spear was wrenched free. Displaced pebbles stung Berkeley's cheek. 'There are others like me,' Thuo hissed, 'who will not do the white man's work for money, who have the warrior's anger in their blood. Tell your people, Mr Berkeley. One day, they will have to kill us all!'

And he was gone, fleet and soft-footed down the shadowed, gurgling ravine.

Hugo scrambled stiffly to his feet, brushed the mud from his greatcoat, controlled the sudden, quivering aftermath. He told the troopers he had stumbled in his haste to seal the trap. He saw the sly, knowing glances that passed between the captives, read their meaning plainly.

Thuo has gone free.

Throughout the long trek to Nyeri, he wondered at the insight

Thuo had supplied. We have created an age-group born to fight, and have denied them the blooding of their spears. They do not steal for wealth or status, but for the sheer excitement of the chase.

And it is our fault.

We placed settler farms between the warring Kikuyu clans. Then Leo and I moved the Masai, thinking it would bring the ridges peace and plenty.

One day, we may have to kill them all.

I will have to warn H.E., he decided, and keep a close eye on the farms in Nyeri district. Especially Leo's farm.

Briefly, the thought cheered him – until the motive for it brought him up short. It would give him a chance to make peace with Rebecca.

It must be nice, he thought, going home to a woman like that: a woman who is faithful, beautiful and proud. Which brought him to one final, uncomfortable truth.

In my heart of hearts, I've always envied Leo. Now, in all our dealings, I must conceal an even darker secret.

I envy him his wife.

23

THEY WERE PUTTING UP the rafters, the day the cattle came.

Axeblades hummed and glittered, wood-chips fountained wide and white, the clang of steel on timber echoed from the hill. Tribesmen perched like sleek brown crows on beams that formed a yellowed lattice against the mare's-tail blue. The air smelled of industry and clean, sharp sap.

Stripped to the waist, his hair bleached flaxen, his skin tanned dark walnut, Leo laboured like a man possessed. Rebecca watched his muscles roil and clench, breathed his fresh sweat and felt her knees go weak: she marked the place where he was standing and made a private vow: one day, we will make love just *there*.

Make tea, my lady. Keep your fantasies controlled.

Duma first noticed the invasion, raised a slim pink palm and stopped the singing dead. Setting the kettle aside, Rebecca turned and saw them too: small, hump-backed creatures, black and white and grey, meandering up the long green slope.

'Surely you needn't *all* go?' she complained, as men swung lithely down and tools fell ringing to the floorboards. 'They want to count our wealth,' grinned Leo, like a truant schoolboy leading the escape.

She swept sawdust, stacked the gleaming simis, heard chants and deep-toned cowbells draw near. Then Leo came back, his amber eyes ablaze. 'We're in luck, Rebecca. Three in calf and one about to pop!'

They grouped like anxious male midwives around the piebald heifer, *eehing*, neighing, nodding curly brown heads. Within the hour, a boma was constructed: an enclosure of thorn branches, a lean-to shelter made of poles and thatch, spread beneath with fresh-cut hay. Lucky little cow, Rebecca thought. While her house is completed, mine must watch and wait.

Twilight came. Doves and ibis called, a fine grey mist settled on the river. The midwives murmured, the heifer lowed piteously. 'Let me help!' Rebecca pleaded. She saw Leo shake his head, sensed the exact tone of the sudden hush, read it plain in Duma's dark and level gaze. *It is man's work.* Sighing, remembering the last time all too clearly, she withdrew to the hut and made supper ready.

Presently, the lowing reached a frenzy, reminding her of dark hyrax cries. Then Leo returned, bloodied but triumphant.

'A fine bay bull-calf who will one day sire a splendid herd!'

He ate distractedly, while drumming thundered from the huts; he prowled like a captive leopard around the dim mud floor.

'For goodness' sake,' she grumbled, 'he is safe and snug and full of mother-milk. Come to bed!'

'I must go, Rebecca. I must be sure he's well.'

She dozed, deserted and disgruntled, and woke much later to an empty bed. Furious, she slung his greatcoat on, marched down through the soft darkness which had once so terrorised her to the shelter where a single yellow lantern swayed.

And wondered at the scene inside. Leo, sleeping on the straw, with a bedraggled, big-eyed bull-calf cuddled in his lap.

Anger faltered, tiptoed from her soul. Cautiously, she burrowed into milky birth smells, laid her head on Leo's shoulder, pulled the greatcoat round all three. There is a little boy within him, she thought. I am doubly blessed, for I love both man and child.

She called the bull-calf Blondel, because of his colour, because he was their talisman. Duma showed her where the sweetest grasses grew, the safest drinking pools along the river. Leo taught her milking, which he'd learned from the Masai.

As each day broke, she squatted on the wooden stool and called the cows by name. She loved their great, dark liquid eyes, their meadowsweet breath, the pulse and squirm of udders in her fingers, the steamy, creamy spatters in the pail. At sunset, she strolled beside them through the scented pasture, past smoky huts where tribesmen grinned and waved for *her*.

In daylight, while the cattle grazed, the hammering and sawing echoed on.

Leo seemed to be everywhere at once – kneeling on the roof-ridge, his grin aglow with nails; using his great strength to place grey stone in yellowish mortar; building thick thorn fences to keep the cattle safe. Each evening, he would eat enough for three, race down to the river, return, slippery clean and shivering, to the little bedroom. There, behind drawn curtains and by shaded lampglow, she would coax warmth into his body and hardness to his loins.

He was sweet and strong and vivid, urgent yet genteel. He always made the flower in her body bloom and burst. But sometimes, as she hovered at the edge of love-spiced sleep, she knew she had yet to fully rouse him. He was too tender and constrained, as if he feared some wildness deep inside might erupt and hurt her.

She owned his heart and spirit, of that she had no doubt; but until she could completely claim his body, she knew she would not conceive his child.

Suddenly, the house was finished; seemed at once in keeping with the land. Nestling in a hollow halfway up the hill, the stout walls quickly weathered, the shingles lost their raw, rough-hewn look. Inside, it was light and airy, with panelled walls, natural stone hearths, and zebra skins scattered across polished wooden floors. Each morning, Kerinyagga's craggy, blue-grey, snow-capped splendour filled the broad lounge window. Each evening, weaver birds clung like golden fruit clusters from the sheltering blue gum tree behind the kitchen door. The charm endures, thought Leo, the dream begins to live.

And he took Rebecca to a campfire celebration among the tribesmen's huts.

The smell of freshly roasted goat brought back fond childhood memories. Its gamey succulence filled Leo with delight. Beside him, shawled in sapphire blue, her beauty tawny-toned by ember-glow, Rebecca grimaced and nibbled daintily.

The drums saved her, rumbling through the risen sparks. Dancers appeared, four couples clad only in yellow breechclouts. The throbbing deepened, sensual and insistent. The dancers swayed and quivered, their faces rapt, their thrusting, oiled brown thighs agleam. Rebecca leaned on Leo's shoulder, pliant and smoky-eyed. 'They are urging us to fill the extra bedroom.' He slid his hand beneath the shawl, cupped her sweetly swelling breast. 'Here is all the urging I need!'

The rhythm died abruptly. The dancers paused in mid-gyration. The charged, maize-beer-scented air took on a sudden chill.

Leo saw a ragged figure cross the pool of brightness, hawk and spit thin slime at Duma's seated form. He felt Rebecca's flesh crawl beneath his steadying arm, watched hatred glitter in dark, familiar eyes.

Mwangi's eyes.

He teetered over Duma, reeking of hard spirits, wearing cast-off white man's clothes. 'All my life, you humbled and ignored me. Now you give *my* land to these Red Strangers!'

Duma rose in firelight and grizzled dignity. 'I see no stranger. I see the man who rid us of the Masai. He was born here, he belongs here. I am proud to call him son.'

'I am your firstborn son. What is yours belongs to me by law!'

'You have no rights, you know no law! You have turned away from Njau and this clan, to play at politics with drunken youths within the town. Now you shame me, before the elders and my friends.'

'Toothless fools,' Mwangi babbled, 'who have grown too old for pride.' Shadows etched deep lines into Duma's face – lines of pity and contempt. His voice cut harshly through the crackling flames. 'Let the clan now hear me and uphold the law. I, Duma, cast out this youth called Mwangi. Henceforth he shall cease to be my kin!'

The tribesmen sighed at this, the most feared of punishments. A low, assenting *eeh* bespoke Duma their support.

Mwangi crouched before the orange embers like some cornered, hot-eyed beast. 'Hear me, you who toady to the white men. Hear and cower under Mwangi's curse. There shall be fire and flood and pestilence upon you, till I return and purify the soil!' He crabbed sideways into darkness. His parting threat hovered among drifting sooty ash. '*Some day, I will have this land!*'

'What did he say?' Rebecca demanded, pale beneath the stars. Leo told her gently.

'*Never,*' she vowed, 'as long as I have life and breath!'

'It's only talk, my love, childhood envy he never could outgrow.'

She shivered, drew the blue shawl tighter. '*They* seem to believe it.'

The tribesmen huddled silently around the dwindling embers, their celebration soured, their faces taut and grim.

Leo led her away towards broad lighted windows, gave her his assurance and his truth. 'We are safe here. No one can harm the Lion Boy.'

Next morning, he rose early, took tools and paint into the misty meadow, fashioned a charm he knew she would believe.

After breakfast, he brought her out to the verandah, under Ker-inyagga's gleaming majesty. He saw the pleasure take her, watched the shadows lifting from her eyes, gloried in her brimming, grateful smile.

He'd hung the sign above the door, one word outlined in gold upon a plain black board: Camelot.

Mwangi sidled stealthily along the grassy knoll towards Njau's solitary hut. The Healer sat outside, his knees drawn up, his arms crossed around them. He wore neither cloak nor anklets, only the pied colobus-skin kirtle. In speckled shade under the high blue gum tree, he looked frail and aged. Once-tight muscle sagged across his chest. Greyish wrinkles scored his coal-black skin.

Yet Mwangi felt uneasy in his presence. Mystery still clothed him, in quiet force an ancient wisdom. He sat unmoving, his eyes glazed milky blue, peering out across the shining river to the hazy ridge beyond. He seemed to be waiting for something. The future, perhaps; a future he alone could see. Mwangi shivered, in the heat of afternoon; shivered and drew nearer.

'Do not plague me with your troubles. You have broken faith.' As always, Njau knew of his approach, knew everything that happened in the valley. He hadn't turned. He sounded harsh and peevish.

Mwangi stepped forward, pointing angrily at the land below. 'Stone huts invade our boundaries, foreign creatures graze our fields, Strangers take what Ngai gave to us!'

'Not much,' Njau grunted. 'Not yet enough for which to risk their guns.'

Mwangi wheeled and gestured at the whitewashed Mission walls. 'Kibe's Christians sing their hymns and dip their children in the river, mock our oaths and ban our circumcision rites. Once, you swore to fight them for our souls. Now, you sit and sigh, and let them flourish!'

'And you run wild with drunken warriors, and lay down foolish curses you cannot yet enforce. Patience, boy, our time will surely come!'

'I will not wait! I won't watch Duma's foundling steal my land! *Give me the power!*'

Njau shifted, glanced upwards, mild and pitying. 'You had the gift. You only had to listen, watch and learn. But your heart was always full of envy. You long to hurt; you never tried to heal. Now you are as any other tribesman. I can give you nothing more.'

Sunlight flickered fiercely on sthe windows of the big house. The rage in Mwangi's heart burned fiercer still. 'You are old and weak,' he growled, 'and wear the Healer's pouch about your neck. I am young, and strong enough to take it.'

Njau rose, slow and creaky, into Mwangi's reaching, lunging shadow. Mwangi's fingers closed on unresisting flesh, clawed towards the secret leather pouch. And halted, rigid and immovable, about the slim frail throat.

Njau seemed to grow into a mighty, muscled warrior. His skin seared Mwangi's fingers, his eyes blazed redder than a forest fire, his voice boomed like tautened drumskins inside Mwangi's skull. 'You have abused my trust and soiled my person. Tremble, now, before true healing force!'

Mwangi stumbled backwards as if from some great wind, his arms dangling, useless at his sides. 'Yours is the power of darkness,' Njau hissed, and each word drove Mwangi farther down the slope. 'Some day, it will surely turn inwards and consume you. Now, I, Njau, cast you out. Take your childish evil and be gone!'

The spell broke, the rigour left Mwangi's limbs. With terror in his heart and Njau's towering image in his mind, he turned and fled into the forest.

He knelt beside a sparkling stream and soothed his scalded fingers. The fear, he knew, would stay with him for ever; but it could not still the anger in his soul. It is *my* land, some stubborn part of him insisted. Leo is a white man, even Njau grants me some small power.

And Njau is growing old.

Slowly, liquid coolness reassured him. His shattered brain began to work again. The tribesmen did heed my curse, he thought, I saw the apprehension in their eyes. I will not be driven from the valley until I can be sure they will remember, and be properly prepared for my return.

Somewhere in his mind, a memory stirred, a rumour sent by far-off drums along the northern ridge: a rumour about cattle and disease.

Mwangi smiled, beneath the slyly rustling leaves. I will go forth, he thought, and buy an unclean goat.

Short rains greened the ridges, setting new richness to the pasture, and bringing flowers into bloom round Camelot. Two more heifers calved easily. The herd flourished, the milk-yield grew apace. For six months, Rebecca dwelt in near-complete enchantment.

She went calling, early one evening, beside the river. The herd looked up, swinging lazy tails at buzzing flies, above their blurred reflections in quiet, shining waters. She said their names, admired the sheen on their flanks: my lady Rebecca turned milkmaid, finding great joy in the task.

Then she turned and stiffened as she saw a skewbald goat fall, dying in the sun. Its swollen stomach spasmed. Jets of thin brown foulness soiled its quarters and the grass. Rebecca shrank from the mad gold centre of the darkly rolling eye and watched the spark go out.

Poison, she thought. The stupid creature has trodden on a snake. Nothing else kills so suddenly and surely. I must not bring the cattle here again.

She never did.

She heard a frenzied wallow, watched her beloved Blondel thrash the shallows into foam. The same ugly bloat deformed his belly, the same vileness darkened the clear waters. With horror in her heart and Mwangi's curse resounding in her head, she raced up to Camelot, crying Leo's name.

'I'll have to bring Hugo,' he said. 'D.C.s know about these things.' And he drove the grey mare at full gallop towards Nyeri, leaving her to watch and wait – and weep.

Hugo went to his knees in icy water, opened Blondel's lifeless jaws, smelled corruption, watched pus seep from bloody ulcers along the yellowed tongue. It *is* a curse, he realised, sent not by Mwangi nor upon the Lion Boy alone. It kills all cloven-footed creatures. Uncontrolled, it could wipe out half the livestock in the district. It has a name, three short sounds to make a stockman tremble. Rinderpest. 'Thicken the fences,' he told Leo, 'round up every goat and cow. You dare not let it spread.' He took a deep breath, told them the worst. 'Chances are you'll have to destroy the whole herd.' He saw the colour dwindle from Rebecca's face, watched Leo move to comfort and support her. He was wearing his Rumuruti look again, tight-lipped and yellow-eyed.

But this was a battle even he could not hope to win.

Then Leo led Rebecca up the slope to blighted Camelot. She moved like a wounded antelope, as if she had the sickness too.

And glared at Hugo as if, in naming it, he had himself visited it upon them.

'*I hope we can be friends,*' he had said. Now, he could only help them see it through, and hope they would not become enemies. He turned and set off sadly towards Nyeri Hill.

Each morning, Rebecca woke and longed for Blondel's gentle lowing. Numbed, bereaved and helpless, she could only haunt the verandah and watch the plague take hold.

It spread like windswept grassfire through the valley, killing ram and ewe and cow alike. Tribesmen stalked the ridges like stricken pale brown ghosts, counting the dead, seeing their wealth decay. The Boers stood guard along the river, their rifles primed for any diseased beast that ventured near. Leo laboured, stony-faced and silent, to preserve a dwindling stock of healthy beasts.

In vain.

'It's over,' he admitted, on the seventh blood-drenched eve. 'It would be better if you didn't watch.' But she couldn't forsake the dream: she had to stand beside him and endure the nightmare.

Scattered lamplight yellowed the pasture, swollen insects hummed, grieving voices called and cursed. Upflung blades gleamed dimly, fell squelching into rotted goatflesh. Blood and sickness prowled the dark, smearing men's bodies, searing their limbs like rank hyena breath.

Lights and tribesmen gathered, carcasses loomed against the stars. There were long moments of silence, a sense of shared horror for what must now be done. Then Duma crouched and set the spark, blew it upwards through the kindling. It broke and spread and lapped the unclean feast with small red tongues. Sinews popped, sour fat crackled, and the reek of scorching hidehair made Rebecca retch. Women's voices rose in ululation, tore high and harsh into the polluted night. The men looked hardly human in that fiery light: wild-eyed, blood-soaked creatures dwarfed by grief and flame. 'I overcame the Masai,' Leo whispered, 'I lived through German shot and shell, but no one taught me how to fight the gods!' She had never seen his face so pale and ravaged, never felt his body so tight-strung. There, among mourning villagers and swirling, tainted ash, she sensed the lurking power of this country.

A year of love and labour lies burning in the night, and the Lion Boy is driven to despair. I will not be defeated, she vowed, I will not be broken by some vengeful, heathen god; somehow I will make the dream survive. She led Leo home, rinsed the stench away, sat beside him while he entered chill tormented sleep. At dawn, while black smoke soured the sun, she stood beneath the golden name-plate and gazed across the desolated pastures, wondering how on earth she might replenish Camelot.

For days, the smoke pall hovered, the tribesmen huddled round their huts, and Leo's spirit sickened. 'They're expecting me to save them,' he said. 'They want the Lion Boy to restore their wealth. It can't be done. I'll never keep cattle again.' And he would ride off to the forest, returning with game meat and hides – and lingering sorrow in his eyes.

Then, one morning, Rebecca saw a small black motor car wheeze down the cart-track from Nyeri. While red dust flew and tribesmen *eehed* with alarm, it disgorged a rawboned, peg-legged man some ten years Rebecca's senior, and a tiny, black-haired, birdlike woman in a bright pink dress.

'Eric Stuart, who fought beside your husband in the war,' the man announced, in rolling Scottish brogue. 'We heard of your misfortune and came to cheer you up.'

And on the verandah, Leo managed a faint smile.

Within minutes, Stuart was stumping up the hill, pounding Leo's shoulder, gesticulating broadly with his walking stick, talking enthusiastically of terraces and irrigation. Molly Stuart watched the two men fondly, her black eyes twinkling. 'Old soldiers, och, they're such great boys! Now let's see this nice wee house of yours.'

She loved the view, she said, the built-in cupboards and the natural wood furniture. 'But oh, those tatty cushions! And forgive me, dear, you're looking a trifle tatty yerself. Come, I'll ferry you to town.' She tossed her glossy head, gave Rebecca a knowing, beaky smile. 'Nothing like a good binge to chase the glooms away.' And seeing the concern Rebecca couldn't quite conceal. 'If it's the bank's money, so much the better!'

'But what about Eric and Leo?'

'They'll be talking war and agriculture till the crack o'doom. Up with you, I'll brook no refusal.'

Molly's driving proved as impulsive as her speech. They zoomed up inclines and swooped across fords in glittering silver spray. Molly used the bulbous, braying horn liberally, waved gaily to startled beaded elders and gawping brown-skinned children. The sheer exuberance made Rebecca's spirit heal and rise.

They swept down under Nyeri's hazed hill, rattled across the wooden bridge, drew up in a screech of brakes and a flurry of dust outside the sprawling, timbered White Rhino Hotel. 'Lunch here later,' Molly announced, 'and gin to ease the parch. Meantime, we're off to beard the Shahs.'

She tripped like a short, pink flamingo along the sunstruck street and a line of dukas – trading shacks crammed with calico, hardware, grocery and hides, smelling of spice and joss sticks, run by plump, sallow Asians. She knew them all by name, disputed their prices fiercely, drank their weak, tepid, condensed-milk-sweetened tea with regal condescension. 'Mrs *Reid*,' she said firmly, when final payments were agreed, 'open an account.'

'Pretty hair,' each Shah said like common litany, and eyed Rebecca with covert lechery. 'You come back quick, get good rates and long credit, isn't it?'

At noon, Molly Stuart led a file of native porters to the car and supervised the loading. Sea-blue gingham curtains, already cut and hemmed, fresh vegetables, a side of bacon, a bottle of French wine. And a white cotton dress with huge orange sunflowers which Rebecca would not have chosen, but which suited and fitted her perfectly. 'When Africa growls,' Molly said, 'you stand tall and kick her in the teeth!'

They sat beneath a jacaranda tree. Iridescent starlings bickered around their chairs. An African waiter in snowy robes and a red fez brought gin and tonic in tall, frosted glasses tinkling with ice. Molly drank deeply, sighed contentedly, fanned her pinkened cheeks with a small, beringed hand. 'There now, Rebecca Reid. Isn't that better?'

It was much, much better. As midday heat burgeoned and the gin loosened her tongue, Rebecca told her story from the very beginning.

'You're wise to mistrust Coetze and his hungry green leer. I'm glad we live four ridges away. Hard to blame him, when you see his wife: a fat, suety sloven. Still, he's right about some things. Beware of goats, and don't get overfriendly with the Kyukes.'

'Ah, Molly, they're almost Leo's kinsfolk.'

'Even so, they're mebbe tender-hearted, but worse than children underneath: self-centred, ungrateful, inconsiderate and lazy.' She smiled, suddenly hard of eye and tight of lip. 'Eric has a saying, cruel but true. Africans are totally reliable. They *always* let you down.'

Perhaps it's true, Rebecca thought, whilst Molly bantered with the barman and paid the bill. Perhaps we should preserve a distance, joke with them in public, disdain them in our hearts. After all, their goats did plague our herd. But I know Leo doesn't feel that way, and so far Duma has never let us down. Wait and see, Rebecca. Work, and watch and wait.

And even this reservation faded, as the steaming, dusty car jolted over the last rise, and she looked down on Camelot. Despite deserted pastures and the lingering whiff of fiery death, for better or for worse, she was coming home.

At Molly's prompting, Rebecca slipped into the new dress, brushed red dust from her hair, dabbed light cologne across her cheeks. 'Nothing like plonk and perfume to stir the downcast laird,' Molly confided, with a knowing grin.

And was soon proven right. The men came downhill, laughing boisterously. She saw the startled, almost comic appreciation in Leo's eyes, and basked in the balding Scotsman's open admiration.

'We've shared some thoughts,' Stuart declared, 'and a wee dram from the hipflask. I reckon the future's looking somewhat brighter.' Then, as Leo and Molly traded shopping notes, he drew Rebecca aside. 'There's wildness in him, girl, and a powerful urge to roam and conquer. Give him a place to love and bairns to cherish. Men like him will be the making of this land.' Then, softly, as small crow's feet of pain tightened round his eyes, 'He saved my life, you know. Call on me, if ever you need help.'

The day was fading, as they climbed into the car. Molly crashed the gears, swore cheerfully, turned the grumbling bull-nosed bonnet northwards. Eric leaned out, offering a flat brown-paper parcel. 'Oops, almost forgot. Little present.'

Dust flared, following them like a long red plume across the greening slope. The parcel was addressed to 'The Lion Pride' and labelled 'Anti-gloom juice'. Inside were two full, square gin bottles: His and Hers.

Leo's marvellous golden grin broke free. His warm whisky-flavoured breath caressed her cheek. 'You look good enough to eat,' he murmured. 'Suddenly, my appetite is back.'

He carried her to the bedroom, closed the new blue curtains, made slow, glorious, joyful love to her. As the flower in her spread and bloomed, his grateful moan rang deeper and more certain. It's getting closer, she thought, in drowsy pleasure. It will happen soon.

Later, as twilight cooled their mingled bodies, he spoke of maize and coffee and raising cross-bred sheep. He stretched, restored, rekindled. She savoured the new determination in his voice.

'First, we build a dam.'

24

LEO ROSE AT DAYBREAK, mustered tools and tribesmen, led them up the slope towards the forest. There, on a rockstrewn plateau beneath a misty sun, he took a pick and cut a circle in the turf two hundred yards across. He saw doubt in covert sidelong glances, heard low-voiced grumbles as he passed. 'If Ngai had meant this for a pond, he wouldn't have made the sod curve upwards.'

'Are you witless monkeys?' he bellowed. 'Are you feeble herdboys? Will you who saved the Lion Boy from Schutztruppe guns now cower from a little honest toil?'

Duma faced him, eyeing the pick disdainfully. 'Digging is women's work.'

'Women?' Leo echoed incredulously. '*Women?*' He threw off his shirt, strode to the biggest boulder he could see, squatted, prised his fingers underneath. Bracing his feet, breathing spicy dust, he lifted the great weight, duckwalked the entire width of the circle, and set the rock down at the centre of the plateau lip. Straightening, dashing sweat from his eyes, he gave them his most contemptuous glare. 'Shall I bring *women* to help me with this task?'

Duma wagged his head in wonder, bent and took a shovel. One by one, sheepishly, the tribesmen followed suit.

A rock wall grew along the plateau edge. Leo joined the singing, revelled in the bite of wooden shaft within his palms. For the first time in my life, he thought, I'm creating, not destroying. For the first time in their lives, these warriors are working on the land.

Together, we will make the dream bloom again.

Rebecca was blooming too. The sun had set a tawny sheen upon her skin, bleached her hair to fine-spun silver. As she rode the grey mare up the evening meadows to greet him, she did look like some medieval princess sprung from Camelot.

But she brought him a more practical demand.

'You must teach me to shoot.'

He glanced up along the mare's sunset-pinkened flank, masking his concern with dark humour. 'Indeed? Has rinderpest converted you to slaughter?'

'Of course not. But the dam will keep you busy for weeks. Meanwhile we must eat.'

'Then I will send Duma hunting.'

'And who will make the others stay with you?'

A telling point. Leo nodded in acknowledgement and changed tack. 'You won't be chasing foxes over gentle English downs. In this land, hunting's not a sport for ladies.'

'*Look* at me, Leo!' Her vehemence stopped him short, making the mare bridle. She sawed the reins, her slender hands controlled and steady. 'I will be your lady whenever neighbours call. I will be the woman in your bed. I will *not* weave useless tapestries beside the river while you toil alone!' She sat erect against the pale blue twilight, her beauty pure and strong; it filled him with great love and pride, and not a little awe.

'Very well,' he murmured, hiding a smile, 'I will teach you shooting.'

At first, she found the rifle too long and heavy. The barrel wavered, the report made her jerk and flinch. Powder stung her eyes, the recoil bruised her shoulder. 'I warned you,' he muttered. She turned to him, her small face tight and pale, her eyes asmoulder. 'For goodness' sake, it's only a bit of pain!' He marvelled at the toughness of her spirit, the force that dwelt within her willowy frame. Until, one lowering evening by the river, she stood and aimed and fired steadily, placing four successive bullets at the centre of the target he had raised. She grinned at him, in elfin triumph. 'Now we can go hunting.'

On a weekend free from digging, he took Duma and the mare on a safari round the forest fringe to Kerinyagga's foothills. In the shiver of their first dawn sortie, Duma tensed and breathed one piquant word.

'What did he say?' Rebecca demanded.

'*Swara*. It means buck – and meat.'

'How does he know?'

A good question. They had been trudging downhill through waist-high grass and swirling mist. Leo could hear little and see less. 'He smells them, I think.'

'Indeed? And what do *we* do?'

'We copy him.'

Duma crouched like a taut brown pointer, head cocked, nostrils flaring. 'We wait; in silence, if you please!'

Even as he spoke, the light broadened. The mist paled and parted, revealing a broad defile below: stunted, bottle-green bushes, emerald pasture, the steely glint of a mountain brook. An impala ram stood at the water's edge. Weak sunlight played on rufous flank, a snowy chest, a fluted flare of horn. Leo unslung the rifle, hearing Duma's expectant grunt and Rebecca's wistful gasp, sensing a moment of truth.

'No targets here,' he growled. 'This one is real.'

He saw doubt take her, followed by pleasure and a flash of bold defiance. And, from the corner of his own eyes, Duma's beseeching glance. *It is madness, bwana, don't let her waste prime meat!*

Rashness, certainly. The breeze in their faces was shifting, turning. The impala advanced a few steps, its black snout raised and questing. A tricky shot at the best of times: downhill, crosswind, a long carry in deceptive light. So it should be. Now we shall see.

She took the classic stance, feet well set and spread, butt tight to the shoulder, left elbow braced and pointing straight down. She levelled the muzzle, nestled her cheek to the well-worn stock. A steady, indrawn breath, an instant fixed in his mind for all time.

She squeezed the trigger gently.

The recoil and the flash rocked her, though not as much as he'd expected. Following hard on the blast, he heard the whump of a solid hit. Duma was already gone, a flying, dark-skinned dervish seen through thin blue smoke. His upraised knife shone silver, his cry of triumph echoed to the sky.

'That was well done, Rebecca.' Leo turned towards her, speaking his mind whatever the cost. If she chose to gloat, so be it. She had earned the right.

Her head was bowed, her green-clad shoulders trembled. Sun-bleached hair veiled her face. She had set the rifle-butt down and was using it as a crutch. A single teardrop glistened on the grey-blue barrel. 'He was so alive,' she whispered, 'and now he is no more.'

'Will you go squeamish on me, after such a coup? Ours was the need and his the misfortune. There are many more of his kind!'

'You don't understand. I cannot abide the loss of – lovely things.'

'Then for all your markmanship, you can never hunt. The messy business is still ahead.'

'Oh?'

'Skinning and butchery.'

'Moron!' She shoved the gun into his hands and marched away, a slender, stiff-backed figure in the growing day. After a while, he followed, scratching his head in confusion.

By the time he arrived, the tracker was drinking, and Rebecca squatted by the carcass. The skin lay spread and intact, the cleanly severed head near by. The air smelled of death and acrid digestive juices. On her knees, up to her elbows in blood and offal, she spared him a single, contemptuous glance. 'Squeamish, you say? No woman can afford such scruples.' Her grey eyes narrowed, her chin tilted proudly. 'You have set the test and seen the proof. From now on, I shall be your full and equal partner!'

Leo followed the mare past the raw red hollow in the plateau while Duma loped towards the huts, spreading news of memsahib's prowess and portions of fresh meat. How lucky I am, Leo thought, I have a lady, an equal partner and a lovely woman for my bed.

If only she could give me a child . . .

He woke early one morning a week later, saw brightness through blue gingham, felt the ache of digging in his body – and heard a distant goatbell chime. The tribe has rallied to a distressed clan, he realised, given the villagers animals to rebuild the flocks. Soon the rains will come, cleanse the pasture, prompt new breeding, fill the dam.

We must strengthen the walls.

Beside him, Rebecca's hair lay like a silken cobweb on the pillow. Narrow sunslants set a peach-like sheen across her cheeks.

Sleeping Beauty.

As he leaned to kiss and wake her, he heard a curious mewling cry and noticed an unlikely chill upon the air.

The front door stood ajar.

Waiting, tense, on smooth cool boards, he sensed no threat, no ill-willed presence near. He pulled the door inwards, stared down in utter disbelief at the basket there.

Unfocused navy eyes gazed back. Minute fists waved feebly, the tiny mouth made sucking shapes – and mewling cries. The baby lay swaddled in soft brown monkey pelts, snug within its woven wicker crib.

Somewhere far inside him, a faint foreboding stirred, mystery he simply couldn't fathom. No Kikuyu would abandon such a healthy child. Custom might frown upon an unwed girl, an errant warrior; but the baby would be counted free of sin.

He bent and looked more carefully, saw straight black wispy hair and honey-coloured skin. And began to understand.

This was a half-caste babe.

I am the Lion Boy, he remembered, granted a special place among the clan. Someone has entrusted me with this most precious gift, someone who dare not own to parentage.

The hungry cry grew louder, filling him with tenderness. He reached out to offer comfort, drew breath to call Rebecca – and paused again, suddenly hard of heart. Warning pictures focused in his mind: Wanjui's broad brown anguish when foster brothers quarrelled, Father Andrew's eagle face when God and Ngai clashed; and Duma's firelit agony while casting Mwangi out. Some day, he thought, I will have children of my own. I cannot let this shameful birthing blight them.

Duma will know what to do.

Duma had sent word to the village. Tribesmen cooed and chuckled over the basket. Already, Leo could hear approaching women chirrup. 'Show me where you found her,' Duma said.

They followed clear dark footsmears from Camelot through dew-sheened grass towards the forest edge. Once within, Leo could only follow Duma's lead. It is like old times, he thought, watching Duma tracking unseen signs in dim green shade. But there was a haunted urgency about the old man's stride, a frown deep-etched into his brow.

Presently, on a mossy bank under a stunted fig, Duma found a wisp of monkey fur, a trace of fine grey ash, a single yellowed maize pip. He bent and sniffed, touched a fist-sized russet stain. 'She gave birth beneath a sacred tree and hid until she knew the child would survive. We must hurry!'

Leo's unease deepened.

Why did she flee, he wondered, what does she seek, which power drives her further from the daylight?

At noon, they found the answer, in an eerie glade where leaves lay dank and soggy, where ugly creepers coiled and no bird sang. Duma halted, sighed and pointed upwards. Leo's blood ran cold.

She dangled like some bloated, broken fruit among warped branches. A plaited yellow liana cut deep into her plump brown neck. Her pallid, rigid soles flickered ghostly. The air already reeked of sweet decay. 'A village maid,' Duma whispered harshly. 'She saved the babe but could not face the cost. Uncircumcised, she bedded with a white man. The village would have cast her out. *It is the law.*'

Leo forced himself to look at her bulging, suffused features, blank, glaring eyes, a black, protruding tongue. His soul clenched in pity for such innocence defiled. The dripping foulness slimed his skin and made his stomach heave.

For the first time in his life, he was ashamed of being white.

Rebecca's eyes were like a stormy sky on Kerinyagga.

'The child was brought to us, and you forsook her!' He held her gently, kissed her tear-salt cheeks and took refuge in the tribal lore.

'The maiden's family will raise the child. A tabu will be set upon the birthing. No one will ever mention it again.' Presently, her sobbing eased, but she spoke with poignant yearning. 'I hope you're right, Leo. She wouldn't have lacked for love.'

Leo was wrong.

Three days later, drums and rumour rumbled through the valley.

At Rebecca's prompting, Leo went to the village and returned shamefaced and embarrassed. 'The Boers have laid claim to the baby. The clan is in ferment. Hugo Berkeley must hear the case at Nyeri Court.'

'So much for tabus,' Rebecca snapped. 'So much for sins absolved. It is partly our fault, Leo. I, too, will go to court.'

The hearing began at ten o'clock, under a cloudless sky, with Nyeri Hill seen dimly through a rippling haze. Chief Maina and the dead girl's sister led the village elders. The Boers sat opposite, thin-lipped and sober-suited. Taking her place within the thatched and open-sided gallery, Rebecca watched Hugo Berkeley begin the proceedings. Today, she conceded, he looked the part – with a snowy tunic, navy trews, polished calf-length boots.

Would the man match the appearance?

He called Duma first, and established times, places and the kinsfolk of the dead. While he wrote, a breeze ruffled papers on his desk, and pied crows bickered in the branches overhead. Then Kibe's wife Esther rose to mourn, her broad brown face bright with godliness and sorrow.

'Her name was Ruth. She was a recent convert, studying for communion. May the Lord send justice on whoever soiled her, and grant her soul His everlasting peace!'

Rebecca's eyes misted, the elders ceased to chat, even the crows fell silent. Wisely, Berkeley let the moment linger, then summoned Chief Maina to the desk.

Maina stood in the full flush of Kikuyu manhood, his blue and yellow armlets gleaming, his greased brown skin aglow. 'The girl Ruth died that shame might not demean us, according to the law and Ngai's will. Now Ruth's married sister claims the offspring as her own. In return, she'll gain the girl-child's bride-price, when she is grown and wed.' Maina drew himself up, sent Berkeley a sullen, threatening glare. 'It is our law. We need no outside judgement.'

He sounds so cold, Rebecca thought, so mercenary; and he talks about *offspring*!

Berkeley returned the stare, all at once erect and stony-eyed. 'The greater law will be applied; call Kobus Coetze.'

Coetze came forward, carrying a soft black leather Bible. Wearing dark grey serge, his sunbleached hair and beard neatly trimmed, he looked every inch the sober, stolid deacon. 'You know the law about which this man speaks – unclean ritual, pagan gods, the rule of semi-naked lechery! You heard the pastor's lady. This child's mother sought pure Christian light. Let us take her in and cleanse her. Let white folk purge the unknown white man's guilt. Let her flourish in true law, and know the one true God!' Rebecca mistrusted the pale green fervour in his eyes, shrank from his strident theatrics. There are false notes here, she mused; *methinks he doth protest too much!*

At which point, Helena Coetze waddled to the stand.

Despite the brand-new, pale pink dress, despite the carefully braided mousey hair, she looked much as Molly Stuart had described her: shapeless, uncomely, and suet-faced. But she spoke simply and laid the issue bare. 'All my life, I've hungered for a child. I swear to you, your honour, she shall inherit all the love I own.' Rebecca's heart went out to her humble ugliness. She saw swiftly suppressed sympathy in Berkeley's shadowed eyes, and consternation among the elders. The dead girl's sister muttered, hatchet-faced, at Maina's shoulder.

The chieftain crouched and hissed his warning out. 'If this child be taken, she shall grow in misery. Our Healer's curse shall fall on her and those with whom she dwells!'

'*No!*' Helena Coetze's cry cut through the babble, drowning Berkeley's gavel. She pushed her husband's restraining hands aside, stood weeping before the judgement desk. 'Do not let this happen! Rather she should go to them than live, accursed, with me!'

Rebecca waited fearfully for Berkeley's decision. He rose in dappled shade, his tunic gleaming, his pale face sombre, and spoke with certainty and poise. 'Because of this child's mixed blood,' he began, 'tribal law does not apply. Neither is religion a crucial issue. Judgement must address a single question: how may an innocent life be best preserved? Only one among you gives an answer – Mrs Coetze, who would forfeit her claim rather than bring ill will upon the child. I therefore grant custody to Kobus and Helena Coetze.'

Very noble, Rebecca thought bitterly, as Coetze preened and the Boers applauded vigorously; what about the curse, what about Maina and Ruth's sister, who were muttering ominously?

But Berkeley wasn't finished.

'Nevertheless, a girl-child has been lost, a future bride-price is made forfeit. In compensation, I order Coetze to provide the customary fee – thirty goats or three prime heifers.'

A long approving *eeeh* rippled from the clansfolk. Ruth's sister capered, joyful, Maina looked every inch the triumphal warrior chief.

It can't be that simple, Rebecca thought, as the opposing factions mingled, and Mrs Coetze dried her grateful tears. Where has all the enmity gone, why is everyone so palpably relieved?

She saw Molly Stuart elbow through the crowd, wearing bright canary yellow. 'Wasn't that fun? Didn't young Hugo handle it superbly? What's wrong, my dear? You look utterly perplexed.'

'I am,' Rebecca admitted. 'I seem to have missed the point. What exactly *did* he do?'

Molly grinned, beaky and knowing. 'Come to the White Rhino. Ask him yourself.'

Berkeley stood in the corner of the cool, shadowed bar. Molly marched straight up to him, made unnecessary introductions. 'I must go and talk to Esther about her plans to stop this beastly circumcision. Rebecca's puzzled; give her of your wisdom.' And was gone, a vivid yellow figure with a mischievous grin.

Rebecca was acutely conscious of Berkeley's wariness, and memories of their first uneasy meetings. 'Buy you a drink, Mrs Reid?' he asked diffidently.

'For goodness' sake, my name's Rebecca!' Seeing relief and wary admiration in his eyes, she added, 'I'd rather know what happened out there.'

He shrugged, toasted her over his beer, sipped gratefully, and set the glass aside. 'Pure theatre. The clansmen didn't really want the child. Lasting shame and stigma, you see. Coetze played the Good Samaritan to salve his own conscience. Only poor, sad Helena was honest.'

'I'm sorry,' Rebecca said. 'I still don't understand. Why should Coetze have a conscience?' Berkeley glanced around, lowered his voice. 'You haven't seen the baby recently. She has bright green eyes. I wasn't playing Solomon: just enacting ordinary paternal law.'

Rebecca felt gooseflesh prickling her arms, felt the blood draining from her face. 'You're saying Coetze drove that girl to suicide, you're saying he's the father?'

'I never have. I never will. There is no single shred of proof.' Berkeley was watching her, his brown eyes sombre and sympathetic. 'I know. An ugly little story.'

'How could you do it?' she pleaded. 'How could you let him take the child?'

Berkeley turned his empty glass, watching thin white froth slither in the stem. 'Call it natural justice, shall we? He daren't acknowledge fatherhood, admit he coupled with a black. So he did the religious act. An enormous risk, a curious kind of bravery. And I just made the best of an unpleasant job. Rest assured, Rebecca. The child will be well cherished.'

'And Coetze will be for ever in your debt!'

'Don't you believe it. He's no fool; he won't thank me for guessing the truth.' Berkeley set his glass down, gave her a rueful, wounded grin. 'Sorry. I've upset you again.'

She was already regretting her outburst, beginning to sense the quiet strength in this man whom Leo loved so well. Awkwardly, hesitantly, she offered recompense. 'It takes two to be at odds. Come and visit us some time, Hugo.' And his sudden, flaring pleasure was the only brightness in the whole, sad, sordid day.

25

MWANGI LAY IN LEAF MOULD at the forest fringe, watching Leo lead the singing tribesmen down the sunset slope. Black cloud hid Ngai's home on Kerinyagga. Yellow lamplight flickered from the big house windows.

A pity, he thought, that they had overcome disease. Talkers said the fair-haired woman and bwana one-leg Stuart had helped the Lion Boy regain his pride. One day, perhaps, there would be a reckoning with *them*. Meanwhile, there was work to do here.

He had watched the digging, understood its purpose, chuckled at how well it fitted his plan. Now, as the first star winked and the first owl hooted, he weighed the simi in his hand and sniffed the wind.

Grinning, Mwangi smelled the approaching storm. You don't have to be a Healer, he rejoiced, to make a curse come true. You only need a hunter's eye for weather, a feel for people's fear, a place to hide and a cold, clear plan.

He worked quickly and quietly, lopping down thick branches, dragging them along the path, piling them up within sight of the dam. Then as darkness deepened, he bore them one by one across the wall and thrust each deep into the soft silt in front of the sluice.

When it was done, he knelt, laid his cheek upon wet soil and watched the water's silent, deepening push against the blockage. No need to cover his tracks; the rain would do it.

Far away, lightning glowed, showing him the crouching waters, the looming, waiting forest. He scuttled crabwise through the thickening undergrowth, settled in his cosy hide beneath a mossy bank, drew his soiled blanket tight around him.

The first fat drops pattered on the canopy above. The forest creatures stilled their chatter. Mwangi thought of waterfalls along the swollen river, and hugged himself with glee.

Lightning lit the bedroom, brighter than a thousand moons. The thunder followed instantly, shook the walls and made the rafters rattle. Rebecca came upright to a sharp reek of ozone, a seething roar outside, and Leo's tousled figure in the doorway. 'The dam is breaching!' he bawled. 'Stay here and block the door!' And vanished into the raging night.

Briefly, sheer savagery cowed her: then she realised Leo would need help.

She needed all her strength to force the door. In that moment, broad sheet lightning burned silvered chaos into her brain. Black torrents drowned the furrow and surged across the pasture. The whole forest seemed to lean and flutter, its steely branches clawing at the sky. Leo faltered, halfway up the hillside, his body bowed: a dark and ragged outline dwarfed against the storm.

She pulled the cotton nightgown tighter, set her teeth and drove into the gale. Solid rainrods lashed her face and drowned her vision. The bellow of the outflow drew her on.

Somehow, she made it to the top, huddled in relative calm beneath the plateau edge.

There, while the storm glared and rumbled like artillery, she tried to make sense of glittering chaos.

She saw brushwood, trapped and crackling in the sluicegates, an upper yawn of furrow almost dry; white water leaping high above the ramparts, ripping the sod away, surging into the outflow further down; and Leo, waist deep, hurling huge dark dripping logs aside. Even as she watched, the sluices cleared. She plunged across the furrow as the first great wave smashed through.

A screaming silver fork seemed to rend the sky for seconds, revealing the true source of Leo's fear. The dam wall centre gushed and buckled outwards. Unless it could be plugged, the whole grey wind-lashed mass would rampage down.

She saw Leo wade into the outspill, haul a ragged rock into the breech. The current parted in two faster streams around it. He blocked the first, bent and lifted once more. She could actually hear the spatter of the single narrow torrent against his flesh. In the next searing flash, she saw the instant of balance, when the thrash of water exactly matched the weight of rock and Leo's mighty, ebbing effort. She fought her way through fine spray, pressed herself into his back, threw every ounce of strength forward. He half-turned, his face gaunt with effort, his eyes dark with anguish and alarm. 'Go back,' he cried. 'For God's sake get to shelter!'

It was only a minute shift of force and posture; it was enough to let the water win. She heard his snarl of fury, saw the boulder slip and slither past, and was struck a glancing blow and wrenched away: turning, whirling, buffeting in pitch-black slimy wetness. Then strong arms closed round her, flung her upwards on to soggy soil.

Chilled to the bone, too spent to walk, she was carried in beneath the bucketing branches, laid on a bank of moss, shielded from the wind by Leo's sodden, shuddering body.

Dimly, she could hear the flood cascading. Dimly, she feared for Camelot. For the moment, it was enough to know they were both safe, to feel warmth and life seep slowly back into their nestling flesh.

Only then did she realise that they were naked.

Presently, he stirred, touched her wet hair gently.

'Ah Rebecca, you might have been killed.'

'Damn you!' she hissed. 'It's my dream too!'

Clinging, snarling like an animal in anger and relief, she sensed the sudden flare and stir of him; saw, in lightning dimmed by rippling branches, golden, loving hunger in his eyes. His hands were urgent at her breasts. Stroking, trailing her fingers down his spine, she touched the bunch and splay of muscle there, felt her own thighs drench and part. Then she was astride him, breathing his musk, glorying in his hardness and the pale heat of his smile. She rode him, moaning softly, turned on her back and drew him further in. The rhythm of his thrusts was like a long, slow ocean swell, opening her, moving ever deeper. She locked her thighs around him, gnawed his shoulder, felt the last strange inner barriers yield. This time, his release exactly matched her flowering: a shimmering, shared eruption that stilled the storm and made the lightning pale. While the earth rocked beneath her and silver seared the sky, she was crying out her joy and triumph, feeling his hot seed spurt inside, knowing it must surely cling and take.

Morning broke, in still, grey aftermath. The flood had left Camelot undamaged, gouging a great raw gash into the slope. Leo prowled the verandah, wearing his gaunt warface, oiling his rifle. The splendour in the storm might not have been. Turning from the devastation, he gazed up at the forest and spoke bitterly. 'Back to the hunter's way. Back to eating game meat and selling hides. I'm sorry, Rebecca. We'll never tame this land.'

Oh yes we will, she thought.

Presently, she took a shovel and marched to the place where upflung slime browned the pasture. She worked steadily, shifting muck and rubble, nursing the living secret far within her, reciting the opening lines of the fable to herself.

On either side the river lie
Long fields of barley and of rye,
That clothe the wold and meet the sky.

It will happen, she insisted. I will *make* it happen.

After a while, she heard them coming; turned and saw the tribesmen bring hoes and picks to help her. Leo led them, striding tall and golden, smiling only for her.

'Woman, will you never let me rest?'

'When it is done,' she retorted. 'Only when it is done.'

Watery sun broke through, gleamed on sweat-sheened skin, made the river shimmer, matched the warmth that blossomed in her heart.

When it's done, there will be a child in Camelot. She smiled in surprise and pleasure at the impulse that possessed her, which would seal an older friendship and excise the recent past.

Hugo Berkeley shall be the godfather.

Mwangi squatted in the dimmest corner of a Nyeri drinking hut, wearing his colobus kirtle, swallowing warm maize beer – and tasting only cold tart failure.

Once more, the pale, silver-haired woman had defeated his plan, restoring Leo's spirit, luring foolish tribesmen back to the land.

He needed help to fight the Red Strangers.

So, following the rumours, he had slipped into town, to witness a new power in the land.

The lost youth of the ridges crowded round him. Among them he recognised only Thuo, who had been Leo's childhood friend. We are two of a kind, Mwangi thought. Like me, he hungers for lost status. Like me, he looks to Harry Thuku, the newest hero of our forsaken age-group.

Harry had been to England, learned the white man's tongue, observed the way they organised their work. Returning, he had vowed to unite Kikuyu labour, abolish crippling hut tax, and force the Governor to raise the daily wage.

Tonight, wearing khaki trousers and a pale blue shirt, he drank bottled beer and brought his message to the restive company. 'Once,' he began, 'there was a pack of jackals in the forest.' His broad brown face had hardened, his eyes took on a strange green glow, his voice rang soft and deep. The chatter ceased at once. He *does* have power, Mwangi realised; and he let the story draw him in. 'Each observed the jackal law. Each had a special hunting ground. When times were good, they danced. When times were hard, they shared food. Then one day, as the jackal leader bore a dead hare home, a lion stepped into his path and spoke. The jackal couldn't understand the words. But he saw sharp claws and long white teeth, and knew what he must do. He dropped the hare and ran.

'So the lion settled in the forest.

'Each time he killed, he drove the jackals off. Each time they killed, he stole the meat. The jackals hunted harder than ever before, and ate scraps. The lion hunted little and grew fat.'

Thuku paused and sipped. Around him, through ember-glow and beer fumes, Mwangi saw eager eyes and rapt faces.

'A young jackal wearied of this hunger. Next time the lion took his kill, he yipped and yapped until his brothers came. They couldn't stop the lion, but they worried him and made him leave more scraps. One day, the whole pack answered the young jackal, and drove the lion from his kill. It became a long hard struggle. Some jackals were hurt. But finally, the lion went back to the plain where he could kill and eat in peace.' Thuku finished his beer, smacked his lips and sat down.

'That is a story?' called a disappointed voice.

'That is a story,' Thuku agreed. 'It is for you to find the purpose.'

There was much heated argument. In Mwangi's mind, a meaning hovered. Struggling to grasp it, he heard Thuo's excited shout. 'The lion is the white man. The old jackals are our elders, the young are warriors, like us!'

'Good,' grinned Thuku. 'And what is the purpose?'

'To take up arms and drive the white man out!'

Thuku raised his hand, stilling the warlike whoops. 'You have forgotten teeth and claws, weapons which are too strong for us. How did the young pack overcome them?'

248

'Together!' Mwangi cried, in sudden understanding. 'Yapping and worrying together.'

'Very good. Not fighting hopeless battles; working all at once, all the time. That is how the lion was defeated.' The *eehs* rumbled, approving and triumphant. Thuku began to talk of unions, and something called an 'hourly rate'.

And later, when the backslappers released him, he came and spoke to Mwangi privately.

'You are a Healer?' he asked, eyeing the kirtle with respect.

'Not yet.'

'Such knowledge, and your quick wit, could be very useful. Will you come with me and learn the white man's language?'

Thuku's eyes had taken on that green glow again. Within them, Mwangi saw defeat for not just the Lion Boy, but for all the whites who trespassed on this land. 'Where you lead,' said Mwangi, 'I will gladly follow.'

'Kenya settlers,' said the Governor, 'are the bane of our existence. Yet we must protect them: we're funded from the revenue they raise.' He stood beside chintz curtains, a little stooped, a little greyer in the whiskers, but wholly in command.

He had warred and weathered well, Hugo reckoned; he had cut down on drink and given up his harem. Now in April 1922, he addressed the assembled District Commissioners of Kikuyuland.

Old hands, these. Like Hugo, they sported white shirts, khaki shorts and weatherbeaten faces. While motor vehicles rumbled past and pipe-smoke rode the sunslants, H.E. patrolled the polished boards and named the latest threat.

'Thuku, Harry,' he began, 'a mission-trained Kikuyu. He's been to war, seen whites bleed and whimper; he knows we're only men, not godlike Strangers. Like all his tribe, he covets well-tilled land: settler land.'

'An upstart,' somebody muttered, 'a flash in the pan.' H.E. rounded, his pale blue eyes glinting. 'Wrong! He speaks and reads English, has strong support among Westminster's avant-garde. Calls himself a trades unionist, rallies the defunct warrior class to his cause. He's dangerous: he must be stopped.'

Sauntering to his desk, folding the skirts of his fawn hunting jacket, H.E. sat and steepled his fingers. He had their total attention.

'Thuku is speaking at Ainsworth tomorrow. Big crowd, big party.

Be there. Keep an eye out for known villains from your district. Be ready to round them up at short notice.' He shuffled papers, flicked a buff file open. 'Next, we have a new Head of Police: Elliot, ex-colonel, K.A.R.'

'Pincer Elliot,' breathed a sotto, scornful voice. 'A brave but brainless fool.'

H.E.'s anger stilled the general murmur of assent. 'He has Whitehall's full support. Be sure you give him yours. That will be all, gentlemen!' Then, as throats were cleared and chairlegs scraped the floorboards, 'Berkeley? A private word with you.'

The door closed. Footfalls and banter faded down the corridor outside. H.E. sat straighter and launched his opening salvo. 'Still cuddling up to Reid and his winsome young filly? Have cosy little chats, do you, about Countess Tara and rough nights out at Lola's?' The same old H.E.: the same malicious, omnipresent eye, the same red-fringed grin reminding Hugo where the bodies lay. I still have the dirt, he was saying, I'm still prepared to use it. Hugo mumbled something neutral, conscious of the red in his own cheeks. 'Two special tasks, then,' H.E. continued. 'Keep a close watch on the Nyeri faction. They're after Reid's farm, I hear. Tricky, since he never filed a claim. If that one goes, the rot could spread. Second, stay close to Elliot tomorrow. Trouble with soldiers is, they're apt to start a war.'

Ainsworth was a grassy knoll enclosed by mature gum trees overlooking the Nairobi River. Arriving at mid-morning, as April rainclouds thinned, Hugo took the highest ground, tethered his chestnut gelding and watched the crowd collect.

They came in vivid gaggles from every compass point: greased brown-breasted maidens in cowhide skirts, chubby chanting children, bald and beaded elders stained grey by travel dust. The usual blur of multicoloured movement, the usual stir of greeting, mirth and gaiety. There was one cautionary note: the presence of young men in tattered trousers, laceless shoes and crumpled, oft-washed shirts. Their eyes bleak and watchful, their faces dark and closed, they seemed to cast a shadow on the gathering. Tawdry white man's clothing stole their dignity, giving them an air of sullen masquerade.

They mean no harm, Hugo told himself. They carry no weapons.

The meeting opened innocently enough, with drums and dances, polished limbs and flashing smiles. By this time, Elliot's force had assembled: men in navy sweaters, khaki shorts and kepis, their shouldered rifles glinting under diffused sun. They spread out around the perimeter, grinning, swaying gently to the soft, insistent drums.

Then Harry Thuku mounted the wooden dais, and the drums fell silent. At first, he seemed just another nondescript, rather moon-faced Kikuyu in a faded grey shirt and khaki slacks. As he spoke, he seemed to gather stature. His passion made the cool air roil and quiver.

'Are we cattle, to be herded in reserves? Are we slaves, to labour for the white man's silver coin? Are we foolish children, who must carry printed cards that bear our names? *Are we?*'

A long, low rumble shook the hillside, a sound of ominous discontent. 'You are right, my brothers: we are not! We are the Kikuyu, who bled and battled to protect this land – land the white men fatten on, whilst we toil and hunger in the fields. Tell me, my brothers, shall warriors sleep while this injustice smoulders?'

The rumble rose, becoming an angry roar. Hugo saw policemen scowl and stiffen, sensing militance and violence on the prowl.

Thuku sensed it too, lowered his voice, took a gentler tone. 'Patience, warriors. Do not give the white man cause to prime his guns. Go calmly to the ridges, hire lorries from the Indian traders, fill them with these stupid printed cards. Then bring them here, and pile them high – let fire and flame devour them before the Governor's eyes!'

The crowd was milling now, chanting, cheering, holding up the hated cards. 'Burn them,' they cried, 'take them to the big white house and turn them into ash!'

For the first time, Hugo saw Pincer Elliot's strategy succeed. The police moved swiftly inwards, their rifles levelled, their teeth bared. Elliot himself appeared, wearing a royal-blue tunic and a chalky white topee. He spurred his bright bay charger through the cowering throng while policemen filed from all sides to the dais, like the spokes in some great blue and khaki wheel.

'Thuku!' Elliot bellowed. 'I arrest you for riotous assembly!'

Thuku smiled, blissful and martyr-like, used the honeyed tones and inverse meanings of traditional Kikuyu double talk. 'Peace, my warrior brothers, do not fight. Do not gather weapons to release me. Be good timid cattle – go home!'

Perched on the suddenly hushed and clouded hillock, Hugo

watched once-cheery faces set in sullen anger, as they acknowledged Thuku's cleverness, and knew it was not over.

Rain pocked the puddles left by last night's storm. Cloud thickened above the Norfolk Hotel's high green gables. To his left, Hugo could see the conical, thatched, white police lines, the low, square greystone jailhouse and Thuku's brown moon face behind steel bars.

To Hugo's right, a smaller, quieter crowd was forming. They stole up from the river, those same ragged cold-eyed youths. They wore no beads, called no greetings, sang no cheerful songs. They walked in the drizzle and in silence, under the looming purple sky.

This time, they bore arms.

Elliot deployed his force across the jailhouse portals, forty men in two straight lines, one kneeling, one erect. At his command, two score breechbolts rattled, two score blue-grey rifle barrels levelled. Mounted on the further flank from Elliot, Hugo smelt the chestnut's fear, stroked its silky ear, leaned tensely against the swirling damp.

The chant broke, full throated, harsh with menace. '*Thu-ku, Thu-ku!*' Fighting to control his horse, Hugo saw policemen flinch and upraised simis flicker, heard Elliot's bold, brash military shout. 'It's just a gutless rabble. Brace up, you men, stand firm!' Briefly, it seemed he would prevail. The rain eased, the sky lightened, the leaderless mob wavered.

Then the women came.

They came in angry, high-pitched ululation, their bare breasts bobbing, their tan cowskin kirtles held up around their waists. Turning as one, screaming obscene insults, they flaunted naked buttocks in appalled police faces. Hugo sensed discipline departing, heard policemen cursing in return, watched helpless crimson outrage flare round Elliot's monocle.

And saw two tattered youths run forward, crouch before the guns, make taunting signs and masturbating motions. The mob surged forward. Elliot's warning cry rose sharp and shrill, and the whole police line belched yellow flame.

Furiously, desperately, Hugo drove the chestnut out across the line. He felt no fear, had no thought except to stay the slaughter. Craning sideways over open gunsights, he bawled his protest into stinging smoke and hot-eyed bloodlust. 'These are *your* people! For Christ's sake hold your fire!'

The shooting stopped. Women's voices rose in grief and terror.

Navy-sweatered figures broke rank, plunged among the stragglers, swung rifle butts and dragged their captives in. The mob fled, shrieking, down the puddled street.

But not all the mob.

Seven women lay in the indecency of death, with shattered breasts and wide-flung flaccid thighs. A dozen youths sprawled like heaps of soiled discarded clothing, leaking scarlet into spreading, shiny pools. Strange, Hugo thought, as bile rose to his throat, strange how peacetime victims bleed brighter than those cut down in war.

The chestnut skittered sideways from a small, sickly-looking Kikuyu, who coiled and spat like a cornered serpent. He glared up at Hugo, his face wet with tears and gaunt with fury. 'Mzungu, fucking white man! I saw you give the orders. I saw you ride them down. I will remember you!'

And Hugo remembered him.

Remembered the same distorted sneer, the same contemptuous hiss, from a sunstriped wedding at the Kerinyagga mission. And knew that he, like Leo, had earned Mwangi's enduring curse.

For two days, while armed soldiers patrolled the sullen, rainswept streets, Hugo laid low at the Norfolk and tried to bathe the stench of innocent blood from his skin.

On the third evening, he was summoned to the presence.

Bloodshot and unshaven behind his file-strewn desk, H.E. took a harsh tone of defiance. 'Thuku's power is broken. He'll be exiled to the Northern Frontier; let him try to unionise the camels. The warriors have seen our strength, the ringleaders are behind bars.'

'And seven unarmed women were killed,' Hugo snapped.

'Inciting violence,' the Governor drawled. 'Acts of gross indecency. Elliot moved to preserve order in the face of extreme provocation.'

'Elliot didn't move at all!'

'Dicky heart, poor chap, brought on by war hardship and enormous stress. Retirement with honour and full pension. Don't curl your lip at me: would you rather it was us?'

'I'm ready to resign if it's necessary.'

'Necessary? I'd call it bloody spineless! You did your duty; now you'll pay the price. Oh yes, there always is a price for silence. A thousand prime acres for Colonel Elliot's dotage, in recompense for health impaired and service rendered.' As rain battered the window,

H.E.'s familiar, foxy grin appeared. 'Salve your conscience, Berkeley, take up your cross and bear it to the north. Elliot's plot is in Nyeri district, quite close to your friend Leo Reid's.'

Rebecca winced, clutched the crisp white sheets, and eased back against the pillows. Fresh cut flowers and a whiff of pine disinfectant filled the sunlit room. Outside, iridescent green sunbirds plied the morning glory, and fluffy cloud veiled Kerinyagga peak.

Inside, the baby was kicking again.

How strange it feels, she thought, to be a patient. How lucky that the sweet-faced Irish nun is a trained midwife. Now I only have to bear the labour bravely; bear Leo the son he so dearly craves.

'Away with you then,' Sister Bernadette had chided, shooing Leo's tall, tense figure out. 'She's a while to wait yet. The good Lord works His mysteries best by moonlight.'

'This is a Reid,' Leo retorted, 'and anxious to arrive. I'll wager it happens before nightfall.' And had left, with a chaste kiss and a sympathetic squeeze of Rebecca's hand.

So she was surprised, in mid-afternoon, to hear a motor car approach, and a familiar breathless Scottish voice. 'Dinna fuss, Sister, she'll be grateful for the company.' Then Molly Stuart bustled in, spread her yellow skirts, and settled in the bedside chair. '*Such* a blether, dear, last night at the White Rhino; your Leo and my Eric, every settler for twenty miles around. Yon Colonel Elliot made his presence felt. "We need a club," he says. "No need to live apart, like lepers."'

'Good idea,' Rebecca murmured; but Molly had gone pink with indignation. 'White Christian gentlemen only, Elliot said, with service in a decent regiment. No Jews, no foreigners, women at their husbands' invitation.' Molly paused, shook her head in bemused reminiscence. 'Kobus Coetze answered; never thought he had it in him. You know that holy look of his, that funny, pinched accent? "Good luck, menheer," he said, "for you'll have a membership of one!" Elliot went brick red, fiddled with his monocle, snorted like a cornered warthog. "Harummph," he growls, eyeing Kobus meanly. "Forgot about you chaps. Fought for King and Country, what? 'Spose you'll have to be included." "Damn decent of you," Eric shouts. "Who says we'll let *you* in?" What a nerve, after that fiasco in Nairobi! It might have got quite nasty, then, but for Hugo Berkeley. Calmed things down, and made them talk practicalities.

Funny, about Hugo – so slim, so unassuming, but everyone respects him.' Rebecca nodded absently, feeling the first faint spasms, watching her bulging tummy ripple under tight-stretched linen. 'Polo,' Molly breathed, in wistful expectation. 'A dancefloor and a bar, a breath of civilisation in the bush! Brace up, my dear, deliver young Reid promptly, come and join the *fun*!' She was on her feet, vivid and birdlike, her expression tight with anticipation and concern. 'You're looking peaky. Should I call Sister?'

'Thanks, Molly, for keeping me amused. And yes, I think you should.'

And when Bernadette's bewimpled smile glittered in the doorway, Rebecca set her teeth and fought the growing pain, and murmured a fervent, silent prayer.

Dear Lord, let it be a boy.

He couldn't believe it was over so soon, couldn't believe the serene radiance of her smile, the storm of pride and tenderness that rocked his soul. Just a tiny, dark-haired, pink-skinned bundle at Rebecca's swelling breast, a sturdy sucking sound, a cosy, milky whiff.

And a sunset room which harboured everything he loved.

He tiptoed forward, kissed her damp, silky hair, laid unsteady hands upon his son.

'You were right,' Rebecca whispered, her eyes misty silver with content and gratitude. 'About Ruth's child, I mean. I could not have loved her quite like this. Smile, Leo. Smile for Lancelot.'

The name rang false, too big and grand for such a tiny creature; but he couldn't find it in his heart to argue, would let nothing interrupt her joy. For the moment, it was enough to stand beside his woman and his child, let peace and pleasure flourish, and savour all the joyful years ahead.

Presently, the Sister came, and laid the baby in his crib. She drew the gingham curtains, settled Rebecca down and ushered Leo out. 'Rest easy, Mr Reid. They are in the good Lord's keeping, this and every night.'

And in mine, he vowed.

He went out to the verandah, gazed across the repaired pasture where pale green seedlings sprouted, down towards the sparkling river's edge. There, so many years ago, he had defied Masai lances and become the Lion Boy.

Lance, he thought, that will be his name.

He will be tall and straight and valiant, clever, proud and true. Rebecca will wean him with that great tenderness which first drew us together. Then she and Duma will teach him the rhythms of the land. When he is older, he will learn to hunt with me; learn the secrets of the forest and the splendour of the kill. If he weeps at first, as she did, that will be fitting, too.

Drums were rumbling, into the fall of eve. Sunset and birdsong burnished Camelot. The legend lives, thought Leo, and mingles with the dream.

And one day, Lance will own this land.

'We have to stay together,' Mwangi told anyone who would listen, after the Norfolk Hotel massacre. 'We have to make Thuku's plan come true.'

But even those who listened paid no heed.

'It was rash and foolish to face the troopers' guns. Two score were killed. Thuku is in jail, and we are no better for it.'

'Why should we fight the white man? We have land in the reserves, work on the big farms, and new medicines to cure our ills.'

'They are taking away our laws,' Mwangi would cry, 'teaching our children to dishonour their elders!'

'We hear no complaints from the elders. They grow rich and happy in Ngai's grace.'

'Because the white men give them power and money! Because they are old and blind and afraid of war.'

'Don't speak of war here, young man. Have you forgotten what happened in Nairobi?'

And so it went on, in a circle Mwangi couldn't break.

Until one day near Thika, in a dim, rank bar, he found Thuo again, and told him what he, Mwangi, had seen.

'Berkeley,' Thuo groaned. 'I should have killed him when I had the chance.'

'You agree?' Mwangi whispered, in wonder. 'You are ready to fight on?'

'I'm a warrior. What else can I do?'

He stood there, sturdy and well muscled, his dark, angry glare aiming north towards Nyeri. 'I too have scores to settle in the valley.' His downward glance turned hard and scornful. 'How can you help? You were always weak and puny.'

'Teach me!' Mwangi hissed, and let the Healer's rhythm take his voice. 'Teach me how to cast a spear. Show me the soft parts of a man, where simi-steel bites best. Take me to the forest, make my limbs grow strong. I will learn, Thuo. *I will learn.*'

He saw Thuo flinch, revelled in the rebirth of his power. 'These are our enemies. Say them after me. Duma, Berkeley, the Silver Woman – and the Lion Boy.'

It will be a long hard struggle, he thought, remembering Thuku's prophecy as Thuo's obedient voice echoed the names. It starts today, in Thika.

It will not end until we take my land.

26

THE PUPPY CROUCHED BESIDE bare childish toes, its brown eyes gleaming, its tongue lolling pinkly over sharp white teeth. 'Watch, Duma!' pleaded Lance. 'Watch Simba do his tricks!' The falling sun touched his slender, six-year-old body, coppery hair and long straight limbs. He has his father's boldness, Duma thought, his mother's grace, and Morgan's colouring. 'Fetch, Simba!' The stick arced out against the deep blue sky. Stick and boy and puppy went whooping down the slope.

Simba, Duma mused, a tawny scrap of fur named for the lion, growing strong and clever with this latest lion boy. Raising them brings pride and purpose in advancing age. Why, then, do I feel this sense of shadow in the valley?

Perhaps it is because of all the changes.

Faintly, borne on meadowsweet breeze, he heard singing from the Mission. Once a month Kibe came, and half the village went to church. Herdboys learned from small black books and Esther turned the maids from circumcision. The old laws are fading, Duma thought, are the new ones strong enough? What will happen when the Healer dies?

He gazed up the slope where dam water glinted between dark green coffee bushes. Soon, the memsahib said, the first crop would ripen, bringing wealth and ease into the valley.

River ducks were winging towards the dam, like broad dark arrowheads. Duma heard a deep, double report, saw blue-black smoke eddy, watched the leading arrowhead fold and fall. The memsahib is up there now, he realised, with her favourite little shotgun. Soon, she will ride down flushed with pleasure, and show Lance how to pluck the still-warm birds.

She has nursed her man and her land through fire, disease and flood, borne a worthy son, and grown into the bloom of womanhood. She, like Leo's mother, is tougher than she looks.

Why, then, when Leo isn't looking, does she sometimes walk alone beside the big house, hunched and pale as if she hurts inside?

Perhaps it is because she has so little time with Lance or because there have been no more children, or because Leo is so often away.

It had begun, Duma remembered, about three years ago when the dam was complete, the coffee had been planted and the sheep had settled in. When the work became routine and unexciting.

And the new club opened in Nyeri.

Leo had taken to a game the whites called polo: riding horses to a lather, chasing a small white ball. He went all over Kenya to play, was frequently away the whole weekend. At other times, he brought Berkeley and Stuart to the huts, to drink maize beer and speak Kikuyu and remember all the Schutzetruppers they'd killed.

Once, at sunrise, he had seen Leo up beside the dam. He was gazing north, beyond Mount Kerinyagga's blue-grey mass. Silver glinted in his hair. His face was gaunt with misery and longing. He wants to hunt, Duma realised. He craves the wink of spears, the whiff of powder, the boil of battle fever in his blood.

A Lion Boy needs enemies to fight . . .

Noises broke the daydream: a puppyish squeal, the thunk of wood on living hide. They have alarmed some creature at the river, Duma thought, a tusked wild hog, a lurking leopard. The young ones are in danger, and under Duma's care!

He scurried down the twilight hillside, yearning for a weapon, cursing stiffened joints and absentmindedness. The squeals rose sharper from a shaded thicket, filling him with urgency and fear. He plunged through a clatter of startled doves and thorns that raked his chest – and stopped short, before the violence raging there.

Lance crouched, snarling, in thick yellow grass, flailing wildly with the shattered stick. Each stroke made a solid, soggy thwack.

No cornered warthog snorted, no spotted leopard roared. A small tawny creature yowled and cowered underneath the rain of blows.

Lance was thrashing *Simba*.

Duma plunged forward, grasped the slender, upflung arm, awed by its wiry force. He wrenched the boy away, flinching from the savage, twisted face. Lance's dark blue eyes were veiled, the fine lips flecked with froth. 'Bad dog,' hissed Lance. '*Bad dog!*'

And thrust splayed, splintered wood into Duma's face.

259

A hunter's reflex saved him, a swift straight lunge that struck the boy's wrist squarely, sending the raw stick spinning away. Duma felt the nightmare falter, saw recognition soften Lance's gaze.

'Hello, Duma. Why are you holding me?'

Cautiously, he let the limp arm drop, slipped his hand around slim, shaking shoulders, made soothing noises to the battered pup.

'What's the matter?' Lance mumbled. 'Why is Simba whining?'

'Don't you know?' Duma whispered, feeling coldness gather in his soul. 'Don't you remember?'

Slowly, wonderingly, Lance raised his right index finger, turned it into fading pink light, showed Duma the tiny red puncture in the skin. 'Simba bit me. Mummy said he must be punished when he plays rough. Simba *bit* me.' His eyes were dark and clear again, his smile as innocent as a new dawn. The puppy fawned around his feet, its tail stirring faintly. Just a boy and a dog, Duma thought, in a sunset thicket where the river gleams.

He is his father's son, Duma told himself silently. He has the battle fever. When he is hurt, he gives hurt in return. It is nothing to worry about. I will tell no one.

I will keep soul-coldness to myself.

He heard a hoof-fall, smelled heated horse, felt the mounted shadow slide across him, and turned upwards into memsahib's cool grey gaze. 'What's the trouble, Duma? Is everyone all right?'

'No trouble, memsahib.'

He saw her eyes narrow, watched her puzzle over trampled grass, the dispirited puppy, the discarded shortened stick. She leaned down, tight-lipped, lifted Lance on to the saddle in front of her, called the puppy to the grey mare's heels. 'You have some explaining to do, my boy.'

Voices and hoofbeats faded up towards the big house. Duma sighed and took the rising slope slowly, making for shadowed huts within this deeply shadowed valley. The unease was stronger now, locked in an inner image of a young boy's savage snarl.

A snarl that sent his mind back to a campfire celebration, to an older, darker boy whose face he'd struggled to forget – and a question which still plagued him in the night.

Does Mwangi's curse yet linger in this place?

The gum trees round the polo field stood tall and black and still, like inked outlines on a dim blue, faintly spangled wash. Practice had ended, men and horses trooped towards the distant yellow lamplight of the bar. Hugo trod through dewfall and the scent of horse manure to the near goal where Leo knelt and cleaned his bay's hind hoof.

'I smell trouble,' he announced, as Hugo neared. 'More aggravation from our beloved Colonel.'

Whatever else ails him, Hugo thought, his instincts still hold true.

Elliot had become their self-appointed, non-playing polo captain. As pompous and insufferable as ever, he shouted scathing comments from the sidelines, ran practice sessions like a martinet, took credit for each victory and disowned them when they lost.

But they could not disown him.

His army contacts ensured regular matches, his war service stood the club in good stead. If Leo had become Nyeri's star player, Elliot remained their indispensable talisman.

'He says you are too reckless,' Hugo muttered. 'You take too many chances and concede too many hits.'

'I also score the goals,' Leo retorted. 'Besides, I can't play any other way.'

'Quite. You'd better go and tell him.'

Leo straightened, running his forearm wearily across his brow. '*You* tell him, Hugo. He seems to take these things from you. Besides, I need a drink. Coming?'

Hugo hesitated, glancing pointedly at the fresh-sprung stars. 'It's late, Leo. Your people will be waiting.'

'*Et tu, Brute?* Will you, too, desert a friend in need? Just my little joke, Hugo. I'm going, like a well-trained pup.' He swung, sighing, into the saddle and turned the bay's head southwards towards invisible Camelot. Hugo bent and picked up a package abandoned on the ground. 'Is this yours?'

'Oh yes. Rebecca's mail. Thanks, I'd forgotten.'

Troubled, Hugo watched him ride away, a tall, somehow diminished figure on a tired horse.

Three tiny, trivial matters: an argument avoided, a bitter jibe, letters no one in this outpost would simply *forget*. It was so unlike the Leo Reid of old, who fought his own battles, chose his own path, needed no well-intentioned friend to guide him.

It has happened gradually, Hugo realised, strolling through the scented night towards bright lights and laughter. As Camelot prospers, Leo's strength and spirit seem to wane. Those of us who love him can only watch and mourn.

He paused, cocking his head, hearing Eric Stuart's hearty Scottish accent from the bar. Eric, who owes him a life, who represents this district on the Legislative Council, whose courage and shrewdness is respected by all.

Perhaps I will have a drink, Hugo thought, and a little heart-to-heart with Eric Stuart.

Leo hesitated at the hinge of Lance's door, hating what he was about to do. Behind him, he could hear lamp hiss and rustling papers – Rebecca studying the mail. Even with his back turned, he sensed the force of her impatience.

She was demanding that he do a father's duty.

'Something happened,' she had insisted. 'Something cold and ugly. The dog was terrified, Lance looked as if he'd seen a ghost. Duma's face was positively grey! I've warned you before, Leo, I've told you about his screaming temper tantrums. He has to be controlled!'

'He's only a child, Rebecca, stubborn and strongwilled – like someone else I know.'

But Rebecca would not be mollified. She stood, her arms akimbo, her eyes as grey as gunmetal. 'He looks to you for his example, worships the ground you tread. If you don't punish him, I will!'

And now, as Leo hovered and flexed the carpet slipper, he could feel that glare upon his back, that same indomitable will urging him to act.

He eased the door open, glimpsed Lance's huddled, cowering form, felt rebellion rising in his heart. Then the boy was upon him, a rigid, fragile, sobbing body pressed against his chest. 'I didn't mean it, Daddy, I couldn't help it! It was the pain, and the red haze in my eyes! Oh Daddy, Daddy, I'm so sorry!'

Leo closed the door behind him and eased his son away; he tried to set some sternness in his voice, tried to remember Father Andrew's litany of sin. 'Sit down, Lance. Be calm. Tell me about it.'

He was shown a pin-pricked finger, heard of sticks and tricks and Duma's fading attention.

'Red haze?' he repeated, puzzled. 'You mean the sun got in your eyes?'

'I don't know. I think so. I only meant to tap his nose, like Mummy said. But I couldn't *see*!'

He could see now, though. His sage-blue, pop-eyed gaze never left the slipper in Leo's hand.

In Leo's mind, a tall grey phantom stirred: a priestly, eagle-faced phantom with a slipper in his hand. Shuddering, remembering hours of anguish in a whitewashed mission room, remembering the sting of cracked leather on bared, boyish haunches, Leo knew he simply couldn't do it. This is my son, he told Rebecca's stubborn image, not a foundling to be forced into some godly mould. He raised the slipper and his voice – and winked solemnly at Lance. 'You must be punished, boy. Bend over!'

He saw Lance's eyes narrow in sudden understanding, shine in gratitude and conspiracy. Then, with a grin and a flourish, he drove the slipper smartly six times against the wall. 'Shout,' he whispered. 'Daddy's beating you!'

Lance shouted, six high-pitched, pitiful, thoroughly convincing squeals. He burrowed under clean white sheets and beckoned Leo closer. 'I knew you wouldn't hurt me. I'll never be naughty again!'

'Promise?'

'Promise!' Slim, surprisingly strong arms enfolded Leo's neck. Sweet childish breath warmed his cheek. 'Oh, Daddy, I love you best of all!'

Rebecca waited, ashen and aghast outside the door. 'Did you have to be so brutal? Let me go and comfort him!'

'Leave him be, woman!' Even in feigned anger, he could not give the direct lie. 'I have done your bidding; he won't forget tonight in a hurry. Now bring me a drink, and get on with your reading!' And for once, she obeyed him wordlessly.

It was only a minor evasion of responsibility, he consoled himself, sipping gin on the moonlit verandah. Lance was truly frightened, made duly penitent; no harm was done to woman, child or dog. Why, then, do I feel so uneasy, as if in some way I deceived myself?

Is it because of the red haze?

He had no time to ponder. Rebecca called him in: she was actually laughing. 'Isn't life strange? We bicker over tantrums while great events unfold!' She sat at the desk, transfigured, holding a letter in each hand. 'This is from the bank. The coffee's sold, the overdraft is cleared. We're free, Leo. Camelot is ours!' He moved dutifully to her, trying to reflect her joy. She held up her hand, smiling ruefully. 'This one's from England. Brother James died three months ago. No need for pious looks, man, we owe him nothing!' She cleared her throat, assumed a plummy pedantic tone. '"As Seton's sole living relative, you are the beneficiary of his estate. Be advised, however, that outstanding debts are likely to exceed the value of existing property and chattels. Should there be a credit balance, it shall be forwarded in due course. Enclosed please find various family deeds and documents."' Rebecca brandished a packet of musty, yellowing envelopes. 'You see? We owe him nothing!'

She took his hand, murmuring apologies for making him beat Lance, spreading her delight like some soft aura across the moonlit land. He stood beside her, still troubled, still unable to smile.

I should be happy, he thought. Seton's death removes the last faint shadow from the past. The moneylenders have no further claim on us. My son sleeps cosy in the house behind me, my lady sighs in pleasure at my side. Camelot shines in steely splendour all around me. The dream awakes, becomes reality.

And it is not enough.

Somewhere far inside, the lion grumbles, yearns for fiercer, harsher times: the glint of Masai warshields, the flying bullet's whine, a bruising battle for the land. But the lion is in bondage, made meeker than the lamb, held by the silken, smothering ties of love.

Rebecca leaned against him, pliant and sweet-scented. 'Isn't it beautiful?' she breathed. He kissed her, gazing above her silvered head to the great silvered starburst of the mountain. Help me, he pleaded silently, as familiar fires warmed his blood and willing bodies kindled.

Send me a new mountain to climb.

The Stuarts' black bull-nosed car steamed gently in the yard. Red dust plumes still coiled above the dark green coffee. Molly suborned Lance with 'treaties' from her bag. Eric had raised his trouser cuff and let the boy knock upon his wooden leg for luck. But the Scotsman's face was gaunt, and painful crow's feet arrowed around his pale blue eyes. He shooed Lance away, and led Leo to the quiet, shaded end of the verandah.

'I'm quitting the Council, Leo. Politics exhaust me, the wound won't give me peace.' Leo mumbled something sympathetic, watching Lance and Simba performing for the women. Molly oohed and aahed, leaned close and murmured urgently in Rebecca's ear. 'It's a hard life,' Eric continued, 'representing settlers who can't agree among themselves, crossing decent men like Hugo Berkeley. Hard on the women too, who have to stay at home and tend the farm. That's what Molly's doing here: preparing the way with your Rebecca.'

Leo sat quite still, sensing a weighty, sunlit Sunday moment; sensing a watershed in all their lives. Stuart smiled faintly, bestowing unspoken congratulation. 'The people hereabouts want you to take my place.'

The Legislative Council, Leo thought, in sudden, soaring excitement. The highest forum in the land. A seat at the hub of power, a voice in state affairs, a chance to shape this youthful, vibrant country.

A new mountain!

'Think on it then,' Stuart was saying, 'and fetch me a dollop of your special firewater.' But though he clearly shared Leo's pleasure, he couldn't sustain social banter, couldn't keep discomfort from his face and voice. Soon, despite loud protests from Lance and Rebecca, Molly helped him to the car, and rattled him away along the dusty track.

'Of course you must accept,' Rebecca cried, before Leo could even ask. 'It's an honour and a credit to us both. Oh Leo, I'm so proud!'

'Come and play, Daddy!' Lance pleaded. 'Make me fly, like Kree the kite!' He kissed Rebecca's golden, glowing cheek, letting her see the gratitude he felt, and went light of heart and foot on to the bright, green-velvet lawn.

Leo settled on his haunches. The sunlight sparkled on his silver streak. Lance burst from the pink-flowered bougainvillaea bush, his bare knees twinkling, his coppery mane aglow. 'Watch, Mummy! Whee!' He launched himself, fast and fearless, from several feet away. Leo caught him, springing upright, thrusting him aloft. 'I am Kree the kite,' piped Lance, 'I am Kree, the red kite!' He cocked his head, hooked his arms like raptor's wings, whistled sharp and shrill. 'Run, Daddy, make me swoop and glide!'

Leo ran, with strength and grace and power, under the blazing sun. Watching, Rebecca felt her spirit rise and join them. This is the dream, she thought, this is the way I always saw it. The house, nestling in greenery and flowers; corn rising yellow all along the silvered stream; Lance held high against the cloudless blue; and Leo, ablaze with joy and beauty.

It's cruel to bind a legend, Rebecca realised, to trap him in one place, harness his great power with our love. Like Kree the kite, he must be keen of eye and fierce of soul, free to soar and ride the changing winds. In order to hold him, I must let him go and serve the Council. This way, I know he will always come back home.

And Camelot will live for ever in our hearts.

27

LEO HATED paperwork.

For five months after Eric's visit he'd managed to defer it. There were crops to plant, dam walls to strengthen after heavy rains, a need to make things function smoothly before he left. Sensing change, Lance proved unusually demanding.

'Teach me to ride, Daddy.'

'Your Uncle Hugo is a better horseman.'

'Teach me to shoot, then!'

'Not before Duma is happy with your bushcraft.'

The ensuing tantrum prompted more mock beating.

'Next time,' Leo warned, meaning it, 'I will not beat the wall!'

Two weeks later, Hugo came, bringing flowers for Rebecca and grave adult courtesy for Lance. 'Hold the reins lightly but firmly. Feel the rhythm, let your body rise and fall.' And, as copper-headed boy and chestnut pony moved as one, 'You're a natural, like your mother!'

When the glowing child had gone to bed, while a whiff of roast lamb drifted from the kitchen, Hugo made a casual promise.

'I'll drop in once a week, to keep an eye.'

'Call it riding lessons,' Leo advised, 'that way, you won't be denting Rebecca's pride.' Hugo grinned, dark-eyed and wistful above his whisky. 'I shouldn't do you favours. Soon, we'll be on opposite sides!'

Sound, sensible Hugo, who'd grown in strength and stature down the years; who would be a formidable political adversary and yet remain a trusted friend. While I'm away, Leo thought, those I love will be well protected.

He could hear them outside now, son and mother frolicking with

Simba. There was sunlight through the window, a scent of new-sprung grass, and not much time before the Council session.

Leo sighed and settled to his numbers.

Presently, he wrote the healthy credit balance: they would not want for ready cash. He flexed his cramped fingers, stretched his aching back. His raised knee jogged the desk. A package tumbled from an alcove at the back: Seton family papers.

He rifled through, and came upon a sealed envelope which brought him upright and alert. 'For Laura Howard only, to be opened after I am gone. George Seton, April 1896.'

It had come among the family documents, and lain neglected ever since. The date gave Leo pause. The spidery script made him feel the sad, slow weight of time. George Seton, father to Rebecca and James, had penned this letter unaware that his sister-in-law was already dead; and he had himself been killed some years later. In Leo's mind, old questions rose anew. An image formed, of Laura's weathered cross beneath the Meru oak. The envelope rustled seductively in his hand. Her mysteries are mine, he thought. No one has a better right to know. He broke the dull red seal, unfolded musty paper, read the black looping words.

Words that froze the sunshine and dimmed the river's roar, that set a clammy shroud around his soul. They leered and capered far within his brain, forming a single obscene word too terrible to name. Darkness took him, darkness sprung at noon; it fixed him, numb and sightless, staring inwards at the wreckage of three lives.

Slowly, night retreated. Outside, on a rain-greened lawn between pink bushes, Rebecca chided Lance. He heard her soft mock anger, the boy's endearing laugh.

Outside this sudden prison, they were for ever out of reach.

All the love and labour, all the tears and joy, were reduced to godless horror by a man's confession read years too late. She has to know, he realised. Some day, she too must see these words, and understand this sick, stark truth. But not while the wound still feels so deep and mortal, not until I'm sure *I* can survive.

He pushed the letter back into the envelope, locked the tainted package into the lowest drawer, slunk through the kitchen and away across the yard. Away from those he loved so dearly and had so hideously wronged.

He walked without conscious volition, heedless of birdsong and the champ of goats. He trod a footpath through the risen maize, across a fallen tree trunk above the swollen river, between clinging thornbush to the further ridge. And gazed down on Camelot defiled.

There on cold grey rock beneath an ice-blue sky, he fought the horror boiling in his blood.

It was far worse than the discovery of Morgan's desertion, this secret shame in Laura Howard's past. Though all his instincts clamoured to deny it, the voice of reason whispered – *it is true.*

I know now why Rebecca never seemed a stranger to me, why her face seemed so familiar when we met. I know why Lance has tantrums, why the red haze sometimes blinds him. He is tainted by the very force that sired him. Father Andrew would have called it sin. Duma and his tribe call it tabu.

In ignorance and joy, we call it love.

I can't go back, he thought. We can never be the same again.

A kite wheeled above him, its rufous wings ablaze. It woke his gift of pictures, conjuring Lance's handsome, eager face. *'Make me fly, Daddy!'* The image dimmed and silvered, showed him Rebecca's lithe and naked splendour in the storm. *'Damn you, Leo, it's my dream too!'* Resistance kindled, lighting a stubborn flame within his heart.

They are words on paper, having meaning in no other mind but yours. Go back and burn them, spread the ash on Laura's grave, let love and Camelot redeem the past. We were innocent, we did not know. Rebecca is still innocent, need never suffer from her father's sin.

He was edging slowly down the slope, letting warmth restore him, feeling his power stir. Set me a test, you gods who deem me sinner. *Show me a sign!*

The sun shone blithely. Camelot's lawns and flowers shimmered in the haze. The river rippled, ragged, in between. Usually here, it made a long slow glide. Today the current spumed and chattered, twelve feet deep and forty yards across.

The river between.

It *is* a test, he realised. If I can cross, the sin will be washed away, the Lion Boy will prosper, the legend will endure. If the tabu is too strong, let the gods deny me; let these brown, boiling waters take me down.

He made himself one last bright beckoning picture – *something I am prepared to die for*: a sunlit birthing room, a suckling, fresh-pink boy, Rebecca's serene, ash-blonde loveliness. *'Smile, Leo. Smile for Lancelot.'*

Leo smiled, and dived.

Noise and cool silk violence sucked him in, rolled him over, flung him upwards like a cork. Seen distantly through muddied spray, the green bush on the further bank went racing past; too fast, too far away. I am the Lion Boy, his inner force was crying, I dwell within the Healer's charm! His strength held, his stroke steadied. The picture and the people in his mind grew brighter. He surged towards them, winning, coming home.

He never saw the half-sunk log that hit him, felt only its clubbing impact and the soggy crunch of stove-in ribs. He went under, flailing, tumbling, clinging desperately to breath and consciousness. Pain knifed through him, sharp and savage, forcing him to double up and gasp. Icy water scoured his throat and nostrils, forcing air and light and purpose out. Lance and Rebecca dwindled in his mind, leaving him, weeping, calling their farewells. And, in a darkening corner, the crippled lion stirred. It circled, yellow-eyed and triumphant, opened bloody fangs and lunged at him.

He knew then that the charm had failed him, that the gods had judged him guilty and the river would prevail.

Knew that he would never enter Camelot again.

Yet even as the great jaws tightened round him, even as great sorrow seared his soul, the Lion Boy found one last cry of defiance, gloried in a poignant victory. Camelot will live, because the secret sin dies with me.

Rebecca will never have to know!

Duma destroyed the dream.

He hunched on emerald greenness, his hawk face gaunt and grey, his voice harsh with tragedy.

'The Lion Boy is drowned.'

She heard his words, but refused to grasp their meaning. She sagged against the wall and clutched the rough-hewn railings, feeling the small pains clearly: white-hot sunshine into suddenly dimmed vision, a splinter in her palm, angled brickwork chafing at her hip. The larger pain was just a gaping inner void.

Silent tribesmen bore him through the high green maize, laid him on the verandah settle, crossed his hands upon his broad, still chest. He lay naked, bronzed and perfect, but for the pallor at his loins and livid bruising at his side. Sunshafts touched the sodden silver streak, breaking golden on his curled, closed lashes.

He looked like some peaceful, potent, sleeping god.

She longed to tear her clothes off, rouse him to swift passion as she'd done so often when he raced up from the river. But Lance appeared, staring, raised a stricken face and an anguished outcry. 'Make him sit up, Mummy, make him smile for me!'

A corner of her mind stayed calm, recalling the comfort Scottish Nanny had once offered. 'Be brave, Lance, he's with the angels now.'

'He *isn't*! I can *see* him!'

Mourning drums and ululation echoed down the ridge. She held her son's hot quivering body, held her husband's lifeless hand, watched the twilight conquer Camelot. She saw approaching dust-plumes, heard a car door slam, heard Eric Stuart's stumping gait. Then Molly's bone-white beaky face loomed and Lance was lured away. 'Can't *you* wake him, Molly? Can't you make Daddy smile?'

Relieved of Lance's weight, Rebecca could not straighten. She crouched and hugged the place where pain was growing. She heard urgent hoofbeats and hurrying footfalls; saw Hugo Berkeley standing to attention and weeping, unashamed.

Why can't I cry? she wondered.

Eric Stuart draped a dark grey blanket over his nakedness, and held it above the lovely, empty face.

'Not yet,' she pleaded, 'please, not yet!'

He faltered, and folded the shroud under Leo's chin. She knelt and fondled tawny hair, kissing the smooth pale brow. Coldness seeped down from her lips, through her breasts and deep into her body. Leo, she whispered, *Leo*, knowing she would never hear an answer, knowing that a part of her had set for ever stony.

Hugo took her hands and raised her. 'Anything, any time – you only have to ask.' His dark-eyed fervour briefly pierced the pain: a promise for a future too bleak to contemplate.

Night fell. Lance found fitful sleep. The tribesmen stood dark vigil on the lawn. The village women's high-pitched grief tore at Rebecca's heart. She let the Stuarts usher her inside.

'God took him in his prime,' said Molly. 'Take comfort, dear. He never will grow old.'

'Drink this,' urged Eric, 'it will warm you.' He gave her gin, which tasted vile and left the pain undulled.

Someone mentioned funeral arrangements. Her decision formed at once, without the smallest doubt.

'He will lie beside his parents, beneath the Meru oak, facing Ker-inyagga.'

'You'll be needing shipboard passages,' Eric said. 'You'll be wanting to go home.'

'Home?' she cried. 'This is home!'

Some time in the small hours, after Hugo left and the Stuarts had talked themselves into torpor, she tiptoed to Lance's door. Moonlight sparkled on his fine, clean features. If there is a dream, she thought, it lives in him. Oh Leo, how shall I bring him up without you?

Alone and afraid once more within the rustling night, she could not stop the long-blocked pain's advance. It began at her most secret centre, rippled up and through and out: a silent scream of grief and fury echoing in her brain. Now, at last, the hot tears broke. She stumbled into yellow lampglow, past her slumped, would-be com-forters, across blurred boards and on to the verandah.

There, while moonlight turned once-golden Camelot to frosted steel, while black bats swooped and the river murmured malice, she stood beside her shrouded knight and mourned the loveless years ahead.

Oh Leo, it should not have come to this.

In the rhyme, the river took the lady.

28

EACH MORNING, DUMA brought herdboys to tend the sheep, and chirping, beaded women to weed among the maize. He patrolled the boundaries, kept the dam sluice clear, supervised the tribesmen at their work. Each evening, Hugo checked the coffee, fed the horses, swept the stables out. He sat beside her when the twilight lowered, trying to keep her strength and spirits up. She valued his affection, and knew in time it might grow deeper. If Duma was her faithful, file-toothed shadow, Hugo was her slimmer, darker knight.

Between them, they kept the farm alive. In her heart of hearts, she knew it was not enough. Without Leo to inspire them, the tribesmen moped and lazed. Slowly, week by week, the profits faltered.

Rebecca worried only about Lance.

Too hurt to help, too young to hide his grief, he dogged her every footstep and demanded all her time. He cowered from the river, flinched from swooping kites, started at any unknown sound. He trailed her skirts by daylight and stole her rest at night.

It began soon after Leo's funeral, his dream of marbled death. He woke screaming, stood rigid and blank-eyed in her embrace.

'Bring him back! Make him smile for me!'

'I'm here,' she breathed, smoothing his coppery hair.

'Go away. I want my *mummy*!'

'It's me. Your mummy's here!'

He peered straight through her, stamping, slavering, calling her yet again. The violence stunned her: it took her minutes to dispel it and made her fearful for his sanity. Finally, some word or touch calmed him, bringing him out in a cold sweat and a crooked smile of recognition. Then his face crumbled and his tears flowed, and he set up a heartbroken wail.

'I want my daddy back!'

Such fits came upon him several times a week. Soothing them only kept her own wound open. She learned to dread his sleep.

And everywhere she turned, she saw Leo.

She saw him riding upwards to the forest, his tawny mane gleaming, the rifle flashing from the saddle sheath. She saw him stand against the morning grey, stripped to the waist, his body glowing while the bright axe leapt and clove hearthside logs. She heard his voice in nightwind from the forest, his footfalls when dawn coldness shrank the boards. Each night, she felt the comfort of his arms, smelled his musk, dreamed the pleasures of his urgency. Each morning she woke to an empty bed, a barren body and an aching heart. Camelot was dying, within her and without.

Rebecca had forgotten how to smile.

Then, one blazing morning, Big Flynn invaded Camelot. He came along the cart-track from Nyeri, driving a battered, tattered covered wagon drawn by two rangy iron-grey mules. Pots and pans twinkled from the buckboards at the side, dust swirled like thick red fog. Flynn sat astride the bootbox at the front, exactly as Leo had once described him: massive, bullet-headed, blue-jowled and ham-fisted, cracking the whip, singing the mules onward in a melodious Irish tenor. He brought the clattering vehicle to a halt at the back door, bowed low and introduced Rebecca to his 'darlin' blackbird Bertha'.

She stepped like a dusky Amazon from the canvas flap, tall, superbly proportioned, wearing a snowy smile and a low-cut scarlet dress. ''Tis sorry we are for your trouble,' she said, in a garbled copy of his accent; and three vibrant, coffee-coloured Flynnlets came brawling in her wake.

'Ian, Liam and Brian,' Flynn announced proudly. 'Liam's handsome and sweet-natured, like herself. The others, poor wee souls, take after me.'

Nonplussed, temporarily speechless, Rebecca saw Flynn's button-eyes widen, sensed the hovering presence at her skirt.

'You'll be Lance, no doubt. Out with ye, then, there's folk for you to play with.'

Lance hung heavily on Rebecca's arm. His face took an all-too-familiar pucker.

'What's this?' cried Flynn, 'tears, from the son of Leo Reid? He's up there, y'know, smiling at Himself's right hand!'

It was the first time anyone had spoken Leo's name in Lance's hearing. Rebecca held her breath, awaiting the outburst.

Lance stepped forward haltingly. His dark blue eyes were moist and narrow. 'Did you know my daddy?'

'*Know* him? And didn't he lay Big Flynn low with but a single punch?' Flynn went to his knees, bobbing and weaving behind great rock-like fists. 'Come on then, show us you're your father's son!'

Suddenly, Lance was prancing in the dust, swinging at Flynn's sun-browned pate, while Bertha raised exasperated eyebrows and the big Irishman feigned distress. 'Ow, cease, enough! Bejasus, 'tis a fighting man y'are! Brian, Ian, Liam, take this murtherin' heathen off, show him the treasures in the wagon!'

Brian grinned, a grubby, mischievous miniature of Flynn.

'*We*'ve got a rocking horse,' he said.

And then there were four.

Four small boys, gesturing and gabbling all at once, vanishing like a minor red tornado into the dim, arched wagon. Presently, still tense and unbelieving, Rebecca heard a sound she'd feared she'd never hear again.

Lance was laughing.

'Mr Flynn,' she whispered shakily, 'excuse my manners. It's hot. You must be dying for a drink.'

'Bless you, ma'am, I thought you'd never ask!'

Once inside, nursing a neat whisky in a massive paw, Flynn turned briefly sombre. 'Like Bertha said, we're sorry. He was a mighty man. No word of mine can heal you, that's best left to the Dear. Meanwhile, Bertha and the boys will see to Lance, and I'll be putting Camelot to rights. No arguments. Call it tribute to the Lion Boy.'

'You're very kind,' Rebecca murmured, through the threat of grateful tears, 'but Duma and Hugo Berkeley are in charge.'

'Och, we're pals from way back. We'll get on fine. Make peace with living, girl. Let Flynn and Bertha worry for a while.'

Bertha cooked and brought the garden into bloom. She moved in tranquil beauty, oozing calm and goodness from each ounce of gleaming ebony skin. Flynn put verve back into the tribesmen, and soon had them singing as they worked. Unburdened, visibly relaxed, Duma played nurse and tracker to the youngsters. Sitting on the verandah in gentle soothing shade, Rebecca watched them scrum and tumble by the river: four boisterous boys, a growing pup, and an old brown man who was beginning to stride freely once again.

Only Hugo seemed put out by the invasion. Arriving late one afternoon, he had a solid handshake for Flynn, a soft smile for Rebecca – and a startled, sheepish, almost fearful gaze for Bertha. 'They're right,' he told Rebecca, 'you are more yourself already.' He wouldn't meet her eye. His polished riding boot scuffed the dust. 'I'll leave them to it, then. Duty calls.' He rode off quickly, without a backward glance.

It was a small mystery which nobody explained and which Rebecca soon dismissed. That evening, she went up the sunset slope to the high green Meru oak where now four wooden crosses stood. There, while crickets hummed and doves crooned, she sought comfort in bright memories and the beauty of the land.

The land that Leo loved so well.

I have to *live*, she told the silent, still-raw grave. I have to conquer pain, if only for Lance's sake.

And thought she sensed his spirit smile and nod. Her first fierce desolation faded. Slowly, grief was giving way to mourning, and altogether softer, sweeter pain.

Next morning, Flynn emerged from the wagon carrying tools and lengths of iron pipe. With much clattering and banging, with black grease to his elbows and an Irish ballad on his lips, he started out to 'modernise' Camelot. He set up a charcoal boiler, channelled water from the dam outfall, plumbed the kitchen and the bathroom. 'Hot and cold running,' he grinned. 'Smart as any city hostelry.'

He dug the long-drop deeper, produced a brand-new toilet pedestal from the wagon's wondrous depths, and set the swing door just below eye level so that, seated, the occupant could ponder on Mount Kenya's peak. 'A loo with a view,' he declared.

But his masterpiece was the Great Coffee Shute.

For years, the tribesmen had complained about humping heavy coffee bags down the hill. The slope was too steep and broken to take an ox-cart; Leo wouldn't demean his ponies with such menial labour. Flynn vowed to solve the problem 'in one fair, fell swoop'.

A few days later, after more mysterious hammerings and sawings, he led them all out into the pasture, and gloried in the product of his toil.

It snaked down from the dam wall on the plateau, a V-shaped

timbered channel supported on ever shorter struts. 'Simplicity itself,' Flynn crowed. 'You toss a bag on top and it comes sliding gently down.' He stuck two stubby fingers in his mouth, waved his other arm, and gave out a piercing whistle. Far up on the slope, beside dark green coffee leaves and the glitter of dam water, a small brown matchstick figure waved and whistled in reply.

The boys cheered. Simba yapped feverishly. Presently, the timbered V began to quiver. Standing ten yards directly below it, arms folded, bullet pate agleam, Flynn raised his chin in pride and demanded due respect.

'Hush there, hold your peace. 'Tis an engineering marvel you're beholding!'

Rebecca heard a sudden whoosh and rattle, and saw a hempen coffee bag go leaping from the shute, arc across the space and cannon into Flynn's barrel chest. The Irishman went down like a ninepin. The bag split, green coffee beans fountained against the clear blue sky. Simba growled and 'seized' the wind-blown bag. Flynn groaned and spat out coffee beans.

And four-year-old Liam, pop-eyed in utter joy, shouted, 'Do it again, Daddy!'

Flynn stood up, cursing, only his pride damaged. Bertha giggled with relief. The dog yipped and capered, the boys were hooting with mirth.

And suddenly, in the sunstruck dusty pasture beside bright Camelot, Rebecca was laughing too.

The mess had been cleared up, and Rebecca won a promise that the shute would be dismantled. 'So much for engineering,' Flynn rumbled, rubbing his chest ruefully. ''Twould seem the old ways are best after all.' He took Bertha's arm, walked her gently down towards the wagon. As they passed, Rebecca witnessed a very private communion. Just a glance between man and mate, quickly delivered, instantly accepted – mutual need and tenderness more potent than any words. It made her very sad, very envious. They have eased the shadow over Camelot, she thought, but I still have to live here, on my own.

When her vision cleared, she found herself gazing north towards green Nyeri Hill, wondering when Hugo would return.

BOOK IV

LANCE
1929-1939

29

HE PACED THE DIM BROWN boards in Hugo's office, his monocle aglitter, his outrage unrestrained. Behind him, morning sunshine lit the window, touching whitewashed police huts and crowflight over Nyeri Hill.

'They're plunderin' the forest,' Colonel Elliot growled, 'shootin' down a dozen buck a day. Bloody Boers – knew we shouldn't let 'em in the club!'

'I'm busy, Colonel,' Hugo sighed, pointing at the mounded files on his desk. 'Can you prove the accusation?'

'Everybody knows it, man! What are game laws for, I want to know?'

'My men are fully occupied with drunkenness and stock theft. Game laws are poorly framed and very tricky to enforce.'

'Nonsense! I'll wager you'll find proof at Coetze's place: a smoke house full of biltong, a floor knee deep in pelts.' Elliot's muddy glare narrowed. 'You're dodgin' the issue, Berkeley, spendin' too much time with young Reid's widow!'

Feeling the flush rise to his cheeks, Hugo bit back a sharp retort. For several weeks, for his own uneasy reasons, he'd avoided Camelot. But Elliot was astride a favoured hobby horse. 'I've done *my* duty, by reporting the infraction. If you don't do yours, I'll be writin' to H.E.!'

How nice it would be, Hugo mused, to give this pompous oaf the short, sharp treatment he deserves. But there *is* a crime, there is a duty. He muzzled pride and gave polite assurance. 'Very well, Colonel. I'll look into it personally.' And scowled in self-disgust as Elliot swaggered out.

Briefly, peace and paperwork prevailed. Then he heard a clatter of high heels. Molly Stuart bustled in. She wore peacock blue, and fresh henna in her hair. Her small beaked face was bright with battle fever.

'How long are you going to sit there and turn Nelson's eye while Rebecca makes a spectacle of herself? Don't give me that innocent brown look, Hugo Berkeley, you know exactly what I mean. It's those *awful* Flynns!'

'They were Leo's friends, and mine.'

'You were rather more than *friends*, Eric says! Can't you see the bother they create? Joined in sin and a squalid gypsy wagon, raising half-caste brats on Camelot? My dear, the whole district is aghast; and *what* an example to the natives!'

Since Leo's death and Eric's reinforced recall to the Council, Molly's bubbling gaiety had soured. Her campaign against female circumcision had grown strident. She flaunted her religion like a flag. This morning she looked shrewish. Her Scottish accent grated like a file. 'It's disgraceful and immoral. You must make her see some sense!'

'If you feel so strongly, why don't *you* enlighten her?'

'You're our spokesman, Hugo, it's your job to keep common decency!'

'I'm the D.C., not the parish priest.'

Molly flounced to the door and took a vengeful, bright blue stance. 'If you don't shift the Flynns, you'll forfeit my respect – aye, and that of every Christian man around!'

For a second time this sunlit morning, Hugo was left to ponder the burdens of his calling: to uphold the law and foster Christian virtues, to strive for justice where conflicting cultures clash. The community must take precedence above the individuals, the issues must be thrashed out face to face. I have been avoiding trouble, he acknowledged, ignoring Boer transgressions, hoping Flynn would slip away as quickly as he came. Now I must confront the Coetzes and parade Bertha's dubious past before Rebecca.

Because these are my duties.

Hugo paused outside the Coetze homestead door. Behind him, the tethered gelding snorted, the river gleamed, the warm breeze ruffled half-grown wheat. Close to, the whitewashed walls looked grey and flaky. Rusting ploughshares littered the dusty yard. The noonday air smelt of half-cured hides and looming confrontation.

Sounds inside deepened his unease: childish whimpers, a woman's chiding voice. He swallowed and rapped sharply on the weathered wood. The noises ceased. The valley seemed to cringe before some ugly revelation.

The door eased ajar. A broadening yellow shaft entered Coetze's gloomy kingdom, lighting sacred texts and pictures on the dark daub walls, bronze buckskins on the red stone floor, a blackened cauldron steaming above glowing ash.

And a semi-naked child huddling in the dimmest corner.

A little girl whose turquoise eyes were moist and glazed, whose raven hair hung lank on high-hunched shoulders, whose hands writhed like hunted mice between her close-clenched thighs. In that first fleeting instant, with a pulse of shock that jolted through his veins, Hugo thought he saw faint weals criss-crossing honeyed flesh.

Then Helena Coetze's shapeless grey-serge-swathed body blocked the doorway. Her pallid features formed false welcome, her voice rose far too bold and bland. 'Say hello to the Commissioner, Karen.'

Presently, a toneless childish voice obeyed.

Hugo edged forward. Helena's face set hard. She pulled the door tighter to her vast grey hips.

'You can't come in, menheer. It is against the custom while the husband is away.'

A custom she'd invented, Hugo reckoned, within the last half minute. 'Then I'll wait,' he snapped.

Helena shuffled, cleared her throat, avoided his eye. 'Try the waterfall, a furlong up the river. He sometimes goes there at this time of day.' The door closed. Hugo thought he heard whimpers start again.

Outside, the hot, still air seemed tainted. The ugly aura haunted him upstream through thickening, musty undergrowth. He intended no concealment, but shadow masked his movements and falling water drowned the noise of his approach. Presently, beneath a canopy of pale green podo leaves, he came on Kobus Coetze, un-aware.

At first, Hugo thought he must be hunting, so tense was his stocky body, so fierce his pale green eyes. Moving now with studied caution, Hugo eased behind him, following his ardent unwavering stare.

And he saw Rebecca through a rainbow sprung from sun and spray. She leaned against a mossy rock beside the tumbling brightness.

Her hair trailed like a silken web across the living green. She wore an ivory silk blouse, a long grey skirt and an air of poignant longing. She comes here for remembrance, Hugo realised. This was one of Leo's special places.

Coetze comes to watch her.

Surely, Hugo reasoned, there is no harm in watching. Her loveliness has already eased my troubled spirit. Then the wind shifted, the rainbow disappeared, and Hugo saw with renewed, icy clearness.

Saw sunshafts pierce the silky sheerness and light the swoop and curve of flesh beneath. From here, he could guess the shape of Rebecca's body. From Coetze's stand, she might as well be naked to the waist.

He could almost taste the heat of Coetze's hunger, almost feel the flare of unslaked lust; he was like a bearded satyr carved from the brooding shadow, poised to pounce on unsuspecting beauty. The ambience of the homestead lingered around him, something rank and dim and sensuous. The ugliness was urgent now. How long would Coetze be content to watch?

Hugo moved, loudly and deliberately, broke the evil spell, let Coetze see his anger and disgust.

And marvelled at the man's hypocrisy.

There was only a tiny, guilty start: the hot green leer softened, the sensual tautness became a pious slouch.

'So menheer, you spy on me while I commune with nature and the Lord!'

Hugo curbed the suspicion for which he had no proof, put his fear for Rebecca's chastity aside, and settled for the lesser, surer charge. 'I've come to see your smoke house. I'm told your people have been poaching game.'

'*Told?* Told by so-called English gentlemen, no doubt! Come then, we have nothing to conceal.'

Seven fresh-killed carcasses hung from dull steel hooks amid the buzzing blowflies and the reek of decayed meat.

'Impala,' Hugo murmured. 'Your licence only permits two.'

'I know the law, menheer.' Coetze's sneer was pink and contemptuous. 'They were trampling wheat. Farmers have the right to guard their crops.'

Sensing defeat, though reluctant to concede it, Hugo played his final card. 'I'll see the house and check the skins.'

'The great D.C. may enter as he pleases!'

Helena met them, visibly relieved. Hugo noted Coetze's anxious, urgent glare, her almost imperceptible nod. *What has she done with the child?* he wondered. Eerily, exactly on cue, Karen's voice echoed in the dimness.

'Welcome home, Father.'

She sat exactly as Hugo had last seen her. Her tone had the same flatness, her eyes held the same opalescence. Coetze bent and kissed her cheek, running a hairy paw across her honey-coloured skin.

Skin that quivered at his touch, yet shone without the smallest blemish in the flickering, faintly medicated gloom. They have drugged her, Hugo realised, and masked her disfigurement with some healing salve. He turned away, the taste of defeat sharper on his tongue.

Coetze lounged against the door-frame, cradling an ancient muzzle-loader, counting hides as Helena spread them out. '. . . five, six, seven. All correct, menheer, and each one was taken with a single ball.' The rifle swung casually upwards. The muzzle was an oiled black eye trained on Hugo's stomach. 'God guides our aim, Berkeley, when creatures trespass here: remember, when you pass this way.'

A covert threat, an open, smirking triumph; and Hugo could do nothing.

There was no proof.

Outside in sudden sunshine, he saw the door swing shut, heard Coetze's low-voiced, gloating chuckle. The aura was upon him again, a sense of wanton cruelty and dark, unnatural urges. He shivered, recalling his bold judgement at Nyeri Court, appalled at the ordeal little Karen must face daily; and he knew his own ordeal wasn't over.

He must confront Rebecca, warn her of the voyeur, tell her to keep Lance away from Karen.

'Come with me,' she snapped, when he'd tallied Mollie's protests. She led him to the bathroom and showed him the bright new piping, freshly painted lime-green walls. 'Flynn did that. He's outside now, digging a proper soakaway.' Faintly, Hugo heard the rasp of spade on soil, and a snatch of 'The Wild Colonial Boy'. Rebecca was off again, her grey skirt crackling, her ivory blouse aglow. She opened Lance's bedroom and gestured at the bed. 'See the patchwork quilt? Bertha sewed it, fifty separate pieces, by lamplight in the wagon, late at night. See how the whole place sparkles? That's Bertha's work!' She marched to the verandah and pointed down towards the river. Within the bush and scudding purple afternoon shadows, four boys and a tawny puppy romped. 'They've cured Lance's nightmares, showed him how to be a child again. And you want me to turf them out, because Flynn chose a black girl? I'll be *damned* if I do!'

In anger, her loveliness was stunning. The Flynns *have* worked wonders, he acknowledged: Lance is not the only one restored. 'It's not that simple,' he muttered. 'Bertha has a somewhat lurid past.' Rebecca waited, arms folded, foot tapping. 'She was a – professional lady – in Nairobi. She's been to bed, for money, with half the white male population!'

'So that's why we haven't seen you, why Lance has missed so many riding lessons!' He shrank from the sudden half-amused, half-contemptuous knowledge in her voice. 'Hugo Berkeley, pillar of the district: she's slept with *you*, too!'

Dimly, through hot-cheeked, tongue-tied embarrassment, he thought he glimpsed a hint of sympathy.

Swiftly gone. She drew herself up, fixed him with a level, steel-grey glare. 'On Sunday when the club is full I'll bring the Flynns to lunch. Reserve the central table. I'll wait on it myself. Let those who have objections make them to my face!'

He went, bowed by her fury and his own guilt, appalled by the image she had conjured: a white woman, serving Lola's famous blackbird in the Polo Club.

The scandal would resound throughout the land.

And he still hadn't warned her about Coetze.

'Beg pardon, Mrs Reid. You and I must talk.' In a welter of warring emotions as Hugo left, Rebecca scarcely noticed that the shovelling had stopped. Flynn loomed on the verandah steps, with red dust smeared along his brawny forearms and rare disapproval in his voice. 'I heard that little donnybrook: you're making a mistake.'

'Don't *you* start. My mind's made up.'

'Even so, you'll hear me out awhile.' Suddenly it was an order, enforced by greater years and bulk, and near-paternal firmness.

He climbed into the shade, held a chair for her, folded himself down beside her and lit a battered pipe. Around them was birdsong and river-gleam, a distant whoop and yap of boys and dog. Camelot lay basking in the fall of eve.

'A grand spot,' Flynn murmured presently. 'A fine and noble place.'

'Thanks to you, it may yet prosper.'

'You'll be staying then, building things for Lance?'

'Where else should I go?' Flynn's great dome dipped in acknowledgement. His pipestem pointed at the wagon.

'Whereas we'll be moving on. Our home has wheels.'

'You needn't go! I won't let them drive you out!' Flynn smiled, softer than the breeze, but there was iron in his tone.

'*No one* drives the Flynn away. We travel when and where the fancy takes us. The work is done. It's time for moving on.'

'Come to the club with me!' she cried. 'Show them they can't dictate our lives!' Flynn sighed, blowing out tart smoke. 'You'll be fighting a terrible fierce land, raising a boy to manhood; you'll need help from those who live about you. Why cross them, for the gypsy Flynns who'll soon be far away?'

'I owe you a debt. I mean to repay it.'

'Even when it hurts the ones to whom you would do honour?' His craggy face was suddenly tight with pain. 'D'you think my Bertha wants to sit amid sly winks and murmurs? D'you think I want to see my children pitied? Keep your blessed club, Mrs Reid. I'll take freedom, and the love of a dark-skinned woman!'

'Oh Flynn,' she breathed, glimpsing tragedy behind the comic blue-jowled mask, 'I didn't think. Forgive me, I'm so sorry!'

'Don't be. Some day, when there are fewer like Colonel Elliot and the Boers, when there are more like you and Hugo Berkeley, maybe we can sit and dine in public. Till then we'll value friendship, and go our separate ways. Don't cry, m'dear. I chose my loyalties, long ago – to hell with blinkered minds. That's life; and you have one to live!'

It took them an hour to pack the wagon, harness the mules, round up the puzzled boys. They did it in gathering twilight and the face of Rebecca's genuine dismay. 'How dare you go, without even a bite of supper?'

Flynn rocked on his heels, wearing his familiar, battered grin. 'Look at yourself, m'dear. 'Tis a fine fighting fettle that you're in, and no need for further coddling.'

As early stars twinkled and pale mist wreathed the river, Flynn bestrode the bootbox and aimed the wagon north. 'One last word,' he murmured, while Bertha bade Lance and Duma tearful farewells and the Flynnlets clamoured under the breeze-tossed canvas. 'Years ago, Mr Berkeley did us a great service. 'Tis he your scheme would damage most, being both club president and D.C. Which is another good reason not to do it. Be easy on him, Mrs Reid. Clear the blindness from your eyes. Some day soon, you'll need a man again.'

'Why, Flynn, whatever do you mean?'

'He's addle-pated for you, it shines through every move he makes.'

Flynn hullooed and snapped the reins. The wagon swayed and clattered up the Nyeri track. Brian, Ian and Liam bellowed their goodbyes. Bertha's snowy smile blazed bright. Rebecca watched the tail-lamp dwindle into dust-spiced darkness with teardrops on her eyelids and the warmth of Big Flynn's insight glowing in her heart.

Then Lance's cool, forlorn hand closed around her arm. She looked down at his crumpled starstruck face. 'Mummy, why did Hugo send the Flynns away?'

'He didn't, dear. They were only passing through.' She held him close, smiling gently in the dusk, feeling something thawing far inside her. 'Hush now, don't cry. We'll soon have you on a horse again. And it's still *Uncle* Hugo to you.'

Eric Stuart perched uncomfortably at the crowded club bar, nursing a whisky in one hand, kneading the stump above his peg-leg with his other. Behind him, the white-robed barman dispensed beer as fast as he could pour it.

'Indians,' Stuart growled, 'still intriguing for the highlands, and half of Whitehall raising their greasy sleeves. There's talk of freeing Thuku, a gold-rush in the west, and Happy Valley playboys fornicating like jack rabbits.' He swallowed, grimaced, rubbed his leg again. 'And Molly's stirring up the locals about blasted circumcision. What's *your* trouble, Hugo? You look as if you've lost a pound and found a ten-cent piece.'

'Duty,' said Hugo shortly, unwilling to confide. 'Kobus Coetze and the game laws.'

'Rather you than me.' Stuart leaned closer, pitched his voice below the hubbub.

'If it's any consolation, they think well of you down south. There's a whisper of promotion on the grapevine. Cheer up, then, it's your round.'

Funny, Hugo thought, with little humour. When you're drinking with a Scotsman, it's always your round. He caught the barman's eye, bawled his order, collected two amber refills and elbowed out of the crush.

Just in time to witness Big Flynn's entry.

He stood swaying in the doorway and a sudden outraged hush. Red dust smothered him from head to foot. His button eyes bleared darkly. 'Nectar!' he bellowed, scenting the air like a great bull-headed mastiff. 'Barman, bring a dying man a snort!'

He shambled forward, rolling his shoulders, scattering drink and settlers, apologising to no one. The barman cringed against the rack of spirit bottles.

'Stir your stumps,' Flynn shouted, crashing a dusty fist on to the bar. 'Me throat's like Satan's furnace!'

Then Colonel Elliot surfaced amid the still-stunned crowd and waddled to the fore. 'This is a members' club, sir. You can't drink at this bar.'

'Indeed?' drawled Flynn. 'Which brave bucko's going to stop me?'

Elliot looked him up and down, adjusted his monocle, gulped audibly. His panicked gaze traversed the room and came to rest on Hugo. 'Do your duty, Berkeley. Show this oaf the door!'

'Mr *Berkeley!*' Flynn echoed, in slurred, feigned delight. 'I do declare I've heard the name before! In wartime, sure it was, when Mr Berkeley rode a terrible fine steed, and troopers scurried to obey him. Be upstanding, Mr Berkeley. Do your worst!'

'Don't be a fool, laddie,' Eric Stuart hissed. 'Buy him two quick doubles and he'll fall into your arms!' But Hugo was aware of bated breath and taut expectant faces – and one short, unavoidable word.

Duty.

Somehow, he kept his hands and voice steady. 'You heard the Colonel. I must ask you to leave.'

Flynn's great booming laugh made the lamps jiggle. Oddly, Hugo caught no whiff of booze. 'We're gennelmen, me and Mr Berkeley. *Gennelmen* go to war outside.' A heavy paw fell on Hugo's shoulder. A heavier hand closed around his heart. Long dormant childhood terrors prowled his mind. He was committed to the night, to a granite-fisted drunkard, and the kind of confrontation which had always terrified him. This time, duty would bring pain.

Then there was darkness, a whiff of dust, and a sober Irish whisper in his ear. ''Tis a debt long overdue, for Bertha and the loving years between. I've smoothed your path to Camelot. This affray will buy you lasting fame.' The bar door opened. Yellow light and anxious voices filtered out.

'You all right, Hugo? Shall we fetch the quack?'

Flynn snorted, driving his own fist with a meaty thwack into his own palm. 'Enough, Mr Berkeley, you're too much for me!' And tumbled, moaning, into upflung dust. Then for Hugo's ears alone, 'Be off and play the conquering hero. Faint heart never won fair lady!'

Hugo mumbled incoherent thanks, strode blinking up the spangled golden lampshaft between pounding hands and sagging jaws. Eric Stuart actually bought a whisky. Colonel Elliot actually shook his hand.

'I don't know,' he answered astonished questioners truthfully. 'He just sort of folded up.'

Later in his tidy D.C. quarters which no fair lady had yet shared, he poured a final nightcap and pondered the surprises in a long surprising day: on duties which were starting to oppress him, dark, unconfirmed suspicions and laws that didn't work. On debts owed and paid by dead and living, on promotion he might no longer want.

Unwitting, no doubt from the purest motives, Flynn was forcing him towards a choice: the career he'd built from such unlikely beginnings, and the woman he had so long secretly admired. He swallowed whisky, scowling at his own presumption.

After today's confession, you'll be lucky if she lets you past the door.

He found her in the freshly plumbed kitchen, plucking bronzy feathers from a brace of river duck. She wore the same ivory blouse and a sheepish air that promised him reprieve.

'I'm sorry,' he began.

At exactly the same moment, she said, 'I didn't meant to cause you trouble.'

There was a brief pause, a sense of shared relief. Late sunshine made a halo of her hair. Weaver birds chattered in the gum tree outside. Presently, she brushed her hands together, scattered silvery down, nodded at the empty yard. 'They left, last night. Flynn said he owed a debt.'

'He paid it.' He outlined Flynn's performance, knowing she would hear of it, omitting only the last private exchange.

'Why?' she marvelled. 'Why would he do a thing like that?'

He breathed deeply, and took a calculated risk. 'Perhaps so that we should be here like this.'

'Then he's an interfering old Irish washerwoman!' But she blushed becomingly, taking on a vulnerability which brought him to his central purpose.

Coetze.

She listened, nodded calmly.

'I know. Coetze has been ogling me for years.'

'You still go there? You're not afraid?'

'You should have looked more closely. I always take a shotgun to the river. But I'm grateful for your concern.'

Her casual self-reliance awed him. Mutual tenderness rode the quiet, faintly bloodscented air.

'Hugo?' she asked softly. '*Did* you sleep with Bertha?'

'Long ago and far away.'

'There has been no one since?'

'No.' He fidgeted, under her steady, sympathetic gaze. 'When I'm in Nairobi, I visit – an old friend – at Lola's Funhouse. For goodness sake, Rebecca, I'm a *man*!'

'Poor Hugo.' Briefly, her warm hand rested on his arm, sending a sweet, swift pulse along his veins. She was standing very close, her pupils dark and smoky. He reached for her, drawn like a moth to a flame.

She stepped back, her head cocked, her breathing fast and fragrant. He heard boyish footfalls and her urgent, warning whisper. 'Don't rush me, Hugo. It's still too soon!'

The kitchen door flew open. Sunset flared in Lance's coppery thatch. 'Hello, Uncle Hugo! Is it too late to ride?'

Hugo was acutely conscious of Rebecca's blooming pinkness and his own awkward breathless stance. He saw the coltish silhouette stiffen, saw Lance's sage-blue eyes set hard.

'Tomorrow,' he muttered shakily. 'There'll be lots of time tomorrow.'

Lance took Rebecca's hand and a plaintive, possessive tone. 'Read me a story, Mummy.' Hugo watched her regain composure and touch the youthful, sunbrowned face consolingly.

In wooing the fair lady, he realised, I must also win the boy.

30

LANCE NOCKED HIS LAST arrow, breathed deeply, and drew back on the string. Behind him, the river lapped and sparkled. Reflected sunlight softened the furrows in his brow, setting his teeth agleam: small, even teeth, bared in effort and concentration. The target gleamed too, a broad pale gash cut from a podo trunk. It could be the same one, Duma thought, that Leo used to hit. Oh Ngai, let Lance hit it this time.

Briefly, it seemed that he might. Briefly, bow and boy were joined in perfect stance: feet well spaced and set in line, left arm braced and pointing, head still, right hand inching back across the slim, taut chest. A goatbell tinkled, faint and far off. The bush was still, expectant.

As always, Lance held the point too long. A tremor began in the outthrust cords of his neck, rippled across his shoulders into the hard, arced wood. His breast fluttered, his left arm buckled. Duma heard his furious sob and the dull thock of mistimed release; he saw the shaft dip and wobble like a wounded bird. It fell short and wide, without force or direction, not even piercing the soil.

'Collect your arrows, boy,' he sighed. 'Let us try again.'

'I won't! The bow is too thick and strong!'

'Ah, Lance. Yesterday, you blamed your old one, saying it was only fit for a child.'

'And now you have made this great stiff pole. You did it on purpose! You don't *want* me to aim true, you want to keep me from my father's guns!'

Lance flung the bow aside and glared upwards. Tears of shame and frustration flooded his cheeks. His slender, sun-flecked face quivered with emotion. 'Ever since my father died, I have worked as hard as any tribesman – tending sheep, weeding the coffee, splitting wood for the fire. You haven't even noticed. Like Mother and my Uncle Hugo, you only give me *lessons*! Take me to the forest, Duma. Teach me to hunt!'

'You are not ready,' Duma sighed, reluctantly. 'First you must be steady with the bow.'

'Give me the gun!' the boy beseeched. 'Then I will show you!'

'I cannot. That is for your mother to do.'

Lance stumbled into untilled pasture, among the startled soft-eyed sheep. He turned there, up to his knees in green, outlined against a bright blue sky. 'Some day, you'll be sorry. Some day you will know that I am the Lion Boy's son!'

Duma trudged and stooped, gathering scattered arrows. Barbed briars raked his wrist, jagged nettles stung him. Small pains, these, when set against the sorrow in his soul. Poor Lance, who, while his parents worked so hard to make the valley bloom, had been brought up almost like a young Kikuyu; whose skills could not yet match those of his father's ghost; and who, like everyone else in the valley, must wonder when his mother would take another man.

Why, Duma wondered in his turn, does Berkeley hover around her like an uncertain hawk? They have hungered more than two years for each other. Why does she not simply take him to her bed, and give the boy the strong male presence he so clearly needs?

How can clever white folk be so blind?

Duma came up from the river, breathing sheepscent, fingering an arrowshaft absently. Lance was a distant, stick-like form among the fresh-sprung maize, with faithful Simba at his heels, and the colour of kite plumage in his hair. Son of the Lion Boy, Duma thought, and that is the real issue.

His vision blurred. His mind went back to the council meeting . . .

It was the first secret meeting Duma had ever known. The Christians were not told. It was held at night, in Maina's hut, before elders who now came from Duma's age-group. In flickering firelight, beneath the sooty rafters, Maina looked like his dead father, Gitau: he had the same balding head, the same chieftain's monkey-skin cloak, the same taste for blue and yellow armlets.

And the same concern for land.

'The crops grow fair around the big house,' he began, eyeing Duma over steamy maize beer in the drinking horn. 'Coffee bushes bowed by beans, full ears upon the corn, green pasture to fatten sheep and goats. Is it not rich soil?'

Assenting *eeeh*s rumbled through the smoke.

'It is like many other big farms,' Duma pointed out. 'It costs many silver coins and even greater labour.'

'It is *not* like other white farms,' Maina retorted. 'It was never put on paper at the D.C.'s office. It was never parted from the valley.' The fire crackled. The elders nodded wisely. Duma waited, sensing trouble.

'Is it not a strange thing?' Maina asked softly. 'This fine land without a man to claim it?' His voice grew stronger. 'Is there any law which says a woman can hold land? Let the council answer!'

The council answered no: a long low growl which set Duma's teeth on edge.

'This was Duma's doing,' Maina continued. 'What does Duma say?'

'Why do you ask?' snapped Duma. 'You know the land was given to the Lion Boy, who lived within the Healer's charm and turned the Masai back.'

'The Lion Boy,' echoed Maina, with a pious smile, 'to whom I owe a life. May Ngai bless his soul.' He drained the drinking horn and smacked his plump red lips, rounded swift and sudden in the gloom. 'But the charm is broken, the Lion Boy is dead. Nothing of him lingers in this place.'

'There is a son,' Duma cried, 'a boy who grows daily in his likeness!'

'Born of pure white blood,' Maina sneered, 'who never dwelt within our huts and never knew our laws. Let the council answer: can *that* boy claim the charm?'

Duma tasted bitterness amid the beer fumes. This is why they keep the Christians away, he thought. So I must stand alone against Maina's greed, and hear the council steal my land away. He saw their grizzled heads nodding, watched their flabby chests rise to shout the victory.

And heard a chink of metal from the shadows by the hearth.

He came, colobus-kirtled into the ember-glow. His hair gleamed like the snow on Kerinyagga's peak, his eyes had taken on a milky cast. But he was still Njau the Healer, whose power held them breathless, whose voice still wove a soft, slow, snaky spell. 'Which of you knows how to tend the coffee?' he demanded. 'Will Maina's war-horn save you from the D.C.'s gun? Why are you so silent? Can the council say no word?' The council couldn't, Duma realised, because Njau willed it so. 'The Lion Boy brought plenty to the valley,' he reminded them. 'His son may yet hold blessings for the clan. There is a strangeness in him. It is too soon to tell.' Duma felt the magic weaken, sensing the effort it cost Njau to speak again. 'While Njau breathes, the charm endures. Watch and wait till Ngai sends a sign. Let the council so agree it!'

The smoke roiled, the obedient *eeeh*s rang out. Njau retreated, jingling, to his shadows. Even as relief raised Duma's spirit, he caught Maina's sullen glance and knew the matter wasn't finished. Njau has won some time, he thought. I must use it to fashion another Lion Boy.

Duma blinked, shook his head, heard sheep call and saw evening take the pasture. The air hung hot and still, the unease inside him deepened. Because when Lance raged and threw the bow aside, he had not looked like Leo.

Lance had looked like Mwangi.

Mwangi was sick of his sour, unwashed smell. He had lost count of the shifting seasons, the years of hardship in the deep bush, the hot-eyed youths who'd joined them briefly, only to desert when nights grew cold and food ran short. He'd grown tired of the rumours no one could confirm. Some said the Lion Boy was dead, and the farm was sliding back to pasture. Others said the pale-haired woman still tended it, with a half-grown son. Mwangi was sick of rumours, hunger, homelessness – and Thuo's company.

A vision kept him going, born of dim red embers while hyenas prowled and chuckled in the dark. In this vision, the big house had burnt down: Mwangi's hut stood in its place; Mwangi's goats grazed the cropless pastures; Mwangi the Healer ruled the clan. His power filled a valley free of white men.

One day, he vowed, it shall come to pass.

The colobus-skin kirtle had grown lank and stiff with dirt. Mwangi's limbs had hardened, his hair hung in a woolly, unkempt mop. Thuo had taught him wrestling holds, put a warrior's fire in his belly, showed him how to make a spear fly true. A little of Duma's bushcraft had stayed with him. The need for stealth and the constant fear of pursuit brought it to full bloom. He'd learned the

295

leopard's patience, and could wait in silent stillness for hours beside a starlit waterhole. He'd learned the jackal's cunning in ambush for small game, he could move like a thin black ghost through the thickest undergrowth.

He was moving like a ghost now, in broken woodland north of Fort Hall. His belly growled with hunger, his mind burned with suspicion. Thrice in as many mornings, he had woken to find Thuo's blanket empty.

Thuo, he believed, was robbing snares.

He sidled down a shady, dew-cooled gametrack, his head cocked to test the breeze. He was nearing the first snare. Thuo's familiar rank body smell grew stronger. Mwangi's suspicion turned to brooding anger.

A shadow shifted up ahead, a ragged, stocky shadow which took on Thuo's mocking, red-eyed sneer. He crouched above the first snare. A plump brown hare dangled, slack-necked, from his hand.

'That is *my* snare,' Mwangi growled.

'I got here first.'

'Give me the hare.'

Thuo's sneer became a warrior's grin. 'Come and take it, *Healer*!'

The hunger and the fury bubbled up in Mwangi's breast. Thuo's heavy muscles could no longer deter him. He went forward in a flailing rush, and Thuo came to meet him.

He gouged at Thuo's eyes, lashed out at his groin. Hard, greased arms enfolded him, flinging him into dewy thorns. They fought like beasts, locked together, rolling over and over through dim undergrowth: clawing, biting, snarling savagely. Mwangi's left hand clutched the still-warm carcass. He scrambled to his knees and wrenched. Thuo squatted, leaning back, pulling with all his force. There was a soggy, yielding sound. The hare was ripped apart. Blood sprayed, yellow entrails drooped from Mwangi's fist. Thuo was laughing, harsh and breathless.

'Enough for two, my brother. Be happy for a share.'

Meat scent overwhelmed the lust for battle. Mwangi grinned too, sank his teeth into torn flesh, felt saliva flood his tongue, gorged the salty, coppery fluids. Thuo was crunching into frayed brown fur. Bone splinters and gut-juices smeared his lips and thickened his voice. 'You are as strong as me, my friend, as ready as you'll ever be!'

It's true, Mwangi realised, relishing the reek of blood, feeling the awful hunger ease. I am a sickly medicine boy no longer. I have become half-man, half-animal.

And wholly a warrior.

'We will go north,' he said.

'Let us eat well once before we reach the valley,' Thuo had suggested. 'We will need strength to take the land. I know where stock-theft's easy. The white man only has one leg and cannot move quickly. His labourers grow fat and lazy.'

They lay for three days in a copse above Stuart's farm, watching routines, checking livestock, making plans.

'That one,' Thuo decided. 'That skewbald calf looks tender and well fleshed.'

'Wait till darkness,' Mwangi cautioned, 'when we can strike in safety.'

'One-Leg pays Masai to guard the herd at night. No need to risk their spears. We go at noon when the white folk rest and the labourers are idle.'

Now Thuo slept in midday heat and fly-hum, while haze blurred the low, pale-timbered house. Mwangi glimpsed the forest edge above the distant valley. I am going back, he thought, with new strength and old power, to defeat the pale-haired woman and take my land again.

He dozed, grinning.

A sense of danger woke him, sudden, very close. He heard harsh whining, parted leaves, and felt his neck prickle.

They came racing up towards the copse, their brindled coats shining, their yellow fangs agape.

'Run!' he hissed at Thuo. 'They've set the dogs on us!'

Fear drove him headlong through clawing thorns out into the blazing sun. Out to where Stuart's men were waiting.

They stood, plump-fleshed and grinning, their levelled spears agleam. One-Leg Stuart lounged there, his shotgun hooked on one brown-furred arm. 'You stink,' he said, in mangled Kikuyu. 'If you're after thieving, you ought to have a wash.'

Sensing Thuo's cornered crouch, Mwangi watched the shotgun rise and stared into death's twin black eyes. The vision was fading. Failure was a fire in his gut.

He'd lost count of the seasons; he'd grown into a warrior and come within a day's march of his land. And lost it, for the want of one good meal. He hawked bile from his throat, spitting it into hot, red dust.

'Mzungu!' he snarled. 'Fucking white man!'

Duma sensed a sickness in the air.

He had never seen the kites fly so high, never seen the sun so brassy over these green ridges. He'd come to round up strays and check the dam. The water lapped slow and oily, stirred by a fitful breeze. Duma faced north-westwards, from whence this clammy current seemed to come. There, above Nyeri's hazy hump, a ragged broad dark cloud stained the sky.

As he watched, the darkness spread and lowered, shadowing the valley, blotting out the sun. It was twilight in mid-morning, an eerie, ugly gloom, filled with the rustle of countless tiny wings and the shriek of carrion birds. The swarm settled round him like slowly whirring bullets, pattering hard and spiky on his flesh. The ground underfoot became a hopping, seething mass. Already, he heard coffee branches cracking under sudden weight. He ducked through whirling green bodies, chased the sheep downhill, raced among the huts and roused the tribesmen.

Told them the locusts had arrived.

All day long the drums rolled, tribesmen bawled and capered in the maize. The darkness never lifted. The winged green host never seemed to end. All night long, Duma urged his men along the fences, carrying flaming branches, treading small, charred corpses, breathing the reek of scorched insect fat. Across the river, shotguns boomed and smoky redness blossomed as the Boers toiled to keep the swarm at bay. As dawn's first grey fingers clawed the night away, in the same mysterious way as it had settled, the locust cloud rose and clattered southwards down the ridge.

Exhausted, hoarse and gritty-eyed, Duma trudged the slope behind the big house and watched morning break along the line of flight.

It was as if Ngai had laid a lightning bolt across the land, above the maize and far into the forest: a wide, dead swathe within which nothing green remained, only dying insects, bare boughs and naked soil.

Not a single coffee bush survived.

Across the river, yellow Boer wheat stood almost undamaged.

Tribesmen slumped in hutshade, eyeing the destruction, whispering Ngai's name. Lance stood wide-eyed beside his mother, pointing upwards at the bareness round the dam. 'What does it mean, Mummy?'

'It means we are poor again.'

Sooty streaks stained her silvery hair; her eyes were bleak and moist as mountain mist. It was the first time Duma had seen her weep since the Lion Boy died.

But it was not her grief that chilled him, nor the damage to the crops.

It was the rumour of Mwangi's return, and the knowledge that the clan would count this as a sign.

Hugo had been offered the post of Provincial Commissioner, Coast. Promotion, hard-earned and well deserved, reward for a vocation long and faithfully pursued. The letter lay on his desk beside a second document – an assessment of damage to the farms.

Camelot topped the list.

He'd been there the day after it happened, and had stared in dismay at the devastation round the dam.

'What will you do?' he asked her.

'Hunt,' she answered crisply, 'as Leo did when the dam burst.'

'Alone, in the forest?'

'Duma will protect me.'

'And who'll protect Lance?'

'We'll manage, somehow.' She drew herself up, lovely, proud, unyielding. 'Camelot endures, Hugo. It always has, it always will.'

'You won't consider moving?' he suggested, thinking of luxurious provincial quarters at the coast.

'Never!' And he knew she meant it.

Ever since, the images had haunted him: a beautiful, beleaguered woman beside sunlit waters; a brooding, bearded watcher in the trees; a white boy running wild among the tribesmen; a cowed and quivering, dull-eyed half-caste girl.

There are many kinds of duty, he had realised.

He turned to a more personal assessment, rechecked his own calculations: the current value of his service pension, the cost of coffee seedlings to replant twenty acres.

The figures almost exactly matched.

Three sheets of paper on a polished wooden desk, embracing

promise, loss and hope. The locust plague had created an unlikely opportunity, a chance for firm decision and bold action.

But first, there was a formal duty to enact.

First, there was a case to hear.

The prosecution arguments were damning and concise. Thuo's stock-theft record went back many years, Mwangi had been wanted since the Norfolk Hotel riot. They had been caught red-handed. No one came to speak in their defence; the hearing had attracted little notice. Yet, as he faced them across the polished judgement bench, Hugo sensed a turning point in all their lives.

They stood side by side in early sunshine, beneath the near green arc of Nyeri Hill. They wore ragged cloaks and bright steel handcuffs, greasy, threadbare kirtles and rusting ankle chains. Thuo, who once had almost killed him, looked weary, shorn of menace, overawed. Mwangi looked murderous.

Something red and feral in Mwangi's eyes sent Hugo's mind back through the years to an English Wealdland village and a younger urchin thief: the same heedless fury, the same intent to hit and hurt and maim. Despite the chains, despite armed native troopers, Hugo flinched from Mwangi's glare and was secretly afraid.

This is Leo's adoptive brother, he thought, who set a curse on Camelot not so very long ago. He meant it then. He means it now.

Suddenly, Rebecca's proud blonde image was in the quiet court-room.

She is out at Camelot, Hugo reminded himself, with only frail old Duma at her side. Mwangi means her harm – one danger from which only I can protect her.

He had never before used power for personal motives; he had tried to leaven punishment with mercy. Such is duty, he had maintained. For the second time today he realised duty could take on different forms.

Rebecca's image tipped the scales of justice.

'Have you anything to say in mitigation?'

'I spared your life,' Thuo pleaded. 'I turned the spear aside.'

Mwangi's sneer was savage and remorseless. 'One day, it will be *my* turn to judge!'

Hugo's decision hardened, instant, free from doubt. He brought the gavel down, imposing the law's full weight. 'Seven years' hard labour in the Northern Frontier!'

And saw the rage in Mwangi's eyes burn brighter.

Returning to the office, Hugo realised that the slips of paper were meaningless. Back there, in the court he'd always served impartially, he had just acknowledged a higher duty to Rebecca.

Mwangi had enforced his choice.

He shivered, mindful of what he stood to lose, awed by what he might yet gain, knowing that *she* must make the choice.

Faint heart never won fair lady, he remembered, and saddled for the ride to Camelot.

Lance met him, with evening sunshine in his hair and Simba at his heels, and a ten-year-old's disdain for disaster.

'We're poor, Uncle Hugo. You must teach me to shoot, so that I can hunt with Mummy.'

'We've been through this before, Lance. Tether the horse, fetch firewood. Your mother and I must talk.'

'She's not here.' Lance's small face turned petulant, with the fixed, oddly adult glare he often used when crossed.

'Where shall I find her?'

'By the falls, I s'pose. Don't you want to talk to me?'

I do, Hugo thought, every day for the rest of my life. But he couldn't say it, yet. 'Later,' he promised, 'when your chores are done.' He dismounted, handed on the reins, leaving Lance forlorn and tight-browed by the stables.

She was standing in dappled sunset, watching the water foam and tumble. She wore a simple buckskin skirt and a fawn cotton blouse. Her colours blended with the woodland. Her sombre beauty brought a dryness to his throat. All at once absurdly tongue-tied, he lingered in the shadows and rehearsed his lines; then went forward through scented ferns and the rumble of the falls.

She saw him step into fading daylight and felt the sadness deepen in her heart. The years have been kind to him, she thought: they have set strength into his finely sculpted features and added authority to his lean-limbed grace. And put not a hint of greyness in his hair. Ever-faithful Hugo, whose quiet, steady presence has helped us through the storm.

How shall we ever get along without him?

She found a misty smile, a suitably enthusiastic tone. 'Congratulations, bwana P.C. When will you be leaving?'

He halted, pale and stunned in dim green half-light. 'Who told you? How did you know?'

'Ah, Hugo, you left the letter on your desk. Clerks gossip; Molly said not to tell a soul. That means at least half the district knows!'

'Damn,' he muttered, '*damn!*' He looked downcast and ill at ease, like a small boy denied a promised treat. He began to mumble about replanting coffee, touching her emotions, wakening her pride.

'Certainly not!' she snapped. 'I won't take charity from you or anyone else.'

'I don't expect you to. I'm offering partnership.' His dark eyes beseeched; still she missed the point.

'Impossible, Hugo. You know officials aren't allowed to own land.'

'I wouldn't be an official.' He moved closer, making no attempt to hide his urgency.

'What are you saying, Hugo?'

'I'm asking you to be my wife.'

She stood quite still, feeling the drum of water on the earth below, feeling the quickened throbbing in her veins, waiting for some echo in her soul. 'You're doing it for Leo,' she accused, 'so that Lance can have a father and because the locusts came. You are forfeiting a life's work to a woman who'll be forty in three years. By then you may have learned to hate her for it!'

'All right,' he growled, 'all *right!*' He went to his knees on soft green moss and took her hand, his brown gaze pure and proud. 'I love you, Rebecca Reid; have loved you long before I dared admit it, will love you as long as I shall live. Now: will you marry me?'

The weight of lonely years ahead was suddenly upon her. Far inside, the stoniness was melting. It cannot be as it once was with Leo, she acknowledged, yet neither can I doubt this good man's truth. Whatever happens, he will cherish me. If that's not love, it's surely the next-best thing.

She raised him, went on tiptoe, kissed his cheek. 'We'll have to ask Lance.'

'You don't escape so easily. We'll *tell* Lance!'

And that felt exactly right, too.

He turned from the waterfall, slipped his arm around her waist, led her gently back towards the pasture. There was a sundance on the river, a croon of roosting doves, a renewed sense of *going home*; and a single poignant question in her mind.

Can love take root again in Camelot?

Duma saw them from the hutshade, saw them walking like one person beside the dim red river; and gave thanks to Ngai.

Now it didn't matter that Mwangi might return, or that Maina might see locusts as a sign. The Healer's charm would silence them, the clan would honour it, the land would soon restore ease and wealth. Lance would be well cared for, the house would glow with love.

And Camelot would have a man again.

Lance saw them, too.

Saw their locked and lingering stroll beside the dimming river, his sleek dark head beside her where once a golden head had shone; heard his mooning murmur, glimpsed her pleasured smile, and sensed a bond between them that made his stomach churn.

He hadn't meant to spy on them – he had brought Simba and the simi to gather firewood. Even now, he didn't try to hide, stood in plain sight and long damp grass below them, waiting to be seen and called, and told to hold their hands.

They walked straight past, looking only at each other. They are nearing my father's grave, he thought. She always goes there after she has been beside the falls, to ask his comfort for the night and gain his strength to meet another day. Soon, she will send Hugo away, and go up to the big, rustling Meru oak.

They walked on, beneath the first cold, steely star, away from the Meru oak, still joined together, still murmuring. Already, Lance thought, they are forgetting my father. How long before they forget *me*?

He felt the hotness kindle in his blood.

There was a drum, far inside him, that beat at times like this, rumbling like the ones the tribesmen played. It ruled his movements, making his anger burn. It drove him now through misty meadows to the river's edge. He heard Simba pattering behind, felt the simi heavy in his hand. Something was going to happen, something that made his chest fill and flutter, and set a bitter taste on his tongue.

He waited while the drum inside beat faster, until his whole body seemed to pant and throb. Simba sat beside him on wet grey pebbles, panting too. Simba, named for the tawny lion; Simba, who would never forget him, never walk straight past with someone else.

'Simba,' he said, in a thick harsh voice he scarcely recognised. The shaggy head cocked. The plumy tail brushed softly on yellow silt. Two brown eyes gazed upwards, full of love and trust.

Then the sun dipped, bloody, across the further ridge, struck square in Lance's eyes.

And the red haze was upon him.

It stole his sight and boiled his blood and brought the drumroll to a single, solid roar. It raised the simi in both hands above his head, made him cry out 'Simba!' and bring the bright blade crashing down. Dimly, he felt the soggy jar of impact, heard one short, quickly cut-off yelp, felt hot gooey spatters on his legs. Then there was only noise and rage and redness, and the simi chopping somewhere below, until the sun sank and brightness faded, and the river's coolness brought him back.

Back to a fiery ache inside his skull, to tremors in his shoulders and sobs deep in his chest. Back to a mangled, leaking, tawny huddle, dark sticky stains on the pebbles and his flesh, and blowflies gathering for the feast. He cried for Simba then, standing in cold clear water, rinsing redness from the simi and his shins.

That is why it had to happen near the river, he thought, carrying the torn, dripping carcass, tossing it into deeper, faster currents, watching pinkness flare and spread and dwindle. So that I can clean the mess, so that Simba can be swilled away.

The lion dog, who like the Lion Boy himself had been taken by the river; who like the Lion Boy himself, would soon be forsaken and forgotten.

But the Lion Boy's son would live on.

Presently, Lance dried his tears and cut some firewood and went up, shivering, to the big house.

Alone, as he would always be alone now, to tell them that Simba had got lost.

31

RAIN WOKE HER, drumming on the roof. She shifted beneath the blankets, eased her swollen belly, rubbed her aching back. For a while, it was all right to be lazy, and watch Hugo dressing in the thin grey dawn.

There was a hint of silver at his temples now. It makes him look mature, she decided, adding distinction to his handsomeness. He still moved with elegant economy, his pale, well-proportioned body gleaming – a body which had brought her back to life.

He had been so patient and considerate during those early weeks while Leo's ghost still haunted this one room. Gradually, tenderly, he had used his voice and hands and lips to rouse her, containing his own great need. At first, she had been absurdly shy, conscious of the fullness passing years had added to her hips and thighs.

'You're amazing,' he told her, nuzzling her breasts, his brown eyes bright with admiration, 'as smooth and supple as a sixteen-year-old.'

'Why, Hugo,' she whispered, in wide-eyed mock surprise, 'you are a delicious old ram!'

'Sign of misspent youth,' he retorted. 'I had professional tuition. And not so much of the "old". I'll be ready again in fifteen minutes!'

He brought laughter to their loving, and a kind of easy languor she had never known before. Lying beside her, warm-fleshed and richly male-scented, he made her feel gloriously wanton, giving her new pride in her ability to move him. Now Hugo's child quickened in her belly, and his love set Camelot aglow.

He leaned over her, his yellow oilskin crackling, his lips gentle on her cheek. 'Take care, my love, your time is near. Don't be hard on Lance. It's a difficult time for him, too.' He grimaced wryly at the spattered window. 'I won't be long. Not much to be done in duck's weather.' There was a creak of the door and a gust of damp air, and Hugo had gone out on the land.

Land to which he'd taken as if it had always been in his blood.

He seemed to know by instinct exactly when each ewe was due to lamb. He introduced the latest dipping routines, produced the finest fleeces and the sweetest meat in all the district. He had a countryman's eye for weather, unerring judgement of what and when to plant. Duma and the tribesmen learned to value his advice and use his unexpected talents to improve their own plots. Already, the coffee plantation was flourishing again. The farm was poised to prosper, the locust nightmare might have never been.

How lucky I was, she mused, to find a man who can so completely fulfil me.

The child inside her stirred. She heard childish footfalls in the passage, reminding her of one conquest Hugo had yet to make.

Lance.

It had begun, she remembered, about the time that Simba went missing: the night Hugo had proposed. She'd never quite decided which had upset Lance more. He had been strangely shifty about the dog, mourning the loss daily, yet stubbornly refusing a replacement. And rejecting Hugo's riding lessons.

'I don't need them,' he'd growled. 'I can ride as well as you already. Anyway, you never score goals!' When Rebecca intervened, he threw a glowering tantrum. 'Uncle Hugo doesn't care about me. Even when I do ride, he only looks at *you*!'

'Give him time,' Hugo advised. 'He'll settle down.'

But Lance didn't settle. Soon there was trouble with the Boers across the river.

'They hate me,' Lance complained. 'Their children whisper behind my back and won't let me play with them. It wasn't like that till Uncle Hugo came.'

'It is my fault,' Hugo admitted. 'They can't forget I was the D.C. They think I send Lance to spy on them. Just as well, perhaps. I don't want him mixing with the Coetzes.'

'Who *can* I play with?' Lance demanded. 'You don't want me to have fun!'

Once again, Duma came to the rescue, taking Lance under his wing and teaching him bushcraft and tracking. Sometimes, from the vegetable garden, Rebecca saw Lance among the village boys: a gangly, pale-skinned, flame-haired figure running, wrestling, throwing a wooden-tipped spear. 'He is quick and strong like his father,' Duma reported: and added hopefully, 'Some day he will be a fine hunter.'

But Lance could never be a hunter, and Rebecca told him so. 'You have manners to learn and lessons to prepare. Soon, you must go away to school.'

'Why? My father never did!'

'He didn't have a mother who cared, and wanted the best for him.'

'If school is so wonderful, why are your eyes all red?'

Because I don't want to lose you, she sobbed inwardly; but she dared not tell him so, because she knew he'd only resist more fiercely.

Lately, as her heaviness grew and the time for schooling neared, he had seemed more cheerful and resigned. One evening he rode up with her to the dam, where sunset made bronze flashes on the wings of inborne ducks. 'I'll retrieve,' he said, 'it will save you work.' He paddled in the shallows, came back grinning through a drift of gunsmoke with a feathered corpse in either hand.

How marvellous, she thought, to see him smiling in the sun.

'Duma's pleased,' he murmured. 'I'm as fast as any herdboy, and deadly with the spear.'

'I know, I've seen you. Well done.'

'I'm also as good as Duma with the bow.' Suddenly, his boyish face was stark with adult longing. 'Let me use the gun, before I go to school! You know my father promised me I could.'

'You'll have to ask Hugo.'

'I'm sorry,' Hugo said, at supper. 'I won't have time to teach you until the ploughing's done. Besides, you're still too young.'

She saw the anger take him, heard the clatter of his fork on the plate, the scuffle of his feet along the passage, the slam of his bedroom door. And knew the brief bright truce was over.

After that, he fretted when she made him sit and work, and raged whenever she corrected him. 'You don't teach me fairly, you *want* me to go wrong!'

Today, she thought, it will be worse. The rain makes prisoners of us, pregnancy plays havoc with my patience.

She clambered out of bed, dressed clumsily, ran a jaundiced eye

307

along the bookshelf. And brightened, at the sight of an old friend: *Morte d'Arthur*.

Pageantry and valour, romance and intrigue, couched in vibrant language and stirring rhythm. Today, she vowed, Lance will quicken to the knight for whom he's named. Today he will learn to enjoy learning.

The rain came on harder than ever. The lounge felt gloomy, chilly and enclosed. She stared in dismay at the two short sentences, scrawled in scornful haste across the page. 'Arthur was a foolish king who couldn't keep his queen. Lancelot was a cunning thief who stole another's wife.'

'That's *all*?' she demanded. 'That's all you can write, after so much reading?'

'That's all there is. They didn't have guns or cars, they couldn't talk properly, they didn't even find the Holy Grail. And everyone knows the sword would rust, in that stupid lake!'

He was watching her defiantly, sneering. The down is darkening on his upper lip, she realised; and felt a sudden ache of failure. For twelve years, we have toiled to carve his kingdom from the bush, and his imagination withered. I show him a legend; he sees rust.

'I can't mark this. You'll have to try again.'

'I won't! I'm tired of being cooped up like a robber!'

'Sit down, Lance!'

'I'm going out!'

She moved to block the doorway. His down-thrust coppery head struck her midriff. She spun, awkward and unbalanced, stumbling heavily against the table-edge. The impact made her gasp. A painful spasm rippled down her back. 'Oh Lance,' she cried, 'the baby!'

He glared up, flushed and raging, his eyes like dark blue embers. 'It was your fault, you got in my way!'

She was weeping, crabbing sideways to the bedroom. Weeping for two children who might be irreparably damaged, praying for Hugo to come home.

Lance lay rigid on his bed, listening to the storm outside, waiting for the inner storm to break. He'd heard Hugo enter, heard his eager greeting turn into an anxious gasp, heard the sobs which echoed from their room. Now, fast flurried footsteps were approaching. I don't care, part of him insisted, it serves them right for making me so miserable. I do care, his heart was crying, please God don't let her be harmed!

The bedroom door swung inwards. Rain-blurred light fell on Hugo's face, a face that Lance had never seen before: bone-white cheeks, eyes like dark brown flints and lips which seemed to hold no blood at all. 'I won't beat you for what you did. I'll beat you for what you *didn't* do. You didn't comfort her, you didn't come for me!'

'No one beats me,' Lance snapped, 'not even my real father!'

'Don't lie, boy, your mother told me how you used to howl!'

Hugo stepped forward, flexing a limber bamboo cane, and Lance had a moment to rue past deception. Ah Daddy, you played the part too well. Then Hugo was growling orders. 'Stand up. Turn round. Bend down!'

The drum began to throb in Lance's brain.

If Hugo hits me, he thought, something bad will happen: worse than Simba, worse than anything I've done today. Hugo came on. The drumbeat quickened.

Rebecca's thin scream froze them both. The cane fell, clattering, and Hugo was gone. The pounding in Lance's head and chest faded. All his defiance crumbled. He ran along the passage, blubbering his sorrow and his fear. 'Will she be all right? It was an accident, I swear!' Hugo brushed him aside, scurrying to the kitchen, setting a pan to boil, racing back towards the bedroom. 'Uncle Hugo? Let me help, I've *said* I'm sorry!'

Hugo turned on him, paler and tighter-lipped than ever. 'Out of the way, boy, can't you see it's started?'

'But I didn't mean it! Let me *do* something!' Hugo's hooked hand clamped his shoulder, spun him round to face the window and the surging, scudding rain. 'See that? We'll never get her to Nyeri, and nobody can reach us in time. Don't you understand, Lance? *You've done enough already!*' He disappeared into the big bedroom and slammed the door behind him.

Lance slumped against the wall and let the hot tears flow. A new outcry sent cold shivers down his spine. The screams came at regular intervals, lashing at his mind and body. He slid down the wall, squatted in the corner, closed his eyes and covered his ears, but he could still hear. It was worse than any beating, harder to bear than anything Hugo could have done. It's my fault, he whimpered, it's all my fault!

Then, as pain and guilt threatened to overpower him, a small spark of defiance lit in his brain. It wasn't me, Hugo. It wasn't me who started this, weighed her down with that great belly, made her suffer all this pain.

It was you.

Hugo stepped into a cockpit of agony and keening. Her flesh shone slick and yellow beneath the lamp he'd lit. She lay unclothed, a nude and rigid starfish tossed on a painful sea. He stood appalled, while spasms shuddered through her limbs and clawed her bloated belly. Her legs flexed and parted, her face convulsed again. 'Don't just stand there,' she gasped, '*deliver me!*'

'How, for God's sake?'

'On your knees, between my thighs. You've been there often enough!'

But never like this.

Bending he flinched from the violet splay of her, the bloodied blonde fringe, the quivering cleft of pinkness. As he watched, her buttocks jerked and stiffened. Roundness protruded, hard and dark and shiny.

'Help me,' she panted. 'When I push, *help me!*' The last two words broke in a strangled shriek. Open-mouthed and breathless he saw the livid head emerge, heard a slow, wet slither, cupped the huddled form and eased it free.

'Quickly – cut the cord!'

He fumbled for the kitchen knife, amazed at the sudden flatness of her body. The blade flickered brightly.

'Not with that, you'll bleed us both to death! Use your teeth, man.'

Of course, he thought, it's like with sheep – the natural way. Kneeling, hearing the floorboards creak, he held the purple cord gingerly, tongued its rubbery breadth and set his jaw.

'Don't bite,' she warned, 'gnaw!'

He swallowed once and did it. His mouth filled with metallic blood and salty fluid. The very essence of all three of us, he realised. Now we are truly joined.

'Hang him by the heels,' she urged. 'Pat his back – *gently!*'

How alert she is, he thought, to have already seen the pink, tasselled sex. Thank God she's been through this before. Thank God one of us knows what to do.

The baby coughed, and set up a lusty wail. New life was strong and sudden in his hands. He gazed down in awe on this mewling, squirming portion of himself.

'Is he all right?' she whispered urgently. 'Was he hurt?'

'He's fine,' Hugo said, blinking back tears of gratitude and pride. 'He's a perfect little prince.'

'Prince *Hal*,' she murmured. 'Don't you agree?' A strand of sweat-darkened hair lay across her cheek. Her eyes were weary, wide and grey, amazingly serene.

'Hal,' he repeated, savouring the sound and the noble image it prompted. 'Yes, that will do nicely.'

She lay back on the pillow and let Hal suckle, taking pleasure in his sturdy, hungry pull. The rain had stopped. Thin sunshine slid between the curtains. Birds were singing, outside. There was a smell of freshly watered soil.

She shifted drowsy Hal to the other breast. Hugo came and sat beside her, taking her hand. 'Rebecca,' he said; the joy in his voice and the softness in his eyes left no need for other words between them. Despite the memory of pain that lingered in her body, she felt a soaring lightness in her spirit and an unexpected clarity of mind. Here, in this charmed, birth-smelling circle, she sensed a new beginning, a future full of love and light and hope. First I married a legend, she thought, and tried to make him fit a girlish dream. Now I have found a real man, and have given him a son. Together we can build a real life.

The door opened. Lance stood in a watery slant of sun. She saw the teartracks on his cheeks, the tightness in his shoulders, the sheets of paper in his hand. She sensed his guilt, the horror of the wait he had endured, his urgent longing to atone.

'I've done what you asked,' he said. 'Will you mark it for me please?'

'Of course I will,' she began – but Hugo interrupted.

'Later, Lance. Can't you see how tired she is?'

She saw the slender figure flinch and stiffen, saw his blue eyes focus on the baby, watched them darken in rejection and dismay. In a moment of poignant insight, she sensed his exclusion from the closeness in the room. Slowly, almost ceremonially, he laid the papers on the bed and spoke to her alone. 'First it was my father, then Uncle Hugo. Now you have another son.'

The adult weariness in his voice hurt her more than any boyish rage. He was bleeding inside, an unintended wound she might never be able to heal. 'It's all right, Mother,' he said. 'I understand why I must go: there will always be someone you love more than me.' He slipped out of the sunlight, leaving an aching emptiness in her heart.

'Go to him, Hugo,' she pleaded, 'tell him it isn't true!'

But even as Hugo obeyed, and Hal nuzzled sleepily at her breast, she was deeply afraid it would be true.

Hugo tried hard, in the weeks that followed Hal's birth. He took Lance with him as he tended to the farm, showed him how to dip the sheep and how to test the maize for ripeness, showed him when the coffee beans were ready to be picked. But Hugo's dark eyes never softened as they did for Hal. He couldn't conceal the fact that he *was* trying hard; so, as far as Lance was concerned, it didn't count.

And Hal took up almost all Rebecca's time.

Why does she love him so? Lance wondered. He is a small purple bundle who eats and sleeps and cannot even smile. He wakes her at the dead of night and when the dawn is grey, puts weary lines into her face and heaviness in her step.

She never did mark my work on *Morte d'Arthur*.

So, as always, Lance turned to Duma.

He found refuge in the smoky, goatmeat-scented hut, and in the tenderness the old man never had to force. 'Tell me about my father,' Lance would plead, 'tell me how he saved the Fighting Horse Brigade.' He never tired of the story. Duma made it seem so real – the pound of hooves, the reek of gunsmoke, the bright red blood and swirling dust. 'Will I learn to be brave, Duma? I don't *feel* brave about going to school.'

'It is not something you learn. You are the Lion Boy's son. When the time comes, you will find the courage. Come now to the forest. We haven't much time left for hunting.'

The hurt would leave him then, with the bow in his hand and Duma's lean, still-young stride beside him, the scent of game in his nostrils and the heat of the hunt in his blood. Sometimes, up in the quiet, green-gold forest, he would feel his father's presence upon him and sense some greater purpose to his life. Camelot seemed small and far away, Hal seemed unimportant – even the thought of school caused no unease.

There is something beyond all this, he thought, a sense of far bright freedom and a greater love than any I have known. Some day, it will lead and I will follow, and these things will be clear to me. Some day, when I am grown.

After I have been to school.

There were three trees at Lorigumu: stunted acacias whose roots clawed among the rocks around the well, whose branches cast meagre shade across the governor's quarters and the chaplain's house. The only shade, the only greenery for a hundred miles in any direction.

Mwangi leaned against rough bark, running the wooden rake through grey-green, thin-bladed grass. He could see the other prisoners toiling in the sun that stood, white-hot, directly overhead. Hard men, these, who fought their captors and each other, who broke rocks and whitewashed concrete cellblocks, beginning at one end, finishing at the other, then doing it all over again. They did it boastfully, despising meeker, weaker inmates, glorying in the warders' curses, growing harder in their bodies and duller in their minds.

Leaning on his rake, watching dark-winged vultures wheel above the refuse heap, Mwangi despised the hard men in return, remembering the secret he had learned so early in his sentence . . .

It began as a pale flutter in the middle distance, seen through narrow steel bars. It drew nearer, like a drunken white butterfly in rippling haze above the scalding, sandy soil. Mwangi inched towards the cell window. Midday in Lorigumu prison, hotter than a hundred campfires, and the smallest movement made salt sweat gush.

The figure stumbled closer, broke through the haze, became a man in a soiled white prison smock. Olang the thief, Mwangi realised, who had gone missing three days ago.

Now we shall see if what they say is true.

He heard boot-tramp, craned forward, and saw Amin the chief warder prepare the flogging post.

Amin was a huge, purple-black Nubian who always wore heavy khakis. He was held in awe for the savagery of his beatings, and because no matter how fierce the heat, no one had ever seen him perspire. A thick bamboo rod glittered at his side. Olang went weeping to him, like a guilty child beseeching a beloved father. 'Beat me, bleed me, make my ribs run red, but let me back into my cell!'

Amin smiled, thick-lipped and smug, swished the rod and raised his voice. Mwangi knew the whole jail was listening. 'We need no fence at Lorigumu,' Amin bragged. 'You may walk away at any time. Tell them what it's like out there, Olang. Tell them why you'd rather take a beating.' He buried his free hand in Olang's woolly hair, wrenching the thief's glistening grey face upwards. Even so, Olang's voice was thick with gratitude and truth.

'Better the rod than the desert. When you have seen the death, you will bear the wounds in silence!'

'Hear him!' Amin bellowed. 'Go meekly to your labour and think on Olang's words. There is no escape!'

Mwangi winced and turned away from the steady, soggy pound of rod on flesh.

Later, Mwangi had gripped the cool, smooth bars and gazed into the blood-red sinking sun. The haze had cleared. There was bare brown emptiness as far as he could see, without landmarks, without water; heat which fried the brain by day, cold that froze the soul by night and sent men back here weeping.

And no escape.

Lamplight flickered, under thin-leaved acacia boughs; the soft yellow light, green shade, stout walls and creature comforts beckoned to him, making him remember the big house under Kerinyagga, where he had vowed to live and rule.

There *must* be a way out, he thought. I cannot endure seven years of this.

He heard Olang's whimpers, and the prison priest's useless Christian prayers; just like the ones he'd heard so long ago at Kerinyagga Mission. Presently, the priest stepped out of Olang's cell.

He stood in the fall of evening, tall, grey-haired, green-robed. Lampglow reached across the barren compound, lighting his sad spare face; and lit flaring hope in Mwangi's breast.

Mwangi knew him!

So was Mwangi's secret born.

Ever since that day, Mwangi had shunned the hard men and curried favour with the warders, and won a privileged place of work – the governor's garden. Now he leaned on the rake, watching the chapel doorway, waiting for a chance to slip inside.

There could be a way back, he thought. It will take time and patience and a careful, cunning plan.

First, I must get into the chapel.

32

AFTERNOON SUNSHINE WARMED mellow yellow sandstone buildings. The lawns were fresh-cut green and alive with boys in royal-blue blazers, grey shorts and knee-length socks. Boys who whooped and whistled at each other, and eyed newcomers scornfully.

'Berkeley, isn't it? Glad to have the ex-D.C.'s son aboard. *Woodfall's* the name, master in charge of Livingstone House.' A weedy man, Woodfall, wearing a shiny brown suit and a starched white collar which had chafed his scraggy neck. His centre-parted hair lay dark with brilliantine. Black tufts sprouted from his nose and wrists. Behind pebble spectacles, his eyes were hard and bleak. Beneath the genial tone, Lance sensed instant dislike. Hugo didn't notice, carrying the trunk across vast playing fields to the low grey dormitory.

Inside, blank-faced boys stood to attention. Ignoring them, Woodfall trod pale flagstones to the dimmest corner. 'They're mostly Afrikaners, Mr Berkeley. We don't believe in national barriers here. So, Lancelot, this will be home for the next few years.'

An iron bed, drab green blankets to match the bare walls, a pine-wood desk and chair, a battered cupboard. The nearest window was yards away, barred and uncurtained.

'The Spartan approach,' said Woodfall. 'Breeds character, we find. Let's do the paperwork, Mr Berkeley. The boys will make him welcome.'

Don't go, Lance pleaded silently; Hugo had already turned away.

'Best unpack, worm,' advised a brawny, straw-haired adolescent in a thick Boer accent, 'or Woodweed'll have your guts for garters.'

'*Lancelot*,' someone gloated. 'You will be knighted, tonight!'

They trooped out, sniggering, leaving Lance alone.

I can't stay in this dim green prison, he thought, at the mercy of the very Boers Hugo taught me to despise! I *won't* stay here!

He slunk between shady shrubs and the scent of mowing, crouched beside the gravelled drive until the coast was clear. Then three quick strides, a fumble with the rear door that always jammed, and he was cowering between the seats of Hugo's parked Ford.

Knowing, in heart-pounding, gut-wrenching despair, that this would be the first place they'd look.

He heard Woodfall, oily and assured, above Hugo's anxious murmur. 'It's common, on the first day. Straight talk always does the trick.' A metallic click, a waft of cooler air, and cruel fingers grasping Lance's arm. 'Out, boy. Shake hands with your father like a man!'

He saw pink shame on Hugo's cheeks, felt the reluctance in Hugo's brief, cool touch, read the denial in Hugo's brown, disdainful eyes.

This is not my son.

Watching the black, box-like car rattle down the drive, Lance felt utterly disowned. Something broke inside him, tearing his heart and making the hot tears spurt.

'Dry your eyes,' snapped Woodfall. 'Your new chums will take you for a *girl*!'

His trunk had been overturned. Clothes lay strewn and crumpled. Books and pencils littered the pale floor. 'New chums' lounged and eyed him as if he were a leper.

'Going to blub again, worm?' the straw-haired lout demanded. He had pale blue eyes, a bruiser's nose, and stubble on his chin. 'I'm Frikkie Jansen. You can call me Boss.'

'Careful, Boss,' a second Boer voice warned, 'he's the D.C.'s boy!'

'Poor little Berkeley,' Jansen taunted. 'Woodweed made him weep!'

They were closing in, trampling his belongings, hounding him into the corner. Tears prickled his eyelids, threatening to damn him for all time.

Deep inside, a drum began to throb.

He was saved by sunshafts sliding into green-walled gloom as someone entered the door: a small figure, dragging an enormous black tin trunk.

'Hell,' breathed Jansen in delight, '*another* worm!'

They swooped like blue-winged carrion birds on their new-found prey.

Lance leaned on cool green stone and let the drumroll die. Reprieved, he longed to join the chant, become one of the crowd, visit humiliation on someone else. He eased into the circle and assessed his fellow worm.

He crouched beside his trunk, thin-cheeked, fine-boned, half a head shorter than anyone else. A domed hump distorted his right shoulder. When he moved, metal callipers on his left leg twinkled, and a thick black boot clumped awkwardly.

'Stumpy,' they chanted, 'a humpy, stumpy worm!' They plundered his trunk, tossing his possessions to and fro.

'I say, you chaps,' he piped, 'play the game!'

Jansen seized some grey socks and read the name-tag. 'The Hon. Rupert Finchley-Malpas. A blue-blood, doncha know!'

Someone had stolen a framed portrait. 'Hey, man, a picture of his mama!'

'Please,' the newcomer implored, 'it's the only one I have!'

'Aaaah, isn't that sweet? Catch, hyphen Stump!'

Finchley-Malpas lunged, teetered, tumbled. The portrait fell and shattered.

Lance saw anguish in the bone-white upturned face, heard gloating chuckles, and remembered his own too recent desolation. 'When the time comes,' Duma had said, 'you will find the courage. You are the Lion Boy's son.' Lance felt resolution growing round a single sentence.

My father would not have let this happen.

He stepped to the centre of the sneering circle, picked up a long, curved glass-shard, and made it hum and glitter in the sudden hush. 'Come,' he invited, 'try a worm that bites!'

'Scrag him!' someone muttered. 'Go, Boss, he can't cut us all!'

Somewhere far away, a bell was ringing. Jansen smiled, cold and confident. 'No, man, tea's up, we'll do him later.' They went together, chuckling, through the door.

'You shouldn't have done that.' The crippled boy crouched amid the glass-glint, clutching the picture to his chest. 'You'll only make things worse.' He stood, pained and lopsided, but found a sweet pale grin. 'But I'm jolly glad you did! Tonight, I'll repay the kindness.'

'What happens tonight?' Lance asked.

'Initiation.'

Lance lay in darkness on the rock-hard bed, hearing stealthy rustles all around. Between tea and lights out, Rupert had helped him to unpack, and showed him the ablutions – outdoor basins, cold showers, pit latrines. 'My big bro came here,' he explained. 'It's bearable, he says.'

But now the night was sharp with tension, and Lance found it very hard to bear.

Brightness flared: a blue-flamed hurricane lamp. Jansen's scowl loomed into it, sinister with gargoyled shadows. The windows had been masked in green. Lance heard door-bolts rattle into place. There were footfalls at his bedside, whispered warnings in his ear. 'Take it like a man, you won't get hurt. Struggle, and we'll tie you up.' He said nothing, his mind flinching from whatever evil 'it' might be.

Jansen hung the lantern overhead. Pyjama-striped figures ringed the hunchback's bed; eyes and bared teeth gleamed in expectation.

Rupert sat naked on the sheets. His head looked too big for his body. The withered leg shone like dead man's flesh. Yet as Jansen neared and the watchers quivered, Rupert smiled like a small, sad saint.

Then Lance saw what Jansen carried: an open tin of boot-black, a small, stiff-bristled brush.

The whispered chant began.

Spread it dark and spread it thick,
Spread it on his little dick,
Be he strong or be he silly,
Shine his balls and black his willy.

Lance felt his own scrotum writhe as he imagined the bite of bristle, the unclean slime, the sense of violation.

Still Rupert smiled.

'Why the grin, worm?' Jansen challenged.

'I'm thinking of the beak's face, when I show him in the morning.'

'You'd tell? You'd go sneaking to the beak?'

'Certainly!'

A brief, incredulous hush. Then a new chant rose: 'Cowardy cowardy custard, dip his wick in mustard!'

'Sing,' Rupert urged them, 'you'll sing a different tune tomorrow.'

318

'Ah, leave the stumpy mama's boy. Let's do the other one.'

Lance stiffened, pulling the blanket higher. And Rupert paid his debt.

'Touch either one of us, and I'll tell on all of you!'

'Snivelling *roineks*!' Jansen snarled. 'You'll be a laughing stock!'

'I am already,' Rupert whispered, 'because of my hump. D'you think I care what names you call me?' There was sudden strength in his frailty and utter certainty in his voice.

Jansen glowered, tore the blankets down, and ordered his sullen henchmen to their beds. 'We won't forget, Stumpy. You'll be sorry!'

The lamp dimmed. Rupert's cheerful voice rang out. 'Night, Lance. Sleep tight!'

'Night, Rupert,' he called, grinning.

But he didn't sleep, not yet.

Today, he thought, I've learnt a new kind of courage: Rupert's kind, that needs quick wit and a steady spirit. But the best time was when Rupert grovelled in the glass and the fire lit deep in my belly. That was my father's kind of courage, that was the most important lesson. Hugo was right. I am not Lance Berkeley, even though my mother insists on this name.

I am the Lion Boy's son.

'You're big and handsome, Berkeley. Do you have a brain? Stand up, boy!'

First day in class. Sunshine probed the window, burnishing wooden desk-tops and white shirtfronts, glinting on Woodfall's pebble specs. The air smelled of ink and chalkdust. Obeying, sensing ill-intent, Lance gave himself a private warning.

Don't let him taunt you. Remember who you are.

'What is the capital of Persia, Master Berkeley?'

'I don't know, sir.'

'Which English author wrote *Northanger Abbey*?'

'Don't know.'

'Who was England's youngest Prime Minister?'

'I'm sorry, sir.'

'*You're* sorry, Berkeley? It is *I* who must mourn, confronting such awesome ignorance! Can you count, boy, can you manage simple sums?'

'I think so, sir.'

'I'm overjoyed to hear it.' Woodfall's smile was broad but treacherous. 'What is the square root of five hundred and twenty six?'

Lance felt the heat climbing to his cheeks and heard sniggers rising behind him. Then, in the corner of his eye, he saw Rupert push a paper to the centre of the desk, and watched him write numbers.

'Twenty-four, sir.' A faint hum of disbelief. Woodfall's grin narrowed.

'A lucky guess, no doubt. Multiply fifteen by seventy-two.' Lance lowered his head, watching Rupert's pen move.

'One thousand and eighty, sir.'

Woodfall plunged along the aisle, swift and batlike in his billowing gown. His pointer flickered and crashed on to the desk. The hunchback wrung his bruised fingers. The tell-tale paper fluttered. 'So,' Woodfall murmured, 'a giant numbskull and a deceitful dwarf.' He waited till the mocking laughter faded. 'Take separate desks in future. Tonight you'll spend free time writing lines. *Sit*, numbskull. Let us exercise your tiny mind.'

The Boer boys made Rupert sorry, hounding him unmercifully.

'Make my bed, Stumpy, else I'll twist your arm.'

'Clean my boots, cripple, that's what worms are for.'

'Swab the toilet, Hyphen. Look, Boss, the little pig has widdled on the floor!'

Seeing Rupert's halting, grey-faced fatigue, Lance knew it was his turn to pay dues. He swept and scrubbed and polished until the whole dorm shone. Rupert taught him facts and figures against the next Woodfall inquisition.

'We'll beat them yet, Lance. Brits against the Boers, right?'

'Right.'

Games afternoon, with the older Form Two boys. The sun was low and cooling, the grass was vivid green, and Woodfall plotted new humiliation. 'Play centre for the reds, Berkeley,' he called, and went into a huddle with the blues.

The kick-off travelled, high and looping, straight at Lance. He stretched to catch it. Two stocky blues smashed him backwards, leaving him dazed and winded on the turf.

'Numbskull,' Woodfall taunted. 'Butterfingers!'

He sat up, rubbing his ribs gingerly, tasting salty blood from a split lip.

Rupert's touchline voice cut through the buzzing in his head. 'Go, Lance, let's have one for the Brits!'

No, he thought, we'll have one for the Lion Boy.

He waited until the ball ran loose, stooped and swept it up. He shoved the first blue tackler off, swerved around another, stepped inside the third's despairing lunge. The way ahead was clear: empty, sunstruck greensward stretching to the white, H-shaped goal.

He ran as he had run with Camelot herdboys: strong, smooth-striding, perfectly balanced. He ran with the wind in his hair, oiled leather in his hands and the sounds of pursuit falling far behind. He felt as he had felt that time whilst hunting – a sense of something just beyond the skyline, a place of freedom, love and joy. This is *me*, he exulted, this is the talent that makes me different from the rest!

For the first time in his life, he felt totally at peace with himself.

The reds gave him the ball more often. He made two more long touchdown runs.

'Lekker game, Lance,' a Boer boy muttered, later; and not even Boss Jansen ever called him worm again.

'If you play like that,' Woodfall enthused, 'Livingstone House will be unbeatable!'

From that day on, he offered help, not mockery in the classroom, and gave Lance extra marks for 'trying hard'.

'He does it for himself,' Rupert warned, 'not because he likes you any better. You're a hero and a scholar. You don't need me any more.'

'Don't be daft! You're the best friend ever!'

'You'll have to get along without me. I'm leaving.'

'Why? *When?*'

'My folks have found a special school in England. I sail next week. I'm going home tomorrow.' He looked up, pale and wistful. 'You won't forget me, will you?'

'I'll never forget you, Rupert!'

This time, as a large, grand car crunched down the drive, Lance was close to tears of real sorrow. Rupert had come in the darkest hour, while Hugo's desertion rankled and the red haze hovered near. He'd stood firm against the Boers and Woodfall, taught Lance to use wits as well as strength. He was like a frail and clever younger brother, someone to trust and cherish and keep out of harm's way. This is Rupert's last lesson, Lance realised. I must try to be like that with Hal, when I get home.

Icy moonlight crept between the bars of Mwangi's cell, drawing him, shivering, to the window. He gazed along the road that wound like a pale snake across the grey wasteland, south to sweet green pastures under Kerinyagga. Once a month, the dark blue prison lorry wheezed up this road, bringing stores, mail and new inmates. Sometimes, it took survivors back to the world of goatmeat and warm maize beer.

The knowledge added force to Mwangi's plan.

He built a group of comrades – Thuo and five others from the Nyeri clans. First, he taught them Harry Thuku's words. 'Like jackals, we must haunt the lion. Plague the settlers, bring fear upon their womenfolk.'

'When?' Thuo hissed. 'How shall we escape?'

'Strike through the desert. Steal camels from the nomads.'

'They are few and scattered. We will die of thirst before we find them.'

'Wait beside the road,' Mwangi suggested. 'Ambush passing travellers.'

'Who travels there?' Thuo demanded. 'Only the prison lorry with armed guards.'

Mwangi shook his head, content to plant the seed. Days later, as Mwangi knew he would, Thuo found the answer. 'The lorry,' he breathed. 'We must take it *here*, at the prison!'

'Who will drive it?' someone protested. Other voices joined the doubting chorus.

'What about the warders' guns?'

'Amin will surely flog us if we fail!'

'*Some jackals may get hurt,*' Mwangi reminded them. 'With cunning and surprise, it could be done.' Woolly heads nodded over chipped enamel plates. Grubby fingers probed the thin grey gruel that passed for porridge. Mwangi left them to it, and slipped back to his cell where he still had work to do.

He moved from the window, pulled the threadbare blanket tighter and opened the Bible stolen from the chapel. The moon was bright enough to make out words – foolish English Christian words he had to know to make the plan succeed. Another tiresome labour on the long road back.

He sat on hard cold stone, turning the flimsy pages, picturing those who had driven him to this: a pale-haired woman, a one-legged settler and Berkeley, the D.C. They will pay, he vowed. Some day, somehow, *all of them will pay* . . .

Rebecca laid the last parcel underneath the tree, stood back and savoured the effect. Tinsel and paperchains, cotton-wool snow and, outside, the warm, soft Kenya night: the paradox of Christmas in the tropics.

She tiptoed to the bathroom and undressed before the mirror. A few more crow's feet round her eyes – laugh-lines, Hugo called them; more plumpness at her breasts and hips – love-handles, Hugo said. Another year gone by, and mostly for the better.

A bumper coffee crop, high returns from fleece and mutton, a wage rise for the tribesmen, an Arab horse for Hugo, more time for shopping and the club; and Hugo had at last filed proper deeds.

Sometimes she felt guilty about Lance, trapped in spartan bareness while they enjoyed such luxuries. But life *was* simpler without his glowering presence. She could revel in raising Hal, and take pleasure in his daily growth.

Sometimes, she had dreaded Lance's return.

Then Lance came home, and she marvelled at the changes in him.

He had grown almost as tall as Hugo, and was already broader in the chest and shoulders. There was darker down on his upper lip and new calmness in his sage-blue eyes. Most of all she marvelled at the way he took to Hal.

'Crikey, he's a *person*!' Lance exclaimed, as Hal sat in the highchair and burbled through his groats. 'Can I hold him, please?'

She held her breath, when Lance held Hal, seeing the quizzical set of Lance's jaw and the dubious frown on Hal's small round face.

'I'm Lance,' the older boy said cautiously, 'your big brother.'

'Bwuvver,' Hall repeated, chuckling, clapping his messy hands, and winning Lance's broad, besotted grin. Rebecca blinked back happy tears and let her breath out slowly.

On the strength of this and a glowing school report, Rebecca took a special plea to Hugo.

'I don't know,' he muttered, 'there's very little time.'

'You could do it if you tried, you always can.'

'Flattery will get you nowhere, my love. He's still very young.'

'*Please*, Hugo, just for me.'

'How can I refuse? But it's against my better judgement.'

Tomorrow, Rebecca thought, smiling tensely at her own reflection, Lance had better vindicate my judgement.

Christmas morning, cloudless blue, and heat already blurring Mount Kenya's snowy peak. Camelot smelled of pinesap and plum pudding. Shiny-eyed in Rebecca's arms, Hal clutched a new pied toy and chortled merrily, 'Pan-da!'

'Clever boy,' Rebecca said. Beside her, tousle-haired and youthful in a grey silk dressing gown, Hugo looked every inch the doting father. 'Come, let's see what Santa brought for Lance.'

A long flat package lay beneath the tree, labelled 'Lance' and wrapped in red crêpe paper. It was heavier than he expected. Books, no doubt. They always bought him books for Christmas. I won't show disappointment, he vowed, I won't spoil Hal's day.

He unwrapped a hard brown leather case with brass-bound corners. There was a tight, expectant hush, a sudden tremor in his fingers.

It *can't* be, he thought, please don't let this be some cruel joke!

'Go ahead,' said Hugo softly, 'open it.' Something in his smile made Lance's heart beat faster – a sense of sins excused and manly pleasures to be shared. He sprung the clasps and raised the lid.

It lay in steely splendour and a nest of soft green baize. Sunlight blued the barrel. A sharp, clean whiff of gun-oil stirred his blood. He stroked the polished wood, traced the silken curves of butt and stock. 'Oh!' he whispered. 'Oh Uncle *Hugo!*'

'It's a big responsibility for a thirteen-year-old. Don't thank me, it's your mother's idea.'

'A reward,' she said, 'for being brave and doing well in school.'

He went to her and held her, ruffled Hal's hair, saw misty grey gladness in her eyes and felt an answering prickle in his own.

'Pan-da.' Hal said again, and they all laughed.

Standing in sunshine and mutual warmth, Lance felt an old, dull sorrow lifting. I *am* part of the enchanted circle, he realised. Without me, it cannot be complete. How foolish, to envy Hal their love. We are brothers. They love us both.

Beyond the sparkling window, the distant forest swayed and beckoned. *What* a holiday I'll have up there, he thought, with Duma and the gun. What tales I shall take back to the dorm!

Perhaps, after all, Camelot is my place of light and love.

*

The party began at three, after Hal's nap. The yard filled with dusty cars, the lawn filled with unfamiliar settlers: weatherbeaten men in short-sleeved shirts and khaki slacks, women wearing sunhats and the latest knee-length dresses.

'New friends,' Hugo confided sheepishly. 'We get out more, when you are away. Serve some grog, there's a good chap.'

Obeying, he encountered Molly Stuart, black-haired and sharp-tongued as ever. She gave him a knitted tartan sweater he'd never wear, and a lecture on 'abhorrent native customs'.

'You bore that like a trooper,' Eric murmured, winking. 'Here's a fiver, give yourself a treat.'

'You're growing up, boy,' Colonel Elliot bellowed. 'Soon be fit for polo. Fetch us a whisky soda in the meantime.'

Briefly, he revelled in his near-adult status, this casual acceptance among Hugo's peers. As drink flowed and talk turned to agriculture, the novelty palled. He longed for someone younger, someone who would covet his new treasure. Most of all, he longed to try it out.

The sun blazed, the conversation rumbled. Women cooed and clucked around Hal. No one will miss me for half an hour, he reasoned.

He slipped inside, collected the rifle and a dozen shells. He knew exactly where to go: the big pool, where the falls would muffle gunfire. There's no harm and no danger, he told his conscience. It's only a few sighting shots.

It was cool and shady by the river. Fine spray damped his face, reflected sunshine made him squint. All the better: it would be a sterner test.

He chose a dark knot-hole in a podo trunk on the far bank, sixty yards away. The rifle rose, smooth and sweetly balanced to his shoulder, feeling at once like an extension of himself. The first shot cut a yellow groove, high and right, going whining through the leaves beyond. He reset the sights and hit low. After another small adjustment, the next three bullets struck dead centre. He held the stance, savouring the scent of cordite, the small pain of recoil at his shoulder, the smoothness of the stock against his cheek.

The sweetest, truest gun in all the world, he rejoiced, and it's *mine*!

Rebecca was displaying Hal to smitten female watchers. Lance had disappeared. A queue had formed at the lean-to bar.

'Two beers and a brandy, Hugo!'

'Hey, how about my gin and tonic?'

'And a sweet sherry for the Ball and Chain!'

'I say, what's the hold-up? I've got a dredger's thirst!'

Hugo juggled bottles, couldn't find fresh glasses, felt yuletide cheer yield to irritation. He heard ironic cheers and looked up in time to witness Lance's entry.

He came down the steps, poised and self-possessed, carrying a laden tray. Sunlight struck coppery in his hair and gleamed on polished tumblers. 'Gangway,' he cried. 'Rescue is at hand.' He had a polite 'excuse me', for those who baulked him, and a glowing, boyish grin for Hugo alone.

Dear Lord, let the moment last, Hugo pleaded. Let pride and pleasure join us, let him become my well-loved elder son.

Lance worked at his shoulder. The crush began to clear.

Then, through sunstruck, drink-flushed faces, Hugo saw two figures cross the fallen tree above the river and march up towards the lawn, their grim, determined plod wholly at odds with the occasion.

Coetze led, bible-black and bushy-bearded, hard-eyed as a vengeful prophet. Behind him, like some reluctant acolyte, came his daughter Karen. Short and plump, with sallow skin and black hair scraped into a bun, she wore a pink, puff-shouldered dress and white ankle socks. She looked sullen, overawed, much younger than her fourteen years.

'Merry Christmas,' someone shouted. 'Come for a noggin, have you?'

'It's Christ's birthday,' Coetze snapped. 'You have made it a drunken orgy!'

He cut through the crowd and planted himself in front of Hugo. 'Someone has been shooting over my land!'

'Don't be silly, old man. It's a party, can't you see?'

'Show him, child.'

Karen raised her hand. A spent, distorted bullet glittered on her small, pale palm. Her voice was less accented than her father's. Every word carried clearly. 'I was walking near the falls. I heard a whine. This thing hit the tree beside me. It's the truth. I swear.'

'I don't doubt you, girl,' Hugo began, 'but no one here has even brought a . . .' He faltered, recalling an unexplained absence, feeling an ugly tautness in his stomach, glimpsing Lance's stricken face; and knew his earlier prayer had gone unanswered.

In the sudden hush, Hugo's eyes set cold and hard. Through a fog of guilt, Lance felt the effort the apology cost him. 'I'm sorry, Kobus. No harm was meant, I'm sure.'

'Harm was caused, menheer. Our prayers were interrupted.'

'I'm sorry,' Hugo repeated, through clenched teeth. 'It won't happen again.'

'I want to know who did it, man!'

'You have my word the culprit will be punished.'

'She could have been killed, while you swill like swine around the trough!'

There was real antagonism in the hot, still air. Coetze's beard bristled furiously.

Hugo wore his bone-white, lipless glare. 'Do you *doubt* my word, sir?'

Coetze's green stare smouldered, wavered, dipped. He took Karen's hand, left them with one final contemptuous gesture at the bar. 'You're no better than the kaffirs, you ought to be ashamed!' And hauled his chubby daughter in his wake.

'Drink up, fellows,' Elliot commanded, 'don't let beastly Boers spoil the fun!'

'Too right! Another port and lemon, Hugo!'

The bravado rang false. The air hung sour. Hugo's whisper cut it like a lash. 'Inside, Lance. I want a word with you!'

'Do you enjoy it?' Hugo began, with weary scorn more hurtful than rage. 'Does it please you to see me grovel to that bloody-minded Boer, in front of all my friends?'

'I didn't mean it! I never thought . . .'

'You *never* think, until the harm is done! You betrayed our trust, Lance, proving yourself unworthy of the rifle. Bring it here!'

'*Please*,' he begged. 'I promise I'll be more careful!'

'Do as you're told!'

He trudged to his room through suddenly chill sunlight. The rifle was a deadweight in his hands. Hugo made him rack it in the gunsafe, made him turn the key himself. 'When you're more responsible, you might get it back. Now stay out of my sight until the party's over!'

Later, while car doors slammed and falsely gay farewells filled the yard, his mother came and made things much, much worse. For the first time, she looked worn and middle-aged. 'It took days to persuade Hugo. You wrecked it, in less than half an hour. Oh Lance, can't you do *anything* right?'

The door closed behind her. The red dust of departure eddied past the window. He fought unmanly tears, hating Kobus Coetze and his fat, prissy daughter.

So much for holidays, he thought. So much for my high bright place. I'd rather be in school where no one knows about the gun, where I'm the rugger hero who refused to have his willy blacked.

Where I can be Lance *Reid* again.

33

THREE PRISONS IN FIFTEEN years, Father Andrew thought, bowed by the midday heat before the chapel altar. Lord, is there a better way to scarify the soul? A twilight half-life among bestial warders and the scum of this dark land, shared with governors who drink too much, care too little and ignore the viciousness around them.

At first he had sought converts, promising redemption from the often hideous evils they had done. They laughed at him, stole from his chapel and his quarters, demeaned his faith and scorned his charity.

Then he heard of Leo's death, and realised that the sacrifice had been in vain. Old guilts returned to haunt him. Another steady inner light burned out.

Now, like the governors he despised, he was serving out his time at Lorigumu. He held one ill-attended service every week, ministered to Amin's victims, conducted all-too-frequent funerals.

'Dead convicts make the only worthwhile converts,' Hargreaves, the present governor, had remarked. 'You *know* they will never sin again!'

Forgive me, Lord, Father Andrew pleaded, I'm beginning to believe him.

He heard a stealthy movement among the wooden pews, turned and goggled in astonishment. A prisoner knelt behind him, a slight, hunched figure in a sweat-stained smock, his dark head dipped in homage, his lips framed a quiet Kikuyu prayer.

A prisoner at prayer, in Lorigumu!

'Help me, Father, lead me to the light.'

'Don't mock me,' Father Andrew growled. 'What worldly favour do you seek?'

'Don't you know me? I am Duma's firstborn son.'

Father Andrew stiffened, recognising this thin, dark spectre from the past, feeling an ancient anger stir. 'Get out, Mwangi. Take your pagan powers from God's house!'

Once-fierce eyes gazed up at him, luminous and mild. Mwangi spoke softly, in English. *'Joy shall be in heaven over one sinner that repenteth, more than over nine and ninety that need no repentance.'*

Soft, stunning words, that hung on the stifling air, words that could not be more aptly chosen. The holy gospel, letter-perfect – as if Satan had arisen, singing psalms. Hope bloomed in Father Andrew's heart, born of desperation and long years of hopeless failure. 'What do you want?' he whispered.

'To serve.' Mwangi's hands spread in supplication. 'I have scars on my back and pain in my soul, because of the evil I have done. Heal me, Father, let me take the Word among the ridges when I'm free!'

He looked and sounded abject; but this was still Lorigumu prison, he was still Mwangi. Take care, a weary, worldly voice warned Father Andrew.

Put him to the test.

'Will you help me at the weekly service? Will you stand before this altar and lead the men in prayer?'

'I will.'

So it began. It was in many ways like watching an older, leaner Kibe come to God again. Mwangi was jeered and cursed and spat upon, isolated by all the other men save Thuo. He bore it like a martyr, learned the prayers and scriptures, sang the hymns with saintly fervour.

Yet doubts still lingered in Father Andrew's mind.

Sometimes, as Mwangi's meek, white-smocked figure knelt at prayer beside him, he remembered the sunstriped Kerinyagga wedding and the red-eyed, colobus-kirtled creature that had cursed it.

Which is the real Mwangi? he wondered.

Until the day Mwangi warned him of the mass escape plan.

'You must promise to move me and Thuo. They will know who informed, and will surely kill us if we stay.'

'I cannot, Mwangi. You have two years to serve.'

'I don't ask release, only to be taken south, far away from here.'

'If I win this promise, will you tell the governor the whole plan?'

'Yes.'

330

'You will give names, betray your comrades?'

'They are not comrades, only godless fools. You have seen how they abuse His servant!'

He stood at the altar, with sunlight through stained glass upon his dark, determined face. There *is* a power in him, Father Andrew realised; no one can deny his holy fierceness, nobody can doubt the risk he takes. He is prepared to die in the service of the Lord.

He has passed the test, and brought new purpose to my life; for if Mwangi can be saved, no prisoner on earth is beyond saving.

Nearing his sixteenth birthday, Lance had outgrown Hugo, was almost as tall as his real father. Despite his rugby prowess and good academic progress, the rifle still languished in the gunsafe. 'Next year, perhaps,' Hugo grunted. 'Meanwhile, stay away from those damned Boers!'

The restlessness took Lance in the middle of another boring holiday: a secret, greening force deep inside. It had to do with shaving, and the strange, heavy spice which sometimes eddied from the double bedroom. Dreams began, dreams he couldn't quite re-member. They woke him with hardness at his groin and dryness in his throat, and a sense of somehow shameful pleasure.

He couldn't tell Hugo. Hal interrupted his one fumble-tongued attempt to tell his mother. 'Mummy, come and see my smashing picture!' The moment passed. Lance's confusion lingered.

In the end, he told Duma.

Sitting on a green bank outside his hut, Duma looked like a wise, iron-grey-haired tortoise.

Duma always had time for Lance.

'There are no girls?' he asked, when Lance had finished. 'No women, at this school of yours?'

'Of course not!'

Duma's eyes narrowed. 'I have seen you, watching maids at work, watching the sunlight on their bare brown flesh. Do these dreams not give you the same feeling?'

Lance felt the flush spreading across his cheeks, and clumsiness returning to his tongue. 'Well . . . er, yes, sort of.'

'You are almost grown,' Duma told him. 'Soon, you will not speak so scornfully of girls.' He uncoiled with easy grace that belied his years, and brought Lance a short throwing spear from the hut. 'Go to the forest, find some small beast to kill.'

'Will that stop the dreams?'

'No. But it will cool the fire in your blood.'

He found the spoor in soft ground beside a brook that smelled of wild balsam. Forest hog, he thought, with quickening interest. They've been rooting in the maize. If I kill one, Hugo might return the gun.

It began, then, just as Duma said it would, the hunting fever which puts dreams to flight.

He moved as Duma had taught him, noiselessly, every sense alert. The spoor was a narrow, damp green tunnel beyond which little else existed. Twice he thought he heard nearby rustles, echoes of his own passage. When he turned, there was only windsigh in the high dim canopy, and filtered sunshafts on empty undergrowth.

The tunnel yellowed, opening on to a clearing beneath an old, dark fig tree. He heard grunts and snuffles, smelled faint, rancid musk. Crouching, circling, he parted hanging creepers and squinted into brightness.

They snouted busily among gnarled fig-roots, their charcoal-grey hides bristling, their trotters churning rich brown soil: a sleek fat sow, two piglets, and a silver-maned, yellow-toothed boar. *What* a trophy, what a prize to take to Hugo!

It would have to be a clean kill, he knew, striking deep at tender throatflesh. There was awesome power in the hunched hindquarters, and danger in the curving razored tusks. He drew the spear back slowly, cocking his wrist for one fierce, fast thrust.

A high, shrill, wordless cry broke, sharp and startling, close at hand. Foliage at the far side of the clearing rattled as to a fresh-sprung gale. He heard the boar's alarm-snort, saw the sow and piglets scatter, and plunged forward through crackling undergrowth. Urgent and off-balance, he caught his foot and fell. A rock-hard anthill winded him. The tumbling blade bit into his thigh.

He rolled over, hunched in pain and fury, clutching at the wound. Blood oozed stickily along his fingers. Its coppery sweetness seemed to fill his lungs. A pulse rumbled in his head; his breath came fast and fiery, his jaw began to twitch. The sun struck, hot and scarlet, in his eyes.

The red haze was upon him.

Shadow slid across him. He scrabbled for the spear. A whiff of wildflowers drowned the scent of blood. Briefly, a small soft hand soothed his nape. A voice broke through the turmoil in his mind:

female, faintly Afrikaans, vaguely familiar. 'I'm sorry, I didn't mean to hurt.'

He felt the fever flowing to her touch, freeing him from pain. He tried to speak. It came out as an incoherent snarl. The touch withdrew. The shadow lifted.

He sat up slowly, seeing sunshine glint on separate grass-blades, hearing a rainbird call, smelling leaf mould, feeling tackiness on his fingertips.

Feeling utterly himself.

But the clearing was empty and his anger flared anew. As his senses focused, he knew the hunt was lost, and recognised the voice which had destroyed it.

Karen Coetze's voice.

He could feel her fat pink presence somewhere. Bitterness broke out in boyish spite. 'Go on, hide, you sneaking *yaapie*! Already you have cost me a fine gun. Now you drive my supper off!'

'You weren't after food, *roinek*! I saw you aiming at the boar. Poor beast didn't have a chance!'

'That's all you know. It's jolly risky, with just a spear.'

'Well, I'm glad he got away!'

He stood up, craning, trying to place her by direction. It was she who followed, he realised in grudging admiration. She's pretty good in the bush – for a girl. He reined his anger, tried to coax her out. 'The least you can do is bind my wound: or are *yaapie* girls afraid of blood?'

'No, man, you growled at me!'

'Ah, I wouldn't hurt you.'

'Promise?'

'Englishmen do not make war on *girls*!'

'Well, all right – if you drop the spear.'

He obeyed. Off to his left, a dense green thornbush parted. Lance stood absolutely still, feeling his jaw sag, wondering if this too might be a dream.

She had grown lithe and slender, only half a head shorter than Lance himself. She moved as gracefully as a long-legged deer of the forest. The fawn buckskin dress outlined her body: a high, full bosom, a tiny waist, sweeping curves of haunch and flank. Crow-black hair waved softly around her heart-shaped face. Her eyes were sea-green, wide and wary. She looked tense, a little timid – and wholly beautiful.

333

Karen Coetze had become a woman.

'What are you gawping at, *roinek*? Close your mouth, you'll swallow flies.'

'You're – different,' he mumbled. 'You're so grown up.'

'And *not* afraid of blood. Take off your shirt. I need bandages.'

Again he obeyed, conscious of her warm assessing interest, grateful for his own hard, well-tuned muscle and the impulse which had forbidden him to shave.

'You've done a bit of growing yourself,' she said, as she ripped the shirt to long white strips.

She bent, her hands working swiftly. Her breathing tickled his thigh. He could see the sweet cleft valley down her spine, a shaded span of honey-tinted skin. The green force stirred. The dreams were suddenly vivid in his mind. He wanted very much to hold her, breathe her female essence, run his fingers through her hair.

The pain had eased beneath her gentle touch. The bandage felt firm and comfortable.

'Karen . . .' he began, and she stepped quickly back, her eyes bright with warning.

'Keep your distance!'

'I only wanted to say – thanks.'

Her face softened. She watched him, curiously intent. 'What happened, man? It's only a scratch: you were as rigid as a board.'

Only then did the enormity strike him, the full understanding of what she had achieved. 'You made it go away,' he breathed, in wonder, 'you made the red haze go away!'

'You are different, too,' she murmured, as if confirming some private belief; then, with urgent loveliness, 'Tell me about it!'

He faltered; he had only ever confided in his father. 'Walk back with me,' he invited, 'I'll try to explain.'

'Look at you, man: a big bold *roinek* naked to the waist. If Oupa Coetze saw us, he would kill me! I must return as I came – alone.'

It wasn't a threat, just a simple statement of the barriers between them. I am Coetze's daughter, you are Berkeley's ward. He felt the bitterness again, this time for a foolishness no act of his could alter. A feud kindled in a half-forgotten war, kept smouldering by opposed beliefs, fanned to flame by years of enforced proximity.

Yet, in this quiet, sunlit glade, he felt her reaching out, felt his own green force grow stronger.

'Sometimes,' she whispered, 'when the moon is high and Oupa

334

sleeps, I walk beside the river. It would not be my fault if a certain wounded hunter found me there.'

She was moving, swift and sinuous across green-gold brightness, pausing briefly at the shadowed edge. A flicker of crow-black hair, a teasing grin. 'Are you man enough, *roinek*?'

Then she was gone.

I am man enough, he vowed. Not all the Boers in Christendom could stop me!

She was waiting in the shadows beside the moonlit waters. She wore a long, dark, supple cloak with fur at the collar: fur that mingled with her breath-plumes and shimmered round her face, making a soft grey halo for her beauty. She wouldn't let him touch her. 'First, I must know all your secrets.'

He took a deep breath, broke the last bond with the past, and told her about the red haze. 'It comes suddenly, without warning, in times of pain and threat. I cannot call it up, I can't fight it. Until today, it always ran its course, leaving me weak and fevered with fresh blood on my hands. Only you can stop it. Only you can make me whole again.'

For a long time she was silent, her gaze rapt and inward beneath the waxing moon. At first her voice was very low. He had to crane to hear her. 'When I was young and high-spirited, Kobus beat me. When I grew older, he began to stare and touch.' He must have started, made some gesture of disgust. 'Don't worry, Helena stopped him, reminding him of godly duties. They are not evil, Lance, only dull and – *hard*. For seventeen years, I've been their servant, living in pious gloom and wearing animal skins. Soon they'll choose a man, and I will be *his* servant: tend his fields, bear as many children as God decrees and my body can conceive. At forty, I'll be fit only to haunt the stoep and sew the Word in thick gold thread. *Listen*, Lance. This is a Boer woman's life!' She moved. Moonlight struck her upraised face, pure with silvered beauty, bitter but unbowed. *'But I am not a Boer!'*

He reached for her; she held him off. He watched her battle misery – and win. Her hand swept up, pointing to Orion's Belt, which blazed in icy brilliance against the deep blue sky. 'I want to live! I want to know a world outside this valley! I want a man who'll catch the stars and make a necklace for me!' She turned to him, let him see the starkness of her hope. 'The first words you spoke made

335

me look beyond your beauty, made me think you might be the one. We are *different*, you and I!'

A short way upriver, sudden yellow lamplight flared. Lance smelled cooking, glimpsed Coetze's bearded silhouette in the homestead doorway.

'Watch for me by moonlight,' she whispered, 'think of me at night. Keep the difference safe and strong for me!'

Father Andrew stood in the chapel, peering out across the blinding sand. The dark blue prison lorry stood with its back doors open. Unloading was complete. The guards lounged and gossiped with Amin.

Mwangi waited in the aisle, his eyes closed, his wrists cuffed in steel, his dark face prayerfully serene. Thuo hunched beside him, mop-headed, wide-eyed in fear.

The escape attempt began exactly as they had predicted.

The outburst was sudden and violent: tin plates pounding, warcries rising behind the cellblock wall. A decoy, Father Andrew knew, to draw the three duty warders off. Forewarned, they stood their ground until the ragged, white-clad mob burst from the dining hall and came pelting through upkicked dust towards the vehicle.

Weight of numbers, Mwangi had explained. They know some will be shot, but enough will survive to overrun the guards. It would have worked, Father Andrew realised grimly, if we hadn't known in advance.

Six more warders stepped from the back of the lorry and levelled their rifles.

It only took one volley, one thundering, smoking cannonade of flame. Three men went down, their white smocks blooming crimson. The rest milled in the dwindling dust, their hands high, their voices raised in a collective, animal howl of grief and rage. Amin was strolling through a drift of gunsmoke, his cane poised, his voice harsh with victory. 'Bleed, you dogs! *There is no escape!*'

Mwangi and Thuo walked the white-hot gauntlet.

First, there was an abrupt, appalled hush, then one short cry of betrayal. The mob's fury boiled anew, with contemptuous curses, vile Kikuyu oaths, a roar so fierce and savage that the warders trained their guns again and even Father Andrew cowered. Thuo bolted into the cab like a terrified hare.

Mwangi strolled, untroubled, his hawk-grin cold and proud.

336

He paused in the cab doorway, sent back one last glance: a glance of godly triumph that made Father Andrew's soul swell with gladness. This was the first and greatest convert, the darkest of the heathen brought into pure white light.

'Do something for me,' Father Andrew called, 'when you are set free!'

'Anything, Father.'

'Seek out Leo's widow in the valley. Take her my good wishes and the blessing of our God!'

Mwangi's smile was blinding in its fervour. His eyes blazed with urgent, amber force. 'Oh I will, Father,' he breathed, '*I will!*'

It was hotter even than Lorigumu in the jolting, juddering, dust-stifled cab. Mwangi's smock lay plastered to his body; the handcuffs chafed his wrists.

'Nyeri?' grunted the fat, plum-black driver with a pistol strapped to his khaki-covered thigh and the keyring in his belt. 'No such luck, my friend. You're bound for maximum security at Voi.' He grinned, gloating. 'Far south you said, far south you get.'

'*Voi!*' Thuo hissed in dismay. 'The worst prison in the land!'

'Quiet,' Mwangi warned him. 'Be thankful you're alive.'

Ever since, while the sun climbed overhead and the dustcloud thickened, Mwangi had been watching the driver. Only three things matter, he decided: the wheel to steer the way, the foot pump to make the engine faster, the long hand lever that makes the vehicle stop.

He waited while they laboured up a winding, blinding scarp into the bare blue sky, and chugged across a rocky ridge. Off to his right, above the steaming, dust-dulled bonnet, he saw green: green hills, green trees, green pasture, a gleam of flowing water, a glint of living goathide.

He had come as far south as he meant to ride.

He waited till the road turned red and the bonnet angled downwards. There was bare grey rock along the near side, and empty open space beyond the driver's door. 'What's that!' he shouted suddenly, pointing right. The driver turned to look.

Mwangi braced his feet, hauled the handbrake on, seized the wheel and jerked hard left. The lorry slewed and skidded, smashing into solid rock. The driver's head lunged forward and crashed against the windscreen. He slumped, bleeding, senseless, over the

337

steering wheel. His weight straightened the wheels. The lorry slithered forward, going straight, inching towards nothingness on the right.

'Stop it!' Thuo screamed. 'We're going over!'

'Get the keys,' growled Mwangi, pulling on the brake with all his might.

The lorry halted, swaying, its offside front wheel spinning gently above a narrow, foaming stream a hundred feet below. Thuo sat stone-still, bolt-upright, with fat sweat pebbles all along his brow. 'Don't move!' he whispered, 'please don't move!'

Mwangi leaned casually across, plucked the keys from the driver's belt, unlocked the handcuffs. He felt the power in him growing. 'Ngai has brought us this far. He will not desert us now.' He pushed Thuo's greasy, rancid body out, jumping lightly down beside him. The lorry shifted, creaking, leaning further out.

'Watch,' growled Mwangi, recalling old Njau's words. 'Watch and tremble at a Healer's force!'

He threw his weight against the hot, dark blue metal, felt the balance shift, and stepped quickly back.

The lorry fell.

It tumbled end on end, dusty red on iron blue, growing smaller. It struck with a crash which seemed to shake the very earth. A red flame kindled, growing into a broad golden flower. In the whoosh of quivering, upthrown air, Mwangi smelt petrol and scorching human flesh.

Thuo watched him, wide-eyed in awe.

Mwangi turned from sizzling destruction, walked a little way along the ravine edge. He could smell hutsmoke, goat-grease and well-watered pastures. On the southern skyline, faint and far through purple haze, he could see the hump of Nyeri Hill.

'This time,' he commanded, 'there will be no "good meal to give us strength". This time, we will watch and wait until the time is right.'

'So be it,' Thuo whispered humbly. 'As the Healer orders, the warrior will obey.'

Now, at last, thought Mwangi, all the hardships are worthwhile. I'm going home, to land which still belongs to me. I'm going with new hardness in my spirit and the Healer's power blooming in my heart. I take two vital scraps of knowledge with me.

How easy it is to deceive the whites.

How easy it is to kill a man.

34

DUMA HEARD IT FIRST from the goatboys on the upland pasture. They gathered in grey dawnlight, their eyes round and shiny, their voices shrill. I must go and see, he thought. If it is true, there will be trouble.

Women in the village stood silent and uneasy. No one greeted him, not a single infant cried. Even the birds forgot to sing. He angled left towards the Healer's knoll, following a narrow, muddy path. The elders had gone before; Maina's great weight left the clearest spoor.

He came over the rise and stopped, shocked by the destruction.

A bough had fallen from the gum tree which shaded Njau's hut. Struck on its peak, the hut had split like empty eggshell. Sooty thatch and shattered rafters glistened in the sun.

Njau lay in the ruins, lifeless but unmarked. He looked somehow smaller – a shrunken, curled-up, snowy-haired child. It was an awesome sight, this dead Healer who had ruled the clan for so long. Ngai is angry, the herdboys had cried. He has sent a curse upon us. Duma felt his nape-hairs prickle at the power of this sign.

Maina paced the splinters, his belly a little lower, his jowls touched with silver. There was fear in his eyes, and his voice shook. 'We are helpless before sickness and ill omen. What shall we do?'

'Go to the sacred fig,' an aged, weary voice suggested. 'Pray for help and guidance.'

'Perhaps Ngai will hear us,' another elder pleaded, 'perhaps a new Healer will come.'

In the weight of sunlit silence and the reek of rotten wood, Duma knew what they were thinking: knew every one was thinking Mwangi's name.

Duma thought only of Lance.

He is not yet grown or proven. Somehow, I must help him show that he brings worth to the clan. Until I do, the curse will stay upon us.

Unless I do, the Healer's charm will die.

A January morning on the upland pastures. Mount Kenya stood white-capped and steely-shouldered under a cloudless pale blue sky. A slack time on the farm: the annual pause between harvest and fresh planting, before the short rains came. Tribesmen lazed and gossiped and weeded their own plots. All the village boys were in the forest, daubed in pale river clay, eating roots and berries, preparing for the ceremony which would make them men. Lance gazed across the riverbend towards the Coetze farmstead and felt his own manhood stir.

She is so close, he thought, yet so far away. We may never bridge the gulf between our families. Yet I dream of Karen, and I know she dreams of me.

She had said so, during rare, stolen meetings by the river, while starlight made a poem of her beauty. 'Be patient, Lance,' she'd whispered, trembling in his tentative embrace, 'be strong and constant – grow up fast!'

In that one way, he mused, I am already grown. When she lets me touch her, when her breath is sweet and needy on my cheek, there is a manly force in me which could sweep us both away. When she turns aside, her smile is soft with promise: a promise which will comfort me through one last year of school.

For a while, in heat and clover scent, he lay still and let the daydream grow.

He awoke to full awareness and vague unease, to sound and movement far across the river.

They came down the distant blue-green ridge, a line of swaying, canvas-covered carts. There was whip-crack and wheel-creak and the bellowing of oxen, a snatch of song, a wide red pall of dust. Drawing near, the seated figures took on form and colour: bearded, weather-beaten men in buckskin, sturdy, broad-faced women, brown-shawled against the dust. They were singing, as their wagons rocked and jolted, a rousing Christian hymn in Afrikaans.

The Boers of Kerinyagga went to greet them.

340

Briefly, he glimpsed Karen, slim, erect and golden, like some exotic flower among drab womenfolk. He couldn't understand the talk; the air of mass excitement carried clearly. He saw fat Helena carrying fire-blackened pots and pans to the wagon in the yard. Coetze drove a team of iron-grey oxen from the paddock, inspanned them to wooden yokes and flat brown leather leads.

Karen went to help him.

Lance sensed her reluctance, saw the furtive glances she aimed at Camelot. They have found us out, he thought, and are taking her away! He left the sheep untended, slipped down the sunlit slope with a single desperate hope in his mind. Surely she will find a way to meet me, if only to say goodbye!

She came to him at twilight and their secret place, with sunset in her crow-black hair and sorrow in her sea-green eyes. She stood in dappled shade and reflected river glow and raised a warning hand.

'They are trekking, and I must go with them.'

'But you will come back?'

'Oh yes, Lance, I will come back.' She said it quietly, without a hint of promise. Her head was bowed, her lovely litheness drained away. 'The elephants have gathered in the north. It only happens once in fifteen years. There will be a great slaughter, a haul of ivory, much feasting and celebration. All the women must go, for the butchery and skinning.'

'I can wait,' he said, 'it won't be for ever.'

'You don't understand. They have come from all over the ridges, men in search of wives. Already, three have spoken for me to Oupa Coetze. He will watch the hunt, pick the strongest, best provider. He will give his blessing; I will be betrothed.'

The first star winked, the sky turned deeper blue. Darkness deepened over Lance's soul. 'You can't let it happen! You're a *woman*, you have the right to choose!'

'It is their way, Lance. I warned you, long ago.' She turned sideways on, her profile pure and sad against the water's fading brightness, her hand sweeping up across the fall of night. 'We dreamed here, you and I, like foolish children, dreamed of being different and making the impossible come true. But the stars are still in place, we couldn't reach them. I am a woman; you remain a boy. Go back to school, Lance. Find some pretty English girl to share your Camelot.'

He felt it then, the fusion of his green force with a looming sense of manhood, a power and a confidence that would not be denied. He took her by the shoulders, turned her body to him, brought his mouth down firmly on her lips.

She fought him briefly, her cold, still strength astonishing in one so slight. Then her small hands fluttered and tightened on his back. Her lips grew warm and moist, her breasts seemed to swell against his chest. She clung and sighed, arcing her back, parting her thighs. The sweetness and the pleasure ran along his spine, setting a throbbing at his centre and a weakness at his knees. Her fragrance was wild and musky; he was drowning in her, quivering on the brink.

A voice cut through the darkness, high-pitched and Boer-accented, much too close at hand. 'Come, Karen, come and get your *braiflaies*!' She pushed herself away, stood flushed and shaking, almost unbearably lovely in the starlight.

'Kiss them as you kissed me, at the start!' he whispered. 'Be cold for them, keep all your warmth for me. Wait for me, Karen. Wait for *me*!'

And just before she slipped away, he thought he saw a promise in her eyes again.

He trudged up through the pasture-scented, cricket-chirping night towards the gabled loom of Camelot. I may not be a man, he thought, nor am I any longer a boy. She knows, she has felt it; but will it be enough to make her wait?

Boards creaked on the verandah above him. Hugo's neat, lean silhouette rose against the yellowed window. There was tightness in his shoulders and accusation in his tone. 'Where have you been, boy?'

'Walking, by the river.'

'Alone?'

He squinted into the brightness, swallowed, and knew his hesitation had betrayed him.

'I'm always alone.'

'Get inside,' Hugo snapped. 'Remember you had the chance to tell the truth!'

He climbed the steps, feeling the coldness gather, sensing confrontation.

They were waiting in the lounge, standing stiffly before the

342

glowing hearth. His mother wore her middle-aged look again. Clutching her hand, peering upwards, Hal looked pale and frightened, goggle-eyed.

'Tell us what you saw, son,' Hugo urged him gently. 'Tell us who you saw your brother with.'

'He was down by the river,' Hal whispered, 'kissing Karen Coetze!'

Lance rounded on him and the anguish of the day broke loose. 'You rotten little spy!'

Hal flinched, grasping Rebecca's skirt. His face screwed up, his sobs were harsh and broken-hearted. 'I wasn't spying, honest! You scared me, sneaking past so quick and quiet!'

'*That's enough!*' Lance hadn't seen Hugo so pale-lipped since Hal's birth. He was glaring up, his fist bunched, his brown eyes hot and dangerous.

Glaring *up*.

Lance sensed another shift in balance. If he tries to beat me, I won't need the red haze: I'm bigger and stronger than him now. Hugo started forward; Lance felt his own hands clench.

Then Rebecca spoke, and stopped the madness. 'No, Hugo, *please!*' There was naked appeal in her eyes, that great love for Hugo which even now caused Lance a pang of envy.

But not for long.

'You leave the sheep untended,' she began, 'tell a bare-faced lie, and take your spite out on a little boy. And all for a few moments with Kobus Coetze's child!'

'She's not a child!'

'Lance, you are going to be head of school and rugby captain. Woodfall says you are university material. What do you want with a half-caste Boer girl?' Hugo asked, with genuine hurt and puzzlement. Lance waited for his mother to protest, remembering her fondness for the coffee-coloured Flynnlets.

Rebecca watched him, pale and silent, drying Hal's tears. Hugo moved across and stood beside them: three tight, disapproving faces, three minds that didn't want to understand.

He concealed the hurt and let them think they'd won. 'Don't worry, they're taking her away. Can I go to my room? I have books to study for next term.' Leaving, he actually felt the relief that blossomed in the hearthglow, and knew he had hard thinking to do.

*

Lance lay in his bedroom, watching moonlight glitter on the book-shelf. Now is the time, he thought, to judge my feelings clearly.

He remembered the three of them gaping at him as if he were a different breed. I *am* a different breed, he acknowledged without rancour. They are Berkeleys, I am a Reid.

There is no place for me at Camelot.

He watched moonlight play on bookspines and recalled Hugo's eulogy to school. *Head boy, rugby captain, university material.* I have already enjoyed all the hero-worship school can offer. I want no dreaming spires, in some grey town beyond the sea.

School holds nothing for me any more.

He remembered the 'Boer way'. *Kobus will watch the hunt, choose the strongest, best provider. I* can hunt, Lance thought, as well as any heavy-footed Boer. But first, I need a gun.

I could have done this years ago, he realised, standing beside the double bed, hearing rhythmic breath, seeing the gunsafe keys glint dimly on the dressing table. I only needed purpose and a grown man's confidence.

His mother stirred, turned over in the bed. Moonlight touched her sleeping face, her spreading, silvery hair. She looked young and beautiful again. Briefly, he felt sorrow for the parting, and the pain he'd caused.

Swiftly gone.

You made your choice, Mother, many years ago. Live in peace when I am gone, with the second son you always favoured.

He left the gunsafe open. He wanted them to know what he had done. The rifle nestled in the crook of his right arm; the rucksack rested snugly on his back. Now he needed only a tracker for the hunt.

Now, at last, he allowed himself to think of Karen: the imprint of her body, the aura of her musk, the softly swelling yield and cling of her. The puzzle was fitting together, the excitement was building in his mind and body. I will go to the blazing north, he thought, and prove my manhood there. *That* will be my high bright place, *she* will be the greatest love I've ever known!

He moved joyfully through dew-damp grass under far, clear stars towards the old man's huddled, cone-shaped hut.

Duma woke to dying ember-glow, a looming shadow in the dim grey doorway, a sense of the past reborn – and an urgent, deep-toned murmur.

'I am going north. Will you hunt with me?'

'You have quarrelled with the bwana again?'

'Yes.'

'You have stolen the gun?'

'Not stolen. It is mine.'

There was an ache in Duma's bones, a longing for the comfort of the hut fire, a sense of warring loyalties. I should rouse the memsahib, he thought, put an end to this foolishness. Then Lance turned, and firelight struck his pure young face.

'Shall we bicker like weaver birds? Will you spend your old age dozing like a bull put out to grass? *Will you come?*'

He was big and broad and beautiful, the living image of his dead father. The Lion Boy, whom Duma had once loved more than life itself; and had brought to manhood on a northern hunt.

Now Njau, too, was dead.

One more time, Duma thought. I must rouse this ageing body one more time, create another lion boy to charm this shadowed valley. So can I be true to myself, and give one final service to those I've served so faithfully, so long.

Duma hawked; he spat, sizzling into the embers.

'We will need a water gourd,' he said.

Hugo leaned on the verandah railings and shouldered all the blame. 'I should have read the signs, long ago. I was too busy farming, too bound up with Hal. Forgive me, Rebecca. I've driven him away, and caused you pain.'

Rebecca went quickly to him, kissed his palm and laid it against her cheek. Seeking to comfort, she sought the secrets she had never told a living soul. 'Leo never knew his parents, always feared some darkness in their pasts. Sometimes, beside those mouldering crosses, I've sensed it, too.' She shivered, and let Hugo's arms enfold her, let the truths pour out. 'Lance was conceived in violence, the night the dam was burst. It's in him still, Hugo. Don't scourge yourself for things you can't change.' She felt his tension easing. Warmth flowed into their embrace.

Then Hal came through the doorway, his dark, straight hair gleaming, his six-year-old face puckered in concern. 'Where's Lance, Daddy?'

She saw Hugo stiffen, contemplate evasion, and reject it, as Hugo always did.

'He's gone hunting, with Duma.'

'But what about school? When will he be back?'

'One day, son. One day, he will ride in with Duma at his side and a saddle full of top-grade hides.'

'Oh,' breathed Hal, savouring the vision, 'that will be nice!'

She saw Hugo smile at this bright-eyed miniature of himself, went and stood beside her husband and her son. Even if Lance doesn't come back, she thought, gazing out across the bright green pasture, there will still be love and light in Camelot. And though part of her would always journey with him, she couldn't suppress one final cool, clear truth.

It might be better if he stays away.

35

MOLLY STUART ARRIVED EARLY, before the sun had pierced the morning mist. She wore emerald green, fresh henna in her hair, and a knowing gleam in her eye. 'Time for Molly's cure again, to take your mind off a certain – absence.'

'How did you know?' Rebecca challenge. 'Who told you?'

'It's been three days, dear. Never underestimate the bush telegraph. Hurry – I left the engine running!'

Hal was sad, because Lance wasn't with them. As the box Ford chugged through drifting greyness up the damp red road, Molly set herself to cheer him up. '*Nyeri!*' she cried, 'lots of shops, and sweeties just for you. Come on, sing. "Daddy wouldn't buy me a bow-wow!"' She grinned and burped the black, bulbous horn.

'Yes he would!' Hal piped. 'Daddy buys me anything I want!'

'Well then, *sing!*'

They all sang, bouncing and laughing along until they reached the second stream, where milling tribesmen blocked the way. Rebecca recognised Maina, in ceremonial monkey-skin robes, and men from the warrior age-group wearing cowhide kirtles and carrying spears. Their greased bodies glinted dully in the overcast.

Their usually cheerful faces looked closed and resentful. Above the engine wheeze, Rebecca heard women chanting. She peered through thinning mist beyond the windscreen, saw weak sunlight strike rhythmic movement and flowing water. She glimpsed slender outlines standing waist-deep in the stream: Kikuyu girls, she realised, their faces and budding upper bodies daubed in pale grey ash.

Mature women formed a swaying circle round the pool, waving fresh green branches. Their voices joined in joyful ululation. Inside the ring, a silent figure waited, kirtled in black and white colobus

347

skin, wearing iron bracelets: a hunched, skew-shouldered female form, with wizened brown breasts, a toothless grin – and a bright blade in her clawed right hand.

A medicine woman, Rebecca realised, a witch-priestess come to initiate the village girls.

We have blundered into a circumcision party.

'What are they doing, Mummy?'

She shifted swiftly, blocking his view. 'Back off, Molly, get us out!'

Molly gripped the steering wheel, her dark eyes glittering with anger. 'Stay here,' she snapped. 'You're safe enough, beyond the warrior guard. I'm going to put a stop to this!' She slammed the door, slipped past Maina, fluttered like a bright green bird towards the waving branches.

In Rebecca's mind, Leo's voice spoke coldly. Once, long ago, he had explained the ritual. 'The maidens go through months of preparation. They eat special herbs and spend all night in the stream; cold and drugs soothe them; prayers calm their souls. When the time comes, they are completely numb.'

'Sing, Hal,' she urged, trying to distract him. 'Sing "Run Rabbit!"' Even as she mouthed the words and beat the rhythm into dusty leather, she couldn't tear her gaze from Molly, poised at the edge of noise and movement.

She saw a tranced and glistening maiden step out of the pool. Two older women seized her arms, sat her down and spread her dark thighs wide. Her plump, round face stayed blank; even from here, Rebecca read the anguish in her eyes.

Leo's voice went on remorselessly.

'It is tabu to show pain or fear. A maid who cries or flinches will be despised for life, and will never find a husband.'

Rebecca saw the witch-priestess stoop, saw the blade swoop silver, buried Hal's face against her breast. The ululation rose to a crescendo. Warriors near the car *eehed* in satisfaction. A sliver of pink flesh arced upwards, splashed into the river, floated free. Rebecca shuddered to Leo's final words. 'They take the clitoris, with very little bloodshed, and salve the wound with leaves. It is the law, Rebecca, the clan's most sacred rite. Heaven help the white man who dares to interfere!'

The maid was up and walking. Hal was squirming in Rebecca's arms. 'Mummy, you're hurting me!' As the second victim was eased down, Rebecca saw sudden leaping greenness, as Molly snatched the knife and hurled it away. The chanting stopped. The tribesmen growled and started forward, blocking Rebecca's view. Molly's fury rose from the hidden hollow.

'... vicious, barbarous mumbo-jumbo! *Look* at the poor wee biddie, crouched in fear and trembling! Be off, ye foul old witch!' Spears gleamed, above slick, brown shoulders. Women urged the maids away. The warriors advanced in hard-eyed silence.

Molly stood alone, unseen, in dreadful danger.

Rebecca laid her shawl around Hal's face. 'Be still, be quiet, we must go to Molly!' She scrambled out and down the grey-green slope, jostled through hard, goat-greased flesh into the warrior-ring.

Molly stood, unbowed, defiant. 'Ah, you great black cowards, will ye threaten babes and women? Do your worst, I'll put my trust in God!'

Rebecca heard the water's sullen murmur, saw righteous outrage in a score of harsh, dark, unfamiliar faces. For the first time in her life, she was truly frightened, cowed by an ancient force she couldn't comprehend, a force which could turn these men she thought she knew to quivering savagery. She scented bloodlust, saw upraised steel shimmer, heard Maina's breath indrawn to give the killing word.

Then Hal stirred in her arms, pushed the shawl aside, gave the looming headman a dark blue, limpid glance. 'Maina,' he chirped, '*aterere*, Maina?' The traditional Kikuyu greeting, spoken with six-year-old delight. Maina blinked and stiffened, glanced almost fearfully at his levelled spear.

He knows how close we were to slaughter, Rebecca thought, as the tension broke and spears were angled down. Only childish innocence could save us.

Molly seemed oblivious. She shoved boldly across the hovering, indecisive circle, strode up the slope into the watery sun. Revving the engine fiercely, she made the horn blast long and hard. '*There*,' she crowed, as if it had been a Sunday school debate, 'that will teach them to trifle with God's law!'

Rebecca held Hal tightly, still frightened, unconvinced, wondering at the secret darkness Molly had unleashed.

Wondering what might happen if the charm were ever broken.

Mwangi squatted in the shadow of Maina's hut, just beyond the firelight's flicker. Roasted goat scent mocked his shrunken stomach. The smell of maize beer made his parched throat writhe. Beside him, Thuo fretted. 'Be silent!' Mwangi warned him. 'Be still, our time is near.'

They had hidden here since sunset, listening to the elders' arguments. Now, despite the hunger and discomfort, Mwangi felt a Healer's power stirring, sensed an end to long, lost, empty years.

The smoky air was shimmering with unrest.

One-Leg's wife and the pale-haired woman had outraged the clan, trespassed on the sacred circumcision grounds, leaving a whole age-group of maidens uncleansed. Kibe had long since moved away. Duma and the Lion Boy's whelp had journeyed from the valley.

And Njau was dead.

Praise be to Ngai, Mwangi thought, who sent a colobus monkey to my snare, that I might wear a Healer's kirtle again. Praise be to Ngai, who made the valley ripe for my return, and turned aside all those who might oppose me. He rose, beckoned Thuo, and stepped into the hut.

'*Mwangi!*' he heard an elder whisper, 'who should be lying in the white man's jail!'

Though smoke stung his eyes, he seized the chance to rule them from the first.

'What jail can hope to hold the Healer, whom Njau trained to take his place? Tell them, Thuo, how we got away!'

'He won the Mission priest to our side,' Thuo said truthfully. 'With one small push, he made the prison lorry crash into red flame!'

Astonished *eehs* sounded. Briefly, Mwangi basked in easy triumph. Then Maina's plump, bald, beaded figure rose before the hearth.

'You are no Healer. You are Mwangi the outcast, whose foolish curses failed!'

'Failed? How did they fail, old man?'

'Look around you, *outcast*. See the crops that flourish where you called flood and fire down.'

'Who owns them?' Mwangi demanded. 'Who lives in the big house and drives the motor car?' He paused, in the dim, ember-lit, expectant hush, and answered his own question. 'Red Strangers! They are not special, they do not live in Njau's charm. Is it not time to drive them out? Let the council answer!'

A low, confused rumble, part agreement, part concern. Then Maina stilled it, with simple dignity. 'I am your chief. You will hear

350

me, before the choice is made.' He stood beneath the single lamp, his monkey-skin cloak gleaming, his round brown face troubled. 'There is some truth in this. The women *did* break our sacred law, the Lion Boy *is* dead. But it is Mwangi who stands here, not Njau. His past is sad and shameful, his power is not proved.' Maina's eyes narrowed. His beaded arm came up in challenge. 'If he truly is a Healer, let him give a sign! How does the council answer? Shall it be this way?' This time, the approving roar was instant and full-throated.

Mwangi's mind was skipping like a marsh frog from memory to memory, bringing them together, fashioning a plan. Let them hear, he thought, let them mark this moment clearly. He crouched before the embers as Njau used to, putting Njau's snaky rhythm in his voice. 'May those who stopped the maidens' cleansing be themselves so cleansed. *May she who stopped their blooding be so blooded in her turn*! That is the sign, O Chief. Remember it, in the days to come.'

This time, there would be no mistake. This time, they had killed a goat and let it ripen, and hidden the carcass in the copse to the north of Stuart's farm.

By early afternoon, the dogs were going crazy, scenting hot north breeze, howling and chasing their tails. Presently, One-Leg came out into the dusty yard and yelled at them; they growled and pointed, and fawned at his feet. Watching from the dimness of the hay barn, Mwangi saw One-Leg's shoulders stiffen, heard him give harsh, pidgeon Kikuyu orders.

'Free the dogs and follow them. Looks like we have visitors again!'

Presently, the whole pack went baying across the pasture, with One-Leg and his spear carriers behind.

Mwangi grinned at Thuo, and led him through hot stillness to the quiet, low, unguarded house.

So many passages, so many sunlit rooms. The smells sickened Mwangi – a reek of kerosene and long-boiled vegetables, a rancid whiff of white man's sweat. Thuo crouched beside him, quivering like one of One-Leg's hounds. Then Mwangi caught a hint of flowery female perfume and trailed it to a plain wooden door. 'She is here,' he growled, 'I can *feel* her.' He breathed deeply, drew the circumcision knife, watched the keen blade flicker in the sun.

And thrust the door inwards.

She sat upright in the huge, blue-sheeted bed, her black hair wild and spiky, her face as pale and sharp as a thin moon. Her mouth gaped, pink and wet. She has no teeth, Mwangi realised in disgust. 'Hold her,' he ordered. 'Keep her silent!'

Thuo pounced like a sturdy, oiled brown leopard, pinned her feeble, cotton-shrouded body to the bed. One broad dark hand clamped her jaws together. The other closed around her scrawny throat.

The room was full of sound and sweat and striving: Thuo's laboured breathing, the woman's strangled gasps, a high, sharp whiff of mortal fear. Mwangi waited till her struggles faded, then wrenched the sweat-soiled nightgown up and back.

Purple veins discoloured thighs as white as a fish-belly. Thin grey hair sprouted from the pubic mound; urine spurted, yellowing the sheets. Mwangi's face contorted at the sound and stench: how could any man take pleasure *here*?

Then Mwangi circumcised her.

He did it with two swift, clean, glittering strokes, hearing the hiss of steel, flicking slippery, severed flesh away, feeling a glow of pride for the Healer's skill. There wasn't much blood. Her body hardly flickered. It was as neat and painless as any maid could wish. 'It's done,' he muttered. 'Let her go.'

Thuo rose from rumpled blue sheets, with great beads of sweat along his brow and wonder in his eyes. 'She bit me,' he complained, wringing his left hand. 'The smelly old cow *bit* me!'

Suddenly, the room was much too quiet.

Mwangi's gaze moved slowly upwards across the red-flecked cotton shroud. Dark bruises stained the upstretched throat. Pink saliva glistened on her lips. Her distorted, sightless face was the exact colour of a ripe pomegranate. 'Fool!' he hissed, 'You've killed her!'

Then they were running like panicked herdboys across the empty yard and up the heatstruck pasture. They ran until they could run no more, slumped into bristly, sun-browned grass on the further ridge and peered back at the farmhouse.

Nothing moved, down there.

'A white woman,' Thuo wailed, his eyes rolling wildly, 'you made me kill a *white* woman!'

'No one knows,' Mwangi panted, in realisation and triumph. 'No one saw us, and the dead can't speak!' He felt the power stirring, grasped Thuo's greasy, trembling shoulders, shook sense and purpose into him. 'The Lion Boy killed his enemies and became the white man's hero. One day when the land is free, the clan will speak

352

our names with pride! You are the warrior who struck the first blow. Keep the secret, and help me bring that day to pass!'

He saw relief in Thuo's eyes, felt the strength regather in his body. 'Yes,' Thuo breathed, 'I am a warrior!'

As they crept together back towards the valley, Mwangi's spirit swelled in warlike joy. We have settled scores with One-Leg, he thought, given the clan a sign: a sign to make them kneel in awe. Now they will be with me, when I march on Camelot!

'*Molly?*' Rebecca whispered, feeling icy dread. 'Oh Hugo, say it isn't true!'

But it was true. Lamplight etched the horror into every harsh line in Hugo's face. She remembered Molly's rashness at the circumcision stream. Leo's warning echoed in her mind. '*Heaven help the white man who dares to interfere.*' The darkness of this land, so long concealed, so easily forgotten, was suddenly upon her. She sat rigid and aghast as Hugo gave the details, then wept in his arms beside the fire. 'Poor, poor Eric. Is anybody with him?'

'He hasn't spoken since he found her. He was drinking at the club when I left. Wouldn't look at anyone, wouldn't say a word. That bar was like a morgue, tonight.'

She shivered, struck by a new horror. 'We'll have to tell Hal. *What* can we tell him, Hugo?'

'The truth, what else? Without the ugliness, of course.'

Before she could protest, she saw him stiffen, heard the hoofbeats, followed him on to the verandah.

They came in line abreast, a dozen silent men on horseback, each carrying a lantern in his hand. Rifles gleamed in their saddle-sheaths; bullets glittered in the bandoliers around their chests. There was an air of deadly purpose in the star-shot, horse-scented gloom.

Eric Stuart led them.

His face was empty in the upward yellow glow. His eyes were dry, implacable, ice-blue. 'Eric . . .' she began, in heartfelt sorrow; he waved it contemptuously aside.

'Save your pity, Rebecca. There's work to do this night.'

'Easy, Eric,' Hugo murmured. 'What have you in mind?'

'Dogs.' He grinned, a skull-like travesty of humour. 'Four-legged dogs found a spoor that led this way. The two-legged kind are somewhere on your land. We're going to burn the huts, until they let me have the dogs I want.'

353

A horse snickered. A low, angry mutter rippled from the ranks. Coldness grew in Rebecca's heart. She hardly recognised these flickering, stony faces, saw not a trace of friendship in their eyes. In this mood, she realised, every one of them is capable of killing.

'Go home,' said Hugo quietly. 'Think about it.'

'Hugo, one of those black bastards butchered my wife!'

'Which one, Eric?'

'Who cares?' someone growled.

'*I* care,' Hugo snapped. 'Find him, and I'll tie the noose myself. Find the proof, Eric. Do it *right*!'

'It's *Molly*, for Christ's sake!' Eric hissed. 'Will you set these heathens above Molly?'

'Come on,' the same impatient voice urged, 'we're wasting precious time.'

Another vengeful rumble, a clink of spurs, a stutter of restless hooves. Hugo walked down the steps and took his stand in front of Eric's horse. 'We came to build a future for our children,' he said. 'We have made the laws and set the standards; we have to prove that ours is the best way! Tonight you answer butchery with burning, as savage as the heathens you despise. For the love of God, remember you are *white*!'

For a moment in that taut, strained dimness, Hugo seemed to be a bigger man. For a moment, with moonlight silver in his hair and utter certainty blazing in his pale face, he might have been the Lion Boy; and words that Leo had once lived by rang in Rebecca's mind.

Such courage must not stand alone.

Proudly, gladly, she went to Hugo's side. 'Molly was my best friend,' she whispered. 'I will mourn her till my dying day. But if you go on with this, you must ride me down, too!'

Lamplight flared and shifted on faces that were becoming familiar again: sheepish, shamed, and turning from her level gaze. One by one, the horses wheeled and cantered off. Until only Eric Stuart sat there, his head bowed, the tears falling like small gold raindrops on his horse's neck.

They helped him down, guided his blind hobble to the lounge, shared his firelit desolation.

'What will you do?' Rebecca asked, when the first fierce spasms eased and warmth had put some colour to his cheeks.

'She'll lie beneath the gum trees on the ridge. She always loved the view from there. I'll not stay. Too much of her about the place.'

His blue eyes filled and hardened. 'It's U.K. side for me, across the water. You'd do well to follow, before they come for you!'

It frightened her to see him broken, this brave friend who'd borne such pain, so long. The darkness *is* all about us, she thought. Perhaps we *should* take Hal away.

But later, with Hugo sleeping warm beside her and stout walls against the night, she let reason reassure her.

Thanks to Duma and the Healer's charm, she mused, our labourers are friends. We have not mocked their customs or infringed their sacred rites. We have nothing to fear. No one in the valley means us harm.

36

LANCE WAITED, TAUT AND STILL against the blinding scree. Hot wind stirred his copper hair. His eyes burned harsher blue than the desert skies themselves. It is more than a hunt, thought Duma, watching, only little less than a war. Pride drives him. It will make him mighty – if it doesn't kill him first.

Gunmetal flickered. Lance unslung the rifle. Turning, Duma too saw movement in the hollow: sandy flanks that blended with the soil, wide black horns that might have been thorn branches. Impala buck, he realised, seen dimly through dense haze.

'Kill cleanly,' Duma warned, 'or the tracking will be hard and long.'

'Tracking is *your* job.'

'Be warned, Lance. Leo would not risk a shot at such a distance.'

'I'm not Leo. See, he runs!'

The buck bolted, hooves aclatter, white rump flashing. Lance moved unhurriedly, raised the rifle, laid his cheek against the polished brown stock; he breathed in gently and pressed the trigger. The report thundered. The impala seemed to crumple in mid-bound, plunging snout first into upflung dust, twitching once and lying still.

Lance's grin blazed through tart blue smoke. 'Speak not of *risks*, old man. Go and make him ready for the fire.'

Strips of liver sizzled over orange flame. Duma breathed their fragrance contented.

'We are eating well,' Lance said. 'Am I not more accurate than Leo?'

'Perhaps. But you have yet to face a lion's charge, or stand before an elephant attack.'

'Do you doubt my courage?'

'Before showing courage, you must first find the game.'

'Just as I have found this buck. Where were the tracker's skills today?'

He didn't notice, Duma realised. He didn't see me trace this spoor and guide him to this hollow. What else has he overlooked?

'Where is the nearest running water, Lance?'

'Why? We have water.'

'And if we didn't?'

'You have shown me, often. Dig in dry luggas. Look for water-plant bulbs.'

'You know these things,' Duma murmured, licking liver juices from his fingers. 'You are better than Leo. So why am I here?'

'You wanted to come,' said Lance promptly. He leaned into the firelight, let his pity show. 'You have grown slow and timid – because you are old, I suppose. Go home, if you want, I'll manage.'

Duma huddled deeper in the shadows, so that his thoughts might not show. 'Let us rest,' he grunted, 'and await what morning brings.'

Duma lay sleepless, watching stars through thin black branches above. The fire sputtered. Redness lit Lance's sleeping, blanket-covered shoulders.

What has happened? Duma wondered. Why does he always choose the steepest path, the longest shot? What did the Boers take from him, that causes so much pain? That drives him ever deeper into the trackless north? Up here, pride *can* kill him, along with blind belief in Leo's charm. Somehow, he must learn this for himself.

Desert chill deepened. The breeze bore whiffs of scorched hide from the fire. Hyenas chuckled, faint and far away. A plan began to form in Duma's mind.

At the heart of the plan was a calabash.

Duma rolled over, running a hand down the cool curve of his calabash. Ah, Lance, you have stolen one more night of old man's sleep . . .

Lance stretched, tasting thin dry air, seeing the sky grow brazen. Another dawn, another northern day to overcome. Turning, he stared in disbelief at the sandy trough where Duma had lain. Only the calabash remained, livid green amongst the drabness, casting an arched shadow on the dust.

'Duma!' he cried, climbing to a point where he could see in all directions. Nothing moved. Echoes mocked him: -uma, -mama -*ma!* Sunlight glared from ochre rock and yellow soil, and the bare, metallic greyness of a hundred thousand thorns. He was alone, dwarfed by endless blue above and the blazing brown below. I'll manage, he had said; Duma had taken him at his word.

The bite of gun-oil filled his nostrils. The calabash made sloshing sounds. Fingering its shiny roundness, he felt his pride revive. Duma taunts me, he thought, dares me to go on without water. Like the others, he would mould me to his way. He's out there somewhere smiling, expecting me to weaken and confess my need of him.

He shouldn't have left the calabash.

I am full grown. Karen's love and Leo's magic shield me. I was born to hunt; now I must live to prove it.

I must go north.

Once, he came upon elephant droppings – dry, straw-coloured, stale. Twice he paused, his senses keyed to unseen pursuit. There was nothing but scrub to see, nothing but the rasping wind to hear.

The distance covered pleased him, as did his own restraint – eating little, drinking less. He blessed the fire he had made, and the impulse which bade him bring the sun-dried impala strips. It had been a good start.

Next morning, he ate salt meat and sipped more frequently. At noon, beneath a white-hot sun, the last few tepid drops slid down his throat. The calabash thumped, hollow, on his chest at every stride. Sweat stung his eyes. Hunting was forgotten. For two searing hours, while his lips cracked and his tongue thickened, he scoured the arid earth for water.

Eventually, he found a gully gouged into the slopes. It led him down between baked rock to a wide white lugga. He had enough wit to seek a bend where a single acacia offered meagre shade. Then thirst drove him, scrabbling, to his knees.

His knuckles throbbed, his sweat starred the shimmering silt, and dust settled coolly on his skin. Wetness touched his fingertips. He lowered his head and lapped, heedless of the bitter taste.

The craving eased. He laid his cloak beneath the tree and hung the rifle high. He was gathering firewood when the first spasm struck, doubling him over, blurring his sight. A cramp, he told himself, from too much sweating. It will pass.

But it didn't. It roiled like molten lava in his belly. He duckwalked from the tree, stumbling out of his shorts. Squatting, breathing his own foulness, he bowed to fiery seizures that voided him again and again. Somehow, he scrambled back to the shadow. Slumped against rough bark, he watched the night burn pale.

First there was a sallow glimmer beyond the dark, stark crags. The moon climbed higher through filigrees of black thorn, blazing silver into Lance's lair. The water was bad, he realised, I am poisoned. I will die unmourned beneath the northern moon, calling Karen's name.

Around him, shadows deepened. An alien presence seemed to hover near. The lugga's brightness flickered. Its radiance took on living form.

The creature seemed to spring full-grown from the softly shining sand: pale and cloven-footed, smaller than most zebra, larger than most buck. It stood milk-white in moonlight, unmoving, unafraid. It can't be real, he told himself, and blinked.

Snowy flanks still shimmered, silvered hooves still trod the soundless sand. And from the centre of the equine forehead, a single long straight horn still speared the stars. I *am* dying, he thought. No man may see a unicorn – and live . . .

Time passed. The fever eased. A breeze sighed, the moon waned; the unicorn remained. Its shadow was dark and solid; its breath smelled of meadowsweet, like Hugo's sheep.

It *was* real.

Lance's head rang hollow to a childhood rhyme.

The lion and the unicorn were fighting for the crown,
The lion beat the unicorn all around town.

I am the Lion Boy's son, he thought, the unicorn is mine by ancient right. I'll take the head to Coetze, and hear no more '*roinek*' taunts.

The creature moved, casting mystic light. The glow drew Lance onward, tottering beneath the rifle's weight. Until, in a dim and jagged gorge, the unicorn browsed on a lone tree and gave Lance his first unhindered view. He took aim at the luminous nearside shoulder. The son of Leo uses but one bullet, he remembered. A legend dies; a new lion boy is born.

He breathed deeply and squeezed the trigger.

Blast and meaty impact rang together. Tremors rippled through the creamy hide. The pale head dipped; the horn plunged downwards, striking sparks from naked rock. Blood welled, dark as pitch, from flaring nostrils. Its coppery odour billowed on the night.

And in that dying instant, black cloud swallowed up the moon.

The strange glow lingered, pulsing fainter, coiling like a halo around the stricken beast. A keening whinny shrivelled Lance's soul, a cry of aching loss and devastation. Sound and lustre faltered, dwindled, died. The silence was total, the darkness absolute.

Lance waited, awed.

The earth beneath him shuddered. Lightning soured the air with brimstone. A gale mauled the tree, shrieking around Lance's ears as if the whole of nature mourned a favourite child. Struggling upright, leaning on the wind, he howled his protest at the cloven sky. 'This beast is mine, d'you hear? *Mine!*'

The storm eased. Lance's certainties dissolved. What if this were the *last* unicorn, whose earthly presence forestalled the Prince of Darkness? Must he, Lance, now become the Devil's boy? I will await a sign, he thought; or morning, whichever comes first. Daylight will put an end to doubt. If daylight ever comes.

Black hobgoblins stalked him, crippled brutes with fiery eyes and drooling jaws. Rank breath scoured his nostrils. Obscene laughter pierced his wakeful dream.

Briefly, sense succumbed to superstition. He shrank before the spectre of the Pit.

A smell of half-digested fodder saved him, and the crunch of splintered bone. Hyenas, not hobgoblins, plundering the dead. The belly had been opened. Exposed viscera coiled like pallid snakes.

Anger drove him, snarling, into the dim mêlée. The scavengers yielded. His prize remained intact: hide and head and horn without which he could never prove his claim. 'Come,' he taunted, 'let's see whose need is greater!'

They came.

The red-eyed circle tightened. The boldness of these carrion-eaters was unnerving – one more eerie happening in this outlandish night.

He couldn't see the forward gunsight. Firing blind won only angry yelps and brief respite. His footing failed. Blackness closed above him, full of slimy jaws and questing muzzles. If there is a charm, he pleaded, send it on me now!

He scented singed fur, sensed sudden space around him. He scrambled into brightness: yellow fireballs falling from the sky.

Hyenas yowled and smouldered. The branches overhead burst into flame. Kneeling beside the carcass, blessed with complete vision, Lance fired methodically until the stragglers slunk from range. The hot wind eddied. The flames above went out. Dawn pinkness probed the eastern sky.

A sunray lit the gorge, quickening the colours, showing him the folly of the night.

The horn, he saw, wasn't central. It sprouted from the left forehead lobe. Where once a twin had grown, only the stump remained. Night had concealed it, fostering delusion. Yet the hide *was* milky, unlike that of any buck he knew. Seeing sunlight glitter pink in lifeless eyes, he finally understood. No unicorn, this, only an albino oryx: a quirk of nature, not a living myth.

Guilt released him. He settled to the skinning. Even as he worked, the mystery lingered. Who or what had called the fire down? Had he after all in some way grown into the charm?

He dusted the bloody inner hide, rolled the creamy pelt inwards and glanced up through sooty branches meshed against the hot blue sky. A slimmer length of wood lay trapped amongst them, equally charred, unnaturally straight. It was pointed at one end.

He stood, seeking proof of his suspicion – and saw half a dozen fire-blackened arrows on the scree. He heard a human footfall, and knew with utter certainty who made it. The terrors of the night were fresh. The nearness of disaster made him shake. He turned and hurled his fury up the slope. 'You could have stopped it!'

'I did,' Duma said.

'What are the lessons?' Duma demanded. 'What have you learned this foolish night?'

'Lessons? Would you send me back to school?'

'I will drag you there myself unless you show more sense! You would be a hunter yet cannot even tell me where you are!'

'If you had stayed, I wouldn't be here! Why did you make me suffer?'

'Pain helps remembrance, Lance.' Duma sent one disgusted glance at dead hyenas and the skinned, flyblown oryx corpse. 'Never hunt without good water,' he growled, 'never kill in darkness. Never stand against hyena packs. These are the first lessons. Now come with me.'

It was still the wild, uncharted north; but Duma led the way, and that made all the difference. In no time he was crossing the lugga and kneeling at the hole Lance had dug. 'Watch,' he murmured, 'learn.'

His fists plunged out of sight. Lance saw sinews ripple in his arms, heard his fingers scraping at the sand. Presently, he raised cupped hands and spilled a small cascade. The liquid glistened opalescent blue. Yellow starbursts lit its fall. 'Beware this colour,' Duma warned. 'It makes you dream in daytime. These sparks can rip your belly. You have already felt their bite.' Mica, Lance knew, tiny golden crystals as sharp as arrowheads. No wonder his stomach had rebelled. No wonder myth and monsters had plagued his night.

'The good water is over there.' Duma pointed along the blinding silt. 'I dug deeper, saw there was no blueness, let the hole half fill, and waited while the sparks fell to the bottom.' He smirked, file-toothed and crafty in the sun. 'Slow old men are good at waiting.' He headed south, at a pace which proved him neither old nor slow. Following, Lance brooded on moonlight fantasy.

The unicorn lived entirely in his mind, misbegotten, of albino blood. Earthquake, wind and storm had sprung from dream-inducing water. The hyenas were real; Duma had made the pre-dawn sky rain fire. Thus could every mystery be explained. Reason pierced the darkness and put devilry to flight.

It wasn't quite so simple. As the air cooled and Duma's marching shadow lengthened, Lance relived a fierce and fevered scene: chill dust underneath him, palsy in his limbs, silk-white splendour gleaming in his gunsight. I did it gladly, he remembered, with full knowledge and belief. In that instant, I was killing a unicorn, forfeiting all virtue. Not to win a Healer's charm, not for gain or glory.

I was doing it for Karen.

Some unbidden instinct made him unfurl the skin. It shimmered softly in his hands. 'Look, Duma,' he called.

Duma turned, his shoulders taut and weary, his brow furled in irritation. 'What is it now? Can't you keep up with slow old . . .' The sentence tailed away, unfinished. Lance saw new strength stir in aged limbs, saw wonder bloom in Duma's old, dark eyes. He came forward, laid one lean brown hand on milkiness. 'In all my years,' he marvelled, 'I have never seen such a thing. Truly, you are Leo's son: and this will be a sign to awe the tribesmen!'

362

Lance sensed his purpose quickening again, feeling excitement bubbling inside. Perhaps, last night, he *had* found enchantment, perhaps his father's spirit *had* possessed him. If this trophy has such power over Duma, he reasoned, how much more will greedy Coetze covet it?

Evening settled, crimson, on rock and scrub and scree. Far to the south, Kerinyagga thrust like a broad grey spear through wavering haze. 'Take me south, grandfather,' Lance breathed. 'Find the Boers for me!'

They came up to cooler country, through pale green fern and purpling heather, across the looming heights of Kinangop, down to the rippling, restless plain beyond.

'The elephants have been here,' said Duma, scenting the air. 'The Boers you seek cannot be far away.' Later that same morning when the mist had burned off, Lance smelt game meat cooking, saw vultures wheel on broad brown wings to distant blue, and paid silent tribute to the old man's skill.

All day they moved through crisp clean air into the constant, keening wind which furled the grass in sandy waves against their knees. Until, beneath a lowering sun, they crested a rise and caught up with the Boers.

The camp stood above a wooded ravine that reached out like a crooked, dark green arm from the body of the forest. The same forest, Lance realised, which at its far north-eastern fringe broke upon the slopes of Camelot.

They had drawn the wagons in a circle. The wind made the canvas flap and rumble, drove campfire smoke in an angled, grey-blue line across the reddening horizon. Tusks lay curved and gleaming beside yellow flame. Lance let meat scent fuel the craving in his stomach; and let Karen's sudden nearness fuel the hunger in his heart.

It is time for a new beginning, he thought.

And time to say farewell.

He saw the wind tease Duma's cowhide kirtle, saw the weariness in his lean brown frame. 'Go back to the hut fire, grandfather. Your part in this is done.'

'What is it?' Duma asked plaintively. 'What do these people mean to you?'

'They have something I want,' Lance said simply. 'Something only I can take from them.'

He saw resignation in Duma's eyes, a hint of pride, a glimmer of understanding. 'What shall I tell your mother?'

'Tell her I am well and strong. Wish her long life and happiness at Camelot.' He heard finality in his own voice, saw Duma recognise it and smile wistfully.

'Will you return? Will you come back to the valley?'

'Some day, maybe.' Lance looked down on the encampment that harboured all his hopes, drawing himself up tall and straight. 'Some day, when I am a *man*!'

Duma took his hand, in a brief, fervent grasp, his look of love and longing more powerful than words. Then he was gone, slipping like a small brown wraith across the advancing evening. Lance blinked wetness from his eyes and called a last salute. 'May Ngai keep you, grandfather!'

And thought he saw Duma's hand rise in acknowledgement and blessing.

Lance waited on the ridge in dewfall, fading wind and deepening darkness. Below, the Boers were finishing supper. He saw firelight on animated faces, breathed a whiff of coffee, sensed an air of unity. Presently, an accordion began to play: wheezy, sweet and haunting. One by one, voices took up tune and harmony, blending in an anthem of thanksgiving. He felt a sharp pang of loneliness. He couldn't see Karen but knew she must be there, joined in another warm, bright circle from which he was for ever set apart.

Has she waited, he wondered feverishly, has the difference proved strong enough?

He unfurled the oryx pelt lovingly. It was snowy in the starlight and silky to the touch.

This is my token, by which she shall be saved.

He made an image of her, as she had been beside the river: moonlit, lovely, yearning for the stars.

This is my future, which she alone shall share.

He breathed deeply and let her nearness move him, remembering the imprint of her body, the aura of her musk.

This is my purpose, which makes my green force stir.

I will go down into that brightness and let them see my purpose. I will lay my token at her father's feet. And throughout all our future, we will carry our own bright circle wherever we may go.

He slipped between the wagons into fireglow, strode through the swelling hymn tune to the place where Coetze sat and tossed the oryx pelt into his lap. The singing died. Suddenly there was only the whisper of the wind, the crackle of the flames, and Coetze's pale green, baleful glare.

And still no trace of Karen.

'I come from the north,' Lance said, into rising sparks and goggling faces, 'and make my claim for Karen.'

'*You?*' Coetze hauled himself upright in the canvas chair. His beard shone tawny grey against the black serge jacket. 'You, an upstart *roinek* boy, would dare to so insult me?'

'I am not a boy, and this is not an insult. I bring proof of hunting power as your custom asks.'

Coetze's hairy paw tightened on the inner surface of the rolled-up hide. His pink sneer split the beard. 'See, *kerels*,' he bellowed, 'the *roinek* seeks to court my daughter. Stand up, Danie van Zyl!'

There was an amused smoky ripple, and movement at the outer circle. A buckskinned figure rose into the yellow light, casting a broad black shadow on the canvas wagon walls behind. He was almost as tall as Lance, twice as thick at chest and thigh and shoulder. His beard was darker than the night, his eyes a deeper blue than Lance's own.

'How old are you, Danie?' Coetze demanded.

'Thirty, menheer.'

'How much land do you own?'

'Seventy rich acres on the outskirts of Fort Hall.'

'How many elephants have you killed, these past four days?'

'Eight, menheer.'

'You hear, *roinek*? He brings me sixteen heavy tusks; you offer one small hide!'

'Open it,' Lance said softly. 'You will never see its like again.'

Coetze's big hands fluttered. The skin unfolded, shimmering, taking on the fire's golden gleam. Lance heard wondering female murmurs and felt his courage grow. 'A token of my love,' he said, 'as rare and beautiful as Karen is herself.' Briefly, he sensed the mood shifting, sensed grudging acceptance on the breeze.

Kobus Coetze cut it down.

'Will rareness feed her children? Will beauty keep her from the evening chill?' His hand rose and pointed at van Zyl, whose sturdy silhouette still dominated the gloom. 'This is a *man*, of property and substance. You are but a foolish boy whose head is full of dreams.

365

That is why, even now, Karen sits in Ouma van Zyl's wagon and plans her wedding day!' He crushed the rippling loveliness and flung it across the space between them. 'Go home, little *roinek*. Take your magic white rabbit skin with you!'

He didn't mind the simple, witless joke. He barely heard their pitying sniggers, scarcely heeded van Zyl's triumphant dark blue glance. His scorned gift hung listless in his hands. The love which had sustained him through the harsh, weird hunt was dying in his heart.

Karen had betrayed him.

He turned his back on their mocking, flame-shot laughter and trudged out of the warm, bright circle he had thought he could possess. There was nothing beyond but darkness, an empty, wind-swept ridge, a dream destroyed . . .

She met him at the very edge of the brightness beyond the wagon ring, a slim, lithe, hastening shadow in the night. Starlight glistened in her hair and set her eyes ablaze. Urgent admiration filled her voice.

'You were terrific, Lance! I saw you stand and face them with beauty in your hands, heard you speak your love for all the world to hear. It was the bravest, sweetest thing I've ever known. Look for me at daybreak. I know a place where we can be together!'

The suddenness of it stunned him. Doubt still oppressed his soul. 'They said you were engaged! They told me you were van Zyl's woman!'

She left him, as swift and silent as she had come, with a snowy smile and two short, thrilling words: '*Not yet!*'

37

THE SUN STILL SHONE, the sky stayed brilliant blue; but Molly's murder cast a pall across the land. Nobody could trace her killer, nobody would admit to fear. Yet all at once, the settlers took to arms.

They carried loaded shotguns in their cars when they went shopping. They snapped rifles to their saddles when they rode around the farms, wore holstered pistols in their belts whilst visiting the club. Even after polo, the atmosphere was taut. People drank too much and laughed too loudly, assuming a forced and brittle gaiety. Eric Stuart haunted them, a hobbling, grey-faced, grief-racked figure, a seldom-sober symbol of horror and defeat.

Rebecca would have none of it. 'I won't ignore him,' she snapped. 'He needs us more than ever now.' She held his hand, and wrote his letters for him, booked his passage on the homebound boat. 'I won't keep the gunsafe open,' she insisted. 'Something terrible might happen to Hal.'

'Just a thought,' said Hugo. 'After all, they did find tracks that led this way.'

'Nonsense! The tribesmen would defend us with their lives!'

But there were times when she had private doubts.

Someone left the sheep pen open. Half the flock strayed across the shrunken river on to Boer land. If Coetze had been there, she thought, he would have shot them all.

One night a dozen coffee trees were vandalised, stripped clean of berry, leaf and branch. Baboons, Maina suggested, driven by drought from the forest, lured to easy pickings. Rebecca wondered what Duma might read in the trampled, bark-strewn dust.

Sometimes, when they thought she wasn't watching, she glimpsed

367

a sullen, inward look upon the tribesmen's faces: the look she'd seen that day beside the circumcision stream. The women, too, seemed downcast, avoiding her eye, forgetting to bring her eggs. Trifling irritations which might have gone unnoticed at any other time; but she still mourned Molly daily, still worried more about Lance than she cared to admit.

Hal eased her troubles and made her feel young again. He had Hugo's looks, Hugo's pallor, Hugo's neatness of movement – and an impish delight in childish jokes.

'Mummy, you said clouds are made of cotton wool.'

'Yes, dear.'

'Then how can there be thunder when they bump? . . .'

'Look Mummy, a pillar-cat!'

'Caterpillar, dear.'

'That's what I said. It'll grow into a flutterby . . .'

'Mummy, why do crows fly high?'

'To catch the bugs, I suppose.'

'No, silly! To make the cows *low*! . . .'

He was clever at his lessons; he made her smile a dozen times a day. And when Duma returned and gave her Lance's greeting, she felt the bad time sidling away.

So, when the nightmare started, she was wholly unprepared.

Another breathless morning, with heat-haze on the mountain and whirling red dust-devils in the yard. Hugo had gone to Eric Stuart's farm to help with last-minute packing. Duma was whittling a new arrow shaft in the shade beside the house. Rebecca stood beside Hal's chair on the verandah and supervised a rare outdoor lesson.

A hot breeze ruffled his dark hair. Sunlight bouncing from the paper made him squint. He was moving the pen carefully, mumbling to himself '. . . are fourteen, three sevens are twenty-one . . .' Watching, listening, her heart brimmed with love and pride.

Then she became aware of another watcher.

Maina stood on the sun-browned lawn, his beads and baldness gleaming. His presence made her edgy. His eyes were hooded, hunted, never still.

'What is it, Maina?'

'Come to the pasture, memsahib.'

'Later, when our work is done.'

'Don't bring the boy, memsahib. Come alone. Come now.' A tone

368

he'd never used before, a hint of thinly veiled appeal. Something has happened in the pasture, she thought, I'd better go.

'Duma, watch over Hal for me.'

'Yes, memsahib.'

She followed Maina's dusty footfalls into glittering heat and an ominous, sickly smell.

More tribesmen had gathered in the pasture, a tight-knit, slack-faced group above the river's trickle. They parted grudgingly before her; parted before an obscene totem pole.

Matted, pink-stained fleece-wool; glaucous, glaring eyes; a purple sun-parched tongue that lolled between yellowed teeth into a buzz of bright green blowflies; a severed sheep's head, impaled on a stake and planted in the pasture.

The stench brought acid bile into her throat, the savagery made her nape-hairs rise and prickle. 'Who did it?' she whispered. 'What does it mean?'

She heard a metallic jingle, saw a small, dark-skinned figure in a pied kirtle.

And recognised Leo's adoptive brother, Mwangi.

The last time she'd seen him, before Lance was born, he had been a wild-eyed, drink-blurred youth calling evil down on Camelot. The passing years had hardened him, laying tight-drawn muscle on his skinny frame, etching unyielding downcurved lines into his hawk-like face. His eyes were deep-set, steady, touched with cold gold fire.

He spoke, sending another shock wave through her shock-numbed body.

He spoke in English, with a lisping sibilance which set her teeth on edge. 'It is a sign of Ngai's power. Already he has taken one white woman who mocked his laws. It is better that you go, before he sends more suffering.'

He's only a little black man, she thought, mouthing superstition under a clear blue sky. Why does his childish menace chill me so? The sheep's head grinned an answer, through fly-hum and the reek of decay. Her fear gave way to anger and she turned it on the chief. 'Will you let this outcast rule you? Will you follow like the silly sheep you should be tending?'

Maina's eyes flickered, but would not meet her challenge. 'He speaks the truth. We hunger for this land.'

'This land was pledged to the Lion Boy! We have made it fruitful, given you good harvests down the years!'

'The Lion Boy is dead. The land is *ours*!'

The tribesmen were shifting again, wordless and sullen, forming a loose half-circle around her with Mwangi at its hub.

Leaving her to stand alone.

'Times change,' said Mwangi softly. 'The clan wakes, the Healer comes and grows into his power. Beware the power, *memsahib!*' He made an insult of the title. His arm swept up, gleaming, pointing at the house. 'Beware what it may do to those you love!'

Suddenly, in heat and brightness, she sensed a shadow over Camelot, saw Mwangi's darkness settle on the land. She summoned all her courage, faced his white-toothed sneer, and let him see the fierce force of *her* will.

'The envy of your childhood has burned your spirit black. You shall not corrupt these people, you shall not sour this land!'

'Brave words,' he hissed, 'from one who is so distanced from her son!'

'What have you done?' she whispered, in real horror. 'What have you done to Hal?'

'What can I do? I am here, and he is there. I cannot save him from Ngai's revenge.'

She saw it in his eyes, then, ancient, yellow evil. In that moment, she knew that he had somehow prompted Molly's murder and set this hideous mask on the pasture.

And lured her here, *away from those she loved*.

She turned on her heel and raced across the pasture, crying Hal's name.

Duma lay spreadeagled on the verandah. Dark blood trickled from his iron-grey hair, pooling and shining beside him. His eyes were open, milky and unfocused. His thin brown chest fluttered fitfully.

Above him on the table, Hal's workbook pages shivered in the breeze.

Hal had gone.

She felt a great, gaping void somewhere deep inside. Grief would grow into the numbness, grief to still the spirit and paralyse the mind.

But not yet.

She went quickly through the silent, sunstruck house, unlocked the gunsafe, loaded Hugo's rifle. The texture of blued steel brought strange, cold comfort. A faint, sharp whiff of cordite cleared her mind. For the moment, Duma's injuries and the long, doomed days ahead could wait. The foolish, bewitched tribesmen must be stopped before they ambushed Hugo.

Duma teetered on the verandah, nursing his head in bloodstained hands. 'Where are you going, memsahib?'

'Hal is dead,' she said, hearing the flat, dull echo far inside. 'Mwangi has killed him, just as he killed Molly. I am going to shoot Mwangi.'

'Thuo,' he mumbled. '*Thuo* killed memsahib Stuart.'

The unfamiliar name gave her pause. 'How do you know?'

'He told me. That is why he wasn't afraid of the big house. Thuo was in jail with Mwangi, and he is also an outcast.' He stood straighter, spoke five brief blessed words. 'Hal is not yet dead.'

'Are you *sure?*'

'They will hide him in the forest until the oathing rite. Then they will kill him.'

She saw strength returning to Duma's body, saw shame and anguish in his eyes.

'*I* let Thuo steal the boy, memsahib. Bind my wound, let me take you to the forest, let *me* take Thuo, before the others come!'

She ought to wait for Hugo, she knew. She ought to alert the settlers, muster tribal police. But she could feel Duma's urgency, sense the flight of time – time which might yet deny her Hal. She bathed and bandaged Duma's head, fumbling with the knot. Her hands were shaking now, her whole being trembled with a hope she could not stifle yet dared not speak aloud.

Hal is not yet dead.

The forest was a rustling deep green cavern, with neither distance nor direction. Rebecca had lost all sense of time. The rifle-strap cut into her shoulder, her skirt caught on a thousand clinging twigs. Her breath came hard in the moist, musty air. Perspiration soaked her blouse and stung her eyes. Duma's bandage led her, flickering like a thin, pale beacon in the gloom. She marvelled at his resilience, the grace and silence of his passage. In the forest, he might have been a boy again.

Dear Lord, let him find my boy.

Every so often, he checked, fingering the bow across his back, cocking an ear, scenting the breeze. She heard nothing but the whispering canopy above, smelt nothing but decaying leaves. And silently willed him to find the spoor again.

Until, waiting behind him, she sensed sudden tension in his stance. She noticed yellow sunrays slanting through the greenness, glimpsed blue between tangled boughs above.

A gnarled and massive fig tree dominated the clearing. Filtered sunlight laid gold and brown mosaics on the trodden earth beneath.

Hal stood in a shaft of brightness, utterly alone.

She saw the fall of sleek, dark hair across his forehead, the shining recognition in his eyes. She went forward, her vision blurred with gratitude, heedless of Duma's warning and the crackle of the undergrowth she broke.

A shadow looming beside the tree became a lunging, reaching Kikuyu man. She glimpsed greased, matted locks above a fearsome scowl, a glint of light on oiled, burly muscles. He moved very fast, despite his bulk.

Too fast.

He was already at Hal's side as she unslung the rifle. By the time she'd levelled it, he was using Hal as a shield. She blinked, struggling for steadiness, trying to lay the aim. She watched one dark hand spread across Hal's nose and mouth, and the other hand raise a simi and lay its silver blade at Hal's slim, tender throat.

'I am a *warrior*,' Thuo cried suddenly, 'I do not fear a bullet if it wins us back our land!'

Hal was struggling now. Rebecca saw Thuo's arm tighten, saw the simi blade begin to bite. She took up trigger slack, waited while the sights stood first on Thuo, then on Hal. The blood was pounding in her head, the rifle was shuddering in her hands. Hal, my darling, for the love of God *keep still!*

She heard a hiss like cobra-strike, saw a slim shaft sprout from Thuo's simi-shoulder. The blade tumbled, glittering. Thuo's bullish bellow filled the glade. He staggered backwards, pawing at the shaft.

And Hal was running to her, radiant with release.

She actually saw the second arrow's dappled flight, heard it thud into Thuo's broad brown chest. He teetered in a small tight circle, his eyes rolling upwards, his snarl spewing bright red froth.

'Run, Hal!' she shouted. *'Don't look back!'*

Then his little body was burrowing to her breasts, his slim, chilled arms were closing round her neck. 'I wasn't frightened, Mummy, I knew you'd come!' Above his head, through his tousled dark hair, she watched Thuo fall, saw dry leaves puff upwards, heard the muffled death-drum of his heels. Duma came forward and wrenched his arrows free. The clearing reeked of blood and satisfaction.

'Is Thuo dead, Mummy? Did Duma kill him?'

She hesitated, remembering Lance's nightmares, fearful of a truth she couldn't hide.

Hal gazed up at her, his small face pure and innocent. 'I'm glad,' he said. 'Thuo was a bad man. Duma is so *good*!' She felt the violence fading and hugged her son, blessing his childish logic.

It *is* fitting, she thought, that Molly's murderer should die this way. It's right that Duma should defy the darkness. The evil spell is broken, Camelot survives. Neither I nor Hugo have blood on our hands.

And Hal is a living, crooning presence, safe within my arms.

The justness of it buoyed her throughout the long hike back. She fought off tears of gratitude, glorying in Duma's restored, ageless stride and Hal's excited babble.

Only when they reached the forest edge and gazed down on the evening-misted pasture did she relive the gaping horror that Mwangi had created there.

And realised that the viciousness might not be over yet.

A rising quarter moon lit Camelot's verandah, gleaming on Duma's bandage and Rebecca's lovely, haunted face. Sitting between them, sharing the ebb and flow of their emotions, Hugo had listened to Rebecca's story: revolted by the savagery she'd had to bear, appalled by the risks she'd had to take, awed by the courage she had shown. 'I have to go to him. I must be sure he's really here.'

'Of course,' he said, kissing her gently, angry that she should be made to feel so insecure, that his beloved son should be so threatened.

He turned his anger unwittingly on Duma, pressing the old man for the uglier details. 'Are you certain Thuo killed Molly Stuart? The raid was cleverly planned: too cleverly for a common stock thief.'

'He told me so himself, bwana. He said she bit his hand.'

'He used the same plan today, you see. A decoy in the pasture while he came here for Hal.'

'He came alone. I, Duma, tell you so.'

'What about the rite, Duma? What did they intend to do with Hal?' Duma's face seemed to shrivel in the moonlight, making a grizzled, fang-toothed grimace of disgust. 'It was an old dark custom: to eat the enemy's brains and drink his blood, to feed on his strength and cleverness before the war began.'

It was suddenly cold on the verandah. The moon seemed grey and distant, the night loomed dark and near. There was a presence at this heart of darkness, a presence Hugo knew he had to name. 'That is not a warrior's business,' he said. 'Only a Healer could perform that rite.'

Duma stood up, bowed and anguished on the silvered boards. His eyes were bright with misery, his voice was harsh with pain. 'What do you want me to say, bwana? That Mwangi killed the memsahib and stole your Hal away? Perhaps he did; but I will never say it. *He is still my firstborn son!*'

He went down the steps and across the dewspread turf, an aged, broken figure under the leering moon. Hugo grasped the wooden railings and leaned into the night, acknowledging the debt he owed. 'Duma? Thank you for *my* son!'

And thought he saw the old man walk a little taller.

This is the conflict, he thought, pacing and shivering, this is the choice the tribesmen have to make. On one hand, Duma: decent, faithful, loving and loyal through all the years. On the other hand, Mwangi: mystic, cruel and devious, hungry for this land.

Which will the tribesmen choose?

He pictured them as Rebecca had portrayed them, standing shifty-eyed and sullen-faced beside a severed head. He remembered them as he had so often seen them: singing while they laboured, grinning at their hearths, dandling chubby children on their knees.

There must be a way, he thought, to make them choose *right*.

He heard a nightjar churring, breathed the dew-damp, darkened dust – and glimpsed an answer. We share their deep attachment to this land, he realised. We share their joy in living, and their great love for children.

That must be the way.

One demonstration, one public act of faith; after this morning's horror, would Rebecca dare to take the risk?

Hal's quiet, rhythmic breathing soothed his starlit room. Rebecca sat beside him, her poise returning. 'Will he always be so safe?' she whispered. 'Is the danger over?'

'Not quite.' Hugo told her, step by step, what must be done.

'You *can't*!' she breathed, appalled. 'You can't put him through it all again!'

'I've fought beside those men, Rebecca, spent half a lifetime with them. Beneath the skin, they're just like us: decent, gentle people.'

'You weren't there, Hugo. You didn't see the violence, sense the evil!'

'Only Mwangi is evil; will you let him rule our lives with fear?'

'For God's sake, Hugo, we're talking about Hal!'

Moonlight through the window touched Hal's sleeping face: the faint blue bloom on his eyelids, the sweet curve of his nose and cheek. Hugo went softly to his bedside. 'He is my only son. We *have* to trust the tribesmen with him.'

'You really believe,' Rebecca marvelled, 'you really do believe the good in them!'

'All my life, with all my heart.'

He saw it then, the bright, blonde pride and courage which had drawn him to her from the very first.

'We'll do it as we always have,' she said. 'The three of us, together.'

The tribesmen gathered on a grassy bank beneath blue gum trees. Sunlight through green foliage played on monkey-skin cloaks and sombre brown faces. Golden weavers chattered overhead. The air smelled of woodsmoke, pepper-dust and eucalyptus.

Rebecca looked pale and drawn in a floral print. Hal wore a white shirt and knee-length khaki shorts. He alone seemed untouched by tension, waving to Maina, grinning at the crowd.

Nobody grinned back; and Mwangi was nowhere to be seen.

They are expecting threats of retribution, Hugo realised. They will get a surprise. 'Some time ago,' he began, 'a white woman was butchered. Settlers came from town that night, with fire in their hands and vengeance in their hearts. We turned them back, telling them you could not do such evil. Some of you saw this; is it not the truth?'

A stiff, begrudging shuffle, a faint, reluctant *eeeh*.

'How did you repay us?' Hugo asked. 'You took the killer in among the huts. You set an obscene sign upon the pasture. You stood aside and let this killer steal my son away. Are these the fruits of friendship? Are you not *ashamed*?'

They cleared their throats, scuffled in the dust. He sensed Maina's embarrassment and scented victory.

Then Mwangi made his entry.

Silvered metal jangled at his ankles, his pied kirtle rippled in the breeze. He crabbed forward, crouched and weaving. Despite the mid-morning brilliance, he brought the darkness with him.

'Hear his honeyed voice,' sneered Mwangi, 'see his thin pale woman, see his smiling son. But do not be deceived! They have force behind their meekness and guns to back their words!'

'I offer no force,' said Hugo mildly. 'I carry no weapon.' A mistake, he knew instantly. He saw the fierce red glint in Mwangi's eyes, just as he had seen it in the courtroom: *intent to hit and hurt and maim.*

Mwangi spoke again, his voice a rasp like lizard skin through dried leaves. 'There are guns in the big house, to turn against the settlers' force and free the land for ever. Let us take the big house, let us take the land, *let us take the guns!*'

Hugo heard the growing rumble of agreement, saw the vacant glaze in the tribesmen's eyes, saw Rebecca's lips set thin and white. The risk was all at once much greater than intended, the clan was sliding under Mwangi's thrall.

He raised his own voice and stabbed a finger into Mwangi's chest. 'Listen!' he bellowed. 'Is this a Healer, hungering for guns? How much sickness has this Healer ever cured?' He took Hal's hand and marched him up to Maina. 'Do you know what Mwangi wanted with my son? To drink his blood and eat his brains and so prepare for battle? Is this your noble custom? *Is it?*'

The glaze left Maina's eyes. Hugo felt Mwangi's power falter, breathed deeply, took the risk. Stepping back beside Rebecca, he left Hal alone between Mwangi and Maina: a small, pale, sunlit figure, bright-eyed and unafraid. 'If this is what you want,' he cried, 'do it in the daylight, in front of all the clan. If this is what you want, *do it now!*'

'Give me the knife,' urged Mwangi, and Rebecca's fingers clawed at Hugo's arm. 'I will do it, for our freedom and this land!'

Hugo sensed the exact moment of balance, the clan's will poised on the brink of bloodshed, hovering between Hal's radiant innocence and Mwangi's dark-skinned snarl. He felt cold sweat ooze across his forehead, knowing that if his faith proved false, all three of them would die.

Then Maina made his choice. 'How much sickness *have* you cured, Healer?'

Suddenly the whole clan was laughing, with explosive mirth which held no trace of humour, only the release of pent-up tension. Suddenly, Mwangi was just a small, ill-favoured black man with bells around his legs.

And Hugo's legs were wobbly with relief.

When the laughter faded, Maina curled his lip and made the choice final. 'You have shamed us, Mwangi, tried to make us more like beasts than men. Go back to the forest. You are once again cast out.'

Mwangi glanced up, and Hugo saw something more disturbing than red fire in his eyes: inward sureness without sorrow or defeat. 'The valley is my home,' he said. 'You cannot drive me out. I will wait here, as I have in other places. Some day, *my time will come!*'

He walked slowly through the silenced clan, erect, pied and jingling, touched with unlikely dignity.

Then Hal was laughing in Rebecca's arms, shaking Maina's plump brown paw, greeting grinning tribesmen by individual name. They milled in scented gum-shade, set up a working chant, and went singing and swaying across the fields to sunlit Camelot.

As if the death and darkness had never come to pass.

Hugo followed, his trust confirmed, his belief vindicated; and followed hand in hand with Hal and Rebecca.

Early the next morning, they went on a shopping spree: in gladness and release, in memory of Molly Stuart's cure. It ended with a lunchtime drink at the Polo Club.

Their news had spread like wildfire. Settlers crowded the bar that smelled of beer and lavender polish. They doffed their dusty hats to Rebecca, offered Hugo hairy, calloused hands, toasted Hal's courage with foam-brimmed tankards.

'Have another lemonade, Hal, you're a real chip off the block!'

'Fine old Af, your Duma. Tell him cheers from me, Hugo!'

'I can put this blasted gun away, thank God. Weapons into ploughshares, what?'

Rebecca drifted out into the gardens, where sunlight filtered through sheltering trees and pied flycatchers fluttered on the lawn. Like the tribesmen and the settlers, she longed for a fresh start, to wipe the recent horror from her mind. Here, in peace and frangipani scent, it was beginning to happen.

Then she saw Eric Stuart.

He stood in the shade with his back to her, staring out across the wooded valley to the high green hump of Nyeri Hill. She started forward, meaning to tell him Molly's murder had been avenged; and checked, struck by his utter stillness. His lean, lopsided body was bowed with sorrow. His face, she knew, was wet with tears.

He was printing the scene on his memory, taking this last bright vision into lonely exile.

How terrible, to be driven from this magnificent, half-tamed land; to leave a loved one buried near the place that you had built, and go into the twilight full of bitterness and pain.

Coldness was upon her again. It was a knowledge she had struggled to suppress.

Mwangi has done this.

In its dark perverted way, Mwangi's spirit dominates the valley, just as Leo's did; but Leo is dead.

It would have been better if Mwangi had left as he did so many years ago, with red fire in his eyes and a drunken curse on his lips.

But Mwangi has not left.

Standing in warm sunshine and the chill of Eric's grief, she felt one more lingering doubt.

Perhaps Duma shot the wrong outcast.

38

LANCE SAW HER FROM HIS lonely ridge and felt the secret force inside him quicken. She moved away from the camp, slight and swift across the umber plain. Her crow-black hair glistened; her fur-trimmed cloak rippled in the early breeze. He ran down through rolling grass with sunlight in his eyes to a place beyond sight of the wagons, running for dear life, and love, and Karen.

He sensed the freedom in her spirit, a girlishness she'd never shown before. 'Oh!' she cried. 'Who is this wild, pale *roinek* that throws himself at me?' Then she was running too, in mock terror. 'I must hide,' she gasped, 'in a cool and secret place where nobody can find me!' He loped behind her, hot-blooded and light-headed, entranced by the smooth sway of her haunches beneath the fluttering cloak. He could have caught her easily, but knew she didn't want him to.

Not yet.

He played the game, endured the tease, savouring the husky promise in her voice.

The path curved down into the ravine. She led him through dappled shade, twisting and swerving between gnarled tree trunks. He drew closer, still playing his part.

'Don't be afraid, *yaapie* girl. I only want to share your secret place.'

'Oh no, you can't, you mustn't. Oupa would not allow!'

He heard the stream, glimpsed its sunlit sparkle, smelt moist, leafy soil. The way was steeper, the light greener, the trees closer together. He sensed nearby coolness, the swirl of deeper water. Reaching forward, he tugged her cloak gently. 'Enough, Karen. This is far enough.'

'Let go,' she hissed. 'You mean to hurt me. I feel your horrid *English* heat upon my back. It's time to douse the flame!'

The cloak flew free and coiled around his head. He heard mischievous laughter and a quiet splash, and stumbled, blinded by her leather, goaded by her scent. Throwing the cloak aside, he stared down on a deep, clear pool. Karen's dress lay on a mossy bank. She floated easily, fifty feet away.

'Those who bathe here,' she informed him sternly, 'must enter as the good Boer God made them: naked.'

Grinning, he tore his clothes off and plunged in.

The water was like iced-green satin. The shock drained his lungs, driving him spluttering to the surface.

'Better?' she enquired sweetly. He caught his breath and went for her in earnest.

She dived and turned and twisted, sleek as an otter, always out of reach. She was under him and round him, her body veiled in bubbles, her smile like liquid gold through muted brightness. Until, waist-deep and winded, he stood in a single sunshaft and admitted his defeat. 'You have webbed feet, *yaapie* girl. Give a Brit landlubber a chance.'

She swam to him, turned on her back, settled across his eager, outspread arms. He could have looked, then; but an inner voice warned, *she isn't ready*, so he watched her face instead. Saw the mischief falter, saw the hunger grow. 'I'm weary too: weary of games and girlhood. Carry me, Lance. I will guide you there.'

He scarcely noticed her weight. Her flesh was firm and cold and slick. He was conscious of her breast against his, her slim thigh brushing his belly, her green eyes glowing; and of his own green force, stirring.

He went up between tortured roots and gleaming rocks, never missing a step. It was brighter ahead: a glade beneath a weathered Meru oak, the grass lush and springy underfoot. 'A secret place,' she murmured, 'where nobody can find us.' She reached up and traced the angle of his jaw. 'Lance, the gallant *roinek*, who brings a magic oryx pelt and puts grown Boers to shame. Put me down, Lance. *Warm me!*'

If the moon became her, forest sunshine set her heart-shaped face ablaze. She rose to him on tiptoe, her mouth wide and welcoming under his. And he rose to her, hard and instant, scenting her urgency, savouring her sigh of pleasure. Heat bloomed wherever their bodies met. 'Be quick,' she pleaded, 'be gentle!'

The grass was velvety beneath his knees. Her knees were wide and lifted, her fragrance overwhelmed him. His spasms grew short and powerful, almost beyond control. Her fingers sought his hardness, closing, shifting, guiding.

And undoing him.

The force of it threw him down and across her, moaning and pumping helplessly. While some deep instinct mourned her loss, he could only wallow in his own release.

Slowly, sense seeped back: he was aware of the sun on his shoulders, the wind in the tree, Karen's quivering flesh beneath his cheek, her need unfulfilled. He felt totally spent, wretchedly ashamed. 'I'm sorry,' he mumbled, 'I'm so, so sorry.'

'Hush,' she consoled unsteadily. 'It is enough that you are close and pleasured.'

'It's *not* enough! Your father was right to choose a man and not a useless *boy*!'

She stirred beneath him, swift and supple. Her fingers stroked his hair. He knew she was leaning over him but couldn't bear to look. 'You faced my father calmly,' she reminded him, 'and spoke your love out loud. Open your eyes, Lance. See and hear *my* truth.'

He gazed up into beauty greater than any dream could fashion: dark-haired, gold-skinned beauty that made his senses swim. 'I am honoured by your seed, Lance. It pleases me to have such power over you. Inside, I am still warm.' Her lips were slightly swollen, slightly parted. Her eyes were dim with tenderness and longing. 'Talk to me,' she pleaded, 'rest with me. Your strength will bloom again.'

It *is* true, he realised; soon we will be truly one. The sun and her certainty were restoring him, pulsing through his body like a Healer's charm. He laid his face against her cheek and spoke her name once like a grateful prayer.

'*Karen.*'

They talked, while the breeze tossed leaves above them and the unseen stream chattered far below. There was laughter and delight, and something warm and timeless growing.

'A high bright place,' he whispered.

'Where we can catch the stars,' she said. She smiled, soft and sidelong. His whole being yearned for her.

Yearned to be her man.

Perhaps she saw it, glowing in his eyes. Perhaps she simply sensed his readiness reborn. She settled back among pale green fronds, stretching sensuously. '*Roinek* man,' she murmured, 'pleasure me!'

Now, at last, he feasted on her splendour, the firm, peaked breasts, the sweeping flare of waist and hip, the lean, clean curve of inner thigh. The risen sun caressed her, laying smoky honeyed tints across her flesh.

He bent to her, moistened his lips, pressed them to her breast; nuzzled upwards, took her nipple in his mouth. It tasted salt yet spicy, and hardened to his tongue. Guided by instinct, spurred by her soft moans, his hand trailed lightly over her belly and found the silky fur below. His fingers trembled, probing gently in moist, fiery folds, until her thighs were fully parted and her mound rose rhythmically against his palm. Her scent was upon him again, rousing and compelling. She called his name, begging him to free her.

This time, the pulse at his groin was slow and solid, enduring; this time there would be no early, uncontrolled eruption. He slid his hands beneath her quivering haunches, eased her upwards, over and around him. The smallest check, the briefest of resistance, then he was plunging deep. The blazing smoothness of it made him gasp.

He was all at once drowning in a whirlpool of sensation: needy breath upon his cheek, silken thighs about his waist, and an ancient rhythm in his blood that seemed to spring from far within the earth. He felt her body spread and arc beneath him, heard her full-voiced, joyous cry. Then he was taut and fevered, pouring himself into her, shouting her name in glorious release.

Gentle touches, drowsy murmurs, soul-deep, sweet content. He was drifting out of boyhood into sleep, feeling the bonds grow stronger, knowing they need never be apart again.

At the very edge of waking, he sensed a broad shadow fall, heard her cry of protest, felt her warmth wrench away. He rolled over, and came to full awareness much too slowly, far too late.

She knelt on the sunstruck greensward, her slender arms across her nakedness. Danie van Zyl loomed above her with blue-black fury in his eyes, a stockwhip in his hand, and guttural violence in his voice. 'Whore! Scheming, fornicating bitch!' The lash uncoiled, too fast for Lance's eye to follow; it hummed like arrow-flight, snapped her tender body into an upflung, quivering arc, scoring a livid purple weal into her honeyed back.

Her agony brought Lance, crouched and raging, into the space between.

He had one fleeting instant to glimpse other gaping bearded faces and realise van Zyl hadn't come alone. Then the lash was hissing like a lean black snake against the blue sky, burning like a living flame around his naked chest. The impact brought him upright, smashing the breath out of his lungs. Hot sunshine seared his vision. His own blood spattered down his flank. Redness folded round him in a boiling, thundering haze.

His seeking fingers closed around the slick, slack leather thong, tore it savagely from van Zyl's grasp – and let it fall. Dimly, he heard his own subhuman growl, and awed murmurs from the watching Boers. Dimly, he saw van Zyl's sun-browned face tighten in alarm, saw him fumble in his buckskin jacket and unsheath a hunting knife.

He turned sideways, drove his shoulder forward, welcoming the sting and glitter of keen steel along his arm. Then van Zyl's thick wrist was bucking and yielding to his force. The knife tumbled, twinkling, to the grass. He swooped and swept it up, and launched his whole weight forward in one smooth, irresistible lunge. He felt the rasp of rib, heard the crunch of gristle, sensed the blade's bite deep in van Zyl's breast. There was a rich, rank fear-reek in his nostrils, warm wetness on his hands, a gust of failing, bloodied breath on his cheek. Then strength ebbed from the burly, shuddering body and light faded in the startled, stark blue eyes.

He eased the knife free, stepped aside, heard the soggy, sighing slump, and felt the red haze growing ever thicker. 'Who's next?' he snarled. *'Who's next?'* The lust was gnawing at him, unquenchable, unslaked. There was soft gold flesh before him, a glint of crow-black hair, a faint, familiar voice. Heedless, he brought the blade up, gloried in its pinkness, and prepared to strike again.

Then Karen touched him, stroked his wounded arm.

She stood in naked beauty, unafraid beneath the knife, her green eyes bright with love and tragedy. He could see each separate upcurled eyelash, smell her lingering incense, hear the distant gurgle of the stream.

The red haze was no more.

He sensed the bearded circle closing, smelt death in the clearing, knowing it was a death he must account for.

'Whatever happens,' she whispered, 'you have been my man!'

There was time for one swift embrace, the wonder of her body warm against him, the sweetness of her parted, pining lips. Rough hands tore them apart, thrusting clothes upon them.

Kobus Coetze shouted into her face. 'Cover yourself, girl! Have you no shame?'

She drew herself up in pride and splendour, letting him wince before the ruin of her back. 'I have no shame for what we did: only for what you made *him* do!'

'Silence, girl! He's no better than a beast!'

'Danie used the *sjambok*, Danie drew the knife! You all saw it!'

'*I saw murder,*' Kobus Coetze said.

Rebecca saw them coming up the river path. Pleasure warmed her at the sight of Lance's tall, straight figure and the graceful languor in his stride. Then she noticed Coetze's grim black plod and the sunlit rope that harnessed them together. She heard Hugo's step behind her, sensing his sudden tension, and gave thanks that on this of all days, she had let Duma take Hal to the pasture.

She knew that Lance was bringing trouble home again.

Even so, Coetze's bald announcement stunned her. '*Murder?*' she repeated. 'There must be some mistake!'

'His mistake, mevrouw. Ask him.'

Lance stared straight ahead, his fine face blank, his sage blue eyes empty. Grease and flour-dust dulled his coppery hair. Dark blood stained his shirtsleeve. 'I killed a man,' he said.

He is capable, she acknowledged, with sudden, deadening honesty. Perhaps I've always known it.

'Say nothing more,' Hugo cautioned sharply, 'until we've seen a lawyer.' He turned on Coetze, his brown eyes hard and accusing. 'If you are so certain, why bring him to us? Why not take him straight to Nyeri jail?'

Coetze fidgeted, plainly embarrassed. 'I don't like you, Berkeley, but I've never doubted your word. Give it, and you can take him in.'

'*Why*, Coetze?' Hugo insisted.

Coetze's troubled green glare finally lifted. 'Because he's *white*, man! Because if he was my son, I'd want to see him first!'

Briefly, Hugo's face softened. 'Thank you, Kobus. You have my word.'

How strange, Rebecca thought, as Coetze trudged into the evening shimmer. In our darkest moment, this tough old Boer offers charity. If he'd done so sooner we might not have come to this.

Hugo had taken Lance inside and was firing urgent legal questions at him.

'The girl came willingly, you didn't force her?'

'Of course not! And her name is *Karen*!'

'You're sure the knife was van Zyl's?'

'I wasn't carrying one.'

'He struck first, and cut your arm?'

'I think so. Don't remember, really.'

'Damn it, you *must* remember!'

It's like the time Simba went away, she thought: the same shifty evasiveness. Perhaps he doesn't *want* to remember. His aloofness chilled her, raising fresh doubts about the past.

Lance stood up and thrust his bound hands forward. 'I haven't slept for three days and nights.'

'You heard what I told Coetze,' Hugo warned. 'You won't try to run away?'

'Where would I go, when everything I want is in this valley?'

He stood half a head above Hugo, a gaunt, bloodstained man-child driven to the limit. The chill inside her melted, overwhelmed by mother-love. She longed to comfort him, but heard Hal's piping voice outside and couldn't let him see his brother in this awful state. She cut the rope, touched Lance's shoulder gently, and watched him stumble to his room.

'Oh Hugo,' she cried, 'what are we going to do?'

'Sleep on it,' said Hugo.

39

REBECCA HARDLY SLEPT at all. In the dim, small hours, daylight doubts loomed larger. Where did we go wrong, she wondered; why must we be punished? She found no answers: only owlhoot from the forest and the river's cold, dark song.

She woke Hal at sunrise, called Duma from the misted huts and told them to hunt butterflies.

'We did that yesterday. I want to stay and talk to Lance!'

'Later. We have grown-up things to discuss.' She saw his small face crumple, knew she mustn't turn another son away. She swept him up and kissed him. 'Do it for Mummy, *please*. Bring a nice big hawkmoth back for Lance.'

His grin was like a blessing, his proud knowledge briefly warmed her heart. 'Silly, it's not time for hawkmoths yet. Come on, Duma, race you to the river!'

How easy it would be, she thought, if boys were always seven years old.

And went inside, to tackle Hugo.

She waited while he brought his second coffee to the lounge, watching the first gold sunray touch the steam above his cup.

'What will happen to him, Hugo?'

'If witnesses confirm his story, he has a good chance of acquittal: self-defence, against a deadly weapon.'

'Do *you* believe him?'

'He shamed the Coetzes and outraged male Boer pride. It's what they say that counts.'

'So he could be found guilty?'

'Manslaughter, at worst. First offence, a lenient sentence.'

386

'But he's only seventeen!'

'Old enough to be responsible in law.'

She leaned across the table, took his firm, lean hand, putting all the years of loving into her plea. 'Give him a gun and your blessing. They'd never find him, in the wilderness out there!'

'Rebecca, Rebecca, you're thinking with your heart. If he runs, they'll know he's guilty. He could never come back!'

'A prison cell would kill him, Hugo. Please let him grow up free!'

'I'll hire the best lawyers and stand by him come what may. I won't see him condemned by default.'

'Hugo, he's my son!'

But not mine, Hugo clearly longed to say; she read it plainly in his grimace of distaste. Aloud, he said, 'It's the law, Rebecca. I gave my word. Must I break it, because he is besotted with a common Boer girl?'

A third voice interrupted, harsh and savage. 'Her name is *Karen*!'

Lance came through the sunshafts in two swift, silent strides. His eyes were raw with sleeplessness. The jagged, half-healed wound on his arm filled Rebecca with foreboding. 'You talk as if I were a tricky problem in some lawyer's book! All right, legal expert: how will *she* be punished?' His face writhed, his hands rose in terrible, clawed supplication. *'What will they do to her?'*

'They will beat her,' Hugo told him, 'to make an example and warn her female playmates to stick to their own kind. They'll send her into exile, to relatives down south, and worthy Afrikaner men who don't know of her fall.'

'No,' Lance said, all at once dangerously pale. 'Oh no they won't. Give me the gunsafe key.'

Hugo pushed his coffee cup aside and came lightly to his feet. 'You're going nowhere, boy: I gave my word!'

'And I gave mine – to Karen!'

They stood poised like rival, rutting bulls at each end of the striped rug. 'Stand clear, Rebecca,' Hugo warned her, 'I should have done this years ago!'

'You should,' Lance growled. 'You're in my way, *old man*!'

He lunged forward. Hugo's left hand flickered, jerked Lance's head back in a small, scarlet spray. She saw his blue eyes darken, heard his snort of rage, feeling the resentment of the years take flame. Lance swung, furious but clumsy. Hugo ducked and rapped his cheek again.

The lounge was full of upflung dust and raw ferocity: taut, warring, unfamiliar faces trapped in sunlight, pale fists slicing through the shadows, the crack of bone on flesh, the smell of fresh male sweat. Rebecca leaned on the rough stone wall, weeping inside for Camelot defiled, praying that neither would be hurt.

Knowing that one of them must lose.

Hugo held his left hand high, leaving that side of his body exposed. He's seen the wound on Lance's right arm, she realised, and knows he can't use it. Oh Hugo, don't be too hard on him!

Lance proved her wrong, bending at the knees, smashing his right fist into Hugo's ribs. She heard the meaty thump, saw Hugo sag and whiten, watched him totter back into the workdesk.

Which shattered, sending him and a hundred yellow splinters sprawling on to the dark, slick boards. Lance was on him instantly, wrenching at his jacket.

'Stop it!' she screamed. 'You'll kill him!'

'No, Mother, I won't make that mistake again. I only want the key.'

He stood up, flushed with victory, glowing with youth and strength, so much like his father that she felt her knees grow weak. He went like a fierce, free wind through the house, and returned with a rifle on his shoulder and a valediction on his lips. 'Say farewell to Duma and give Camelot to Hal when he grows up!'

Then he was gone.

She turned, chilled by the finality of his leaving, fearful of the sudden silence. Hugo lay where he had fallen, ghastly pale, ominously still. She knelt beside him, guilty and afraid. Guilty, because she'd yearned for Lance's freedom.

Afraid she might lose both her men.

Lance had tethered one of Hugo's ponies by the river, a big bay gelding with a white-blazed face – the only thing he'd take from Camelot. He moved, swiftly and silently through the balsam-scented bush. Nothing can stop me now, he thought, not even the entire Boer nation. I have outfaced a grown man in single combat. I have a rifle in my hand, Karen's image in my mind, and the force of our love in my heart.

He paused where the shadows ended, peered out across Coetze's yard. Mid-morning sunlight glinted on a rusted ploughshare. The breeze made wagon-canvas flicker, set grey smoke circling above the thatch. Nothing else stirred. He smelt game-meat stew, heard Helena humming, and grinned tightly in the hazy heat.

It would be even easier than he'd hoped.

He made no sound, raised only small red eddies in the yard-dust. Breathing deeply, levelling the rifle, he thrust the door open and made his intent plain. 'I've come to claim my woman!'

'I thought you would,' Kobus Coetze grunted.

The absence of resistance made Lance feel foolish. Coetze lounged in a hearthside chair. Helena loomed beside him, her broad moon-face untroubled in the ember glow.

Karen was nowhere to be seen.

Battle-lust gave way to sick suspicion. Lance remembered Hugo's warning words. *They will send her into exile, to meet a worthy man.* 'Where is she?' he whispered. 'What have you done to her?'

Coetze eyed him, sleepily and disdainfully, raised a hand and scratched his grizzled beard. 'Karen, your *roinek* pup is here!'

She came from smoky depths into a gloomy corner, with an aged, weary shuffle that made his stomach clench. She wore a drab-grey shroud that covered her from neck to ankles and stood mute and listless, staring at the floor.

'We will not stop her,' Helena murmured. 'She is a woman grown, and free to choose.'

'Ask her,' Coetze taunted. 'If you want her, *ask*!'

'*Karen?*' he breathed urgently; and saw her head come up.

Her face was tight and tragic, her eyes held only pain. 'If you go alone, the Boers will be content that we are parted, and your guilt is proved. If I go with you, Oupa will muster every rifle, and hound you to the ends of earth.'

'*The ends of earth,*' Coetze echoed. 'I swear it, by the living God!'

'Do you think I am afraid? I love you, Karen, come away with me!'

She was weeping, tears that caught the ember-glow and fell like molten lava. 'I cannot come, and watch you die!'

He simply refused to accept it, and swung the rifle into Coetze's face. 'You say she's free. Will you swear *that*, by your living God?'

'You heard it, boy. Don't point that thing at me!'

He turned back to Karen, letting her see his passion and his hunger. 'I have a horse outside. Your oryx pelt rests beneath his saddle. Remember the necklace in the stars, remember your power over me. *Remember the difference we share!*'

Fleetingly, he thought he saw the spark in her rekindle, bringing green fire to her eyes and beauty to her face.

'Remember mustered rifles,' Coetze growled, 'and the hounds of earth!'

Karen leaned forward, racked with hard, harsh sobs. 'I dare not come *because* I love you so! Go quickly, Lance, before they change their minds!'

Then she was gone, fading for ever out of reach into the sooty, righteous dimness of her father's house.

He turned away from Coetze's hot, triumphant leer, from the Afrikaner hymn of praise Helena was already crooning. He trudged back across the sunlit yard that seemed so cold and clouded, back through bush that smelled only of failure. *Nothing can stop me now*, he remembered bitterly.

And nothing will go with me.

Nothing will go with me but an image of her beauty in an upland forest glade, and the memory of a love that once burned bright. When the wilderness enfolds me, when the darkness takes me down, hers will be the image I carry to the grave.

He slumped in the saddle, let the gelding amble to the ford. The river sparkled as he crossed. Camelot shimmered in the haze. Dimly, he thought he heard someone calling: Rebecca, perhaps, offering forgiveness. He ignored it and rode on, haunted by his own bold words so recently spoken. *Where would I go, when everything I want is in this valley?*

Everything I want is now behind me.

The sound came again, closer and more urgent. Turning, breathless, not daring to believe, he saw Karen running up the slope to join him.

She ran as she had run that day beside the shaded stream: free-striding, flowing, fluid, full of grace. Wind moulded the grey shroud to the wonder of her body. Her heart-shaped face was luminous with joy. He leaned down, took her slim, warm, honeyed arm, swung her up behind him.

'Ride for our lives, Lance!' she cried. 'Let the difference keep us from their guns!'

There was sunlight on the pasture, silken warmth against his back, and towering triumph in his soul. The days ahead were fraught with danger, the nights would blaze with tenderness and love.

And the red haze would trouble him no more.

He let the laughter bubble up inside him, flung a wordless victory howl to the listening hills.

And drove the gelding forward, into the high bright north.

Rebecca's panic eased as Hugo stirred beneath her contrite touch. His breathing deepened, colour trickled back into his cheeks. Presently he blinked and sighed and took her unsteady hand. 'By God,' he gasped, 'your little boy packs a man-sized punch!' There was something besides pain in his eyes, an almost conspiratorial brown twinkle.

Suddenly, she understood it all.

'You *wanted* him to win, you laid your left side open purposely! It was the only way you could let him go with a clear conscience!'

'Don't say it,' he warned, instantly serious, 'don't even think it. He knocked me down and stole the key. I've got the bruises to prove it.'

She helped him up, slipped her fingers inside his shirt, touched the swelling gingerly. His eyes were suddenly wide and warm.

'It's mid-morning. The house is empty. I'd say I need a massage, wouldn't you?'

'Hugo, I'm nearly forty-seven, and you've just been severely wounded.'

'I know. Disgusting, isn't it?'

She smiled, and let her breast quicken to his gentle palm. 'I think it's rather nice!'

Later, dozing in his arms, basking in his love-scent, she sensed the storm subsiding, sensed a meeting of enduring love and fresh-sprung grief. We did our best for Lance when he needed us. He needs us no more. He has become a man: old enough to choose his own path, *old enough to be responsible in law*.

And Camelot *is* brighter, without the violence which seems to follow him. Dear Lord, keep him safe wherever he may go.

She snuggled deeper into Hugo's arms.

40

DOZING IN FILTERED SUNSHINE and Hugo's slack embrace, Rebecca heard Hal's light, approaching footfalls. He hovered in the doorway with one grey sock rolled down and faint thorn-scratches on his sun-tanned shin. 'We caught a smashing butterfly for Lance!'

'He's out at the moment,' she muttered cautiously.

'Never mind, I'll give it to him later. Why are you resting, in the middle of the day?'

'Daddy fell and bumped his chest. Don't worry, he's all right.'

'Is that how the desk got broken? Golly, it's a *mess!*'

'I'll clear it up,' she promised, slipping into her navy-blue bath-robe. 'Wake Daddy if you like. Gently, he's still sore.'

Hugo's snort of feigned outrage trailed her down the warm gold passageway. She heard Hal's giggle and the creak of tortured bed-springs: sounds of normality, returning. Then Duma appeared on the verandah, bringing further consolation.

His gestures were lean yet eloquent, his dark eyes wide with awe. He made her feel the urgency of youthful lovers meeting, see the fierce bright splendour of their northern flight. 'The Boers will follow, memsahib,' he warned her gravely. Then his face furled into upward wrinkles like an old brown shoe. 'They will never catch him. I, Duma, taught him all I know about the bush.'

She touched his shoulder lightly, once. 'Bless you, Duma.' He went down the steps and loped towards his hut. Bless you, she meant, for guarding both my sons, for love and faith and courage down the years.

She stood for a moment looking north across green, shimmering ridges, letting her heart go out to Lance and Karen. Stay in health and beauty, she told them silently. Now perhaps the charm will circle Camelot again.

She went inside, to tidy up the lounge.

Hal was right. It *was* a mess.

The desk leaned drunkenly, one side darkly polished, the other split and sprouting pallid splinters. Papers lay everywhere, like large confetti on the zebra rugs. The ink on some had yellowed. They felt fragile in her fingers, smelling of must and mildew and long-past yesteryears. She knelt and sorted them, making a game of it: that to keep, that to throw away, this one for the waste-bin, this for Hugo's files.

Halfway through, she came upon an envelope that brought her upright, keyed and curious: pale vellum dimmed by dust and time, a brittle, faded-red wax seal. 'For Laura Howard only,' she read, 'to be opened when I'm gone. George Seton, April 1896.'

For Laura Howard *only*, who was already dead when the letter was written. Yet the seal had been broken, the letter had been read.

When, she wondered, and by whom?

The afternoon sun was gentle on her back. She could hear Hal and Hugo still romping on the bed. Camelot seemed to snuggle round her, warm and full of love.

She felt a quick, cold quiver of unease. *This one should be thrown away.*

Leo had been working at the desk the day he died. If he had found the letter he would certainly have read it. Aunt Laura was his mother, after all.

Why did Leo try to cross the flooded river?

Laughter from the bedroom seemed to call her to the present. Again, she poised above the rubbish bin.

Again she hesitated.

She sensed the nearness of a final answer, an end to years of mystery. It's in the past, she reasoned, it can't hurt to *know*.

She drew the letter out, smoothed the deep-set creases, ran her eye across black, spidery script.

She read it once in horror, refusing to understand the evil. She read it again, felt the evil growing, and prayed to lose the power of understanding. Camelot was fading all around her, taking on Shalott's grim-towered shade. The laughing voices suddenly seemed very far away.

She never knew how long she stood there feeling dead inside, waiting for the agony to start. She never knew quite how she stumbled to the riverside. When sense returned, she was shivering in sunlight where the water coiled and lisped, and ring-necked doves were grieving overhead: grieving for Laura Howard's secret, and deadly understanding fashioned forty years too late.

Too late, she understood her father's guilty goodnight kisses, his robber's glances at her childhood bedroom door. No wonder Mummy's eyes had set like hard grey shiny pebbles, no wonder she had always seemed so fair and far away.

Now, at last, she knew why Laura's picture had been broken, the eyes put out, the lovely face scored through with harsh red slashes. No wonder little Becky had been lonely and unloved, and the Sussex house had seemed so cold.

The river glittered, heedless and unruffled. The sun was sinking, blood-red, on the ridge. The deadness in Rebecca's heart deepened.

She understood the mystic oneness she had shared with Leo, the curious restraint she'd always sensed beneath his loving touch.

The touch which had given life to Lance.

Now she thought she understood why Simba had gone missing, why van Zyl died, why Lance and Hugo fought. Sins of the past, held dormant down the sweet, bright years, revealed in a long-lost letter and a dead man's anguished hand.

The evening smelled of meadowsweet, the first star glittered, distant, cold and bright. Her hands clenched, she screwed the letter up and flung it out upon the water. The river took it, as it had once taken Leo.

The words remained, branded on her brain.

Branded like Blue-Eyes's never-quite-forgotten accusation; savage, scarlet, irrefutable.

You lied. We lived a lie, she realised, however innocently. Now truth comes swooping like some vengeful carrion bird. The worst of it is only just beginning.

Hugo has to know.

'Mummy, you're shivering, your hands feel like ice!'

'I'm sorry, Hal. I walked too far, too late.'

'Is it because Lance hasn't come back?'

'No, dear. Duma says he'll be all right.'

'He *will* come back, won't he?'

'Go to sleep, Hal. Let angels sing you to your rest.' Why did I say that? It sounded like goodbye!

'Kiss me, then, like you always do.'

'I can't. I . . . I don't want to give you my cold.'

'Blow me one!' She managed it somehow, just as she had managed to cook his supper, taking refuge in routine, trying to pretend she wasn't dying, deep inside. She tucked Hal in, watched starlight smooth the wrinkles from his brow, waited till his breath came sweet and easy.

Sleep well, my son. May you, at least, remain unblemished by it all.

She came into the firelight like her own aged, anguished ghost, all her silvered beauty bled away. She looked as Eric Stuart had the night his wife was killed, the flesh tight-drawn across her cheeks, her eyes like iron-grey pools.

'What's happened?' he asked. 'Is it Lance again?'

'Be patient, Hugo. You have to hear it all.'

She sat stiffly in the hearthside chair. Her hands writhed, pale and restless, in the deep blue lapfolds of her robe.

'Long ago, there were two sisters, born to a poor family some thirteen years apart. Both grew fair and pretty. The elder married a rich man and bore a son called James. The younger came to help with the boy, and stayed as a companion. James grew up and went to college. The younger sister found herself with child.'

'*James's* child?'

'Don't prompt me, please.' He had never heard her voice so frigid; it held a coldness which, despite the glowing hearthlogs, he was beginning to share.

'It was 1892. The scandal would have destroyed them all. She was sent somewhere far away for her confinement. When the baby came – a daughter – the elder sister took her in and raised her as her own. Only the rich man and the sisters knew the truth.'

'It wasn't uncommon, in those days,' Hugo murmured. 'Why all the mystery? What were their names?'

'Wait,' she snapped, 'just *wait*!' Her eyes were darker now, inward and opaque. The tightness in her body made him wince. Her voice droned on, remorseless. 'Can you imagine how it must have been, in that house? One sister caring for a child she didn't love, the other pining for the child she dared not own? Perhaps they fought; we'll never know. We *do* know that James brought two cronies on an African safari – and brought the younger sister too.'

Touched with lamplight, smoke, and faint foreboding, he felt the story gathering around them.

'James was a bully and a lecher. His friends, no doubt, were cut from the same cloth. They drove the younger sister into the arms of a bearded hunter who happened on their camp.'

'*Morgan,*' Hugo muttered, seeing the connection at last. 'The younger sister ran away with Morgan! She was Laura Howard, your aunt and Leo's mother. Buck up, Rebecca, I'm not going to faint because your aunt once had a love-child!'

'I haven't finished yet.' She hunched forward, staring at the embers as if they held an even darker ghost. 'The rich man left Laura a letter. I found it, among Leo's papers. He writes of provision in his will, and begs her to forgive him for fathering her child.'

She was at the heart of it now, her face gaunt with abasement. 'His name was George Seton. Don't you understand? I was the love-child. *Laura was my mother, too!*'

And finally, he *did* understand.

Leo and Rebecca were spawned in the same womb, brought forth from the self-same female flesh. Conceiving Lance, they had broken the oldest, most inviolable tabu, and set an unclean cloud over the valley. It hovered round two simple sounds, a single word he could not bear to speak.

Incest.

He sat distraught and barely breathing in the blue ember-glow. Desperately, she sought to pierce his awful lethargy. 'We didn't *know*, Leo and I; and Lance is burdened with our sin. Must the Boers destroy him? Will you let them claim his freedom and his love?'

Briefly, Hugo rallied. 'We are not alone in family shame. When I go, I will leave a sworn statement with Nairobi lawyers, setting out the truth of Karen's birth. A copy shall be sent to Kobus Coetze. He won't dare bring Lance to court, knowing that his affair with a Kikuyu maiden would be revealed.'

In relief and gratitude, she reached to touch his hand.

It was only the faintest flicker of revulsion, only the smallest cringe of fevered flesh beneath her own.

It felt as if he'd cut her heart away.

He shrank from her, stumbled across dim zebra stripes. Turning at the starlit window, he let her see the silvered teartracks on his cheeks. 'I can't stay here. I cannot live with this!'

'It's over, Hugo, buried with Leo underneath the Meru oak!'

'It can never be over! It's in us and around us like some evil fog. You and Leo coupled in these very rooms!'

'Surely you're not jealous, after all these years?'

'Of course I am, I always envied him, but it's far worse than jealousy now.'

'But we were man and wife, in love and innocence!'

'You were brother and sister! You tainted the whole place with – *indecency!*'

Such cruel injustice flayed her, from one who'd always been so just and fair. She hit back, harsh and hasty. 'You *dare* speak of indecency, you who spent so many nights with common whores?' She regretted it at once, sensing the sudden gulf between them that might never close.

He faced her from the far end of the lounge, his shoulders bowed, his hands spread in a kind of anguished resignation. 'You see? Already we are savaging each other, opening fresh wounds and bleeding old ones. That is no way to live, no way to raise a child. Better we should part in what remains of fondness.' His voice and body hardened, in the stubborn resolution which had seen them through so many trials – and which now made her afraid. 'I will go, Rebecca; and I will take Hal with me.'

'You shall not! He is my son!'

'I have shown you how *your* son can be saved. Now you must allow me to save mine.'

'I'll fight you, Hugo, to my last breath, through every court in the land!'

'And make the whole thing public? And visit Leo's curse on one who is not even Leo's child? For God's sake, woman, *Hal is the only one unblemished by it all!*'

Finally, her agony was blooming.

It was worse than Blue-Eyes's death or Leo's drowning, worse than the destruction Lance had caused. It was the fiercest, deepest pain she could imagine. The very words she had herself breathed at Hal's bedside thrown back into her face, a truth she simply couldn't contest. The past left her condemned, and gave Hugo every right. She could only weep inside, and face the practicalities. 'Where will you go? What can you do?'

'They say Europe's on the brink again – chap called Hitler rattling the sabres. Doubtless there'll be something for an old warhorse.'

'And who'll look after Hal, while you play soldiers?'

'I still have family, in the Wealdland. He'll be safe there when the fighting starts.'

'What will you tell him? It will break his heart!'

'That his mother always loved him; that one day, he will understand.'

'Oh Hugo, how *can* you?'

He came, halt and ravaged, towards the dying fire. 'Nothing can change the way I feel about you, nothing can take away the joy we shared. But I will not risk Hal's future in this shadowed place, and I will not watch our love be slowly smothered. Though it will break all our hearts, it must be done.'

'Then do it at first light,' she cried. '*I can't bear to see you go.*'

She saw him make one final, faltering effort, watched his hand inch out across the fireglow. She closed her eyes and bowed her head in hope.

Just for a moment, Leo's ghost coiled behind her closed lids, naked and shimmering with roused male beauty. Hugo had put it there, she knew, in his taut, pale, unreasoned pride. Yet suddenly, she was deeply shamed.

Coldness hardened in the space between, coldness even the great love Hugo professed could not redeem. She heard him speak the saddest, sourest words of all.

'You can have the bedroom. I'll sleep on the couch.'

He left her, then: left her to her agony and one fierce, futile wish.

I wish the Lion Boy had never seen the light of day.

Rebecca saw the light of day. She saw dawn's grim grey fingers steal into the room, heard the engine putter in the yard, and knew she would have to watch them go.

Some time in night's blackness she had stumbled into sleep. Now the sun was rising on Mount Kenya's snowy peak, and pain was like a hoarfrost in her soul.

The polished boards were cold beneath her feet. Her breath fell misty on the window pane. She watched them cross dew-damp brown dust and shake Duma's hand, saw the old man's helpless, uncomprehending shrug.

Then they turned and looked back at the house.

The first faint yellow sunray touched Hal's tearstained face: a bereft, boyish beauty that made her want to run to him. She held her ground and clawed the window frame, knowing that if she touched him she would never let him go.

Knowing she had lost the right to touch him.

Hugo bent and kissed him, set him in the car, straightened and faced Camelot. In the blush of morning, he too was young again, sleek-headed, as lean and upright as the first day he had ridden up to greet her.

May Hal grow in his likeness, straight and strong and true. Remember me, in the life I cannot share.

Hugo stood erect and still as stone. He is doing as Eric Stuart once did, she realised, forming one last, cherished image to take across the sea.

Remember me!

Tears blinded her. She heard the car doors slam. When her vision cleared, they had already left her, in a small black box receding towards Nyeri Hill, under a plume of dawn-red Kenyan dust.

Taking the best of her with them.

Only then did the grief storm break, tearing her from the window, driving her down across the bed. She cried until the tears no longer gathered, clutching the pillow, breathing Hugo's lingering male scent, clinging to a single, sorry shred of consolation.

At least I still have Camelot.

41

IT TOOK HER A WEEK TO understand how vain this hope had been, and know the agony wasn't over yet.

'*Jambo*, memsahib,' grinning tribesmen shouted as they passed. 'Are you well this day?' As if they couldn't *see* her grief.

'Never mind, memsahib,' piped the village women who came to sell her eggs. 'Perhaps Ngai will send the bwana back.' She envied them their sloe-eyed optimism, their readiness to live one day at a time.

'You need a man,' growled Duma. 'It is not good for you to be alone.'

'Indeed? Why not?' He gestured at the pasture, his wrinkles all turned down.

'Too much work.' He pointed at the forest, his still-sleek hair gleaming in the sun. 'Too much danger.'

'Mwangi, you mean?'

'They say he lives beneath the sacred fig and praises Ngai's name. They say he even tries to heal the sick.' Duma looked and sounded sceptical, clearly regretting the mention of Mwangi's name. He too was estranged from a son.

So Rebecca tried the Stuart cure, wishing with all her heart that Molly was alive to make it work. Alone, the Nyeri journey seemed much longer. Shopping for one became a chore.

The club was an ordeal.

Ashamed of the truth, she used evasions. Even to herself, they sounded false. 'Hugo's got some popsy, U.K. side,' she heard a booze-flushed bar-fly mutter. 'He used to be a devil for the ladies.' She intercepted more than one sly, assessing stare, she felt hungry male eyes on her body. 'When will *you* be looking for a stand-in?' they were asking. 'Are you wed, or do you live in Kenya?' She finished her drink and took the homeward road.

Coffee bushes formed a deep-green garland round the dam. Sheep grazed the higher pastures, like pinkened puff-balls on a broad baize lawn. Further down, maize sprouted, pale gold tendrils thrusting through rust-brown, upturned soil. The air smelled of clover bloom and woodsap.

It was as beautiful as ever; it was no longer home.

Without Hal and Hugo to furnish it with love, Camelot was just an empty shell. Home is a way of living, she realised, not a place. How quickly we learn, when it's too late for learning. How soon we yearn for what is lost, which once we took for granted.

Beneath these latest sorrows, she sensed a purpose growing, a need to make peace with herself and this land she loved.

As always, instinct drew her to the river.

The river, which had taken Leo from her, and where she'd fought to survive their great sin.

The swirl and whirl and chatter beckoned, until she balanced on the grassy brink. She saw her own reflection against the blurred blue sky, her hair more grey than golden, her eyes still dim with pain. The day darkened round her. Visions formed within the cool green depths. One by one, the living and the dead, they came and called to her.

Duma first, under the rustling forest edge. 'It is a good place, memsahib. I will tell them the Lion Boy has found a worthy wife.'

Then Mwangi, slurred and hot-eyed within the campfire sparks. 'Now *my* land is given to Red Strangers!'

Molly Stuart surfaced, beaky and beady-eyed, sipping blue-tinged gin and tonic in a hotel garden. 'When Africa growls, you stand tall and kick her in the teeth!'

Next came Kobus Coetze, tawny-bearded, dressed in grey, pleading for a half-caste babe under Nyeri Hill. 'Let white folk purge the unknown white man's guilt!'

The current coiled, the mirror rippled. Hugo stood in lamplight under horse-borne rifles, staring into Eric Stuart's skull-like face. 'We have made the laws and set the standards. We have to show them ours is the best way!'

Finally, Mwangi reappeared, dressed in the Healer's kirtle, touched by unlikely dignity. 'The valley is my home. *My time will come!*'

She couldn't grasp the meaning. The effort seemed too great. Willingly, almost gladly, she stepped into the stream. Silky coolness soothed her, the purpose egged her on. How easy it would be to drift down through sunlit meadows till every sense and vision paled away.

To be the Lady of Shalott.

Water foamed around her calves. Deeper coldness shocked her into fresh awareness: of the flight of birds, the call of sheep, the pure, green-scented air. She pictured Hal, remembered Hugo's words – *His mother always loved him, one day he'll understand* – and imagined what this cowardice would do to them. It's *too* easy, she realised, there has to be a nobler way.

She began to read the message, see the meaning.

All the tears and laughter, all the love and toil were sprung from that first, fateful union: the weave of Camelot legend and Njau the Healer's charm. We came to make the land bloom and found a dynasty, bring wealth into the valley and ancient superstition into pure white light. We did it in good faith, believing we alone were right.

Everything we did was soured with sin.

A sin so black and evil even Hugo could not bear it, a sin that colours all our rightness wrong. If this is true, I must not heed friends or loved ones.

I must listen to our enemies.

Mwangi, who fought Leo from birth, who plotted Molly's murder and planned to butcher Hal. '*You have given my land to these Red Strangers!*'

Coetze, whose lust drove a maid to suicide, whose Boer intransigence sparked Lance's madness. '*Let white men purge the unknown white man's guilt!*'

She stepped out of the water on to soft, green, sunwarmed grass. She breathed the meadow's richness, sensed the fresh crop stirring in the soil. Courage and purpose fused inside her. She knew exactly what she had to do.

One last act of penance, one final sacrifice, to right the wrongs and cleanse the land and free her soul from incest.

And make her agony complete.

They met as usual, under the trees beside the headman's hut. Diffused sunlight struck rufous highlights from the elders' monkey-skin cloaks. The air was thick with goat-grease and anticipation.

Duma stood among the chattering tribesmen, his iron-grey hair glinting, his face creased in concern.

Mwangi stood apart.

He wore no metal anklets, only the pied, threadbare kirtle. There was brooding stillness in his thin dark body, a sense of unslaked hunger and ambition unfulfilled. Despite her resolution, Rebecca felt a pang of doubt each time she caught his vengeful eye.

It *is* fitting, she reassured herself. No matter how dark his powers, he has suffered jail and exile for his beliefs.

She waited until the elders had drained the drinking horn, and Maina's plump brown beaded arms were raised to demand silence. She waited while the chatter ebbed, until there was only birdsong and the murmur of the wind in grey-green leaves.

'I am leaving the valley,' she said.

She heard the low, communal gasp, saw Maina's jowls sag in consternation.

'Don't go, memsahib. We are happy with you here, even though you have no man.' His glance slid disdainfully to Mwangi. 'We tend the sheep and till the meadows gladly, whatever some may say.'

'Thank you,' she murmured formally. 'But those I love have gone, and I must follow.'

They gave a sympathetic *eeh* which held an edge of anxiousness. Maina gave it urgent voice. 'Which of the white men have you sold us to? What is he like, what kind of man is he?'

'I am not selling, Maina.'

A murmur of relief, and puzzled frowns.

'Then who will buy the seed and sell the fleeces? Who will keep the hearth warm, in the big house?'

'I am returning the land to him who rightly owns it.'

A longer, lower rumble of approval, in which only Mwangi didn't join. Seeing his dull glower, she felt the doubt again, and dismissed it. It was time for ceremony. She spread the paper against a barkless curve of gum trunk, raised the pen. 'Let the elders order it, and witness as I give the land to Mwangi!' The hush was total, slack and sudden. She saw appalled disbelief on grizzled faces, felt collective anguish in the air.

Then Mwangi moved into watery sunlight, with malice in his eyes and menace in his shuffling step.

'*Yes!*' he crowed. 'Let the elders order! See the pale-haired woman yield to Mwangi, see the strongest, truest sign of all! Watch, and kneel before your new Healer!'

403

'Mwangi is an outcast!' Maina bellowed. 'Memsahib, you cannot do this thing!'

'Write it,' Mwangi hissed. 'Write it *now*!'

Mature men and elders rallied to Maina, their faces full of outrage and alarm. Bright-eyed in awe and reverence, younger tribesmen grouped at Mwangi's side. His savage, capering triumph chilled Rebecca's soul anew.

There is *still* some great wrong, she realised. Mwangi will not rest until he's stained the pasture red with blood. I came for absolution; instead, I only tear the clan apart. Is the taint of incest never-ending? Must *everything* I do be so condemned?

'Why?' she cried, in all-at-once ungovernable anger. 'Why do you snarl like scavengers on the gift I bring?'

Her sharpness checked them, halted Mwangi in mid-prance. She was still the pale-haired memsahib who held papers for the land.

Maina answered, dignified yet bitter. 'You have lived here many years, yet do not know our ways. Mwangi has no voice among us. He owns no blade of grass!' His arm came up, pointing to Camelot. Blue and yellow beads flickered dimly. He spoke as to some slow-witted child. 'Don't you see, memsahib? The land belongs to *Duma*!'

And Duma was suddenly the focus of attention, grinning like a wrinkled, bashful brown gnome.

Duma, who had raised the Lion Boy, and helped Rebecca conquer early fears; who had soothed Lance's tantrums, taught him how to prosper in the bush, brought him in his turn to manhood; who had gone, bleeding, to the forest depths and rescued Hal from Thuo's glittering simi.

The land belongs to Duma.

She felt her spirit rising, sensed the clan's expectation, and knew she must play memsahib just once more. Now the time *was* right, all doubts resolved, the purpose pulsing steady in her blood. She let them see the paper, let them watch her sign. 'It shall be as I have written,' she cried, 'and as your elders will. From this day forth, the land returns to Duma!'

The approving *eeeh* became a full-fledged roar. The tribesmen reunited around Duma, clasping his hand, grasping his frail brown shoulders.

Leaving Mwangi cast out and alone.

He gave her one last smouldering glance and sidled up towards the forest.

404

That is as it should be, too, she thought. Mwangi's is one darkness we did not create, now and always in and of the clan.

She left the growing celebration, knowing there would be no more work today.

She paused once, gazing up towards the Meru oak, to the deep green shade where four crosses stood. For the first time in many years, she let Leo's image comfort her.

A tall, wide-shouldered image wielding a great bright axe, making wood-chips hum and spray. There was sunshine on his scarred, bronzed chest and silver in his tawny mane. He was smiling wistfully as he worked, looking north and longing, as he so often did; as if he knew his bold, flawed son roamed there.

Do you hear me, *brother*?

Today I have redeemed the sin we did not know. It could not be more just than that Duma should inherit. By Maina's grace, I did something utterly *right*, and cancelled out our dreadful wrong. The tribesmen are united on the land they always owned, free from bwana's rule and memsahib's whim.

Free to go whichever way *they* choose.

Now I must go, to the empty house that we once shared, and pack away the last few tokens of the legend.

And take my broken heart out of this valley.

'Remember us, Duma, as you doze beside the hearth, Some day, we will meet again.' She took his hand, warmly, softly, once. In the early sun, the joining of her paleness and his brown filled him with a sweet, sharp ache. He saw the silver in her hair, the mourning creases in her ageing, still-comely face. If we meet again, he thought, it can only be on Ngai's shining mountain, when breath leaves our bodies and our spirits are set free. He had no words to name this feeling. He stood straight and let her see the sorrow in his eyes, the honour and affection sprung from bright, lost years.

She left him with one wounded, lingering glance, and grief in every stride. The heavy-laden motor car dwindled into greenness. The dust it threw up hovered, like the thin red ghosts of those she'd left behind.

She was the bravest and the best, he mourned. When Mwangi's darkness threatened and her loved ones stole away, she kept the clan together and gave them back the land.

In the flicker of the hearthfire and the rising of the sun, we *will* remember her.

He walked, slow and burdened, into the scent of thyme, towards the high, green, rustling forest edge.

The forest, where it all began.

The Lion Boy was born in wonder and an ancient, sacred tree. His mystery had prowled the valley long after he was dead; it had in the end driven memsahib away. It is the mystery of life itself, Duma realised. No matter how it hurts, it can't be changed.

Shauri ya Mungu: it is the will of God.

Mist and hutsmoke blurred the village. Weak sunlight silvered roofthatch and the river's lazy curve. From here, he couldn't see the big house. From here, the valley looked as it had looked when he was young.

It *is* the same, he realised in surprise.

Long ago, a bearded hunter roamed the north, and came upon an outcast girl called Laura. Now, with his outcast lover, a grandchild wanders there: all that remains of the Lion Boy. Despite the white man's cars and guns, things are as they were. Goats still graze the pasture, maize still greens the river edge. Despite the long-closed Mission and the herdboys' small black books, the youth must still be circumcised and Ngai's word is law.

Red Strangers entered, Duma mused, liked seeds upon the wind. Now the wind has blown them out again. The land remains, unchanging and unchanged.

One day soon, Mwangi will surely come to claim it.

He looked northwards, where Kerinyagga's cold white head shone through rising mist, and sent Ngai a hopeful heartfelt prayer.

Just once before Mwangi comes let Lance ride into the valley, with sunshine in his coppery hair and Karen at his back, and Leo's love for living in his eyes. Just once before I die, let my old heart rise again; rise and leap to greet the Lion Boy's son!

The guard's whistle sounded, sharp and shrill. Doors slammed, coloured kerchiefs fluttered. The air was thick with steam and tart with sulphur. Somewhere up ahead, the engine stuttered. Great wheels clanked and slithered, gripped and gathered speed. The floor beneath Rebecca's feet trembled.

Though pain still lurked, she felt none for the leaving of Nairobi.

It had become a place of big red buildings, metalled roads and electric lanterns. No one here would miss her; it was nowhere she had ever lived or loved.

She trudged the swaying corridor until she found an empty compartment. On this last Kenyan journey, she wanted only solitude.

The sky was turning deeper blue above Athi's umber plain. The pain was building in Rebecca's heart. She saw sunset on a browsing zebra herd, making pied sleekness into stripes of black and gold. She saw a red road winding up towards a lone, low farmstead, where yellowed windows gave out homely warmth. Outside, the evening would be soft with breeze and dust-spice, the unique essence of this lovely land for ever in her blood.

Inside smelt of engine-smoke and loneliness.

Ahead lay a grey and distant world, another bloody war; more shattered limbs and minds, and the knowledge that no shining knight would pass her way again.

Unbidden, no longer to be quelled, the images she'd fought so long were forming.

The lift of Camelot gables against a clean grey dawn, the river's sparkling sunset gleam. The rustle of the forest, the tribesmen's deep-voice chant, the croon of roosting ring-necked doves. Again, she saw bronze duck-wings flash above the mirrored dam, the glint of stars on Kerinyagga's iced, majestic peak. She heard again Kree's kite-call and the bleat of new born lambs, breathed the meadows' incense after rain.

Images spawned sorrow, sorrow raised her living ghosts: Duma's fanged and faithful brownness: Hugo's fine, pale face; Lance's fierce and coppery beauty; Hal's sweet, impish smile.

In privacy and desolation, even her great courage failed. She leaned against the window pane and wept.

She wept for beauty gone beyond recall, for a father's sin passed on to a son. She wept for everything she'd loved and lost, and would be leaving here.

Bowed and blind, she heard the door slide open, heard the rattle of the wheels grow louder. Dear God, she pleaded silently, spare me casual company and trivial travel talk. Let me bear my agony alone!

She couldn't stop her shoulders shaking, couldn't mute her sobs. She felt hesitance behind her, sensed a presence taut with doubt and pity. Go away, her inner voice was begging, please, please *go away*!

It was just a single word heard above metallic clatter, a word that shut out every other sound.

'Mummy!'

The blood was pounding at her temples, roaring in her ears. She turned slowly, afraid she might be dreaming, terrified by sudden, soaring hope.

Hal swooped like a bright-eyed, nestbound fledgling through her veil of tears. 'We heard you were on this train, so we took it too. Oh Mummy, *let us ride with you!*'

Always, she thought, for ever; may this journey never end!

She stood. Hal felt weightless in her arms. She stared in growing wonder above his dark, burrowing head – into Hugo's brown shame-shadowed eyes. The evil is still with him, she realised. He could not deny Hal a last farewell.

'Can you forgive me?' Hugo mumbled. 'I've been such a fool!'

'Can *I* forgive? What about George and Laura? What about . . .'

'Not your doing, not your fault.' He wagged his head, letting her see the pain their weeks apart had caused. 'We simply can't get along without you.'

'We can't go back. I gave the land to Duma.'

'I heard and was proud. I will always be proud of you.'

Hal was tugging at her sleeve, demanding her attention. 'Will you stay with us? Will you sleep in Daddy's room again?'

She waited, too choked to answer, remembering coldness by the Camelot hearth; and heard Hugo's blessed reassurance.

'Of course she will!'

'Oh good,' Hal purred. He was grinning up at her, bubbling with sweet, familiar mischief. 'It's been awful, Mummy. Daddy *snores*!'

The cramped compartment welled with healing laughter. She sat Hal down, letting him cling to her thigh. This time her arms were spread for Hugo alone.

'Rebecca,' he murmured, like a man reborn.

This time there was only poignant longing in his eyes, only tender hunger in his touch: hunger that drove all lingering doubt away.

'Where are we going?' she asked. 'Where will you work?'

'A desk command in London, my brother's regiment. It doesn't matter, as long as you are there.' He was swaying to the clack and rumble of the train: lean, grey-templed, radiant with joy. The shade of incest might have never fallen. He looked as he had looked that far-off day beside the falls – *I will love you as long as I shall live.*

It's true, she thought in deep fulfilment, there cannot ever be a harsher test. She felt the answering love inside her surging up to meet him, a slow, strong, steady tide of victory. She held Hal tighter, moved once more into Hugo's arms. 'It will be as it always was,' she vowed. 'The three of us, together.'

The night rolled dimly past outside. The train wheels hummed a lullaby. Hal dozed on Hugo's lap. Watching her own restored reflection in the window. Rebecca felt a smaller, sweeter pang.

We have loved and laboured half a lifetime here. The evils of the past have been redeemed. Africa is part of me. I will mourn her fierce, broad beauty until the day I die.

Why, then, am I certain we must go?

Presently, one last bright image formed. The final mystery yielded . . .

She had closed the farmyard gate for the last time. The car stood packed and puttering pale grey smoke. Duma waited, grizzled and stately, bowed by grief he didn't try to hide.

She let her gaze feast once on the great, green-shouldered mountain and the boundless pure blue sky beyond. Standing tall and straight, she bade the pain be still; and gave the keys to Camelot away.

'Here, Duma. It's your land now.'

He nodded, sighed, turned his old face northwards. His arms swept up, encircling all she loved. 'It always was, memsahib,' he said. 'You see? It always was.'